BATTLETECH:
NO GREATER HONOR
A BATTLETECH ANTHOLOGY

EDITED BY JOHN HELFERS
AND PHILIP A. LEE

This is a work of fiction. Names, characters, places and incidents either are the products of the author's imagination or are used fictitiously, and any resemblance to actual persons, living or dead, business establishments, events or locales is entirely coincidental. The publisher does not have any control over and does not assume any responsibility for author or third-party Web sites or their content.

If you purchased this book without a cover you should be aware that this book is stolen property. It was reported as "unsold and destroyed" to the publisher and neither the author nor the publisher has received any payment for this "stripped book."

The scanning, uploading and distribution of this book via the Internet or via any other means without the permission of the publisher is illegal and punishable by law. Please purchase only authorized electronic editions, and do not participate in or encourage electronic piracy of copyrighted materials. Your support of the authors' rights is appreciated.

BATTLETECH: NO GREATER HONOR
Edited By John Helfers and Philip A. Lee
Cover art by Tan Ho Sim
Interior art by Alan Blackwell, Doug Chaffee, Dale Eadeh, Brent Evans, Stephen Huda, Harri Kallio, Duane Loose, Justin Nelson, Matt Plog, Anthony Scroggins, Franz Vohwinkel, David White
Cover design by David Kerber

©2022 The Topps Company, Inc. All Rights Reserved. *BattleTech* & *MechWarrior* are registered trademarks and/or trademarks of The Topps Company, Inc., in the United States and/or other countries. Catalyst Game Labs and the Catalyst Game Labs logo are trademarks of InMediaRes Productions LLC. No part of this work may be reproduced, stored in a retrieval system, or transmitted in any form or by any means, without the prior permission in writing of the Copyright Owner, nor be otherwise circulated in any form other than that in which it is published.

Printed in USA.

Published by Catalyst Game Labs,
an imprint of InMediaRes Productions, LLC
5003 Main St. #110 • Tacoma, WA 98407

CONTENTS

FOREWORD   4
PHILIP A. LEE

CONFLICTS OF INTEREST   6
JOEL STEVERSON

NO TEARS   35
CRAIG A. REED, JR.

DYING DIGNITY   64
CHRIS HUSSEY

THE HAND THAT FEEDS   87
RANDALL N. BILLS

THERE'S NO "WE" IN "MERCENARY"   122
JASON HANSA

FAILINGS IN TEACHING   158
DANIEL ISBERNER

VIEW FROM THE GROUND   177
ALAN BRUNDAGE

NO DUST, NO WEAR   198
JASON HANSA

THE DAY WHEN HEAVEN WAS FALLING   232
JASON SCHMETZER

STRONG AS STEEL   253
MICHAEL J. CIARAVELLA

FOREWORD

When it comes to one of the most prestigious and enduring mercenary commands in the Inner Sphere, no word carries more weight than "tradition." The concept of tradition itself speaks to a longstanding history, and precious few military units in the *BattleTech* universe can claim that distinction.

The Eridani Light Horse, however, has been around since the very beginning. And by the "beginning," I mean two things: the original, first edition of *BattleTech*, published in 1984 as *BattleDroids* (the name "*BattleTech*" first appeared on the game's second edition a year later), and the fall of the First Star League, the most pivotal event in *BattleTech* history.

The first-edition game contained very little background information about the *BattleTech* universe, just six pages of brief detail on BattleMechs and the general state of the Inner Sphere. However, within those six pages, you can find a single short paragraph about a mercenary unit called the Eridani Light Horse. Those six sentences fired the imagination of a generation of *BattleTech* fans, giving birth to almost four decades' worth of stories surrounding this outfit.

But perhaps the most important aspect of the Light Horse is its roots in the Star League Regular Army, which began as the Third Regimental Combat Team in 2702, a formation of two striker regiments and two light-horse regiments. Nearly half a century after the Third was formed, the unit's commander was assassinated by agents of the Prince of Rasalhague, who deemed the RCT an occupation force, not Star League peacekeeping troops.

In response to this heinous act, the Third deployed to all ten worlds in its assigned district. When the Prince sent troops to evict them from Trondheim, the Third fought with such a terrifying swiftness near the city of Eridani that an eyewitness journalist claimed the Star League forces routed the Prince's army "like spirited Eridani stallions chasing after fat Luthien cows." The description stuck, and thus the Third adopted the nickname "Eridani Light Horse."

This Star League pedigree, coupled with tragedy during the Amaris Coup, led the Light Horse to a crossroads after the fall of the Star League. While Aleksandr Kerensky, Commanding General of the Star League Defense Force, felt his best course to prevent future war from engulfing the Inner Sphere was to take the survivors of the SLDF into the Deep Periphery, the Eridani Light Horse believed the best way to honor the Star League was to remain in the Inner Sphere and carry its legacy like a torch. Although the unit transitioned to mercenary service, its leaders and members maintained an unparalleled reputation for precision, professionalism, and martial excellence. This, along with the Light Horse's flagpole ceremony honoring the fallen League, served as a tangible reminder of the valor and values the Star League had stood for.

For this collection, we challenged our authors to take us through every facet of the Eridani Light Horse's legendary history. Among these pages you will witness the early tragedies during the Amaris Coup and the fall of the Star League. You will follow the survivors through the vicissitudes of the Succession Wars, the sudden return of the SLDF's descendants during the Clan Invasion, and the uncertainty and destruction of the Word of Blake Jihad. Then you can witness their glorious return in the waning days of the Dark Age, and into the new ilClan era. Each story demonstrates that throughout the centuries, no matter how ruthless the opponent, how deep their losses, or how close they were pushed to the brink of disaster, the Eridani Light Horse remained steadfast and resolute—a lasting testament to their history, and to the bravery and honor of the soldiers that filled their ranks.

For the sake of tradition, let's all sit back, pour one out for the Star League, and honor its memory together while looking ahead to the future.

—Philip A. Lee, Co-Editor
Catalyst Game Labs
February 2022

CONFLICTS OF INTEREST

JOEL STEVERSON

**ULTRACOM RUINS
ZEBEBELGENUBI
FEDERATION OF SKYE
LYRAN COMMONWEALTH
12 NOVEMBER 2772**

Blinking back tears as she watched the Eridani Light Horse Regiment's procession enter the quad, Major Astrid Karlsson logged a mental note to put in a commendation for Captain Calhoun. The quartermaster had worked his magic yet again. After five years of vicious fighting, the regiment was bedraggled and threadbare, yet somehow Calhoun had scrounged up dress uniforms for the honor guard.

The soldiers at the head of the column wore crisp, olive-drab uniforms with verdant half-jackets and side caps, knee-high boots in butternut and matching leather gloves. The ELH insignia—a piaffing, chestnut stallion on a gold circle with a gilded border—stood brightly atop the lotus-blue Radstadt World Sash running from right shoulder to left hip. Belted, ceremonial daggers completed the ensemble. Their vibrant uniforms stood in stark contrast to the dreary ferrocrete of the quad and the blackened ruins surrounding it.

A solitary flagpole rose from the center of the courtyard. The Rim Worlds Republic flag—a cobalt shark emblem upon a maroon field bordered in white—fluttered in the light wind.

The flagpole was flanked by a wrought-iron brazier on the right and a mahogany lectern to the left. A mixture of soldiers, militia, partisans, law enforcement, emergency services, and civilians filled every available meter of the yard.

As the last of the procession took their places, Colonel Ezra Bradley stepped to the lectern. The ELH's commander moved with an almost imperceptible limp as his artificial left leg swung a hair faster than its organic companion. Near constant combat for the last five years had aged him considerably. His hair was more gray than auburn now, and thick worry-lines etched his face like aged parchment. Crow's feet flared from the corners of his light-grey eyes as he squinted against the bright lights and waited for the teleprompter to spin up. The dedication ceremony would be streamed worldwide.

"Today is about duty," he said in a baritone rumble. "Duty is the obligation we have to one another through our shared belief in something greater than ourselves that compels us to act no matter the cost. It gives us courage when we are fearful, hope when we are in despair, and something to believe in when all else has failed.

"This campus was once Ultracom—the Ulsop Robotics Training Complex—where the Star League Defense Force trained soldiers to operate our Space Defense Systems; a nearly-impregnable network of space- and ground-based weaponry, space stations, and autonomous drone ships that safeguard key Terran Hegemony worlds.

"Technological prowess made the Hegemony a paragon of exceptionalism. A symbol of all that humankind could accomplish. The Modern Chivalrists Movement spread Hegemony values throughout the Star League. The Cameron Star became a symbol of manifest integrity. Confident in the protection of our armored fortresses, the Hegemony dispatched the SLDF to squelch the New Vandenberg Uprising.

"For all our accomplishments, we failed to uncover the traitors in our midst. We were betrayed by Stefan Amaris, the dastardly leader of the Rim Worlds Republic. The Usurper assassinated First Lord Richard Cameron and launched his reign of terror with simultaneous assaults on all Hegemony worlds. In a month, he'd stolen Camelot from Arthur."

Angry murmurs spread through the crowd. Bradley waited for them to die down before continuing, "When the Rim Worlders conquered this world, they made Ultracom their planetary command center, and forced Ulsop engineers to train their soldiers on SDS operations. The resistance tried to stop the training, but they failed. They had a duty to protect the Hegemony, so they tried again. They failed a second time, yet still they tried again.

"After eight failed attempts, they were finally successful in the spring of 2768. They smuggled three tons of SRM inferno missiles into the complex. Forty trainees died in the initial blast, and the resulting fire razed half the complex and injured another one-hundred-thirty occupiers."

Bradley slowed his cadence and poured anger into his next words. "The Rim Worlders responded by executing all three hundred Ulsop trainers and turned the ruins into an extermination camp where resistance fighters, dissidents, and anyone else they disliked spent their final days in conditions intended to cause a lingering, painful death."

A soft whimper drew Astrid's attention to the left. Captain Maeve Ramirez was visibly trembling. Astrid gave a slight smile, hoping Maeve would understand the offer of sympathy, but the younger woman didn't seem to notice. Astrid logged another item for her mental to-do list.

The SLDF had finally retaken Zebebelgenubi three weeks ago. The Seventy-First Light Horse had temporarily transferred from XI Corps to V Corps to bolster the assault. Astrid's battalion had been rounding up straggling Guards' forces when they discovered the Ultracom camp. Her rapid scout company—Maeve's High Flyers—were the first on site. The prisoners were so emaciated they resembled worn skin stretched over too-large skeletons more than people. A third suffered from diseases long since eradicated on all Hegemony worlds, implying the Rim Worlders had been testing bioweapons on the camp's population. Maeve's company found thousands of men, women, and children clinging to life surrounded by rotting corpses. When the prisoners had become too infirm to dig their own graves, the Rim Worlders simply stopped burying them. As the camp's horror came into focus, Maeve summoned every medtech in the regiment, but if half the prisoners survived it would be a miracle.

"Six years of occupation is simply interminable," Bradley said, resuming his normal diction. "I can scarcely imagine how difficult it must have been to persevere. The Rim Worlders desecrated your world. This hallowed ground was a monument to the Star League's preeminent defensive apparatus, and they twisted it into something vile and perverse. I'm sure there were times when giving up was an incredibly tempting option, but you persevered, and Zebebelgenubi is free of tyranny once again.

"This flag," Bradley gestured at the Rim Worlds Republic flagpole, "is a symbol of hatred, violence, and oppression. We will eradicate it, and then dedicate this space to the intrepid souls that survived internment here. Governor Moretti will be following me and speaking to the memorial plans. First, please join me in observing a moment of silence in recognition of the thirty thousand people who lost their lives here."

A trio of soldiers from the ELH's ad hoc honor guard swiftly lowered the Rim Worlds flag and wordlessly dropped it on the brazier. Hungry flames devoured it in a few seconds. When the last vestiges had been incinerated, the soldiers attached the Star League flag—the Cameron Star in white and black on a sapphire field—to the halyard.

"Thank you," Bradley said. "Now please stand for the Star League Anthem."

Astrid found Maeve waiting for the next shuttle back to their field headquarters. She had just missed the previous flight of VTOLs. They would have twenty minutes of relative privacy before their ride returned.

"If you ever want to talk, please know I'm here for you," she said. *That sounded awful. Why am I so bad at this?*

Maeve dropped her eyes and slowly shook her head. When she finally looked up, hot tears rolled down her cheeks. Any other time, Astrid would have encouraged her to see a combat fatigue therapist, but that luxury wouldn't be available until they rejoined the Sixteenth Army in January, and the ELH took care of its own.

"I don't know what I'd say," she managed at last.

"That's fine. I probably won't have any answers for you, but I am a good listener," Astrid said. She hesitated for a moment, mulling her options. It had all sounded good in her head, but the intense pain in Maeve's hazel eyes tangled with her own demons until everything in her head was a discombobulated mess. *How can I compare my pain to hers? Great job, Astrid. Now what are you going to do?* As the silence stretched into uncomfortable territory, the words tumbled out, "When the Nineteenth... Uh, when Oren... I mean..."

"It's okay," Maeve said. She took Astrid's left hand and gave a gentle squeeze. "I know what you're trying to say."

Astrid nodded her thanks.

"Avenge the Nineteenth," Maeve said.

"Burn the Usurper," Astrid replied by rote. *That's not where I was going.*

A year and a half ago, the ELH's Nineteenth Striker Regiment dropped on Talitha in an attempt to destroy command, control, and communications facilities at what was previously the Eighth Army Headquarters. A Rim World spy leaked their plans to the Talitha garrison, and the Nineteenth was wiped out. Astrid's nephew had been one of the first casualties. She drank herself to sleep whenever she could for the first month. Purging that vice had taken considerable effort. *It's been eighteen months and I'm still struggling.*

"I just don't want to see you repeating any of my mistakes, Maeve," Astrid said, trying to salvage her pep talk.

Maeve made a sound somewhere between a cough and a monosyllabic laugh.

"Trust me, I make plenty of them," Astrid admitted. "I just have ten more years of experience at hiding them."

"Hiding what?"

Astrid startled, and her cheeks flushed. *Nothing like demonstrating poor situational awareness for the old man.* She turned to Bradley, but following field etiquette, didn't salute.

"*Good evening, sir,*" Astrid and Maeve spoke as one.

"As you were," Bradley replied. "My apologies, I didn't intend to intrude."

"Oh, uh, we were just talking—"

Maeve cut in, "Major Karlsson was just offering her recommendations on a personal matter."

Bradley smiled knowingly. "I was briefing General Badler when word of this camp came in. The pictures gave me nightmares. I didn't make it here until last week, and all the bodies had been buried by then. I can only imagine how horrible it was in person."

"Thank-Thank you, sir."

"I think turning this place into a memorial will help a lot of people heal. How is your company handling it?"

"It's been difficult for us all, sir. Some are handling it well, or at least giving the appearance, but a few are definitely struggling."

"Is there anything your company needs?"

"Aside from a million dead Rim Worlders?" Maeve said, then stiffened. "Sorry, sir, that was supposed to be a joke."

"Is it? My wife tells me I don't have a sense of humor. It's fine, Captain. I understand where you're coming from—" Bradley glanced at Astrid, "—but hating the enemy isn't the solution."

"Sir?" Maeve asked.

"They have monsters among them, the Amaris Dragoons for one, and a command structure that encourages their predilections, but the average RWR soldier isn't all that different from any other soldier. We estimate that up to a third of their forces have been conscripted."

Maeve looked a bit abashed. "I...hadn't realized that."

"It's not something that's been emphasized in briefings," Bradley said. He gave Astrid another quick look and continued, "The last few years have been difficult for us all. The hardships will continue to get worse. The road to Terra is very, very long, but we have a duty to the citizens of the Hegemony.

"Today's ceremony was meant to give people closure, but for some I suspect all it's done is stirred up strong, uncomfortable feelings. I was thinking it might be helpful to your peers if there was a support group—nothing formal, just a gathering when there's down time. Since you were the first field officer on site,

I thought you might want to volunteer to lead it—assuming the major can spare you, of course."

Astrid marveled at the confident smile that had appeared on Maeve's face. *She's completely turned around. He makes it seem so easy, and he also gave me a message while spending the whole time talking to Maeve.*

Abruptly, she realized Bradley was waiting for her reply. "I'll make sure Captain Ramirez has the time she needs."

"Excellent. I suspect she'll discover that service to others is its own reward."

"I won't let you down, sir," Maeve said.

Bradley nodded. "Do your duty in all things, Captain, and you'll be fine. You cannot do more, and shouldn't do less."

**MCKENNA-CLASS WARSHIP SLS *MCKENNA'S PRIDE*
ZENITH JUMP POINT, VAN DIEMEN IV
TERRA FIRMA PROVINCE
TERRAN HEGEMONY
14 NOVEMBER 2772**

Aleksandr Kerensky, Commanding General of the Star League Defense Force and architect of Operation Chieftain—the campaign to retake the Terran Hegemony—cleared his throat and tapped the record button again.

"Good work on Zebebelgenubi, Colonel Bradley. I knew your regiment would help get the job done. General Badler gave you high praise. I don't have the details, but as you know she's hard to impress."

Kerensky paused for a moment. When he continued, his tone was somber. "I understand your desire to remain on-world. The camp you described gives me chills. Unfortunately, General Marcocelli reports that fighting has bogged down on Lyons. By the time you get there, your Twenty-First Striker and 151st Light Horse regiments will be ready to go in. I need your whole Regimental Combat Team to work its magic on this one. Keep your head down, Ezra. Reports are the Amaris Dragoons have already deployed biological and chemical weapons. *Ni pukha, ni pera*, my friend."

Kerensky tapped the stop button and sat back with a sigh. He had fifty-three messages still to record. If he worked fast, he might get to his bunk by 0200.

AUSTERA ISLAND
SARMENTOSA ARCHIPELAGO, CARVER V
HEGEMONY CORE
TERRAN HEGEMONY
15 JULY 2773

Astrid's reticle pulsed gold and she squeezed her primary targeting interlock circuit. Waste heat poured into her cockpit as the *Phoenix Hawk*'s GM 270 fusion engine funneled power into the 'Mech's lasers. A coherent, green beam struck the *Jackrabbit* just inside its left shoulder. It bored through a weak joint where a vertical armor plate connected to the 'Mech's shoulder and severed its arm. A pair of scarlet rays piled on. The first came within centimeters of the *Jackrabbit*'s angular head. The second found its way through the gaping wound that had been the 'Mech's armpit and into its SRM feed mechanism. The resulting explosion drove the 'Mech ten meters to its right, where it crashed into the burning remains of a Demon combat vehicle.

"Nice shooting," Maeve said.

"Thanks," Astrid replied. "I think that was the last one."

"Agreed, my screen is clear. How are you holding up?"

"The Gauss slug from that Demon definitely wrecked my left foot. The rest of the leg is holding, but barely."

"If there are more Rim Worlders, we're in real trouble."

After liberating Lyons, most of the Eridani Light Horse had continued to Imbros III with the Sixteenth Army. Astrid's Sixteenth Recon Battalion had been detached for extended reconnaissance raiding on the beleaguered world of Carver V.

Carver V was a water-rich, tropical world with no continents, three significant landmasses, hundreds of archipelagos, and thousands of islands. Although it lacked Castles Brian and SDS, it was one of the most heavily fortified worlds in the Terran Hegemony.

The largest island, Quantico, hosted multiple training centers and advanced specialty schools where the SLDF's elite Cavalry, Armor, Aerospace, and Naval (CAAN) regiments honed their craft. Thanks to this infrastructure—and a spirited defense by General Saul van der Kolk's CAAN regiments—Carver V was one of the few Hegemony worlds that hadn't fallen during the Amaris Coup. After linking up with van der Kolk, Astrid's force had spent the last three months harassing Rim Worlders with guerrilla operations, scouting, and avoiding set piece battles.

Amaris Republican Guards General Noriko Milton-Davis had been trying to pacify Carver V for six years. Although she nominally controlled seventy percent of the world, including the Reinhardt island chain and planetary capital of Korce, the CAAN regiments still held Quantico and many key islands worldwide.

Astrid's forces had been sweeping a rocky region three klicks from the beach on Austera Island when they'd been ambushed. Rim Worlders poured out of hidden tunnels ahead of and behind them, Demon combat vehicles and infantry from one, and two lances of 'Mechs from the other.

Wilson's *Wasp*s had taken the worst of it. One 'Mech had its torso cored by a Gauss round and another lost both arms to the opening salvos. Knox's lance of *Firebee*s had fared the best, and all four were still operational. Astrid's Command Lance was at half strength.

Maeve's lance of *Phoenix Hawk* LAMs posed a different problem. An experimental unit, the Land-Air 'Mech was capable of converting between three different modes: 'Mech, aerospace fighter, and AirMech—an interstitial hybrid that looked like someone had glued arms and legs to the front half of an aerospace fighter. The Rim Worlders had concentrated on them. Somehow all four were still functional, but with supply lines uncertain, Astrid couldn't risk losing them.

Maeve's going to hate this. "Evac will be here in twenty minutes—" she began.

"No, ma'am," Maeve cut her off. "I know that tone. I've got just as big a score to settle with these Rim Worlders as you do."

"You're right," Astrid admitted.

"I am? I mean—"

"But I need your lance to bug out now."

"You're not serious?"

"Maeve, you're becoming a solid leader, but right now you're our best scout, and that's what matters. You can cover ten times the ground we can, and we need that intel to stay in the fight. You've a duty to the Light Horse and the CAAN regiments to stay alive and do your job."

"Yes, ma'am."

Astrid could still feel the hate in those two words twenty minutes later when the landing craft beached.

FORT PLEIKU MỚI
CARVER V
17 NOVEMBER 2774

The Eridani Light Horse regiments had been on Carver V for a little over a year. All three had volunteered to reinforce the CAAN regiments and stay until the job was done. Together they had liberated much of the watery world, but victory still seemed a distant dream.

This battlefield spread over a thousand hectares of cratered, ruined ground. Crashed aerospace fighters carved deep furrows and spread debris across the dirt. Skeletal 'Mech remains marked overrun battle positions and sketched the path of the counterattacking Republican Guards. Thick, black smoke billowed from the flaming wrecks of countless vehicles, obscuring the enemy 'Mechs as they advanced.

Radar showed the Guards deployed in an inverted wedge, with the tip of the left flank closest to the Seventy-First's position. The Light Horse were staging a fighting withdrawal in left echelon, anchored by the Eighty-Second Heavy Cavalry on the left. Astrid's Sixteenth Recon battalion, deployed among rocky hills capped with sparse scrub brush, held a salient on the right flank.

The shrill scream of incoming artillery shells pierced the air, briefly drowning the staccato noise of combat. Half a breath later, explosions blossomed to the right of Garba's Gladiators, blocking their advance with plumes of earth and shrapnel.

"They're trying to get around us," Captain Garba said, his deadpan tone further flattened by the radio.

"If they get us in enfilade, it's going to spoil the party," Astrid replied. She zoomed out on her secondary display studying the map. "Drop back and circle around east of hill forty-three. I'll have Jafferbhoy hold there and defilade."

"Copy that," Garba said.

Astrid switched back to her battalion's command frequency and relayed her orders as she watched Garba's lance of *Spector*s execute their maneuver. Garba's Gladiators was the fastest ground force in her battalion; a lance each of *Spector*s, *Mongoose*s, and *Mercuries*. They weren't built for a slugfest, but could easily handle the Guards' screening force.

A second volley hammered the same area west of hill forty-three. The box barrage landed well ahead of Jafferbhoy's advancing company, launching more chunks of earth and shrapnel into the air. *Either the Guards aren't adjusting fire, or this is some sort of area denial.* Astrid throttled back her *Phoenix Hawk* and took a longer look at the map. *What am I missing?*

Jafferbhoy's company moved into position behind hill forty-three. His *Crab*s, *Starslayer*s, and *Griffin*s fired blindly into the smoke, hoping to slow the Guards while the battalion's third company—Maeve's High Flyers—sprinted across the open space. Her entire battalion was now positioned to blunt the Guards' advance. The maneuver would protect the rest of the regiment from enfilading fire along the long axis of their echelon and spoil any attempted envelopment.

A third artillery barrage struck the same spot, but this time it blanketed the ground in thick, dark smoke. Astrid's radar showed the Guards split into two groups of skirmishers with a reinforced company moving toward either side of the hill.

"Contact right!" Garba said. "Mixed lances: *Jackrabbit*, *Night Hawk*, *Phoenix*, and *Thorn*."

The Guards outweighed the Gladiators, but were at a significant disadvantage in speed. Garba ordered his company forward in bounding overwatch, with his lance of *Spector*s taking point. In seconds, their concentrated fire dropped the lead *Phoenix* and damaged its lancemates. Before the Regulars could react, Garba's nimble company had penetrated their line.

Jafferboy's *Starslayer*s and *Crab*s wheeled right around the hill and into supporting positions becoming the anvil to Garba's hammer. The Guards were stuck. If they turned to face Garba, they exposed their weaker rear armor to Jafferbhoy. If they didn't turn about, then Garba would pepper their backs, and they'd be just as dead. Dropping straight back would have been the smart move, but the Guards hesitated, and their indecision cost them a *Jackrabbit*.

"Contact left!" Captain Maeve Ramirez announced.

Astrid's sensors had identified the group approaching through the smoke as a mix of *Night Hawk*s, *Sentinel*s, and *Firestarter*s, with a pair of *Ostroc*s for support. The bulbous heavies were technologically inferior to Astrid's force, but their twin large lasers packed a punch, and they were spry with decent armor.

Astrid started to order her command lance forward, but Maeve cut her off, flooding the comm channel with a string of profanity. Astrid frowned. Her friendship with Maeve had suffered significantly after Austera, and she was still working to repair the damage. Maeve had shown a lot of technical improvement in the last year, but she'd also grown distant and often cold. *It's not like her to break protocol and get emotional. What's got her so rattled?*

Six sapphire and charcoal 'Mechs emerged from the smoke. Each had chains criss-crossed over their front torsos. Gaunt people in tattered rags hung from the chains. Some thrashed wildly. Others were either frozen in terror or already dead. A pair of *Sentinel*s each had one captive splayed over their sloping left torsos. Four gangly *Night Hawk*s had prisoners restrained between their stubby arms and narrow side torsos.

The Guards fired on the move. Emerald beams leaped from the *Night Hawk*'s arms and the *Sentinel*'s Ultra autocannon spat angry slugs. Armor plate sublimated into vapor under megajoules of coherent light or buckled and shattered from kilonewtons of kinetic energy. Unlucky as ever, Wilson's *Wasp*s bore the brunt. One got head-capped, and another had its left leg severed at the hip. It tottered as its MechWarrior struggled in vain to stay upright, but fell seconds later.

Alarmed chatter blended into a cacophony of crosstalk.

"Do we return—"
"Of all the rotten—"
"Sick bast—"
"What are—"
"Kill 'em all—"
"Silence! Silence! *Silence!*" Astrid barked.

Adrenaline-fueled time dilation stretched milliseconds into hours. An incoherent, stream-of-consciousness flashed through her mind. *The Rim Worlders are inhuman... No living thing deserves this... The violence is so...personal.*

It was also well outside her rules of engagement, but there was only one answer.

For Oren.

"Return fire! Hostages be damned!" a ragged, guttural voice bellowed over the comm. A few seconds passed before Astrid realized it was hers.

Her reflexes took over, and she pushed her *Phoenix Hawk* into a run. The rest of her command lance fell in, closing range with meter-devouring strides.

She centered her reticle on a *Sentinel*'s right torso, well clear of the human shield, but anything could happen. The reticle flashed gold, and she squeezed her trigger.

Forgive me...

FORT PLEIKU MỚI
CARVER V
25 NOVEMBER 2774

General Milton-Davis's Republican Guards surrendered the fort four days after she died in combat. The front lines were now fifty kilometers ahead, and the fort bustled with post-battle activity. The Light Horse senior officers were gathered around the holomap table in a large briefing room.

Astrid marveled at Bradley's appearance. *How does he look parade fresh after so much time in the field?* Most of the assembly—Astrid included—had dark circles under their eyes. Several seemed to be wearing more bandage than uniform. Astrid's fatigues were stained with grime, sweat, and blood. A ragged gash, held together by ten staples, ran from just behind her left temple to the base of her skull.

"Next on the agenda is our POWs," Bradley said.

"I think we should execute the lot of them," said Major Kaitanak. The Twenty-First Striker Regiment's XO had a deep alto voice (out of place in her slight frame), almond skin, dark features, and flowing charcoal hair.

Astrid said, "Unless we're going to hold courts martial—"

"They don't deserve it," Kaitanak interrupted.

Several officers nodded their agreement.

"I didn't say they deserved it," Astrid spat.

"These reamers used nerve gas on my battalion—twice!" Kaitanak retorted

"And human shields," Astrid said flatly.

Kaitanak ignored her and said, "It's not just here. They nuked the Fourteenth Army on Murchison, too. They've committed war crimes throughout the Hegemony. We ought to dig a big hole and be done with them."

Supportive murmurs filled the room.

"We knew what they were capable of, and we knew they'd behave even worse when things got real," Bradley said. "I'm surprised we haven't seen more of this."

"I don't disagree," Kaitanak said, "but respectfully, we have to send a message that crimes against humanity will be met with swift, decisive justice."

"And how do you suggest we do that?"

"By executing the lot of them." Kaitanak punctuated her words by thumping the table with her fist.

Several of her peers hooted their support.

When they'd finished, Bradley asked, "How is extrajudicial killing justice?"

"It's what they'd do to us," Kaitanak said.

"You're begging the question."

Kaitanak's cheeks flushed with color, but she said nothing.

"What's the purpose of this campaign?" Bradley asked.

"Reclaim the Hegemony and depose the Usurper," Kaitanak said.

"Wrong." Bradley held the gaze of each of his officers before continuing. "We're not merely fighting for the body of the

Hegemony, but also for its soul. If we mistreat our prisoners, all we've done is prove the Star League Defense Force is just as capable of malfeasance as the Rim Worlds Republic. That's not enough. We have to be better than them—"

"We are," Kaitanak protested.

"Of course we are." Bradley splayed his palms on the table and leaned in. "But how do we demonstrate it?"

When Kaitanak didn't answer, Bradley caught Astrid in his gaze.

At length, she said, "By preserving our honor."

"Why?"

"Honor means doing the right thing even when others don't," Astrid said, "not because someone is watching, but because it's all we have."

"Exactly," Bradley said with a smile. "Either our values truly matter, or nothing matters. We must stand for what is right, and that means due process, courts-martial, and true justice. If we do *anything* less, we dishonor ourselves, the Star League, and everything we're fighting to save."

**FLAGSTAFF ISLAND
CARVER V
HEGEMONY CORE
TERRAN HEGEMONY
21 AUGUST 2775**

The flash of white light was so intense that for an instant it was all encompassing. Astrid's viewscreen automatically dimmed in an attempt to mitigate the effects, but it was a fraction of a second too slow. She blinked to clear the spots from her vision. Then the blast wave hit.

The concussive force tossed her *Phoenix Hawk* to the ground like a rag doll. Sharp pain coursed into her shoulder and thigh muscles where the harness attached, but it kept Astrid in her command couch. Her head slammed into the side panel, and a coppery taste flooded her mouth. Fire burned in her lungs as they begged for air. Reflexively she grabbed at her chest. Darkness started to creep in around the edges growing more pronounced with every passing second. Just as Astrid believed she was about to pass out, her lungs started working again. Her breath came in desperate, ragged gasps.

That was too close. She spat blood and toggled her command frequency. "Sound off."

Static.

Her viewscreen's polarization returned to normal. A towering column of dirt and debris reached into the cerulean sky. She couldn't see the top, but the expansive mushroom shape was a given. The Amaris Dragoons had nuked Flagstaff. Belatedly, the radiation klaxon sounded, and amber light flooded her cockpit.

"Acknowledged," she said.

The klaxon continued blaring its unnecessary warning. Astrid flipped the manual cutoff switch and the klaxon silenced. The rad meter was in the yellow. That gave her a few hours to clear the radiation zone.

Her company was spread out across the island, probing the fortresses defenses from multiple vectors. Her command lance was with Maeve's company on the beach. Garba's was four klicks west tangling with Amaris Fusiliers, and Jafferbhoy was two klicks further out. Both should have been well outside the blast radius.

"Sound off," she said again.

"Garba."

"Jafferbhoy."

Maeve didn't respond.

"We saw the nuke, are you okay over there?" Garba asked.

"Stand by," Astrid said. She switched to her command lance frequency. "Sound off."

"Kowalczyk."

"Cartinez."

"Anyone have eyes on Huang?" Astrid asked.

"Negative."

"Me neither."

Astrid pulled her *Phoenix Hawk* into a crouch. Her new ride, courtesy of LIII Corps, was the heavily upgraded 1b model. The rest of her command lance had the older, but still capable PXH-2 models. The Dragoons *Phoenix* she'd been fighting lay face-down in the sand a hundred meters away.

She tried to align her targeting reticle on it, but her HUD stuttered and skipped. The gray overlay blinked out, but returned a second later. *Close enough.* She squeezed her primary trigger. Manmade lightning cut a jagged path through the air striking the 'Mech in the right shoulder. The beam burned through the joint, severing the gun-arm. The *Phoenix* didn't stir. Its pilot was either dead or unconscious. *The EMP really fried your systems, huh girl?*

Astrid scanned right, looking for Maeve. Her *Phoenix Hawk* LAM was down on both knees arms splayed wide. A length of palm tree trunk had crushed her cockpit.

Astrid screamed and put several more shots into the Dragoons *Phoenix*, ensuring that it wouldn't get up, and then worked her *Phoenix Hawk* to its feet.

The Davy Crockett tactical nuke had turned sand to glass and vaporized everything within a few hundred meters of ground zero. Along the beach palm trees were blown down, their wide trunks sheared through.

A ferrocrete bunker jutted defiantly out of a rocky hill rising a twenty meters above the sandy ground. Its face blackened with soot and withered under the force of the explosion. Its armored turret had been reduced to melted steel, but otherwise the structure was intact.

Her command lance (with Maeve's High Flyers) had been in fire team wedge formation moving south along the beach. The Amaris Dragoons had come out to meet them with a lance of armored vehicles; two Turhans, a Demon, and a Manticore, two companies of infantry, and a lance of 'Mechs—a *Phoenix*, *Hunchback*, *Galahad* and *Crusader*.

The nuke had either detonated prematurely or struck well off target. Most the Dragoon infantry were down, dead or soon to be. The lead Turhan was on fire, but the remaining vehicles were still in the fight, and the 'Mechs were getting to their feet. Astrid's group was at a significant disadvantage.

She gave Garba and Jafferbhoy a quick update, and told Maeve's surviving lancemates to switch to her frequency. "Okay Light Horse, we're blooded, but we need to compartmentalize. We have to move before the Dragoons regain their senses. *Firebee*s, take the *Hunchback*, *Wasp*s, do what you can with the Turhan. The rest of you with me, the *Galahad* is our primary target, then the Manticore."

The bulbous *Galahad* opened up with both Gauss rifles. The weapon used a series of magnets to accelerate a nickel-iron alloy slug to hypersonic velocity. It smashed into the lead *Firebee*'s left torso. Armor plates gave way, showering the 'Mech's insides with shrapnel. One of those shards punched through an SRM ammo bin and the *Firebee* exploded, its arms and legs cartwheeling off in different directions.

The surviving *Firebee*s unloaded on the *Galahad* with their large lasers. The Dragoon 'Mech weathered the storm without significant damage. Heat flooded Astrid's cockpit as her reactor surged to provide power for her ER PPC and ER large laser. The azure bolt missed wide left, but the emerald laser beam was true, and sizzled armor off the *Galahad*'s right arm.

Astrid jogged left, narrowly avoiding a flight of LRMs from the *Crusader*. The missiles caught Cartinez in the right arm and leg, but her *Phoenix Hawk* shrugged off the damage.

Cartinez answered with a large laser, scoring a hit on the *Crusader*'s thick torso. Kowalczyk's shot was close enough to melt paint, but did no real damage. Maeve's lancemates added their large lasers to the mix. The *Galahad* staggered, but stayed on its feet despite losing nearly two tons of armor.

Astrid led the septuplet of *Phoenix Hawk*s forward at a run. They needed to get in close before their heavier opponents picked them apart. The Manticore gunner badly misjudged its LRM shot. Ten missiles tore up the sand two hundred meters behind Astrid's group. Its PPC struck home, and severed left arm from Cartinez's 'Mech. The *Phoenix Hawk*'s left leg was next, torn apart by a gauss shot as the Demon re-entered the fight.

Long-range missiles and Gauss slugs tore at the *Phoenix Hawk*s, smashing armor, weapons, and heat sinks, but the nimble 'Mechs made difficult targets, and for every shot that hit, another two or three only found air.

By the time they were close enough to use their secondary weaponry, the seven were down to five. The *Galahad* dropped first. Then an emerald beam of light cut through the Manticore's armor and detonated its ammo magazine. The turret blew off, landing upside down in the sand ten meters behind the ruined hulk.

The *Crusader* pilot was far too liberal with her LRM shots, and quickly ran her ammo bins dry. The formidable 'Mech still had Streak SRM-2s, medium lasers, and machine guns, and fired them continuously at the troop of *Phoenix Hawk*s. Ruby darts from more than a dozen medium lasers converged on the *Crusader*. They were rewarded with a rumbling explosion as machine gun and SRM ammo detonated simultaneously.

With help from General van der Kolk's CAAN regiments, the island fortification had been breached, and the remaining Rim Worlders surrendered rather than fight a hopeless close quarters battle for the fortress. Light Horse injuries ran near thirty percent, with KIAs just over ten percent. Maeve's High Flyers had lost three, including their leader, but another Rim Worlder force had been defeated.

Bradley stopped by the recovery ward to check on his XO and other injured soldiers. He moved from bed to bed, offering words of support and encouragement for the wounded.

When he got to Astrid, he said, "I'm sorry to hear about Captain Ramirez. I know you two were close."

"Thank you, sir," Astrid replied numbly, unable to sit up.

Noticing her effort, Bradley put a hand on her shoulder. "Just rest, Major. From what they tell me, you're lucky to be alive."

"I hear I have Captain Calhoun to thank," she said. "From what Garba told me, Calhoun traded ammunition with the 151st. If he hadn't given away our machine gun rounds in exchange for more SRMs, I wouldn't be here. The shot that knocked out my reactor also tagged my ammo bin, and the CASE for that bin has been on the repair list for months. I suppose that means I owe him a beer."

"Make sure you take care of that debt."

"I will."

Bradley smiled, then leaned in close. He whispered, "Maeve isn't the only MechWarrior under your command. You have a duty to all of them, and getting killed in a frontal assault is no way to honor that commitment."

Astrid nodded. "I know."

"I know you do. I just thought you could use a reminder."

YELIZOVO, NORTH AMERICA
TERRA
ALLIANCE CORE
TERRAN HEGEMONY
15 FEBRUARY 2784

The campaign to reclaim the Terran Hegemony ended successfully on 12 November 2779. It had taken far longer than anyone predicted, cost one hundred million lives, and consumed half of the Star League Defense Force. The Usurper had been executed for his numerous crimes, but rather than ignite the Terran Hegemony's resurgence, the end of the war had been simply the prelude to a new conflict.

Political brinksmanship had dominated the past three years, and it was all but certain the Star League was doomed to a slow and painful death. The Eridani Light Horse had survived the Hegemony Campaign, but martial skill could not overcome the looming threat.

Yesterday, Aleksandr Kerensky, Commanding General of the Star League Defense force, had gathered his senior officers at a secret meeting on Terra and shared his bold plan for a Star League in absentia.

Following that meeting, Kerensky made time for one-on-ones with many of his officers at his retreat in the town of Yelizovo. The den he now shared with Colonel Ezra Bradley was cozy and lived-in, with tasteful décor reminiscent of his great aunt's birthplace in Kungur. Kerensky had inherited the modest home after her passing in 2730, and often used it for quiet contemplation when he needed a respite from bustling Unity City.

He set his scotch on the ashwood center table, leaned back in his antique leather chair, and gave Colonel Ezra Bradley a warm, reassuring smile.

"Believe me, Ezra, I understand your feelings. It's not hyperbole when I tell you this is one of the most difficult decisions I've ever been faced with."

"You really expect another war?"

"I'm afraid I do. The Council Lords all failed to do their duty to the Star League when the Usurper struck, and they have only grown more recalcitrant."

"I take your point, but it doesn't mean they're looking for war."

"I'm quite certain they're not *looking* for war, but I believe it will find them nonetheless. The absence of House Cameron has created a power vacuum. Each of the House Lords believe they are the smartest person in whatever room they occupy. This naturally suggests each is the best candidate to fill the First Lord's shoes. If there's one thing I've learned for certain, it's that not one of them would deign to take a position subordinate to their peers.

"I suspect—within the next decade at most—one will anoint themselves successor to Richard Cameron. They've already stripped me of my role as Protector of the Realm. It's the obvious next step."

Bradley frowned. "We've been friends, what, twenty years? You've always been a man of integrity and honor. How can exile be the answer? What about our duty to the citizens of the Hegemony? We cannot abandon them in their time of gravest need."

Kerensky looked as though the questions sapped all of his strength. For several long minutes he wore a thoughtful expression, as if considering which answers to provide. When he finally spoke, his voice was weary.

"I have wrestled with that dilemma more than any other. It has become my white whale. Certainly, I have a duty to the citizens of the Hegemony. Notwithstanding that, I have a duty to the Star League. I also have a duty to myself. Each of these compete with the others, pulling me in different directions. Each invokes a different duty, a different aspect of core values I cannot choose to ignore.

"If the SLDF remains, the Council Lords will eventually cast me out. I'm too great an obstacle to their ambitions for them to let me remain indefinitely. Once I am out of the way, they will make overtures to the officers they believe to be sufficiently malleable. No House Lord will bend the bulk of the SLDF to their will, but each will succeed in recruiting some number of troops to their cause.

"They will believe this affords them sufficient advantage, and they will strike. The remnants of the Star League will again plunge into war. Not tomorrow, hopefully not next year, but within a decade at most.

"Going into exile deprives the House Lords of that resource and the temptation to subsume it. Do you remember your ancient Terran history—the doctrine of mutually assured destruction? That is the only path forward here. We maintain the balance of power, so that no one faction has the advantage. There's been far too much war in the last decade."

Bradley nursed his scotch before he replied, "I would never question you publicly, and I cannot tell you how much this opportunity for candid discussion means to me, both personally and as your subordinate.

"Reclaiming the Hegemony has greatly reduced our strength, but we are still a potent fighting force. Our very presence is a deterrent to the schemes of even the most conniving House Lord. What if going into exile removes their restraints and emboldens them to reckless action?"

"Naturally, I've considered that scenario." Kerensky sipped his drink. "But ultimately I must concern myself with those matters directly in my purview. I am responsible for the well-being of the SLDF and their dependents."

"Despite our losses, we still outnumber any single House military," Bradley continued. "The men regard you with deep admiration and a singular affection. I believe most will follow you no matter the course you set. The surviving heirs to House Cameron are all distant relatives with no substantial claim—"

"No," Kerensky interrupted.

Bradley held up his hands. "I did not mean to suggest—"

"Yes, you did," Kerensky said. "It's okay, my friend. You're not the only one to consider it, but it is not an option, and you will regard it as a settled matter."

"Of course, sir." As the silence began to border on uncomfortable, Bradley said, "I'll brief my regiments as soon as I return home. Between following you into exile or remaining at home and facing the unknown, it's an impossible decision. You might as well ask me to choose my favorite child."

Kerensky nodded. "I can think of no greater conflict of interest than the competition of equally opposing duties. Each soldier will need to decide how they can best fulfill their obligations while respecting their intrinsic values. I would not deprive them of such an important decision, but they will need to make it soon."

He leaned forward and locked eyes with Bradley. "We've been friends a long time, Ezra. I appreciate that you felt obligated to make your case, and that you trusted our friendship enough to be frank with me. Let me return the favor by saying I know which direction you're leaning. I want you to touch base with Lauren Hayes. She'll be coordinating efforts with those who remain behind."

Astrid was waiting for Bradley at the airport. His meeting with the general clearly hadn't gone as he'd hoped. In all their years together, it was the first time she'd ever seen him look defeated or at a loss for words.

As they boarded the shuttle, Astrid wondered what could have happened over the last forty-eight hours to leave the general in such a sullen state. She was almost afraid to find out.

ERIDANI LIGHT HORSE PARADE GROUNDS
ELBEUF, RADSTADT
RADSTADT PREFECTURE
DRACONIS COMBINE
8 JULY 2784

"Mister Razaee, are we ready?"

The signal systems tech glanced at his tablet and replied, "Yes, ma'am, local stations standing by, HPG interconnect green; at your command."

They were gathered in a mobile headquarters vehicle parked between the red-brick headquarters building and base parade ground. Outside, a team of videographers, boom operators, grips, managers, coordinators, and more waited for the director's signal.

Astrid blew out a long breath. As the nominal producer, she was in charge of the operation, but in practice she deferred to the director and was little more than a rubber stamp. Still, her palms were slick with sweat.

We're in the dirt now.

"Do it."

"Yes, ma'am."

With a few taps on his tablet, Warrant Officer Razaee activated the channel. The signal was streamed to all members of the Seventy-First Light Horse on world. When the broadcast completed, it would be sent via priority HPG burst to the 151st on Richmond, and the Twenty-First on Balsta.

The Cameron Star filled the screen for a moment, then dissolved into an image of Colonel Ezra Bradley in his dress uniform, standing to the left of the twin flagpoles. The Star League Defense Force flag flew from the left flagpole; the Eridani Light Horse flag from the right one. Both fluttered slightly in a light easterly breeze. A three-person honor guard stood at each flag pole. To Bradley's right, hundreds of ELH warriors stood at parade rest in formation. The camera zoomed in until the general's upper body filled the screen.

He said, "Fifty years ago, when I was a cadet at the War Academy of Mars, I learned the acronym SHIELD. It's a mnemonic for the SLDF core values: service, honor, integrity, excellence, loyalty, and duty. I joined the SLDF because I wanted to live a life that embodied these values. They've informed every decision and action since I first donned the uniform, and they will continue to do so until I take my last breath. They have never been as important as they are now.

"History teaches that a house divided against itself cannot endure. Nineteen long years ago, the New Vandenberg Uprising threatened to sunder our house after nearly one hundred-seventy unified years. We met that challenge. We persevered. Two years later, the Usurper tested us as we could never have imagined. Once again, we met the challenge. We fought for seven years—culminating in the bloodiest campaign the Inner Sphere had ever seen. We triumphed—" Bradley's voice cracked, "—but our House faltered, and then fell." Straining, he continued, "The High Council disbanded. Yet again we were tested as never before, and yet again we endured.

"The Usurper dealt us a mortal blow, and the House Lords are poised to deliver the coup de grâce. Our House is in the preactive phase of dying, and a fourth, arduous struggle lies before us. General Kerensky and many of our peers fear the House Lords will suborn us with their machinations unless we move beyond their considerable reach. General Hayes and some of our peers contend that we must remain a bulwark against tyranny.

"When I shared this news with you in early March, I asked you to make an impossible decision without fear of reprisal or recrimination, so that when the time came, our actions would be guided by conscience and commitment to duty. You've waited patiently these past three months, and now the time is upon us.

"Nearly all of the Eridani Light Horse have chosen to remain and safeguard our homes. From our three surviving regiments, fifteen MechWarriors and their dependents have chosen to join Exodus. They depart immediately, with our blessings and fervent hope that we will be reunited at the conclusion of their successful journey.

"I cannot speak to individual divisions, but the majority of the SLDF will join Exodus. I remind you that this information is classified, and may not be discussed outside our ranks." Bradley took a deep breath. When he resumed, his voice was grave. "Providence alone knows how this will affect the Inner Sphere, but I fear posterity will mark today as the end of the Star League.

"It has long been our custom to observe a moment of silence in recognition of our comrades who have given their last full measure in service to the Eridani Light Horse, the Star League Defense Force, and House Cameron. Today, our remembrance takes on new significance. As the SLDF begins its journey into the unknown, we begin a new tradition in honor of that sacrifice.

"Henceforth, until the SLDF returns from exile, we will leave one flagpole bare in memoriam, and we will fly our own flag at half-staff, not as an expression of our loss and grief, but as a symbol of our fervent hope for their speedy and safe return."

"I'm sure General Kerensky will understand, sir," Astrid said.

"It's not that," Bradley said. "I know he'll understand, but I still feel like we should be going with him...like *I* let him down."

They were sitting in Bradley's office in the headquarters building. His window looked out onto the parade ground. Astrid kept glancing at the flagpoles. The new ELH flag had a black horse on gold with a black border—another symbol of mourning. *Eventually, it will stop looking strange.*

"Do you remember what you told me on Carver V?"

"Actually, no," Bradley said. "That was what, nine, ten years ago? We had a lot of wounded on that campaign, and I visited a lot of soldiers."

"Well, I remember it. I don't think I'll ever forget it. That was the day we lost Maeve, Captain Ramirez. I was so full of blood lust that I led a suicidal charge against a group of Rim Worlds heavies, nearly got myself killed.

"You've always had a knack for telling me things I needed to hear, sometimes without even saying them to me. I'm not as eloquent, so you'll have to forgive my bluntness, sir.

"General Kerensky knew we'd be conflicted, and he wanted each of us to do our duty and follow our conscience. That's why Exodus was a volunteer mission, not an order. So the only way you could have let him down is if you had betrayed what was in your heart. You did your duty, and that's always the right choice."

Bradley pursed his lips and gave a slight nod. "Thank you, Major."

"No thanks needed," Astrid said. "I'm just doing my duty."

CRUSADER
HEAVY—65 TONS

FIREBEE
LIGHT—35 TONS

GALAHAD
Heavy—60 tons

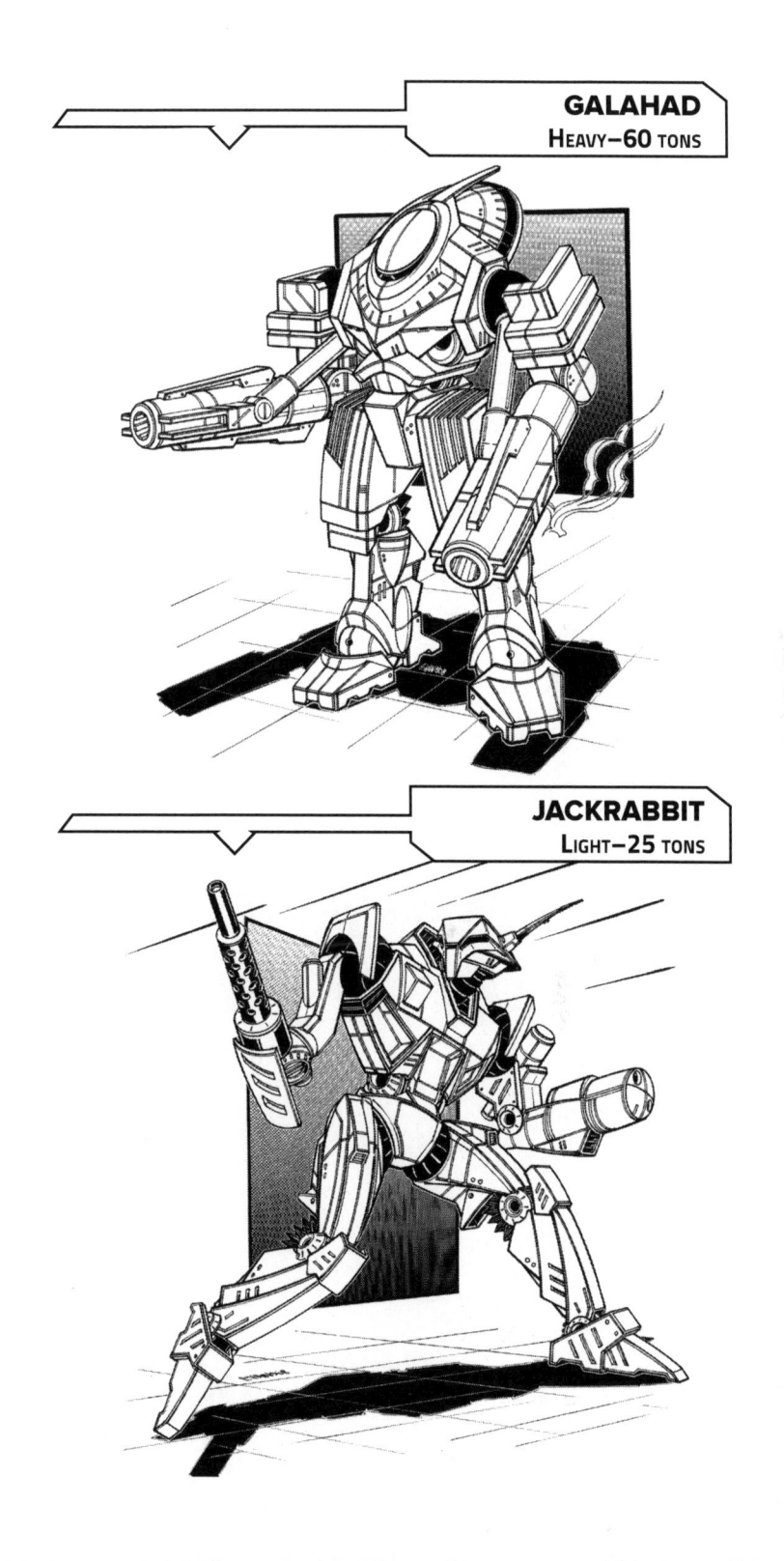

JACKRABBIT
Light—25 tons

PHOENIX HAWK LAM
Medium—50 tons

NO TEARS

CRAIG A. REED, JR.

**AOBA DISTRICT
SENDAI CITY, SENDAI
BALDUR PREFECTURE
BENJAMIN MILITARY DISTRICT
DRACONIS COMBINE
5 JUNE 2798**

The mournful drone of a sole trumpeter playing "Retrieve the Colors" echoed through the half-filled courtyard. It bounced off the surrounding stone buildings, leaving an echo a couple notes behind the actual tune. In front of the headquarters building, a trio of Eridani Light Horse soldiers in dress uniforms slowly lowered the unit's flag from half-staff.

The courtyard was filled with rows of soldiers. Every single soldier in the Eridani Light Horse, except for a handful on guard duty, stood in dress uniforms at parade rest. Behind the rows of soldiers, civilians—men, women, and children who were the soldiers' dependents—stood and watched the solemn ceremony.

With the rest of the Fiftieth Heavy Calvary Battalion, Lieutenant Rafe Fraser watched the flag being lowered. He glanced left, to see if the rest of his lance was paying attention. Next to him, Jason King, his lance second, stood at a stiff parade rest. Next to King, Linda Lawton made parade rest look like slouching. The last member of his lance, Randy Van Faylen, looked as if he was calculating the flag's speed as it came down the pole.

The trumpeter's last notes faded away as the flag reached the bottom of the flagpole. In a measured manner, members of the color guard detached it from the flagpole ropes, two of them carefully folded it, while a third watched every move with a critical eye. With military precision, the trio turned and marched toward the quartet of officers standing a dozen meters away. One presented the flag to the senior officer while the other two saluted. Colonel Bradley took the flag while the other three officers, all colonels, returned the salute of the color guard.

Once he had the flag, Bradley turned to a grizzled master sergeant and nodded. The man's bellow carried across the courtyard and echoed throughout the space. "Soldiers of the Eridani Light Horse! Attention!"

The sound of several thousand boots coming together thundered like an artillery barrage.

Bradley handed the folded flag to Colonel Winston and took a step forward. "Soldiers of the Light Horse!" he said, the courtyard's sound system doing most of the work for him. "As of yesterday, with the backing of the regimental colonels, I invoked the escape clause in our contract with the Draconis Combine."

There was only a low murmur from the soldiers, but a larger one came from the civilians. The Combine was not well-liked among the Light Horse, but invoking the escape clause was unexpected. Most of the soldiers had heard the rumors—Rafe had heard them, and he was sure the rest of his lance had too.

Bradley scanned his command. "We are leaving the Combine because we just learned that the Combine has massacred millions of civilians on Kentares IV, on the orders of Coordinator Jinjiro Kurita." He let the shock settle in for a few seconds. "We cannot, in good conscience, continue to work for a state that massacres civilians."

"More like the colonel doesn't want us anywhere near 'Psycho Jinjiro,'" King muttered.

Rafe elbowed him and followed up with a hard stare. King looked unrepentant, and both Lawton and Van Faylen nodded in agreement.

Rafe sighed. King wasn't wrong. Jinjiro's reputation wasn't as a good leader, and if he had ordered millions to be massacred, it was best not to be anywhere near him.

"Starting after this formation," Bradley continued, "we will begin packing up. I want the entire Light Horse outbound by this time next week." He looked over his shoulder at his colonels. "Regiment commanders, see to your troops."

**AOBA-KU DISTRICT
SENDAI CITY, SENDAI
BALDUR PREFECTURE
BENJAMIN MILITARY DISTRICT
DRACONIS COMBINE
9 JUNE 2798**

The smell of something sweet and warm tickled Rafe's nose when he opened the door to his quarters. He stepped in, closed the door behind him, and smiled at the woman sitting on the chair. "Hello."

Ellen Fraser smiled at her husband. "Hello to you, too."

Rafe walked over and leaned down for a kiss. "Any more of that?" he asked, pointing to the cup of warm, rich liquid in a cup next to her.

She was taller than he, with long, blond hair and a face Rafe could stare at forever. She was dressed in loose clothing, and a book rested in her hands. "On the stove."

Ellen watched him as moved over to the small kitchen. "How is it going?"

"As expected. Administrator Dojiro is being unhelpful."

"I thought he would be. Rafe, I don't trust him."

Rafe took a cup from the cupboard and poured himself a cup of the rich chocolate. "Dojiro's a jumped-up bureaucrat who's scared he's going to be blamed for us leaving."

"That's what worries me. He's throwing up a lot of roadblocks."

Rafe sat in a chair across from his wife. "And we're overcoming them all."

"He may become desperate."

Rafe snorted, then sipped his drink. "And do what? His militia is one step up from useless, their equipment is mostly two centuries out of date, and their training is abysmal. They have less than a battalion of 'Mechs, and the best are part of the Administrator's Guard."

"That may be," Ellen said, standing up and walking over to him. She sat on his lap and stroked his cheek. "How long do we have before you have to report back to duty?"

"Six hours." He smiled at her. "No time for fun tonight."

"I know." She leaned in and whispered something in his ear. Rafe's expression became one of joy.

**MODIFIED *UNION*-CLASS DROPSHIP *RED RIVER*
SENDAI SYSTEM
BALDUR PREFECTURE
BENJAMIN MILITARY DISTRICT
DRACONIS COMBINE
13 JUNE 2798**

The observation room was small and dark, with only a single glowstrip above the hatch giving the compartment any light at all. The small viewport was a meter wide and high, showing a field of stars unmasked by an atmosphere's haze, while Sendai itself took up a third of the view.

The hatch slid open, spilling light into the compartment, and a figure stuck its head into the compartment.

"Rafe?" a female voice asked. "Oh, there you are."

Rafe turned to look at his visitor. "Everything all right?"

Lieutenant Mahault "Manny" Carstens nodded. She commanded another lance in the Fiftieth Assault Battalion's First Assault Company, and was a close friend of Rafe and Ellen's. Manny was short and petite, looking more like a college student than a lance commander. "Still waiting for our dependents to lift?"

Rafe nodded. "They should've finished refueling by now." He sighed. "I've got a bad feeling about this."

"You're just nervous."

Rafe turned to look at his friend. "Ellen's pregnant."

Manny broke out into a smile. "She is? Damn, that's great!" He sighed. "I don't know if I'm ready."

"You'll be a fine father, you'll see."

He nodded, but didn't smile. "But I'm worried Dojiro's going to try something. Ellen's been telling me for a week the bastard can't be trusted. We should've been the last Light Horse group off the planet, not our families."

"I wouldn't worry about Dojiro. He doesn't have the spine to stop us." She cocked her head. "You sure everything's all right?"

"What's the latest intel on the Combine sending forces to Sendai?"

Manny sighed at the change of subject, but stepped into the compartment. "The intel boys have upped the possibility to sixty percent, and they think they'll be in-system three to five days from now. The colonel doesn't want any of our combat units on-planet just in case they show up."

"I won't be happy until Ellen and the rest are in space."

The DropShip's klaxon sounded, cutting off the conversation. "Attention!" A voice barked. "Lieutenants Fraser, Carstens, Hannon, and Ngo, report to the briefing room at once! This is not a drill!"

"Are we under attack?" Manny said.

Rafe scanned the outside through the portal. "I see nothing."

"We'd better get going." Manny stepped out.

Rafe took one last look at Sendai, then followed her. He felt a coldness seep into him. *Please, God, no…*

Rafe and Manny were the last to arrive at the briefing room. Fran Hannon, a burly woman with very short hair, commanded the company's attached infantry platoon. Nancy Ngo was the company's senior aerospace fighter pilot. Both were sitting on one side of the table, while Captain Ethan Reis, the First Assault's commander, sat at the head of the table. The look on Reis' face sent a jolt of fear into Rafe's heart.

"Take a seat," Reis said without preamble. He was tall and muscular, with a shaved head and deeply tanned skin. "Major Kroger will transmit in a minute."

"What's going on?" Manny asked.

"The major will explain," Reis replied, his tone sharp. Rafe saw anger radiating in his eyes.

The two took seats just as the table's holoprojector came to life. The image stabilized, and Major Teller Kroger, commanding officer of the Fiftieth, stood there, stiff and his face hard.

"Officers of the Fiftieth," he said. "We have a situation. An hour ago, the government of Sendai seized our dependents' DropShips and is holding our people hostage."

Ellen!

Coldness gripped Rafe even harder.

"They demand that both battalions return to Sendai and surrender ourselves to them. If we do not, they are threatening to execute the dependents."

The air in the compartment stilled. Rafe's hands tightened into fists, fear and anger warring inside of him.

"They are giving us eight hours to comply." The major's expression softened, looking much older than he had a few seconds ago. "Both Major Stedman and I have consulted with both Colonels Fairchild and Bradley, and we...we have agreed we cannot give in to threats."

The words hung in the air with a cold finality. Rafe felt his heart clench and his stomach drop.

"We..." Kroger swallowed and closed his eyes for a few seconds. "We have to hope they're bluffing. Even if we reversed course right now, it would take us a minimum of twelve hours to reach Sendai's orbit. I am ordering the Fiftieth's DropShips to slow to point-five G's, and Major Stedman of the Eighth Recon is doing the same. Colonel Bradley is trying to negotiate the release of our dependents, and I am hopeful the government will see reason and release our people unharmed. That is all I have at the moment. I will keep you apprised of any developments. Kroger out." The holo image vanished, but the air of hopelessness remained.

Reis was silent for a moment, then he inhaled slowly and exhaled. "Let your people know what is happening. And pray that this can be resolved peacefully."

"And if it isn't?" Manny asked, his tone harsh.

"I don't know. For right now, keep yourself and your people busy. As soon as I know something new, you will be informed. Dismissed."

**MODIFIED *UNION*-CLASS DROPSHIP *RED RIVER*
SENDAI SYSTEM
BALDUR PREFECTURE
BENJAMIN MILITARY DISTRICT
DRACONIS COMBINE
14 JUNE 2798**

As soon as Rafe entered the briefing room and saw Reis' face, he knew the news was bad. The captain looked as if he had aged two decades in a few hours. He motioned to Rafe to take a seat at the table. The others, coming in close behind Rafe, quickly took seats as well. The air hung heavy with despair, and no one wanted to look at anyone else.

The DropShip's loudspeaker blared, followed by a voice saying, "Attention all hands! Message from Major Kroger!"

There was a pause, then Kroger spoke, his tone cold and brittle. "Soldiers of the Fiftieth, I have bad news. An hour ago... An hour ago we received word that the Sendai government has executed our friends and families."

The words hit Rafe like a physical punch to the gut. He doubled over, and only an empty stomach prevented him from throwing up. He knew vaguely that the others were in shock, but all he could see was Ellen.

God, no!

"The Eighth Recon's dependents were also executed. Dojiro sent a video of the executions as proof."

Kroger was silent for a few seconds. When he spoke again, Rafe could hear the anger building with every word. "Both Major Stedman and I have agreed that we cannot walk away. In ten minutes, the DropShips carrying the Fiftieth and Eighth Recon Battalions will flip over and begin a one-point-five-G burn for Sendai."

Kroger paused again, and the fury, now laced with sorrow, was even stronger when he continued, "We are going to burn

Sendai with our wrath. We are going to hunt down and execute every member of the militia, every planetary minister, every bureaucrat we can find. Every government building, every militia building is to be razed. Every militia 'Mech, every militia vehicle is to be destroyed. When we leave, we will leave nothing in the way of a government. The only quarter we will give is Tarleton's Quarter."

He paused again. "If you feel you cannot follow these orders, then you are free to stay on the DropShips, and I promise we will not hold it against you. All that I ask is that you inform your superiors before landing."

Rafe felt like he was collapsing in on himself. He looked up and saw the same expressions on his fellow officers' face. But all around the table, their expressions slowly changed to ones of cold fury. His own anger burning inside of him flared to life, using his grief as fuel.

"What we are about to do will seem like a violation of everything the Eridani Light Horse stands for." Kroger's tone dropped to just above a whisper. "But it is exactly because of what we stand for that Major Stedman and I have made this decision. We will inform Colonel Bradley of our actions once we have reversed direction, and both Major Stedman and I will take full responsibility."

Kroger took a deep breath. "Officers, see to your units. I want the Fiftieth to hit the ground running. That is all."

MODIFIED *UNION*-CLASS DROPSHIP *RED RIVER*
HIGH ORBIT, SENDAI
BALDUR PREFECTURE
BENJAMIN MILITARY DISTRICT
DRACONIS COMBINE
14 JUNE 2798

In his *Guillotine*'s cockpit, Rafe made his last checks. He did them automatically, his mind deadened to anything else but the routine. The sorrow lived there in the back of his mind, but his fury was like a dam, holding it back and letting him function.

Vengeance was the only thing holding him together, him and the rest of the Fiftieth. Their grief would wait.

Only after he had finished his checks did he look at the picture tucked into a corner of his control panel. For the first time since he had heard the news, grief surged to the forefront of his mind.

Ellen...

He had first met her during a meeting of recent hires to the Light Horse, only four years ago. She had been a blue-eyed goddess, long, blond hair flowing down to the small of her back. She was a few centimeters taller than him, but he didn't care. He had fallen in love with her at first sight, and devoted himself to winning her love. His thoughts drifted back to the perfect moment, when she had teared up and nodded after he had proposed to her. Their last night on Sendai, they had made long, passionate love, despite her condition, and he had promised they would be together in only a couple of days.

A promise now broken beyond repair...

He reached out and traced a finger down Ellen's chin in the picture, wishing it was real. "I should've taken your advice, but I didn't," he whispered. "I failed you and our child. Now I'm about to avenge you. Please forgive me."

He wanted to release his grief, to rage and scream, break down, and curl up into a ball. But his anger would not—*could not*—allow him to give in to his pain. He hadn't shed a tear for Ellen and the others. His anger couldn't spare the energy and now, it pushed the feelings of helplessness back into a corner of his mind. Now he had a mission, and mourning would only interfere with it.

His radio cracked. "Rafe?" a female voice asked.

"What is it, Manny?" he asked in a flat tone.

"Have you seen the latest reports?"

Rafe glanced at the map screen. "What?"

"The militia is digging in around the capital. They know we're coming."

"So? It'll make them easier to kill."

"I checked the roster." Manny was silent for a few seconds. "Everyone is committed to this, Rafe. No one's staying behind."

He nodded, the heat of his anger settling into his stomach after pushing back the heartache. "Good."

"First Assault Company," Reis said over the company channel. "We have our orders. The Fiftieth will drop onto Aobayama City, while the Eighth will drop onto Sato. First and Second Assault Companies will land at the city spaceport and drive toward the city center, with Third Assault trailing behind to destroy any targets that First and Second bypass. Command and First Recon will remain at the spaceport and destroy all targets in and around it. Hammer Two, you have point."

Rafe nodded slowly. "Understood, sir."

"Hammer Three, you have the left flank."

"Yes, sir," Manny replied.

"Hammer One will have the right flank. Any enemy, we steamroll. Intel shows most of the militia is digging in around Sendai City, so resistance should be light. We drop in twenty mikes. Make last checks and report back. Hammer Six out."

AOBAYAMA CITY, SENDAI
BALDUR PREFECTURE,
BENJAMIN MILITARY DISTRICT
DRACONIS COMBINE
15 JUNE 2798

Hell came to Sendai.

According to their intel, the city's garrison comprised an infantry regiment, an armor battalion, and a 'Mech company, all using either Draconis Combine Mustered Soldiery cast-offs or home-built equipment.

They had sent most of the militia to Sendai City, but those left were ready to fight.

For all the good it did them.

The 'Mechs of the Fiftieth Heavy Calvary made a low-altitude combat drop onto the city's spaceport and destroyed the militia force defending it in only a couple of minutes. As soon as the DropShips landed, the assault companies moved out from the spaceport, heedless of any damage they caused.

Overhead, the Light Horse's aerospace fighters ripped into the few atmospheric militia craft that rose to challenge them. Several defenders fell onto the city itself, smashing into buildings, starting fires and sending black smoke into the morning air.

On the ground, anger-fueled mercenaries slammed into the city with the force of a hurricane. The resistance—militia, police, and a few civilians—grimly held their ground despite the odds; none were equipped to fight the BattleMechs or the well-trained soldiers of the Eridani Light Horse. The mercenaries took the order for Tarleton's Quarter to heart and left nothing but dead defenders and destroyed equipment in their wake. Tactics were basic and brutal, the enemies' destruction their primary goal.

The city died alongside the defenders. The nobles' district was obliterated, no building spared, only a few broken walls left standing. Every government building and major institution—banks, schools, museums, broadcast stations, train stations, police and fire stations—was methodically destroyed. Weapons fire ripped apart other buildings, either by accident or on purpose, sending large sections of burning debris into the streets. The only buildings that avoided destruction were hospitals, and the casualties soon overwhelmed their resources. Fires raged everywhere, as most of the city's buildings were burning out of control. Smoke and dust hung in the air, turning the day into a hellish twilight.

Near the middle of the city, Rafe watched the combined firepower of his lance shred the last militia 'Mech, a *Trooper*. As the dead 'Mech toppled into an office building, his *Guillotine* strode past it and into the city square. The city's main administration building stood on the far side of the square, a mountain of glass and stone built to resemble a mountain peak. Machine guns scattered around the square opened up on Rafe when he came into view.

"Hammer Two-Six to Hammer Actual," he said, his voice clipped and emotionless. "We've reached Objective Eagle."

"Understood, Two-Six." Reis' voice was almost lost in the static. "We're pushing the militia back to the docks. Destroy the objective and get over here as soon as you can."

"Understood. Two-Six out."

By now, the other 'Mechs of Rafe's lance entered the square, sparks dancing on their armor as machine gun bullets bounced off them.

"All right, people," Rafe said. "We're taking down Objective Eagle. King, Lawton, take the right side. Van Faylen, we'll take the left. Energy weapons only."

He got one-word answers from them, their anger a fire Rafe felt too. King's wife and children had been among the murdered, as was Lawton's own wife and sister. Van Faylen's entire family—parents, siblings, and fiancée—had perished, turning the normally outgoing MechWarrior into a grim-faced man who barely spoke.

The lance split up, King's *Grasshopper* and Lawton's *Griffin* moving right, Rafe's *Guillotine* and Van Faylen's *Exterminator* moving left. Still ignoring the machine gun fire, Rafe aimed his lasers at the base of the building and squeezed the trigger, ignoring the wave of heat that spiked through the cockpit.

Five beams ripped into the building, burning through the stone face and into the structure. Van Faylen added his lasers, and the building shuddered as part of the steel frame dissolved into molted metal.

In the back of his mind, he knew the machine gun fire had lessened, and part of his awareness noted that uniformed people were running from the building. As far as he was concerned, they could wait until he finished destroying the building.

Rafe shifted his aim and fired again, carving another hole in the building's base. The building trembled as its weakened structure buckled under the building's weight. Glass exploded as the window frames twisted and flexed beyond their tensile strength. Chunks of masonry peeled away from the building and joined the shower of glass, becoming a lethal rain falling on the escaping soldiers. Cracks formed across the stone face, growing larger every second.

"It's going!" Lawton snarled.

"Fall back!" Rafe barked.

The Light Horse 'Mechs backed off. The administration building groaned as the surviving support beams tried to hold the building up, but the damage was too great. With an ear-shattering moan, the administration building's facade collapsed into the square, filling most of the open space with debris and thick dust.

Rafe waited until the dust cloud had mostly dispersed before firing into the building. He glimpsed people inside, running for their lives, but shoved any thoughts of mercy aside as his lasers cut deep into the building's structure.

The rest of the lance followed his lead, lasers slashing into the exposed building's interior. Explosions ripped through the floors, and fires roared to life, unhampered by the building's fire-suppression system. In a matter of minutes, the building was engulfed in flames, smoke mixing with the still-airborne dust, darkening the sky above them.

Rafe looked at the destruction with no emotion besides a temporary-sated need of vengeance. "Two-Six to Hammer Actual," he said. "Eagle destroyed. No serious damage to Hammer Two. Moving to your position. Two-Six out."

FIFTEEN KILOMETERS SOUTH OF SENDAI CITY, SENDAI
BALDUR PREFECTURE
BENJAMIN MILITARY DISTRICT
DRACONIS COMBINE
16 JUNE 16 2798

Rafe sat in the shade of a large tree on top of a hill and watched his *Guillotine* undergoing repairs. The heavy 'Mech had taken some armor damage during the razing of Aobayama City, but it was minor.

Around him, the rest of the Fiftieth Heavy Cavalry was repairing and rearming. In the distance, separated by a few rolling hills, he could hear the booms from the Light Horse's artillery shelling the defenses in and around Sendai City. If had cared to look behind him, he would have seen the distant haze of smoke that marked the charred remains of Aobayama City.

A bag of half-eaten stew sat on his lap, while a squeeze bottle of Electrolyte sat on the ground next to him. He ate slowly, chewing the meat and vegetables thoroughly before swallowing. Every so often, he would pick up the squeeze bottle and squirt a mouthful of the vaguely orange-tasting liquid into his mouth to wash down the lingering taste of stew.

"Do you mind?" a voice said.

Rafe looked up. Manny was standing there, a bag of food in one hand, her own bottle of Electrolyte in the other. Like him, she had put on a jumpsuit over her cooling suit.

Rafe shrugged. Manny took it as an invitation and sat next to him.

"How are you doing?" she asked.

"Fine," Rafe replied flatly.

"The captain said we're going to start the push into Sendai City in about three hours." Manny's voice sounded scratchy. She took a mouthful of her drink and continued. "He also said that the planetary militia outside of the city is destroyed."

Rafe watched the techs struggling to remove a damaged piece of armor from his *Guillotine*'s left leg. "Dojiro?" he grunted.

"As far as intel knows, he's still in the city. The Eighth has blocked all northern escape routes, and we've done the same in the south. The aerospace boys destroyed the spaceport and naval port and wrecked every single aircraft, ship, and bridge they found. No one's getting out by air or sea."

"Good."

Manny looked at him closely. "When was the last time you slept?"

"Couple of days."

"Maybe you should take a nap."

Rafe shook his head. "Can't. Bad dreams."

"Ellen?"

"Yeah."

Manny leaned back against the tree. "I've been on my own since I was sixteen," she whispered. "The Light Horse took me in, gave me the family I needed. I didn't lose any blood relations in the massacre, but I lost friends, good friends like Ellen."

"Then why are you here?"

"Because the Light Horse is my family, and my family needs me."

"You're lucky," Rafe said. He took a gulp of Electrolyte. "I still can't cry."

She stared at him, startled by the sudden change in topic. "You'll have to, eventually."

"Not now. There's no time." He closed his eyes, his breathing becoming erratic. "Part of me wants to die, but the rest of me wants to kill every Drac on this planet. Those are my choices—kill or curl up and die. And I can't die yet. Not when there's Dracs to kill."

"I know. I feel the same way. But there will come a time when we must let that grief go. If we don't, Dojiro and his ilk will have won."

"Not now. There's still so much to do." Rafe downed the last of his drink and stood. "I'd better check on my 'Mech."

"Are we damning ourselves?" Manny asked. "What will they think of us in the future?"

He looked down at her. "I don't care about the future," he said. "The future died with Ellen and the others." He started down the hill.

"Damn you, Rafe Fraser," Manny whispered after him. "And damn me for caring about you."

TAIHAKU DISTRICT
SENDAI CITY, SENDAI
BALDUR PREFECTURE
BENJAMIN MILITARY DISTRICT
DRACONIS COMBINE
18 JUNE 2798

The militia fought like demons to defend the city. The Combine 'Mechs, despite being obsolete and having ill-trained pilots, threw themselves into battle with all the fierceness of ancient *samurai*. Militia armor held their ground far beyond any reasonable expectation. The militia infantry, their numbers swollen by police and volunteers, were like ants at a picnic, racing through the rubble and flames to take their suicidal shots at the Light Horse forces.

Despite all that, they died in droves at the hands of both Light Horse battalions. The mercenaries hit the city like a tidal wave—the Eighth from the north, the Fiftieth from the south—and both struck with the anger of Poseidon.

Sendai City died all around them. As the city was already shattered by the intense artillery barrage, neither side tried to avoid further collateral damage as they fought. Entire blocks, some several centuries old, were torn apart by cannon and laser fire, shattered by missiles, or simply leveled by 'Mechs and armor crashing through them. Streets became choked with rubble, parks turned into wastelands, and vehicles were crushed or destroyed. Uncounted numbers of civilians and defenders perished in the battle's firestorm.

None of this mattered to Rafe. First Assault was pushing through the defenses around the Administration District, destroying everything in their way. Flames and smoke filled the air around the *Guillotine*, making Rafe glad he couldn't breathe the air outside his sealed cockpit. Sweat beaded all over his body despite the cooling vest he wore, and the cockpit atmosphere was hot and dry.

"Hammer Two-Six!" Reis' voice barked over the radio. "An armor column is leaving the Administration District, heading toward the docks. Dojiro and his senior staff might be in that convoy. Intercept and stop them."

"Copy, Hammer Six," Rafe said. "Hammer Two-Six out." He studied the map for a few seconds, then switched to the lance frequency. "Hammer Two elements, there's an armor column heading for the docks, and Dojiro might be in it. We are to intercept. Move out on a heading of zero-three-five and do not stop to fight until we find that column. Two-Six out."

The lance dashed through the streets, jumping over obstacles when possible, smashing through buildings when they couldn't. Enemy forces in their path were quickly and ruthless destroyed.

"Six, this is Three," Lawton said, her tone cold. Her *Griffin* had landed on top of a parking garage. "Target spotted. Heading northwest. Eighteen vehicles, twelve military, six civilian, and—"

Two eye-searing bolts from particle projection cannons slammed into the parking garage a level below Lawton, smashing through the concrete and turning several cars into fireballs. Instantly, Lawton launched her *Griffin* into the air. "Enemy 'Mech! *Warhammer!*"

Rafe's smile was wintry. "That's Dojiro's personal guard! Two, Three, engage that *Whammer!* Four, you're with me. We're going to head off that convoy!"

"Be advised there's more than that *Whammer* escorting that convoy!" Lawton shouted. "There's a *Dragon* and a *Marauder* with them!"

"That's the Administrator's Guard all right," Rafe growled. "There should also be a *Gladiator* somewhere nearby, so stay alert! Let's move, people!"

The *Guillotine* and *Exterminator* dashed down the street, while the *Griffin* and *Grasshopper* opened fire on the Combine *Warhammer*. As they passed through several intersections, Rafe glimpsed the convoy speeding on a parallel course a block to the north. "Next intersection!" he growled. "Turn left!"

At the intersection Rafe threw the *Guillotine* into a hard left turn, sending the 70-ton 'Mech skidding across the street. He growled as he fought the momentum, keeping the heavy 'Mech on its feet. The screech of metal on the road surface was audible in the cockpit. The *Guillotine*'s foot struck a car parked on the street and crushed it. As he brought his 'Mech under control again, a blood-red *Marauder* appeared at the next intersection and opened fire, its PPCs and autocannon hammering Rafe's left side.

Ignoring the loss of more than a ton and half of armor, Rafe fired back. Lasers and short-range missiles raced through the air and slammed into the Combine 'Mech. Heat rose in the cockpit, but Rafe ignored it. Behind and to the left of Rafe, Van Faylen added his *Exterminator*'s lasers and missiles to the attack.

The twin attacks hammered the *Marauder*, the crab-like 'Mech losing armor across its front. A sudden spike in heat on his thermo sensors told Rafe the enemy 'Mech had taken engine damage. Behind the *Marauder*, the convoy sped on, swerving and weaving to avoid debris in the street.

Shimmering from excess heat, the Combine 'Mech staggered back, barely avoiding a swerving Chi-ha infantry combat vehicle. Snarling a curse, Rafe fired his lasers again. The volley cut across the *Marauder*'s torso, melting armor. Van Faylen's follow-up strike also melted and stripped armor off the torso and arms, forcing the Drac pilot to concentrate more on staying upright. Behind it, the last of the fleeing convoy passed through the intersection at high speed.

"Charge them!" Rafe shouted. He sent his *Guillotine* forward at a run, with Van Faylen's *Exterminator* charging after him. Forty-five meters from the still wobbly *Marauder*, Rafe hit his jump jets, sending the 70-ton *Guillotine* up and over the enemy 'Mech.

The *Marauder* backpedaled, trying to keep both Light Horse 'Mechs in front of it. Van Faylen sent another volley of lasers into the enemy 'Mech. The *Marauder*'s autocannon suddenly went slack as the lasers found a weak spot in the ravaged armor.

Rafe's *Guillotine* landed in the middle of the intersection and unloaded a full strike into the *Marauder*'s back at point-blank range. The right-arm PPC pod exploded as Rafe's lasers and short-range missiles slammed into it, stripping away armor and ripping apart the skeletal frame. A heartbeat later, the Combine 'Mech's left hip and knee actuators exploded under the laser firestorm.

"I've got 'em, sir!" Van Faylen shouted. "Get that convoy!"

Rafe turned and raced after the convoy, which had opened a half-block lead. In his 360-degree viewstrip, he saw Van Faylen's *Exterminator* slam into the *Marauder* at full speed, sending armor fragments in every direction. Despite the impact, the militia 'Mech stayed on its feet and tried to fight back.

Van Faylen didn't stop, instead wading in and using his 'Mech's fists like sledgehammers. Both smashed into the red 'Mech's side, shattering armor and denting the interior frame.

"*Whammer* down!" King shouted. "We're moving to rejoin!"

"Help Four!" Rafe barked, pushing his *Guillotine* into a run. He began closing some of the distance between him and the convoy. Four civilian vehicles, two of them limos, were in the middle. The rest of the convoy was a mix of armored personnel carriers, Chi-ha ICVs, and cargo-carrying half-tracks.

The two rearmost Chi-has slowed, spun their small turrets, and opened fire with their machine guns. Rafe snap-fired his right-arm lasers, and the scarlet beams burned through the ICV's turret and into its interior. The infantry combat vehicle exploded, shrapnel slamming into its partner. The surviving Chi-ha wove uncertainly, turned, and slowed as the driver tried to get it under control.

Rafe didn't give it a chance, choosing to kick it hard in the side. The ICV's side crumpled under the blow and sent it into the air. The Chi-ha hit the ground and rolled like some sort of mutant die on a casino table, sending out a cloud of metal and plastic every time it bounced off the ground until it crashed top-down into the side of a building, which buried it under debris.

As the Chi-ha finishing its dying roll, Rafe was already running past it. He made it half a block when his sensors screamed a warning coming from behind and to his left. He turned and snap-fired his large laser at the 'Mech coming out of a side street, a *Dragon*. The beam caught it high in the right torso, melting away armor even as the Combine 'Mech fired back. Its stream of autocannon rounds passed over Rafe's shoulder, and the single medium laser melted armor off the *Guillotine*'s left leg.

Rafe screamed and fired everything, ignoring the sudden intense heat in the cockpit. The *Dragon* staggered as most of the *Guillotine*'s volley ripped into it, melting and shattering armor across its body, but the Kuritan MechWarrior rode out the barrage. Return fire removed more of Rafe's armor before the Combine 'Mech spun and disappeared down the street it had come from.

Rafe started after it, but his eyes passed across the picture of Ellen, and the memory of his orders overrode the fury in his heart. The *Dragon* could wait. Stopping the column was more important.

He turned the *Guillotine* around and chased after Dojiro's convoy. The brief fight had given them the chance to gain valuable distance, and they had made the most of it. They were now two full blocks ahead of him.

"Hammer Two-Six to all Hammer Two elements!" he snapped. "Where are you?"

"*Marauder* is still in the fight!" King shouted. "The *Gladiator*'s shown up and brought some light armor and infantry!"

"Kill them now!" Rafe barked.

"We're trying!" King snapped back. "But they're not cooperating!"

"Hammer Four-Six here," Hannon said. Her infantry platoon had been following the company's advance, finishing the destruction of targets and making sure there was no resistance left behind. "We're two blocks behind you and a block south. We'll try to get ahead of the target."

"Copy, Four-Six," Rafe said. "Try to—"

His proximity alarm screamed just ahead of a barrage of explosions blasting across the *Guillotine*'s left arm and leg. Rafe twisted left just in time to see the *Dragon* dart behind a building a block over.

"Hurry, Four-Six!" Rafe snarled. "This damn *Dragon* is keeping me from the target!"

"We'll be there as soon as we can!"

Rafe cursed under his breath as he ran after the convoy. With the rest of his lance tied up in battle, he knew he was the only one who could get to the convoy. No matter what, Administrator Dojiro would pay for his crimes.

Nothing else mattered.

A flash of red from his left, a reflection off the side of a tall building, gave Rafe enough time to twist on the run and fire at the *Dragon* as it darted into sight. Most of his lasers struck the heavy 'Mech, but none of them breached its armor, though the assault rocked it. Its own fire stripped away more armor from the *Guillotine*'s frame, though the missiles missed him by several meters and blasted large holes in the building behind him. Before Rafe could fire again, the *Dragon* disappeared behind a building.

"*Marauder* down!" King cried. "The *Gladiator*'s retreating!"

"Step it up!" Rafe barked.

The next intersection was coming up. The building on the far left-hand corner gave Rafe an idea. The short building, a bank of some sort, looked like it was strong enough to bear the *Guillotine*'s weight. The enemy expected him to stick to the street. It was time to change things up.

Just before he reached the cross street, Rafe ignited the *Guillotine*'s Anderson's jump jets, sending the 70-ton 'Mech into the air. Two streets over, he could see the *Dragon* adjusting its aim at the sudden aerial target. Rafe was quicker, firing his Sunglow as he dropped to the roof of the building.

The laser beam melted through the last of the *Dragon*'s torso armor and drilled deep into the autocannon magazine. A fireball engulfed the Kuritan 'Mech as the remaining shells ignited. The surrounding buildings took the explosion's power, windows shattering, concrete cracking, and steel beams buckling.

Rafe blinked to clear the bright flash from his vision. *Dojiro! I'm coming for you!* When his vision cleared, he saw the convoy was still moving, with a Demon, of all things, dropped back to guard the rear.

"Damn it!" he growled. Intel had said nothing about the locals having a Star-league tank!

He raised the Sunglow again, lined up the Demon, and fired. The beam burned into the tank's rear, melting off vital armor. The turret slewed toward him, its Gauss rifle traversing up and firing.

The *Guillotine* staggered as the Gauss round slammed into the left side of its torso, shattering the last of the armor and breaking several internal support braces. Rafe gritted his teeth and launched himself off the building, using his jump jets to push him in the Demon's direction.

The 70-ton 'Mech landed in the street with a thunderous crash, leaving a burned and cracked crater. As he landed, Rafe fired everything at the massive tank. Five lasers and several short-range missiles ripped into the Demon, punching through the weakened rear armor and ravaging the interior. The tank shuddered and died, smoke pouring out of several shattered armor sheets.

But the Demon got off one last shot, and Rafe's world went dark. Red lights lit up on his damage screen as he fought to keep his *Guillotine* standing. There was a screech of steel and the snap of cables and wires as the left arm, and the Sunglow laser, fell away and crashed to the ground.

Frantically, Rafe struggled with the sudden weight loss. Bits of wreckage fell out of the torso's shattered remains, tumbling and skittering away as they struck the cracked roadway. The *Guillotine* staggered like a drunk, then stopped, fully under control again.

Rafe blinked sweat from his eyes and glanced at his damage screen. It was bad. The left side of the Mech's torso was gone. The loss left him with just three medium lasers, the missile rack, three-quarters of his heat sinks, and reduced jumping distance.

The prudent thing would be to wait for the rest of his lance to join him. But Rafe didn't want to give the administrator any chance to escape. Not with the soul of Ellen and the other, innocent, defenseless Light Horse dependents crying out for justice. Not until Dojiro and the other government officials who had ordered them killed paid the price in their blood.

He glanced into the distance. The administrator's convoy was opening the distance even more. He ran in pursuit, his unbalanced torso forcing him into an awkward gait. "Hammer Two-Six to Hammer Two elements! Where the hell are you?"

"*Gladiator* is down!" King yelled. "We're on our way!"

Rafe was gaining on the convoy again. There was a Chi-ha and two APCs between him and the last civilian car in the convoy. One APC drifted to the left, while the rearmost APC drifted to the right. The Chi-ha remained in the middle, its turrets swinging around to point its machine guns at their pursuer. All three opened fire at the *Guillotine*, chipping armor but doing little damage.

Without breaking stride, Rafe stroked the trigger for the arm-mounted medium lasers, his targeting reticule on the right-hand APC. Two beams slashed into the vehicle's turret, cutting through the armor and turning the interior into a charnel house. The APC shuddered, lost control, and slammed into the edge of a building.

The other APC stopped and unloaded its infantry. Assault rifles joined the machine guns to slow Rafe down. A volley of his SRMs ended the infantry attack and wrecked the APC's rear. Rafe shifted his 'Mech to the left and kicked the APC, caving in the vehicle's side and sending it rolling onto its side.

Rafe moved on. The Chi-ha was still firing its machine guns when it exploded from his lasers boring through it. The two civilian non-limos were next, and they died under the *Guillotine*'s feet.

A pair of Randolph support vehicles, half of Hannon's platoon, roared out of a side street ahead of the convoy and opened fire on the lead vehicles. As the vehicles spun to face the new threat, the other half of the infantry platoon roared out of a street a block farther ahead of the convoy. Machine guns blazing, they charged the head of the convoy, adding their fire to the fight.

Still moving forward, Rafe stomped on the second limo's rear, breaking the rear axle and lifting the limo's front end into the air. With a screech of tortured metal, the limo crashed back to the ground with enough force to break the front axle. The frontmost limo tried to make a hard left-hand turn to escape, but the overlarge vehicle slid sideways, losing speed and distance. Rafe didn't give it a chance to recover, his foot crushing the engine compartment. An APC ahead of the limos tried to turn around, but Rafe's lasers turned it into a fiery wreck.

With the vanguard under attack and a rampaging 'Mech behind them, the rest of the convoy dissolved into panic. Vehicles broke off, seeking any path that would take them out of the kill zone. Laser fire from behind Rafe turned two of the fleeing vehicles into flaming pyres, and he glanced at his viewstrip to see the rest of his lance joining the fight.

Rafe stayed where he was, firing his lasers at any target and ignoring the scattered infantry-rifle fire. More cars exploded, and the panic increased. Two cars crashed into each other as they tried to turn into the same side street, while a truck was T-boned by an APC. People abandoned the vehicles, more willing to take their chances on foot than to stay with what were rapidly becoming death traps.

Another Demon rolled out of a side street and swung its Gauss rifle to target him. Rafe fired at the building next to the tank, and an avalanche of steel and stone collapsed onto the Combine tank. The Demon was buried under dozens of tons of rubble, trapping it and the crew.

Rafe shifted the *Guillotine*, seeking his next target. Smoke choked the street, and flames burned everywhere. Wrecked cars, combat vehicles, and bodies surrounded him, adding to a scene straight out of hell. Nothing moved save for a mild breeze stirring the air.

"You think we got the prize?" King asked.

Rafe noticed movement from the lead limo. Someone opened the rear door, fell out, and was now crouched next to the vehicle. Rafe tapped the magnifier to bring the face into sharp focus. The image of a sweating bald man with a pudgy face filled his screen. A face he had burned into his memory.

Planetary Administrator Kol Dojiro.

The man who had murdered more than two thousand defenseless men, women, and children.

The man who had murdered Ellen and their unborn child.

Rafe pointed the *Guillotine*'s right arm at Dojiro. He smiled grimly as he saw the administrator's eyes widen at the sight of impending death. One stroke of the trigger, and the deaths of Ellen and two thousand innocent civilians would be avenged.

The limo's rear door flew open, and a woman scrambled out. Long blond hair spilled out around her shoulders as she grabbed Dojiro by the arm and tried to pull him away from the limo. She glanced up at the *Guillotine*, and for an instant, Rafe saw his dead wife's face. His thumb trembled, caught between two conflicting emotions.

The woman pulled Dojiro from the limo and dragged him away before throwing herself in front of him. When she looked up again, Rafe realized she wasn't Ellen. She was a couple of decades older than his wife, with sharper features, thinner build, and her hairstyle was all wrong. She looked up at him, and Rafe could see the determined look as her body shielded Dojiro from the vengeance he richly deserved.

No, he thought. *She won't stop me from killing him.*

Two more people spilled out of the car and ran toward Dojiro and the woman. She was screaming something at the newcomers, but they didn't listen, and they reached the pair and hugged the woman around the waist.

Two children.

Children.

One was a boy, maybe eight years old, the other a girl, about six. Both stared up at Rafe with wide eyes and a look of abject fear on the faces.

"Hammer Six Actual to Hammer Two-Six." Reis' voice was sharp. "Is the target alive?"

Rafe looked down at the family under his sights. One simple pull of the trigger would be all it took, four blackened bodies, and a simple "no" uttered over comms would be all he needed to say.

"There will come a time when we must let that grief go," Manny's voice said inside his head. *"If we don't, Dojiro and his ilk will have won."*

He looked at the family. A wife and children. How were they responsible for the orders Dojiro gave?

One finger, he thought. *A pull of the trigger and Dojiro's in hell, where he belongs.*

"No," a familiar female voice—Ellen's—whispered in his head. *"You are a soldier, and soldiers follow orders."*

He closed his eyes, fighting the anger for the first time since he had been told the love of his life had been murdered. He had already done so much killing in the last few days, destroyed everything that had stood in his path between him and Dojiro. His anger demanded the man dead. Unable to tamp down his fury, Rafe did the only thing he could—he reached out for his bottled-up grief. He let it fill him, driving the anger back. He felt numb as the two emotions swirled inside him.

"Hammer Six Actual to Hammer Two-Six! Respond!"

Rafe opened his eyes and stared down at the family still huddled in front of him. His trigger fingers relaxed, and he exhaled slowly.

"Hammer Six," he said, suddenly feeling exhausted. "We have the target, and he's still alive."

"Keep him that way. The major wants him and any other surviving ministers you find to be taken alive."

"Understood, Six," Rafe said. "Hammer Two-Four. Get up here and get this bastard into custody ASAP. Command wants him alive."

"On our way!" Hannon shouted.

Rafe leaned back in his seat and closed his eyes.

**MODIFIED *UNION*-CLASS DROPSHIP *RED RIVER*
HIGH ORBIT, SENDAI
BALDUR PREFECTURE
BENJAMIN MILITARY DISTRICT
DRACONIS COMBINE
23 JUNE 2798**

Manny found Rafe in the same observation compartment. As before, he was looking out at the stars and Sendai slowly getting smaller.

Both battalions were tired and emotionally spent. Once Dojiro had been captured, the resistance collapsed. The militia's 'Mechs and armor were destroyed or stripped for parts. All government buildings were razed, and firing squads executed the surviving governmental leaders. Dojiro himself was executed after a trial, the last act before the Light Horse lifted off. Now most were wrapped in grief or sleeping, but Rafe couldn't sleep, not yet.

Manny stepped inside, uncertain of his reaction. They hadn't spoken to each other since that lunch on Sendai, and she did not know what to expect. "Rafe?" she said. "The memorial service is starting in an hour."

"Thank you."

She fought the urge to leave. "Rafe?"

Rafe turned his head to look at her. A single tear ran down his left cheek. "I can cry now," he said, more tears welling up in his eyes. "I can finally cry."

With a wail, the tears came.

Before she was fully aware of it, Manny had already crossed the compartment and was holding Rafe in her arms. Her own tears started.

"Yes," she breathed. "We can all cry now."

DRAGON
Heavy—60 tons

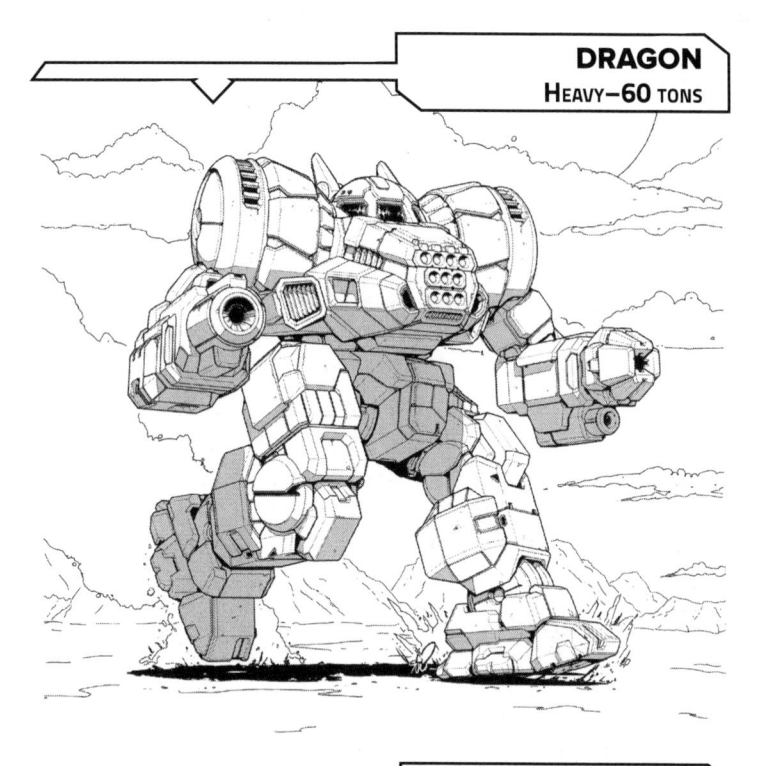

EXTERMINATOR
Heavy—65 tons

GRIFFIN
Medium—55 tons

GUILLOTINE
Heavy—70 tons

MARAUDER
HEAVY—75 TONS

WARHAMMER
HEAVY—70 TONS

DYING DIGNITY

CHRIS HUSSEY

**RIGA POINT
PENCADER
LYRAN COMMONWEALTH
4 APRIL 2853**

Colonel Pro-Tem Idris Majed surveyed the destruction all around him. Lyran 'Mechs and aerospace fighters—in pieces, in many cases—lay scattered and smoking across the pockmarked tarmac of the Riga Point spaceport. The mailed fist of House Steiner, emblazoned on the broken and battered 'Mechs, seemed to stand in defiance of their defeat, but there was still no question that the Lyran Commonwealth Armed Forces garrison had been utterly crushed. The raid by his unit, the Seventy-first Light Horse Regiment, had proved beyond successful. *Bradley will be pleased.*

The raid had gone off without nearly a hitch. Majed's regiment had set down in their landing zone five kilometers outside the Riga Point military outpost unmolested while the 151st Light Horse had struck at a secondary target further east. The rest of the unit was currently back on Circinus, enjoying rest and refit.

Majed had suspected a trap as they marched toward Riga with no Lyran resistance. Only when the scout lances reached the base's perimeter did the Commonwealth 'Mechs and conventional support show up, and even then it had been scattered and disorganized. Only a company of LCAF 'Mechs, with a matching amount of tank and infantry, had turned out to meet the Seventy-First. Far less than what was actually stationed at the base.

The colonel couldn't get over his good fortune. The remaining untouched Lyran 'Mechs would go a long way toward rebuilding the other Eridani Light Horse regiments, which had taken a bit of a beating of late. The Free Worlds League was proving to be a good employer, but the unit was being worked hard.

That hard work meant Majed found himself in temporary command of the entire unit. Despite Colonel Bradley's advanced age—over 100 years—he hadn't lost his mental edge. He might not be able to sit in the cockpit of a 'Mech, but he could still run the ELH.

Ever the wise leader, Colonel Bradley carefully groomed his potential replacements. Each of the regimental commanders served in a pro-tem status over the past few years, and now it was Majed's turn. He wasn't even sure if he wanted the job. He loved running the Seventy-First, but the entire Light Horse? That was something else altogether.

Majed reached the outpost's command-and-control center. Far across the grounds, he saw Light Horse infantry processing the prisoners. They needed to be contained, but wouldn't be taken back across the border. That might be normal wartime practice, but times were a bit different now. The League and their contract only called for nonhuman resources to be taken. Prisoners meant more mouths to feed. Hatred ran deep on both sides of the Commonwealth-League border, and the thought and cost of trying to convert enemy soldiers to fight for your side was out of the question and out of the budget. The same with prisoner exchanges. It wasn't worth the expense. Better to take their 'Mechs and let the enemy feed the Dispossessed.

Majed headed into the center and to his temporary office, his staff saluting and nodding to him as he passed them.

An aide flagged him down. "Sir, Colonel Cirion is trying to reach you."

Majed nodded, stroking his mustache. "I figured as much. I'm curious if they've had as much luck as we did. Patch it through to my desk," he commanded as he quickened his pace.

Closing the door to his office, Majed spun the holoprojector around. As his fingers moved to activate, he looked up, seeing his own reflection in the mirror across the office. His chestnut skin and jet-black hair bore a sweat-induced sheen from Pencader's April heat. But it was the look on his face that concerned him. Dark bags hung heavy under his hazel eyes, and his normally square jaw sagged uncharacteristically. *Maybe I'm more tired than I thought.* He snapped his mouth shut, attempted to tighten up, and activated the projector.

Angelica Cirion commanded the Black Warriors, the other half of the Pencader raiding force. A fellow former-Star League Defense Force unit, the Warriors had set up shop in the Periphery, but forged an alliance of convenience with the Free Worlds League. The ELH was assigned to work with the Warriors to harass and raid the anti-spinward region of the Commonwealth. Cirion and her unit were a little rough around the edges, but Colonel Bradley felt their shared Star League history made them a more palatable unit to work with than the Free Worlds regulars, which had proven to be a mixed bag.

The image flickered to life, static and lag causing it to shift and break up briefly before locking in. Angelica's hardened, angled face stared back at Majed. Her blond hair was pulled back tightly. A can of some beverage briefly appeared in the image and she took a pull from it, then wiped her mouth. "Colonel Majed, talk to me. What's your sitrep?"

"Everything's secured here, Colonel," Majed said. "In fact, it went better than expected. Their resistance was minimal and, quite frankly, disorganized. They only managed to muster around a third of their garrison. As it stands, looks like a lot of their personnel are absent. We're currently trying to locate them."

Cirion pursed her lips. "That would explain it. I think we found them. Resistance here is stiffer than expected. My guess is most of your missing ended up here. They're fielding more 'Mechs than intel reported. They're trying to pull us out of Towerlund City to engage, but I've kept my forces inside the city walls to cause as much damage as possible. We'll pull them back inside soon enough."

She was about to continue, but Majed cut her off. "You're staying *inside* the city? I thought our target was their defense forces and resources? If you march out to meet them, I can send a company from the Seventy-First your way to flank."

Majed watched the hologram shrug. "True, but if there's resources in the city and it's worth defending, they'll come back in. Personally, I think they might be trying to lure me into a trap. But I'll take that company. The Lyrans no doubt know about your success already. If you send some of your troops this way, it might force the issue of surrender."

Majed felt himself growing annoyed. "Colonel, forgive me, but what do you mean, 'if there's resources'? You don't have any confirmed targets in the city?"

Cirion took another swig of her drink. "Colonel Majed, the city *is* a target. Infrastructure is part of their resources. We cause enough damage here, the Lyrans will have to devote more to this world, taking it away from another, possibly on the front lines."

She looked away, nodded, then turned back to Majed. "I need to go. Looks like recon's located some tanks in the streets. Send that company! It's an honor to fight alongside fellow sliddiffs. I'm sure the Big K would be proud!" The signal shifted briefly, then went dead.

Majed sighed. This wasn't the first time the Black Warriors had engaged in such cavalier tactics. Some in the ELH went so far as to call them "dishonorable." He also hated the term "sliddiffs," how the Warriors referred to former SLDF units.

Despite Majed never serving in the SLDF, he had been raised in the extended Light Horse family, finding the traditions and customs a welcome insulation to the chaos and destruction of the First and Second Succession Wars. Growing up, he heard the older warriors and officers spoke in utter adoration of their service in the Star League and what it meant. Majed recognized the importance of maintaining those ideals and code of honor as an oasis to what often seemed like civilization crumbling around him. It bothered him that the Black Warriors, while technically also former SLDF, didn't hold the same ideals. *A conversation for another time, I suppose. And she didn't even ask about the 151st.*

Majed rose from his desk, grabbed his comm unit, and moved with purpose. Flagging down his aide, he finished attaching the device to his belt. "Get me Captain O'Conner. He and his company have new orders."

UNION-CLASS DROPSHIP *BUNGABUNGA*
OUTBOUND FROM PENCADER
LYRAN COMMONWEALTH
7 APRIL 2853

"Tell me again what the new orders are?"

Majed stood firmly, fists on his hips, the viewport of the Black Warriors' DropShip behind him as it sped toward the system's zenith jump point. He stared with concern back at Colonel Cirion, who leaned casually against an instrument panel.

Cirion smirked at Majed's pose. "We're not heading back to Circinus as planned. The Free Worlds League sent us updated operating instructions. We're to proceed to Biloela for another raid."

The corner of Majed's mouth tightened as he looked skeptically at her. "Why wasn't I transmitted these orders as well?"

Cirion shrugged. "Why would you be? With all due respect, Colonel, the Black Warriors are the lead unit in this operation. I'm their commander, and thus I'd be the one receiving any changes in orders." She held up a hand to forestall his next question. "Don't worry, this is still within the parameters of your contract. The Free Wheels respect your integrity and all that."

Majed's irritation rose over her flippant attitude. "It's not that. I just feel that since our unit is being put on the line, and we are of equal rank—"

"Well, let's be fair here, Idris. It's not your *whole* unit. Just half. The rest are back on Circinus, correct?" Cirion's eyes dropped to the bars on Majed's uniform. "And correct me if I'm wrong, but you are just a colonel pro-tem, yes? Colonel Bradley is still the true commander of the ELH, right? You're just sort of… auditioning."

Majed's irritation flared to anger. "That's—" He paused, taking a calming breath, "Correct."

"Thought so. Again, hence why the Free Wheels felt it wasn't necessary." Cirion's expression softened. "Look, we're still outbound. You can transmit any concerns you have back to the boys in purple, as well as to Bradley. We can't wait for their response, of course, but I'm sure it'll be noted."

Majed knew her words were filled with faux concern, but he also knew it had to be done regardless. He set the issue aside. "I appreciate that." Offering his own manufactured appreciation. "What's the objective this time?"

Colonel Cirion straightened and moved across the bridge to a screen adjacent to the command chair. Her fingers flew over several keys. "SAFE agents reported a Lyran task force is slowly gathering on Biloela. They might be prepping for a major anti-spinward incursion. We need to hit what is gathered so far, slow their progress, and make them rethink their priorities. Looks like they are gathering at the city of Arke's Bounty. Targets are the spaceport and as much of their military assets as we can hit. It's a fast in-and-out. SAFE reports there's close to two regiments on-planet, with another three likely en route. We want to get in and out before any reinforcements arrive. We have coordinates for a pirate point to cut travel time in half. The Seventy-First and the One Fifty-First will hit the main forces, and the Warriors will go after the munitions."

Majed took a serious tone. "So just the spaceport and the equipment? Nothing more."

Cirion cocked an eyebrow at him. "Is there a problem?"

He paused, chewing his lower lip, then locked eyes with the Black Warrior commander. "If it becomes something like what we just left, I may have one."

Cirion chuckled, not breaking from his gaze. "Are you *still* upset about the damage to the city? Idris, you're just as much a warrior as I am. If the situation calls for it, that's what we do. Down there in Pencader? That called for it. Besides, it worked. We drew them in and finished the job."

"That's one opinion, yes."

Cirion left the command chair and stepped toward Majed. "No, that's a *fact*. We were on a mission to damage their resources and infrastructure. That's what *we* did. And if the situation warrants it on Biloela, we'll do it again." Her tone was curt, and it was obvious she wanted no reply.

Majed ignored it. "The Eridani Light Horse *does not* and *will not* engage in wanton property destruction or civilian casualties."

Cirion stopped centimeters from his face. "It's admirable that you're clinging to your Star League ways, Colonel. But the Star League isn't here anymore. You have no ideals to uphold anymore. In fact, the only ideal you should be upholding is the one tied to what you are now—*mercenaries.* That cold, hard cash the Mariks are lining your pockets with is the only thing you need to worry about. And the sooner the ELH comes to terms with that, the better off you'll be. If you think some *El-Kaff* MechWarrior's going to respect your Star League honor on the field of battle, you're not going to make it long. They're more than ready to shove those Steiner fists right down your throat."

"Just because the Star League is gone doesn't mean we can't still uphold its ideals, Angelica. The House Lords may act like savages, but that doesn't mean we have to."

Cirion laughed. "Are you serious? Pull your head out of your idealistic ass, Idris. You don't get to sit here and cast that sort of judgment. Just to remind you of your own history, your unit *chose* to stay here when Kerensky left."

"So did yours," Majed retorted.

Cirion threw a finger in his face. "Like hell we did! You know when the Warriors *finally* received the Big K's departure orders? Six months *after* they'd already left. Granted, it didn't affect me none, but I grew up listening to a lot of the vets grow bitter and angry over not only what they felt was betrayal by Kerensky, but also by the Mariks."

Majed frowned. "I'm sorry that happened to them, but if you feel that way about them, why are you even working for the Free Worlds?"

Cirion's voice lowered, and Majed could hear the anger in her own words. "Do we still hate them? Yes. Will we still take their money? Damn right we will. Times change, Idris. We've adapted—and you should, too."

Majed wanted to press the issue. Anger roiled inside him like a storm, but he forced himself to back down. Cirion had won this round. She had the orders. She had their transport. And the ELH wasn't whole. Majed knew when to bide his time.

He nodded curtly. "Understood."

The colonel pro-tem turned and marched toward the bridge's exit.

**ARKE'S BOUNTY
BILOELA
LYRAN COMMONWEALTH
17 APRIL 2853**

Majed steadied himself as he charged his *Black Knight* forward. The Lyran *Pillager* he faced was twenty-five tons heavier and far more lethal. The pair had been playing a game of cat and mouse for the past several minutes. A game Majed found himself losing.

But that was about to change, thanks to a platoon of Zephyr tanks arriving in time to box the massive Lyran 'Mech in at an intersection. The Zephyrs roared in from the side streets of the T-intersection while Majed charged down the center.

Seeing the trap, the Lyran pilot aimed at Majed, intent on fighting their way free. He saw the momentary heat shimmer from the *Pillager*'s dual torso-mounted Gauss rifles, then felt the impact of a slug slamming into the chest of his *Black Knight*. Staggering briefly under the impact, he planted his 'Mech's leg to stay upright. Amber lights blinked across nearly all of his armor icons, with a several accents of red for good measure.

I need to end this now. "O'Conner, get your tanks in close. I don't have much left to give!"

The *Knight*'s right arm jutted forward, sending a beam of charged particles arcing toward the *Pillager*. The azure bolt raked the Lyran 'Mech's right arm from shoulder to wrist. Majed's pair of torso-mounted large lasers stabbed out and met in the same spot above the *Pillager*'s right shoulder. The beams carved a pair of matching trenches down the enemy machine's chest, armor melting off in rivulets to splatter on the street below.

The loss of almost two tons of armor in an instant sent the *Pillager* stumbling backward, causing the ruby beam from its own large laser to go over the *Black Knight*'s head. The pilot did their best to steady the unbalanced assault 'Mech, but only succeeded by using the building behind it to prevent a total fall. It ended up almost sitting on the side of the building, canted over at an awkward angle.

"Close in. Don't let that 'Mech jump out!" Majed shouted to the platoon of hovertanks from the Seventy-First. His cockpit became a sauna thanks to the heavy weapons fire, but the colonel pro-tem resumed the charge.

The *Pillager* thrashed around, throwing broken masonry and glass everywhere as it struggled out of its three-story impromptu chair. Majed saw the telltale heat shimmer of jump jets powering up.

Damn it! The heat was starting to fade in his cockpit, but he knew it wasn't going to be enough. He felt the vibrations of both large lasers and his PPC finishing their recharge. Anticipating, he adjusted his targeting reticule slightly upward as the indicator lights for his weapons flicked from red to green. At the same time, his other hand flew over keys, tying in all his weapons save the small laser to the same interlock circuit.

Bracing himself, he pressed the firing stud.

A bundle of concentrated light, followed with accents from the *Black Knight*'s PPC and missiles from the quartet of Zephyrs, reached out for the *Pillager* as it lifted from the city street, arcing back and away from Majed.

It never made it.

Numerous beams clawed and raked across the 'Mech's surface, stripping away armor and carving through internal supports. The *Knight*'s PPC hit the *Pillager* square in the right elbow. With armor already peeled away, the particle beam crackled through the myomer fibers and supporting structure, snapping it free. Numerous missiles battered the Lyran 'Mech, making the pilot's desperate action even more difficult.

Or more correctly, impossible. The horrendous assault caused the 'Mech to pitch sharply to one side. The jump jets suddenly quit, a sure sign the pilot had lost consciousness. The *Pillager* pitched hard to the right, then dropped with the aerodynamic grace of a brick. Mere seconds after it had launched into the air, the building that had saved it from falling backward would now become its final resting place.

Majed gasped as the heat generated from his strike hit him like hellfire. His exposed skin stung as his body instinctively jerked, trying to escape the hellish assault. His vision blurred as warning klaxons sounded, threatening engine shutdown. He slapped at the manual override, but was either too late or the battle computer chosen to ignore his demands. All lights, except the appropriate glow from red emergency lighting, snapped off, and his screens went blank.

His comm crackled as the heat sinks in his *Black Knight* labored to cool the 'Mech back down. "Colonel! You alive?" It was Benton O'Conner, the tank platoon commander.

Majed struggled to get air as the temperature in his cockpit went from searing to merely sweltering. "Affirmative. I pushed it and I paid. Should be back online soon. O'Conner, I appreciate the assist from your platoon, but link back up with Shifty's company. They're getting a lot more resistance than expected."

"Roger that." The quartet of Zephyrs spun in place and raced away as the familiar hum of the *Black Knight*'s fusion reactor coming back online vibrated through his cockpit. Systems and displays followed. Two 'Mechs from his command lance emerged from side streets, making their way toward him.

Lieutenant Grace Lytton's voice filled his ears. "Apologies, Colonel. When that Lyran lance separated us, we had to call in the reinforcements."

Majed nodded. "It's fine. Much appreciated. Let's make sure this is the last time we underestimate Lyran militia units."

The fact that the Seventy-First had only engaged militia so far troubled him. He'd expected a much larger force of front-line units to be on Biloela. But so far, there was nothing of the sort. Colonel Cirion, who was on the other side of the city, was also only reporting minimal resistance. *Something's not right.*

His 'Mech now fully powered up, Majed called up the sitrep for the rest of the Seventy-First. They were scattered out across the north end of the city. As expected, they had everything under control, keeping the Lyran defenders at bay while the Black Warriors went after their objective across town. The 151st was still back at the landing zone, ready to respond.

Majed hated city fighting, but took consolation that things were being kept to the perimeter. That meant the majority of the civilians were spared most of the heavy combat.

He switched his scans to the Warriors' side of things. There was exceptionally light resistance there, too. His battle computer was showing little more than a company of Lyran 'Mechs; the bulk of the Warriors not even engaged in battle.

Majed keyed his comm to the private command channel. "Colonel Cirion, looks like you have things well in hand."

A happy voice responded, "Oh, Colonel Majed, we do indeed."

"Any idea where the rest of the defenders are? I was expecting a lot more."

"Not sure, Idris. Maybe they are in another city."

Majed was skeptical. "Possibly, but our fighters made the recon as requested, and they reported back a negative. No signs. I'm beginning to think we got some shoddy intel."

"It's possible. SAFE isn't known for their accuracy. More like *un*-SAFE, right?" Cirion chuckled at her joke.

Majed grunted acknowledgment. "Right. Okay, I'm going to start moving our troops back toward the LZ, but I'll send our VTOL scouts over for one more sweep of the city, just to be sure."

Cirion cleared her throat. "I don't think that's necessary, Colonel. I think you're right. We're almost done here. Just head back to the LZ, and we'll rendezvous there. Cirion out."

Now I know something's not right. Majed was liking this mission less and less. He switched his comm to Shaw's aerial-recon platoon. "Lieutenant Shaw, this is Colonel Majed. New orders."

The rhythmic thumping of the rotor blades from Shaw's VTOL accompanied his reply. "Shaw here, Colonel. What do you need?"

"Looks like we've got some bad intel, so we're pulling out. Confirm your area is clear, then take one last sweep of the city. And Shaw, make sure you sweep the southern portion, where the Warriors are, last. Understood?"

A pause, then Shaw's voice came back on. "Yes, sir. Warriors are the tail end before we make for the LZ."

Majed switched back to the unit's channel. "Okay, Seventy-First, this is Majed. Let's break off. We're out of here."

Most of the Seventy-First pulled back in an orderly fashion, with the remnants of the Lyran militia happy to have them depart. As they left, Majed kept one eye on the Warriors and their actions and so far, things hadn't changed. They were still playing cat and mouse with the militia, but the bulk of Cirion's force was still together around what appeared to be a cluster of buildings. *What the hell is going on there?*

His comm blinked. It was Shaw. "Go for Majed."

Shaw's tone was concerned. "Sir, you're going to want to see this. Feed incoming."

Majed routed the signal to one of his visual displays. At first, he thought he was witnessing a standard protection circle, where several 'Mechs form a tight perimeter around a target or a command vehicle. He quickly realized the circle was actually protecting several damaged buildings and a number of armored personnel carriers. Troopers and light 'Mechs worked in concert on the buildings, clearing, carrying and loading something into the APCs.

Majed zoomed in, taking a closer look. His eyes widened when he realized what the troopers were carrying out of the buildings—heavy security containers, the kind that usually contained cash, gems, or precious metals.

Are they...robbing those banks?

"Shaw, am I seeing what I think I'm seeing?"

The rumbles of autocannon fire and missiles could be heard faintly over Shaw's reply. "I believe so. Looks like theft." Shaw paused. "Sir, did we just become thieves?"

We didn't. They *did*, Majed thought. He was about to order Shaw out of there when the signal suddenly blurred as the VTOL banked hard. The image steadied as the lieutenant shouted to the rest of his platoon. "Hard left! Drop us down! Where did that shot come from?"

Majed heard another VTOL pilot answer: "Unknown. I'm not reading any hostiles nearby!"

"Keep your eyes peeled. They might have snuck up on us. Cut left again, through those side streets. We'll get a quick glance when we arc around and through the intersection."

Majed leaned in, keeping a keen eye on Shaw's signal. "Shaw, ID who took the shot, then get out of there. Do not engage. Leave it for the Warriors."

Buildings blurred as the chopper banked and glided down the cross street. Cubes and spires blended together as the VTOL bobbed up and down. The buildings vanished as it hit the intersection, opening up into the street.

The image stabilized as it slowed, enough for Majed to clearly make out the pair of 'Mechs standing at the far end; a *Shadow Hawk* and *Phoenix Hawk*. Even in the split second of the image, Majed spotted the stylized skull and crossbones of the Black Warriors. It was clear Shaw saw it as well.

"Those are Warriors 'Mechs. Looks like it was friendly fire."

Nothing "friendly" about it. Majed jumped in. "Lieutenant Shaw. Get back here. I'll handle this. Repeat, return to the LZ."

Shaw was terse in his reply. "Yes, sir. En route."

Majed killed the video feed. *Damn it, Cirion. What the hell are you doing?*

The wind whipped up a small dust devil that split apart when it hit Majed's bare legs. The dirt from the hard, baked ground stung slightly as it landed, but the Eridani Light Horse colonel ignored it. His gaze was fixed on Colonel Cirion as she walked toward him. Both units were in final preps before dustoff, and normally he would wait until they were off-planet, but the thought of spending any more time with Cirion on her ship made his stomach turn. He was going to have it out with her, right here, right now.

As she approached, Cirion tilted her head and smiled like a child who had been caught misbehaving. It stood in sharp contrast to the scowl on Majed's face.

She held up her hands in a *mea culpa*. "Colonel Majed. I cannot express my disappointment, sadness, and shock at what happened. Thank God your crew didn't get hit." She lowered her hands, stopping a meter from him. "I did warn you though not to send your people there. Why did you dis—"

"Cut the shit, Cirion!" Majed shouted. "You're not upset about the friendly fire, because that was a damned warning shot, and you *know it!*"

Cirion's eyes widened. "A warning shot? What the hell are you talking about?"

"I said, *cut* the *shit*. You didn't want us to see the robbery you were pulling."

"Robbery?" Cirion's hands went up again. "Now wait just a minute, *Colonel.* Lyran militia was dug in inside those buildings. We were rooting them out."

Majed gritted his teeth. "Bullshit. I saw troops—*your* troops, carrying out the containers from the banks. It was a damn robbery, and you know it!" He looked around their LZ. "And I'm guessing this whole little operation wasn't 'bad intel.' It was planned from the get-go with a bullshit cover story. You just needed our help. I bet those orders weren't even real."

Cirion narrowed her eyes, stepping centimeters away from Majed's face. "Did you actually *see* those so-called containers, Colonel? Hmm?"

Majed straightened. "As a matter of fact, I did."

Cirion dismissed the comment with a wave. "Okay, so? And are you seriously going to tell me you've never had a superior officer change your plans while on a mission? Give me a break. Those were legit orders."

Majed opened his mouth to protest, but she cut him off, sticking a finger into his chest. "You know what's *actual* bullshit, Idris? The high and mighty Eridani Light Horse, thinking they're somehow more noble than the rest of us. Oh, you're a Star League unit. You still cling to those saintly ideals. Ideals from a dead empire, and an army that isn't even in the Inner Sphere anymore. With that being the case, are those ideals really worth keeping anymore?"

Majed slapped her hand away. "We're *warriors*. Not *thieves!*"

"You're not?" Cirion raised an eyebrow. "Yeah, it was money we stole. Money that probably would have funded an attack. Now it can't. In essence, we've saved lives *and* helped ourselves survive. The Free Worlds League won't employ us forever, and our people are starving."

She pointed to a Black Warriors DropShip. "That money puts food in their bellies. There's a noble ideal for you. Say what you want about the ELH and your traditions and all the other lies you tell yourselves, but in the end, all you're really fighting for is a paycheck."

Majed's rage made his blood boil, but once again, he forced himself to take a breath and get it under control. "You're right. We fight for money. But at the end of the day, our honor is still intact. At the end of the day, we can still live with ourselves and our conduct, knowing we haven't given in to the chaos around us."

Cirion waved off his statements. "Whatever. You're not changing my mind, and I'm not changing yours. Yeah, we played you, but nobody died, and any damage you've taken is covered in your contract. You got a problem with what we do, take it up with the League. But I'll tell you this: they don't care. They hired us to disrupt the Lyran border, and that's what we do, authorized or not. End of story. Now let's go."

Cirion didn't wait for a response, instead turning toward her DropShip and walking off, leaving Majed standing alone.

Oh, no, it's not over yet.

**BAD LANDING
STARSHINE
LYRAN COMMONWEALTH
5 JULY 2853**

Colonel Pro-Tem Majed couldn't help smiling as the PPC from his *Black Knight* raked the right leg of the Black Warrior *BattleMaster* in front of him. His smile grew even wider at the knowledge that it belonged to Colonel Cirion.

The Black Warriors and the Seventy-First Light Horse Regiment hadn't come to Starshine with the intention of coming into conflict, but that's where they found themselves. In fact, the attack on the Lyran world had started off like many of their previous raids: disruption of Lyran supply lines or hamstringing the Commonwealth's efforts to wage war against the Free Worlds League.

It all changed when the Black Warriors had abandoned their flanking position against Starshine's defenders, the Sixth Arcturan Guards. The Seventy-First were taking on the Sixth, and Majed expected the Warriors to be the hammer to their anvil. The Sixth would be routed, and from there they'd damage the Starshine central spaceport, take or destroy the munitions therein, and pull out.

"I'm sorry, Colonel Majed, but you'll have to handle the Sixth on your own. We've got a secondary mission to undertake." Cirion's words held little regret. Majed knew full well what "secondary mission" meant. Another resource theft. Another act of piracy.

Cirion seemed to delight in taking the Seventy-First on their shared missions since the two had squared off on Pencader. She knew it bothered him to no end. But this was the last time he would accept it. The Free Worlds League might turn a blind eye to their piracy, but Majed no longer could.

As he watched the Warriors' DropShips rocket away, Majed sent an open broadcast to the commander of the Sixth. "Colonel Brubaker. This is Colonel Idris Majed of the Seventy-First Light Horse Regiment of the Eridani Light Horse. I would like to propose a deal."

A near eternal pause stretched out before Majed's call was answered. The voice was deep and bore a heavy Germanic accent. "This is Brubaker. What exactly do you propose, Colonel?"

Majed laid out his case: the Black Warriors' treachery and likely plans. He promised a cessation of the attack and immediate retreat, but only *after* being allowed to put an end to the Warriors. "Just let the Seventy-First strand them here, and your forces can come in and capture them, including their DropShips." He paused. "Colonel, I know this is an unusual request. You have no reason to trust me, but I give you my word as the commander of the former SLDF Third Regimental Combat Team, this is no trick. We've grown tired of what the Black Warriors have done, and as a fellow former SLDF unit, we're embarrassed and disgusted at their actions."

Another eternal pause, then finally Brubaker responded. "All right, Colonel Majed. We have an agreement. Looks like your pirates are heading southwest, toward the Bad Landing island chain. There's an old SLDF base there. Been rumors of a supply cache there for years, but we've never found anything. Nobody goes there anymore. If you want to maroon them there, that's fine by us."

Majed smiled. "Thank you, Colonel."

There was confusion in the ranks of the Seventy-First as they withdrew, but once Majed told his soldiers the what and, more importantly, the why, there were zero objections. And when the Seventy-First dropped in on the Black Warriors at Bad Landing, there was no doubt. It was payback time.

Cirion's *BattleMaster* shook off the hit from Majed's *Black Knight* and pressed forward. The 'Mech's right arm lifted the massive double-barreled weapon it held and returned fire.

The PPC beam slammed into the *Black Knight*'s chest, snapping and melting armor plating. The paired medium laser went high over the 'Mech's shoulder, but the other three lasers found purchase, each on separate limbs. Majed struggled to stay upright as over a ton and a half of armor vanished off his 'Mech in an eyeblink.

Cirion's taunting voice came over his comm. "Finally had enough, eh, Idris? Finally decided to take some action? I never thought you'd be this rash. This is going to end so badly for you."

"Keep telling yourself that, Cirion," he countered as his *Black Knight* backed up, its circular feet digging deep into the wet sand of the beach. He adjusted his targeting reticule lower and triggered his paired large lasers and quartet of medium lasers when it pulsed green. The beams stabbed in concert, all but one of the medium lasers finding their home in the *BattleMaster*'s legs. Rivulets of armor dripped off the 'Mech, mixing with the sand.

The assault caused Cirion's 'Mech to stumble, but she used the free arm of the massive BattleMech to remain upright and countered with a sextet of missiles. Half of them impacted the upper chest and shoulders of Majed's 'Mech. A fourth slammed hard into the pointed tip of the *Black Knight*'s head, making him rock back hard in his seat.

He shook his head to clear his blurred vision just in time to see Cirion on him. The *BattleMaster*'s massive left fist was cocked back like a deadly piston, looking to finish the work the missile had started.

Majed smiled again as the alert pinged, telling him all his lasers were recharged and ready. He angled his 'Mech slightly to his left and fired, just as Cirion did the same.

Lasers from both war machines savaged each other, burning and cutting away armor. Some penetrated deeper, slicing myomer fibers and melting the reinforced metallic bones underneath. Majed gritted his teeth as he watched the *BattleMaster*'s fist close in. Not hesitating, he thrust the right leg of his *Black Knight* out.

A sickening *screech*, coupled with a lowing groan and finally a sharp *snap*, filled Majed's ears as the *BattleMaster*'s massive fist caved in the *Black Knight*'s right shoulder. Warning tones tried to rise above the pandemonium of crushing armor, indicating damage to the 'Mech's shoulder actuator joint.

Majed ignored the alert as he struggled to keep his 'Mech upright, which proved nearly impossible on a single leg as the *Knight*'s other leg slammed with a *crunch* into the *BattleMaster*'s right leg. The power from the kick carried through the damage he'd already done, forcing Cirion's leg back farther than it was designed. Titanium-alloyed steel members inside the limb screamed as they stretched, then snapped free from the 'Mech's body.

Majed leaned his 'Mech forward as Cirion's fell backward. The symphony of chaos played on, filling his cockpit as the pair landed hard on the beach in a clumsy embrace.

Safety straps bit into Majed's skin as he hung nearly upside down. A groan escaped his lips as he fought to clear his senses. As his focus returned, he stared directly through the cracked ferroglass canopy to the damaged and bent dome of the *BattleMaster*'s cockpit. The angry face of Angelica Cirion stared back at him.

Majed's comm panel beeped. "Damn you, Majed!" Cirion shouted. "You think you've won? I'll have your head for this!"

Majed slowly began to stand his 'Mech back up, refusing to break eye contact with Cirion. "No, you won't. In fact, you won't have anything for this. Once the rest of the Seventy-First is done disabling your 'Mechs, the Arcturan Guards will be taking care of your DropShips." He paused above her. "And then, like a proper pirate, you'll be marooned here, with nothing but your broken 'Mechs and your broken honor."

"You'll tell them just *our* unit was destroyed?" Cirion screamed. "That's a lie no one will buy!"

Majed finished his rise. "Yes, they will. The Eridani Light Horse is an honorable merc unit. Our reputation is stellar. We have no reason to lie. I can tell any story I want. Our honor guarantees it's the truth." He punctuated his sentence with a final crushing blow to the *BattleMaster*'s remaining knee.

Majed turned his *Black Knight* away, leaving Cirion to her new home and her new fate.

**ERIDANI LIGHT HORSE COMMAND
CIRCINUS
CIRCINUS FEDERATION
28 JULY 2853**

Majed's face was a mix of emotions as he stood across from Colonel Ezra Bradley. Despite the Eridani Light Horse commander's weak and withered form, the Colonel sat upright in his wheelchair. Though unable to lead in the field in a 'Mech, the aged commander still kept his military cut, a small square of close-cropped white hair standing in contrast to the vast array of cinnamon-colored liver spots that blanketed his skin. Majed wanted to feel pity for his commanding officer, but it was difficult when he knew the man's record and the weight he carried keeping the Light Horse together through the collapse of the Star League and the chaos of the Succession Wars. The respect Majed felt for Colonel Bradley nearly overwhelmed him.

He finished presenting his report. Since the actions on Starshine, the colonel pro-tem had come to regret his decision. Yes, he'd eliminated Cirion and her troublesome unit, but he couldn't reconcile the cost to his own standards and those of the Light Horse. The closer he drew to Circinus and Colonel Bradley, the more he knew he deserved punishment for what he'd done. His report reflected that internal struggle. It contained all the instances of Cirion's treachery and duplicity, culminating in the actions Majed and his forces had taken on Starshine.

He sighed heavily. "I understand the severity of my actions, Colonel. I am ready and willing to accept whatever punishment you feel is necessary. I do humbly request that you direct it all toward me, sir. Spare the rest. They followed *my* orders."

Bradley's bony fingers swiped across the noteputer, while he focused his attention on the report, almost ignoring Majed. After almost a minute of silence, Bradley spoke. "There will be no punishment, Colonel. I'll need you to alter your report a bit, but I'll handle this."

Majed's eyes widened, and his jaw dropped. "Excuse me, sir?"

Bradley finally looked up at him. "You heard me, Idris. There is no punishment to mete out. You did what you had to do, and quite frankly, I agree with all of it."

Majed struggled with his words. "Sir...but, why?"

Now Bradley sighed. "Colonel, you, more than most, seem to fully understand what the ELH is about and what we represent. What we're trying to be as the galaxy appears to almost be crumbling around us."

Majed nodded. "Of course, that's why I feel—"

Bradley held up a hand. "Stop. But you must also realize that such a thing can't exist right now. The Inner Sphere is not black and white. We can create an appearance, but the reality is almost always very different."

Majed looked down at the noteputer, then back to his commander. "What exactly do you mean?"

Bradley gestured for Majed to sit in the chair across from him. "It isn't that complicated. For example, to most, the Circinus Federation looks like nothing more than a group of pacifist farmers just trying to survive the horrors around them. The reality is the Black Warriors are their 'secret' military that supports the Federation through raids. When we contracted with the Free Worlds, they painted our mission as not only raids against the Commonwealth, but also as an effort to protect the 'peaceful' people of the Circinus Federation—or as some might want to call it, an occupation. Under the table, the Free Worlds knew full well what was happening here and offered the Black Warriors a fat contract of their own, sweetening it with the promise of our assistance.

"Now, with the evidence you've presented, if we decided to leave on moral grounds, such an action would be painted very poorly against us, not only to the realm we're serving but it would also work against us in future contracts. We can't have that. Our people have suffered enough of late. They do not need to suffer more."

Majed nodded. "So, what will you do?"

Bradley gestured beyond the office window, to the rest of the base where both the ELH and Black Warriors were stationed. "We are not completely without our ideals. Your actions will quietly show the rest of the Warriors that we won't tolerate such behavior. They won't know exactly what happened to Cirion, but they're no fools. We will fulfill this contract, and perhaps even put in for another, until such time that we can control the story and leave when it best serves us."

Majed found himself recalling Cirion's words about changing times and adapting. "I suppose this is the best we can do for now."

Bradley nodded. "For now. I'd hoped the ferocity and bloodlust would have been quenched with Amaris' downfall, but then I realized the House Lords had never truly gotten their fill during those years."

Majed stood. "Our ideals will keep us intact, sir."

Bradley nodded again, slower this time. "True, but our careful compromises are what will keep us alive."

Majed took in those words as he saluted, acknowledging he'd learned that lesson without even realizing it.

BATTLEMASTER
Assault—85 tons

BLACK KNIGHT
Heavy—75 tons

PILLAGER
Assault—100 tons

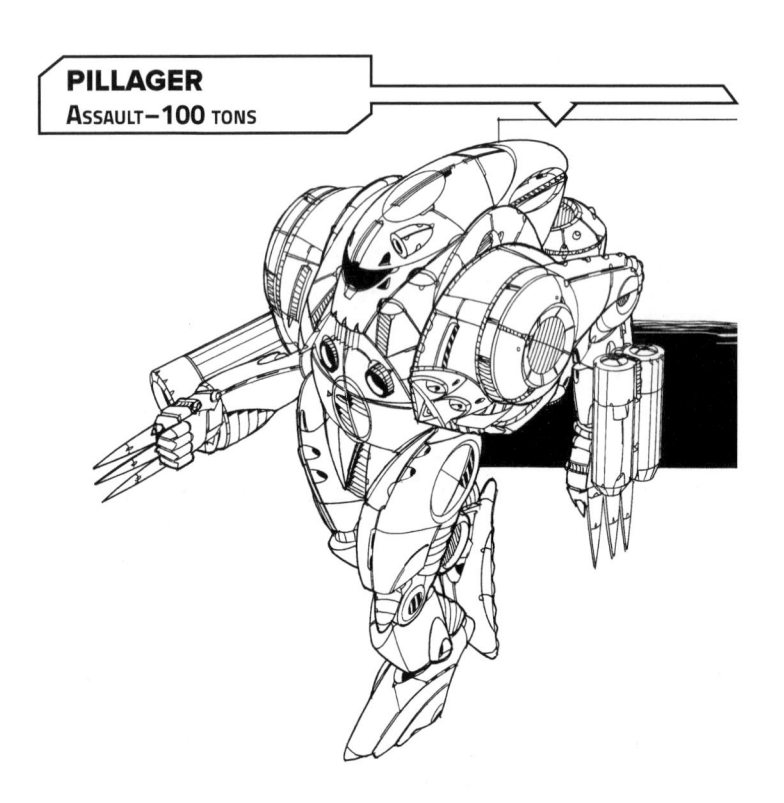

THE HAND THAT FEEDS

RANDALL N. BILLS

**ERIDANI LIGHT HORSE HEADQUARTERS
NEW KARLSRUH, AULDHOUSE
ISLE OF SKYE
LYRAN COMMONWEALTH
2 JULY 2999**

As Brevet Major Ryana Campbell slipped into the room, she smiled mischievously at Major Nigel across the way. He winced sourly back at her. *That's right. Found out about this meeting whether you wanted me to or not.*

While the tension only made her smile more, it turned a little sickly at the sheer amount of brass in the room. She balked at her immediate desire to cut into the pressure. *Maybe in a bit. Let's see where this is at first.*

Despite the number of officers in the room, there was a clear delineation of *us* and *them* that ran straight down the middle. On the left, a phalanx of blue and white, chevroned to a point centered on Hauptmann-General Alexi Garstov. Along that winged chevron, an additional bevy of adjunct-generals and -colonels supported the head of the Liaison in the negotiations. Ryana just kept a whistle from escaping, but she couldn't help shaking her head, which sent her topknot fluttering. *The head of the Mercenary Troops Liaison herself. Not pulling any punches.* Her smile broadened. *Then again, we're the Light Horse. Of course they're desperate to keep our contract.*

On the right side of the usually spacious room—though feeling cramped with so many in attendance—Brevet General Kerston, overall commander of the Eridani Light Horse, along with his own support crew right and left of the general's chair: Colonel Charles Winston, commander of the Twenty-First Striker Regiment, and Colonel Jessica Coolidge, commander of the Seventy-First Light Horse Regiment on the right; and Nathan L. Armstrong, commander of the 151st Light Horse Regiment, and an empty chair to the left.

Despite the meeting having been underway for some time, Ryana caught one or two pairs of Lyran eyes drifting uncomfortably toward the empty seat. She momentarily lost her smile, solemnly nodding toward that chair, always placed when all top commanders were present, in memory of the Nineteenth Striker Regiment destroyed on Amity during Operation Intruder, the reconnaissance raids that preceded the Liberation of the Hegemony campaign from the Usurper, Stefan Amaris. *You still serve the Light Horse.* She could think of no higher compliment.

She also then noted a few select battalion commanders and their XOs beyond that half-circle. *Just not me, eh, Nigel?* She glanced at him again, only to find him frowning at her heavily, as though his displeasure could somehow force her from the room. *Not if Kerensky himself walked through that door!* Her smile returned, as wide as she could make it, as she raised her chin to Nigel, which only made him pale. *You wanted me as XO. You and Colonel Winston both. Not gonna apologize for who I am.*

She focused back on the moment, trying to get the gist of the negotiations. The silence wore heavily on the room, as though it was a dark cloud that actually seemed to steal the light from the numerous fixtures.

"Brevet General Kerston, your position is untenable," Hauptmann-General Alexi Garstov said calmly. "Please, be reasonable."

Trying to keep the tension from your voice. Not working so well, lady.

"We have given concessions in nearly every category," she continued. "Why will you not concede in this one area?"

General Kerston waited a long pause before answering. His hard-planed face gave nothing away; his deep voice filled the room, even as he kept his volume low. "Because you have consistently done us harm with your command decisions."

The tension spiked, if possible. *Damn...straight to the point. Was he this direct before, or did I miss the good parts?*

"I believe you are overstating your case," General Garstov tried again, further failing to keep her voice even.

"And Hesperus?" Kerston managed to make it a slap without changing his inflection.

I have to figure out how he does that!

"If our command had not directly disobeyed the orders of Leutnant-General Mouttheim, we might have lost an entire regiment," he continued, a hand momentarily pointing for emphasis. "Not to mention you might have lost a significant portion of your production on that world."

Ryana's smile faltered, and she couldn't help but shrink just a little against the wall, her stomach dropping, despite all her protestations of defiance. She thought for sure they would all abruptly look at her. *After all, I'm the one who defied Mouttheim.*

Memories flashed: Of standing up to that prig of a general—of a desperate fight against overwhelming odds, and her unusual use of artillery to blunt and scare off the attack—of the instant death of a company of men by her hand. But she should've known she was a fly on the wall. The battle waged between these two powerful individuals cared not a whit for those at the periphery. They ignored her equally.

General Garstov nodded her head somewhat jerkily. "That was an unfortunate incident. But it was an isolated case."

General Armstrong shook his head, as though lecturing a child, regardless that they appeared of age. "There are other examples. Hesperus is simply the most egregious. We have no issues with continuing our contract with the Lyran Commonwealth. In many ways, House Steiner has been generous. But that generosity cannot compensate for those failings. We will no longer accept Integrated Command, but demand Independent Command. We will fight when and where and how we see fit to best accomplish the objectives you provide."

General Garstov glanced down at her noteputer, as several of her aides typed furiously. *You're all digitally connected, of* course. *Blake's Blood, how I would love to know what you're saying to each other.*

General Garstov glanced back up, nodding as though in response to something she had read on her screen. "We can understand your hesitance, General. Perhaps Integrated Command has not worked as well as both parties had hoped. We are willing to adjust that to House Command, provided there is an appropriate shift in another category. Perhaps a five percent cut in your salvage rights?"

General Kerston stared at her until even Ryana felt uncomfortable, though Garstov didn't show a hint of discomfort. *I've never been under that gaze, but I've seen that power on others. You got spine, lady—I'll give you that.*

"I will reduce salvage rights by eight percent, as well as cut three percent off transport reimbursement, and five percent off support and overhead compensations," General Kerston abruptly continued in his low-volume-but-still-fills-a-room voice. "In exchange, you will concede to Independent Command rights."

Ryana almost let another whistle slip out. She didn't know all the nuances of those numbers—even the thought of having to keep track of such things made her skin crawl—but she knew rough figures. *That's one hell of a cut the general just put onto the table.*

She watched nearly the entire Lyran side of the room pause for a long moment of taking that in, and her smile started creeping back on her face. *You are a Great House, like the other four squabbling over the lost Star League. Yet, at your heart, you will always be merchants. Did that much penny-pinching just win the day?*

"That is…very generous," General Garstov responded after nearly a minute of returned silence. "I admit, it is so generous, I would like time to discuss this with my team. May we return here in one week's time? I'm sure we will find a compromise that will satisfy all involved."

General Kerston nodded. "Of course, General."

Everyone stood, respective nods were given, and the Lyran officers all filed out of the room. Ryana watched Kerston nod to a pair of Light Horse guardsmen in the back of the room who followed them out to ensure they all left the building complex that had acted as their headquarters during the duration of their Lyran Commonwealth contract.

No one dared opened their mouth until the general spoke, and it was quickly apparent he wasn't speaking until the guardsmen returned. Ryana edged around the room until she sidled next to Major Nigel.

"I missed the call to XOs," she whispered. "Sorry about that."

Ten years her senior, the major always came across as double that, especially when lecturing Ryana. Despite the resignation in his eyes, he still responded. "I'm surprised you kept your mouth shut. Especially when they mentioned Hesperus," he whispered back, glancing at General Kerston as though ensuring he didn't intrude on that silence.

Yeah, always lecturing. She shrugged. "I can do as I'm told."

"You can?" he replied, standing up straighter, feigning surprise. "I haven't seen it."

She silently looked at him, nails into a board, until he returned his own shrug. "Mostly," he finally conceded.

"You tricked the colonel into making me your XO and sometimes ops commander."

A true smile emerged from behind his usual grimace. "Yes, that's right. I pulled the wool over the eyes of the commander of the entire Twenty-First Striker Regiment of the best mercenary command in the Inner Sphere. And years later, he still hasn't figured it out."

Exactly. She squelched that little voice immediately. She'd done a superb job in her new office, regardless of how much she still wished to just be a company commander in the field. *Perhaps I'll still be able to do that after all this.*

"Regardless, it seemed like the negotiations weren't going well," she whispered, trying to get away from a topic she didn't like.

He subtly waved his hand, as though to shush her.

Ryana frowned at his dismissive motion. *Nobody shushes me!*

"That's putting it mildly," he said, his voice even lower. "I think...there may be a change coming."

Despite wanting to protest, she matched the lowered volume. "Do you think we'll actually leave?" The Light Horse had been on a Lyran contract for more than a century. It didn't seem possible.

A guardsman returned to the doorway, signaling the Lyrans were all out of the building. "I think we're about to see," Nigel whispered before stepping closer to Colonel Winston, as though he would be at hand if asked a question.

"What do you think, Jessica?" General Kerston asked Colonel Coolidge, the commander of the Seventy-First Light Horse.

The tall, gangly woman sneered. "She's taking the week so they can communicate directly with the Archon. But the Elsies will never give us Independent Command. They just can't stomach the idea of placing that much trust in any mercenary outfit."

"Comes from loving money too much," Colonel Armstrong spoke up. "They know how they respond to it. They can't imagine anyone responding any different."

All three sets of eyes settled on Colonel Charles Winston, who brooded, as usual, eyes unfocused as he deliberated. Ten centimeters taller than anyone present and built like a tank, his impassive eyes watched internal scenarios running.

But Ryana was confident she already knew the answer. Because it was her answer. And after years of working closely with the colonel, they often saw eye-to-eye.

"I believe it's time we started looking elsewhere, General," Winston finally responded, refocusing on the here and now and taking in the deciding body of the Eridani Light Horse. After all, the general still led, but he empowered his colonels, and heeded their advice. "It has been a long time, but House Steiner no longer feels like home." He then looked beyond the top officers to all of those in the room, including Ryana—she dared to nod imperceptibly—before pausing at the empty chair of the Nineteenth, and then turned back to the general.

"It is time to take down the flag."

Four sets of eyes bored into each other, before the three colonels firmly nodded in unison, and Ryana let out a pent-up breath as General Kerston gravely nodded in return.

"It would seem the Light Horse needs to find new fields to course. Colonel Winston, I cannot get off-world without raising too much excitement with the Lyrans. I'm delegating the full rights of negotiation to you. Take a discreet crew and travel in person to Galatea. I don't want any communications falling into unfriendly hands. I can drag these negotiations out for several months, if need be. But I want a new deal on my desk by the start of the year. It's five jumps to the Mercenary Star. You'll want to book passage on a trader vessel to allay any fears, so it'll be one, two months to reach Galatea. That gives you several months to deliver."

Colonel Winston saluted. "I'll get it done, General. But that means I should be about the work."

"Yes it does, Colonel. Bring us a new home to raise our flag."

The others kept talking, but Ryana had stopped hearing anything else. *A new home? A new home!* The excitement lit a fire in her belly. Those previous memories of Leutnant-General Mouttheim and Hesperus rose, but this time she popped them like unwanted balloons. *We'll get away from such incompetence. We'll find a home where we're valued, and little men won't get in our way.*

She glanced up to see Colonel Winston and Major Nigel quietly conversing while eyeing her. She smiled, thrusting out her chin again, knowing full well what it meant. *Let's make this happen!*

GALATEA CITY
GALATEA
ISLE OF SKYE
LYRAN COMMONWEALTH
14 OCTOBER 2999

Ryana itched. She scratched. Wrinkled her nose. *Smells like crotch in here.* She scratched her scalp (*I need a shower*) and glanced around the room, realizing she'd been inside these walls for weeks. Leaned back in her chair to stretch her back, her mind wandering beyond the constant, droning voices.

The early days on Galatea had been a whirlwind of excitement. The first encounter with the hiring halls of Galatea City. And entering the largest building, past the huge, rotating doors and the massive rotunda, off which marched three long hallways. Screens absolutely everywhere, bursting with information on every type of mercenary contract imaginable. While, above their heads, a titanic holo of the Inner Sphere rotated. Each world blinking in an array of colors—with various shapes and sizes as well—indicating conflict zones and the corresponding agencies seeking said contracts.

She had spent the first forty hours doing a deep dive just into her noteputer, tapping into that wealth of data. As soon as she'd verified that Colonel Winston had no intention of taking a Free Worlds League contract—she would've had something to say about *that*—she'd spent those heady days digging up whatever details she could find and exploring options she could bring to the colonel.

After all, they were not some down-on-their luck mercenary force, or—she shuddered to think of it (had told her friend Chloe she should stop such dreams!)—a brand new command, without a mark on their resume and only a lance to their name. They were the Eridani Light Horse! Three primed regiments with a legacy that stretched back to the Star League. Their name spoken in the same breath as the best of the mercenary commands in all of human occupied space: McCarron's Armored Cavalry, the Northwind Highlanders (her old command), and the Light Horse!

Wonderfully, beautiful, exciting days…

…which had slowly devolved to this. She glanced around the dull room and the acidic smell of too much sweat and too many bodies in too small a room.

"Colonel," Leftenant Colonel Joaquin De Santos said, his emphasis somehow pulling Ryana back to the moment. The small, swarthy man filled his suit very well, despite the mustache she personally disliked. But he'd been knowledgeable and unfailingly polite.

I will not hate your voice. I will not hate your voice. I will not hate your voice…

"I understand and appreciate your desire to secure Independent Command," the leftenant colonel continued. "Especially considering the incident on Hesperus. But as I've stated before, I believe you can review the last century's worth of mercenary commentary on our employment. There are a few blemishes, to be sure. And I've pointed those out as the exception that helps make the rule. But the Armed Forces of the Federated Suns is the largest employer of mercenaries in the Inner Sphere. It behooves us to ensure that you are happy with your employer."

He paused for a moment, as though ensuring he had their undivided attention, then continued, "I will do anything to advance the cause of House Davion. Not only am I here to personally see that this contract is signed, but I will be your Liaison Officer. While I am far from the throne, I am a Davion by marriage. My wife, Celia Rand-Davion, is not just intelligent, she will be her own boon to you as we always work together. But further, her connection to the throne is my connection to the throne. Is *your* connection to the throne of the largest Great House in human-occupied space. *That* is the importance House Davion places on each and every contract. *That* is the importance we will place on you."

Smooth. So smooth. She'd tried to find a distaste for the man. Especially as he'd used that gambit three times now in the last few weeks. But despite protestations that she hated his voice, she knew an internal lie when she said it. *He's been nothing but up front and professional. And it's simply a powerful point of leverage. Why wouldn't he use it?*

I just hate it because men in power have abused it around us too often. She felt a half-truth, and gritted her teeth to get it all out, even if it was just to herself. *I just hate it because I've been cooped up for so long. Gods, I need to be back in a 'Mech!* She'd even contemplated complaining for a moment, but realized doing so in front of a prospective employer... Yeah, Major Nigel—much less Colonel Winston—would give her a dressing down that would leave her unable to sit for a week. After all, she'd practically begged to be a part of these negotiations. She'd just never imagined it would be so...*boring*!

Seriously, Chloe. If you tell me one more time how you want to start your own mercenary command, I'm going to beat you about the head. Because then you'd drag me into this!

"I've reviewed all of the material you've provided, Colonel," Winston said, leaning back; his tank-like frame made his chair squeal alarmingly. "And as I've also said, House Davion is an impressive employer."

"Why we're here week after week," Ryana mumbled before she could stop herself, earning a dark look from Major Nigel—nothing from the colonel, but she knew he'd heard and ignored it…for now.

"But we must have that Independent Command. It's simply non-negotiable."

Leftenant Colonel Santos rubbed his mustache, then ran his hands down the front of his uniform that sported a burst of gold rays sprouting off his left shoulder, as though he was smoothing a wrinkle only he could see. "I don't mean to countermand you, Colonel. But I am a Mercenary Liaison, and you are a mercenary. Stepping into any negations with a firm 'no' in any category is far too limiting. Perhaps that is why these negotiations are taking so long? As your esteemed brevet major has let it be known." He nodded in her direction, though he kept his gaze on the colonel.

Ryana just kept the heat from showing in her face. *Oh, hell—I'm gonna pay for that later.*

"Perhaps we need to look at this from a different perspective," Santos continued, tapping the noteputer in front of him. "Since our last session, I've received new instruction from the throne. Directly from the First Prince himself. He is very keen to add the Light Horse to our stable. Pun intended, of course," he said, smiling.

Ryana wanted to find insult there, but couldn't. *He's just so…genuine.* She'd spent so many years around House Steiner's social generals and their incompetence, she didn't know how to react when what appeared to be a competent and respectful liaison wanted to engage.

"This Third Succession War is dragging on interminably, with no real end in sight," Santos continued. "Waging a full-scale invasion, even with your potent command, would be costly, to say the least. Perhaps more costly than we wish to bear at the moment. However, that doesn't mean our enemies still do not have aspirations. Aspirations we need to meet and eliminate." He paused, taking a long drink from the glass of water at his side, giving Ryana time to surreptitiously scratch at her scalp again. *So frustrated with this, not taking care of myself.* Chloe would clobber her for that.

"You wish Independent Command," Santos continued. "And the throne wishes to have Liaison Command. Perhaps…we can meet in the middle." He paused again, placing fingers on the noteputer, pursing his lips and looking at each of them in turn. "We have had good negotiations so far, Colonel. But what I'm about to share with you is a hint of future military planning. Showing you this, before we have assigned a contract, is a gamble on my part. A gamble I was given the discretion to take. But I hope you fully appreciate that in doing so, I show the deep respect we hold for the Light Horse, and taking you as men and women of honor as we share these details before said contract is secured."

Ryana sat up a little straighter, fingers practically tingling to look at those details, as Major Nigel and Colonel Winston both nodded gravely.

"We do, in fact, know exactly what this entails and the respect it affords," the colonel responded. "Regardless of whether this negotiation is successful or not, the Eridani Light Horse has never leaked state secrets, and we are not about to start now. You have our oath."

Ryana firmly nodded, silently setting her oath next to that pledge.

Leftenant Colonel Santos inclined his head, accepting the promissory statement. He tapped on the keyboard, bringing up data, and then casually flipping the noteputer around for the Horsemen to review.

Ryana eagerly leaned forward. *Finally. Some real headway!* Her eyes widened as she quickly took in the gist of the details.

"As you can see," Santos continued, "if we can come to an accord and sign you to House Davion, we will not station you on a single world. Instead, our desire is to use your expertise of reconnaissance-in-force by splitting the Light Horse regiments into battalions and stationing them on nine different worlds, spread across the entire borders of the realm with both the Capellan Confederation and the Draconis Combine. You will then be tasked with said reconnaissance-in-force across those borders. And this is where perhaps a compromise can be found.

Each battalion will have its own Liaison Officer." He touched his chest. "And though I certainly will be one of those, which I very much look forward to, others will also be attached to you. All connected to the throne, of course."

He paused, giving them time to devour the details, and Ryana found herself sharing a look with Major Nigel; for once, he seemed to struggle to keep a smile from his own face, but it shone brightly in eyes that matched her own. *We'd be deployed as our own command. Almost guaranteed I'd get into the field!*

"That compromise you were talking about?" Ryana finally said, unable to bank her excitement further. After all, she'd been used as a goad across the weeks of negotiation to catch the leftenant colonel off guard, even if they chastised her now and then for being too much of a stick some days. *But if I'm a stick, I gotta hit something sometime!*

Santos smiled easily, leaning forward to tap up a new screen that filled with bullet-pointed text. "A selection of guidelines will be given by each liaison," he said, "taking their cues from the throne. But each liaison will listen carefully to Light Horse commanders when selecting targeted worlds, giving them appropriate consideration. And if a different target is chosen by a liaison—one not agreed on by the Light Horse commander—the liaison must have the backing of at least two other command-level officers. One a mercenary officer in our employ chosen by the liaison, and one an AFFS officer chosen by the Light Horse. Both will review the details: If the target is not confirmed, the Light Horse will choose from secondary targets. However, if they support the liaison's decision, the Light Horse will move on the target. And of course, even as they move on a target not of their choice, once on-world, the Light Horse will be free to follow their own command decisions to achieve the desired objectives."

Ryana couldn't think clearly for a moment. *After all this time, how did such a brilliant breakthrough happen?* "You've got to be kidding me. What do we give up to get this compromise?" she said before she could curb her tongue. All eyes swung toward her, and her stomach did a slow somersault. She thrust out her chin. *I'm a stick, remember?*

Santos smiled easily. "Just a few percentage points off overhead, transportation, and salvage compensation. Nothing you haven't already put on the table, just a few more points to ensure I can answer tough questions from the field marshal, should they come. But really, this is not my plan. This is straight from the First Prince, you see. A masterfully outrageous plan."

She slowly nodded, glancing at Colonel Winston and Major Nigel, both of whom had guarded expressions. *Do we actually have a new home?*

"Leftenant Colonel De Santos," Colonel Winston said. "While I can appreciate the multiple worlds for battalion commands, we have always held a central world for a base of operations for the Light Horse. I am sure we shall still need this accommodation."

Ryana just kept from nodding. *Always gotta push and see how far they bend.*

The other man smiled easily, pulled the noteputer to him for a moment to tap up another window and slid it back. "We assumed so, of course. The world of Bristol is located in the Crucis March, almost at the tip of the salient between the Capellan and Draconis Marches. An excellent position to coordinate with the battalion commands that will be spread through said Marches. What's more—" he continued, hand pointing to the data on the screen—she could feel all three of them leaning forwarding to read, "—the Ashwood Desert on that planet was once used for SLDF training. The 152nd Mechanized Infantry Division, I believe. There is a burgeoning city there, Derby, that's arisen in the last decades, catering to commands looking for hardscrabble training. The locals there will regale you about how the name is meant to lift the "Southern Curse" after the depredations of the Succession Wars, whatever that might mean."

Ryana could practically sniff the carrot dangling in front of the Light Horse. *We'll probably just find a few broken down walls and long-ago looted lostech caches. And still...you play this game very well. So smooth...*

"This offer may just work," Colonel Winston said slowly, his impassive eyes giving nothing away. "We have rarely deployed like this in the past, nor accepted such an unusual contract. As such, I do not feel comfortable making this decision on my own.

Please make a full addendum to the contract as we've currently negotiated, and I will be heading for the next JumpShip to take this in front of Brevet General Kerston personally. But I will say I believe things are finally where they should be."

They all rose, exchanging handshakes and kind words—the ease and familiarity so stark against the negotiations with General Garstov; hers more a wary treatise with enemies—and watched Leftenant Colonel Santos leave the room before they shared a final look.

"You said to be a goad," Ryana said to Major Nigel, forestalling any recriminations.

"That was more like a club," he responded immediately.

"More like a hammer," Colonel Winston deadpanned.

She thrust out her chin, her topknot fluttering as she stood up straight. "Hammer at your service, Colonel." She could almost joke around him without her stomach fluttering now. *Almost.*

"A kick from a BattleMech," Major Nigel said, but she could see that hint of a smile working past his usual glower.

"Nine worlds. Nine different operations. This is going to be…exciting," she couldn't help saying.

"And dangerous," the major said, though his tone belied the words.

"Of course it'll be dangerous. We're mercenaries."

"So dangerous that despite their protestations of wanting more percentage points, I'm sure the general will want hazard pay."

Ryana nodded, her mind already playing out how she could get back into the field. "Yeah, they'll pay." They all nodded a last time, before heading out themselves.

She stopped for a moment in the corridor, glancing down to see a bevy of mercenary commands and prospective employers traversing the corridors of the hiring halls that fueled the soldier-of-fortune industry in the Inner Sphere. And despite the sweat and tension filling these corridors, it still smelled like sweet, mountain air as they finally moved forward. Ready to pack her few things, knowing it would take at least half a year to reach their destination.

But the Light Horse was heading to new fields!

**ARLUM VALLEY
HOFF
DRACONIS MARCH
FEDERATED SUNS
11 APRIL 3000**

The sun kissed the newly installed flagpoles.

Though Ryana had only been with the Light Horse for a little more than a decade, they were almost as good at inculcating traditions as the Northwind Highlanders, where she'd grown up.

As such, she, along with every single member of the Seventh Striker Battalion and all their dependents, listened to "To the Colors" played on a lonely but defiant bugle while watching with near reverence as the Eridani Light Horse banner of a prancing horse on a yellow shield banded in black was attached to the line by two soldiers randomly drawn from lots for the honor. Then, slowly, the two hoisted the flag up to half-mast before tying it off. The other flagpole remained bare. As the final bugle note echoed into silence, all saluted simultaneously.

Two hundred and sixteen years ago, the Eridani Light Horse lowered their Star League banner for the last time as a combat command of the Star League Defense Force. They'd soon emerged as a mercenary outfit, one of the best in the Inner Sphere. Yet despite all that success, they still bore the scars. *I've only been here ten years, and yet I still feel that mark...that longing to be a part of something greater than ourselves. Will we ever get that back?*

"I'm glad the general let each battalion hoist a flag on our new worlds," Major Nigel said, walking up beside her as conversation resumed after the sacred moment and soldiers began moving off to assigned duties.

She nodded. "Can't break with centuries of tradition, now can we?" she said as the sun finally rose high enough to make her squint in the bright light.

"You wear our traditions well, Campbell," he said.

She laughed. "You gotta be kidding. I mean, I love the Light Horse and all. And it is an honor to serve here; I absolutely think of myself as a Horseman. But I was raised in the Northwind Highlanders, who've got a history that stretches all the way back to ancient Terra. Seventeenth century. With all due respect, the Light Horse are pikers by comparison."

He managed to smile in return. "I guess it's all about perspective."

"It is."

She glanced around at the bivouac that was quickly taking shape. At the end of the beautiful Arlum Valley, nestled up against vertiginous hills that spread around behind them; only jumping 'Mechs could reach them across that defensive perimeter. The elbow-shaped hills ran nearly a kilometer on both sides into the distance, spreading out wider before dropping down to meet the valley floor, which included several hundred square kilometers of rough but beautiful terrain. She glanced up into the distance, at another rearing terrain feature. She could just make out a man-made structure, lonely against the sunrise, swallowed by all the vegetation around it.

"The Belfast Heights," Nigel said as she caught him looking in the same direction.

She nodded. "I can just make out part of the old Star League-era General Circuits company."

"I studied the maps inbound. That's just a small satellite facility. The main ruins are about ten klicks farther on."

Ryana brought up the memory of her own study of the region, orienting herself now that she was on the ground. "I'm sure that's been long picked over. Nothing but garbage left after so many centuries. Can't imagine it being targeted for a strike."

"Exactly. No way the Feddies would allow us to headquarter on this world if there was anything of real value left there. Far too many raids."

"Speaking of raids," she said, nodding at the largest semipermanent Quonset hut at the edge of the bivouac area. "I believe our esteemed liaison is already waiting for us. We've barely got our flag up and he's already trying to buckle on a saddle and point us at a target." A light breeze wafted through, bringing alien scents she'd never encountered. Her skin prickled, as it always did when she touched down on a new world. *A new canvas for discovering what I can accomplish.*

He shrugged as they both began walking toward the Quonset. "They did pay a pretty penny to sign us. Not to mention the hazard clauses. I imagine they very much want to put us to work; make sure they get what they paid for."

She nodded, letting the conversation lapse as she companionably marched toward their new destiny. *And new worlds? And hopefully back in my conn chair again!*

Another minute and they stepped through the open door, finding a large holotank already set up and working. Leftenant Colonel Joaquin De Santos stood easily in green-camouflage Federated Suns' fatigues, stroking his mustache as he peered intently at a noteputer in his hands. He glanced up, a warm smile breaking through the concentration. "Good morning. I didn't want to intrude upon your ceremony, so I've been in here working."

"That's appreciated," the major said, walking up to the monitor, as Ryana joined him, eyes hungrily devouring data displayed by the tank. "We're as ready as you are to get to work."

"Good. Good. We've got three targets I think are the best candidates," he said, passing over the small noteputer to the major, giving them time to digest.

Ryana let the major glance over the details while she continued her study of the holoprojection. It displayed part of the border between the Federated Suns and Draconis Combine, roughly two hundred light-years' worth, some seven jumps anti-spinward to spinward, and about half that coreward to rimward. To that anti-spinward left were the Combine worlds of Markab and Cyclene II. The border then swung spinward, mostly flat, with the worlds of David, Klathandu IV, Breed, Royal, and Crossing all just across the yellow-red interstellar divide, until it reached their border posting now on Hoff in the yellow, with that crossing just over the astronomical line. Then it started tapering up to the right, with the worlds of Tallmadge and Fairfield under Davion flags, before it disappeared off the map. And nearly due coreward, two jumps, the world of Harrow's Sun, which had been the site of two major battles between AFFS and DCMS forces in the past, though the whole region lay firmly in snake hands now.

Ryana knew her history well. Knew the conquests of a hundred worlds during large-scale invasions of dozens of regiments were a thing of the past. Lost to the First and

Succession Wars and the decline of technology. Instead, endless raids were the standard operating procedures of the day. With carefully orchestrated strikes enabling a few precious worlds to change hands. And change hands they did, often so quickly ComStar's astrocartographers couldn't keep up. And so, while the borders of a regional map might appear relatively stable, she knew the reality on the ground. The citizens of a world might salute two different House flags a half-dozen times in as many years, even as both sides denied the three-card monte being played at interstellar scales. Having lived with war for centuries, the people kept their heads down and saluted away, trying just to eke out a life those lucky enough to live on a realm's interior worlds couldn't imagine.

And we're here to see if we can change that flag again. A momentary melancholy swept over her at the thought, but it was soon submerged beneath growing excitement. *This is what I live for. To face off against death and the odds and come out the victor!*

Without even looking at the noteputer, she guessed the three options for potential targeted raids. "Crossing, Benet III, Glenmora. Those three are a single jump from here. If we try going beyond that, we're double-jumping behind enemy lines." She looked up at the major and leftenant colonel. "Not that we haven't done that before. But not sure we want to start with such a bold move. I assume all three worlds have defenders? Who's stationed there?"

The major handed her the noteputer, and she reviewed the latest intelligence. Her eyebrows rose as she glanced back up to Santos. "First Pesht Regulars? What in the world are they doing so far from their Military District? Not seen that before."

De Santos nodded. "Neither have we. However, the Combine hasn't exactly been the power it once was of late. We give as good as we take now. All we can assume is that they are rotating in additional reinforcements from the depths of their House in the hopes of bolstering commands that have perhaps lost their edge."

Ryana snorted derisively. "Stupid. They should've just hired some mercenaries."

"Ah, certainly what we do. But then again, the Dragon is known for not playing well with mercenaries. Their Dictum Honorium leaves little room but to feel superior. And so, they too often instigate the Company Store policy, forcing outfits into bankruptcy and near servitude. Which means any outfit taking their contracts must be desperate."

She sighed. "I know. Like I said, it's all stupid."

"It is. But it perhaps gives us an advantage. We believe the First Pesht Regulars are not that combat ready, having not experienced true combat in several decades. This could be the key to unraveling the Combine's hold on these worlds and collapsing this salient back all the way to Harrow's Sun, or perhaps even to New Aberdeen. Especially as they have no experience dealing with your type of reconnaissance-in-force."

Ryana glanced at the major, who slowly nodded as he took in the border map as well. "Your intelligence indicates their First and Second Battalion are on Crossing," he said, "while their Third Battalion is on Benet III. Meanwhile, Glenmora currently hosts a battalion of the Arkab Legion. Someday I would very much like to face the Legion, and test their mettle. But I don't think that day is now. Instead, Benet III seems the only obvious choice."

"Too obvious," Ryana responded, frowning. "It's the least defended. Of course they'd expect us to strike there."

"I do not believe that is the case," Santos responded. "After all, if we maneuvered anti-spinward before striking into the Combine, we could hit Royal, Breed, or Klathandu IV. None of them has anything more than standard planetary militias, though such actions would net us no real intelligence for future actions. What's more, I'm sure they're thinking they can easily bring in reinforcements from Crossing—or even Glenmora, if it comes to that—before the forces on Benet III could be in trouble. Especially if only a battalion makes planetfall. But again, that's where we believe their inexperience will be our advantage. They have never faced you. They don't understand the speed with which you can move and accomplish your objectives." He paused, a smile playing across his face as he nodded at the two of them. "As it is, with the exception of the outrageous Ceti Hussars, most of our commanders don't really understand how you do what you do."

Ryana itched a little at the ease of him shifting away her concerns, but they were valid arguments. Besides, she couldn't help puffing up at the compliment.

"Well, if we told you," Major Nigel responded, "then you probably wouldn't need to hire us, would you?"

They all shared a chuckle before returning their focus back to the matter at hand.

"So, looking more and more like Benet III is the target?" Ryana said. "Smash and grab? Or more smash than grab?"

"At this time, we are not aware of any significant finds on Benet III that would warrant an extraction. Instead, it's about disrupting supplies that pass through the planet to Crossing and Glenmora. There should be a secret supply cache there we can destroy. As well as seeing how much damage you can inflict on their battalion before withdrawing. What you learn and the damage you do there will open the door to future possibilities and future targets."

"Sounds like we'll be earning that hazard pay," Ryana said, excitement building. *You'll* have *to put me in the field, Nigel*!

Santos nodded. "You will indeed. I'll not be accompanying you directly, but I very much look forward to seeing what the Light Horse can do under the Davion banner."

ARLUM VALLEY
HOFF
DRACONIS MARCH
FEDERATED SUNS
19 APRIL 3000

Ryana sadly laid her hand on the hard, cool metal of her beloved *Claidheamh-mór*—"claymore" in Scottish Gaelic—that towered fifteen meters above the hard-packed dirt of the bivouac.

"Hard to entertain the notion you will be leaving your beauty behind when you head into the field for the first time in years," a cultured voice spoke behind her. She turned to find Chief Tech Olfson, almost as round as he was tall in his usual slovenly looking coveralls, standing beside here.

"One of these days you're going to tell me how you don't get demerits for looking like that. Major Nigel would ream me—much less Colonel Winston or Brevet General Kerston—if I walked around looking like I slept in my togs."

He spit off to one side and smiled; even his teeth appeared dirty. "My lady, I'm afforded my eccentricities because I keep the steeds of the Light Horse fit and trim. Any time the major or colonel wish to attend a cotillion at a moment's notice, their steeds are at the ready. Unlike the slack-jawed yokels most mercenary commands deem fit to call 'chief tech.'"

She shook her head, trying to remember when he'd first gotten away with calling her 'lady'; anyone else she'd have punched. She kept on her grumpy face—it was expected between them at this point, after all—and turned back to her *Highlander* assault 'Mech. If she looked closely, she felt she could still see the blue-and-green tartan underneath the Light Horse olive drab, hearkening back to a previous life. She avoided the inevitable a moment longer before taking away her hand and turning back to the chief tech. "I hear there's another reason they haven't canned you?"

He bowed his head and swept his arm toward the prefabricated warehouse that had blossomed overnight, covering nearly a thousand square meters, before he began his rolling gait in that direction. "There is indeed. I was tasked with the impossible," he said as they walked; despite his ungainliness, he moved quickly. "How to make a brick fly. Especially when the tools at my disposal are always so limited."

She snorted as the shadow of the structure fell over them as they neared the massive doorway, and the heavy clang of machinery and shouting of crews getting work done in a loud environment. "Limited? You receive more funds than most of my old company, Chief."

He somehow managed to puff up bigger—if that were possible—as they entered the Seventh Striker Battalion's salvage-and-repair facility; the din spiked. "I do not cast aspersions on the Light Horse, or the generosity of Major Nigel or Colonel Winston. I simply lament civilization's inexorable decline, my lady. The beautiful accoutrements of the past have been replaced by inferior equipment almost across the board.

I am a man living out of time. Imagine what I could have done with Star League technology!"

She wanted to laugh out loud at his audacity, but their tacit relationship required a different response. "So how have you made a brick fly, Chief?" she groused. "A brick I'm required to pilot because my *Highlander* isn't fast enough for the raid we're about to execute." It felt traitorous to even say the words.

"I might regale you for hours, my lady. But instead, simply take in her glory. And realize how well she now suits the Light Horse." He swept his arm up toward a nearly twelve-meter-tall BattleMech that stood halfway back in the warehouse.

"Brick" did actually come to mind. While many of the anthropomorphic BattleMechs ranged between agile-looking to even lithe, the 65-ton *Thunderbolt* was an absolute brute. Thick in limb and body, with an odd, sunken, off-center head that gave it the look of a bruiser ready to head into the worst of the fight. She'd done her research and knew when it walked off the assembly lines in 2491, it was the first 'Mech designed for planetary assault. And while many machines were larger and carried more destructive firepower on today's battlefields, she knew the *Thunderbolt* was a nearly indestructible machine: it kept dishing out damage and coming on, no matter how hard you slugged it.

She studied it thoroughly, noting the other three identical machines off to the left. "I don't see the machine gun or SRM ports. And the LRM launcher is smaller. You cut those out to mount jump jets? And what, added some extra heat sinks to make up the difference?"

She heard a *slap* and turned to find the chief with his hand over his heart, a stricken look on his face. "My lady. You know not of what you speak. This is more than just swapping some weapons between chassis. Any hack can accomplish such slapdash jury-rigging. This is figuring out which of the aging jump-jet systems will actually *work* to put this brick into the air without destroying itself. *And* without compromising the structural integrity of the BattleMech. It usually takes a factory to accomplish such delicate work, yet we have done it here, in the field! This—" he said, sweeping proudly toward the four 'Mechs, "—is art. And mark my words, others will look on with jealousy as the Light Horse fields this potent variant without the cost and time commitment of a factory!"

This time she couldn't help the small smile that slipped onto her face. "Then I best get to work on syncing the neurohelmet of this machine with my gray bits. Major Nigel is letting me into the field once more, but only by taking this beast. So let's get this testing done. We've got forty-eight hours till lift off."

AURORA BADLANDS
BENET III
GALEDON MILITARY DISTRICT
DRACONIS COMBINE
27 MAY 3000

"You gotta be kidding me!" Ryana's voice bounced inside her neurohelmet and cockpit, the echoes still not sounding right, despite weeks spent at the *Thunderbolt*'s helm. It was a good model. Even an excellent model. But it wasn't her *Claidheamh-mór*.

"I'm not kidding, Ryana," Captain Chloe Reed replied on the comm. Her 55-ton *Shadow Hawk*, a hundred meters to Ryana's right, joined the entire line of Light Horse machines trying to scatter as the sirens of incoming target locks bellowed along comm channels.

"How did their fighters get so close? How many of these damn things do we have to slap down?"

A pair of heavy aerospace fighters swooped low, their delta-arrow look giving them a deadly profile as a bevy of medium lasers stabbed out along their line of approach. Instead of scattering, she stood still, willing to take the strafing attack in exchange for a better chance at striking back.

Ryana quickly raised her BattleMech's right arm, barely waiting for her reticule to change to the golden hue of target lock before pulling into her primary target-interlock circuit that sent her large laser and ten long-range missiles launching toward the fighter on the right.

Lasers lanced at her *Thunderbolt* at the same time her own shot left a glowing furrow across the aerospace fighter's wing, followed by missile explosions that ruptured the fine flight lines, and made the machine wobble. But the fighter flashed by in the next instant; *Slayer*s were not brought down so easily. Meanwhile, her 'Mech's own armor outline flashed at her with changing colors of lost protection.

Ryana typed furiously on her secondary monitor, bringing up maps of the surrounding region, along with a callout of the Sierra continent where they were fighting. The line of march led away from the heavier populated Marquis County where they'd initially grounded, and out into the hinterlands. The intent was both to lead the First Pesht Regulars on a merry goose chase to see which bits they might strip away, but also because there were heavy indications of military movement along this route. Recent movement. Meaning that secret supply cache they'd all hoped to locate.

Something itched in the back of her mind, but she couldn't pull it together just yet...

"Brevet Major," Major Nigel broke into her comm. It was crackling, as they were a dozen klicks farther into the valley between the Iron Mountains leading into the Aurora Badlands. They were called "Iron" for a reason, and it was playing havoc with communications unless both parties were right on top of each other.

"Yes, Major?"

"We were just struck by an aerospace attack."

She nodded. "As were we."

"Did you manage to damage those *Shilone*s at all? We should be able to bring them down if they dare another pass."

She started to nod before her mind blanked for a moment. "Wait, what? Negative. We were hit by a pair of *Slayer*s."

Silence fell on the line as she watched on the viewscreen the company she'd previously commanded—and now was simply attached to—begin to re-form, weapons still visibly oriented toward the sky, waiting for another strike.

"That's too many fighters," Major Nigel said. "The Snakes don't go heavy on their aerospace assets."

"Agreed, sir," she responded. "They believe in quality, not quantity. What does it mean?" The itch was growing more insistent, but she couldn't place it just yet.

"It means that either they've deployed their entire regiment's aerospace detachment here—"

Through the comm she heard explosions against Major Nigel's BattleMechs while sirens rang of incoming fire.

"—or we appear to have found a new battalion," Major Nigel continued calmly, despite the growing cacophony and danger. "Make that at least a reinforced battalion. We are falling back toward your position."

"Wait—*another* battalion?" The itch burst across her skin, tingling with anger and frustration. "That means most of the First Pesht is on-world."

"Perhaps even the entire regiment," he replied.

"I can be on your position within two hours."

"Negative, Major. If the entire regiment is on-world, we are severely outnumbered."

She bristled, fingers convulsing on her joysticks. "When has that ever stopped the Light Horse?"

"When our intelligence is so bad that we had no idea where half a regiment is deployed!" he said, voice raising a notch. "Who's to say that perhaps the Arkab Legion is not here as well?"

A chill ran down her back. They were the Light Horse. But the Arkab Legion was some of the best the Snakes could field. And if they were that outnumbered… She gritted her teeth, reminding herself that this was not a planetary invasion. This was a reconnaissance-in-force. And the reconnaissance was bad news all around. *Time to get out.*

She glanced around at the towering cliffsides nearby and the tortured landscape—badlands indeed—and realized there would be no bringing in DropShips for a quick extraction. They'd need to extract themselves.

"Confirmed, Major. We'll start falling back at half-speed, ensuring there's a clear path back to the DropShips."

"Confirmed."

She tapped her throat mic to change channels. "You heard the Major, Chloe. Time to bug out. But we'll have plenty of swatting to do before we go."

"You heard the woman," Chloe responded to the company. "I want our standard Delta formation. Half-speed, back along our line of march. Dawson and Nikolai, you've got the vanguard.

And keep your eyes glued. If they ambushed the major, we can expect the same thing."

Ryana couldn't help the swell of pride at the calm, quick words in Chloe's commands. They'd only known each other three years, but they'd quickly become like sisters, and she was proud of the speed of Chloe's climb within the Light Horse.

But Ryana couldn't shake the itch that still scrabbled across her skin.

How did they know?

IRON MOUNTAINS
BENET III
GALEDON MILITARY DISTRICT
DRACONIS COMBINE
28 MAY 3000

The night lit up with sporadic bursts of weapons fire and explosions; a mesmerizing kaleidoscope of light and sound. It was nearly beautiful—if it hadn't all been designed to kill them.

Ryana fought through a yawn as she fired the last of her long-range missiles at the *Panther* bounding over the terrain in an effort to flank her position. The last of the Iron Mountains' shattered foothills was on her right before they broke out into the flatter land leading to the Waddi River and their escape.

"You gotta be kidding me!" she said, glad she'd turned off voice activation as the 35-ton 'Mech managed to dodge her last salvo, gaining the higher ground, trying to bring its particle projector cannon to bear.

"Time to show you my own tricks," she growled, stomping down on her pedals that ignited the jump jets within the *Thunderbolt*'s torso. Despite all of her confidence in Chief Tech Olfson, her gut clenched, and she imagined she could feel the magnetically shielded reaction chambers superheat the reaction mass and then vent it out vectored nozzles to launch her brick of a 'Mech into a harsh ballistic arc up onto the same shelf as the *Panther*, coming down right in its face.

The shock of the enemy pilot at being the first Pesht warrior seeing a *Thunderbolt* fly made the *Panther* stand unmoving as though poleaxed. Ryana grinned savagely—she might actually give Olfson a hug—and reared back to slam her left arm straight into the enemy 'Mech's head. She felt the *crunch* of such transferred kinetic energy as an impact to her own hand—even through the conn chair's inputs—and the nearly decapitated 'Mech fell to the ground.

She immediately searched for additional targets, only to find the First Pesht 'Mechs and a handful of combat vehicles falling back into the light forest that spread off toward the beckoning river.

"Do we keep pushing or hold?" Chloe asked, exhaustion painting her voice, causing Ryana to yawn again out of sympathy.

The major should've met up with us already. Even with ambushes and the tortured terrain, they should've been here by now!

At this point, the itch on her skin was a rash she worried at constantly, and the only answers ate at her worse than the damage pockmarking her armor.

"Ryana?" Chloe said again.

Ryana wouldn't have noticed the entreaty in her voice if they'd not gotten to know each other so well. She desperately wanted to scratch her scalp after so many weeks in her own stink.

"The major told us not to hold, but to keep forging forward. The Snakes will be back, trying to break us and cut off the retreat of our main body. We have to stay moving and get back to the LZ. But that doesn't mean we have to be in a rush."

"Quarter-speed it is. Dawson, Mason, lead us off again."

The "*yes, sirs*" across the comm hid most of their exhaustion.

The pounding rhythm of her heavy BattleMech swayed Ryana in her conn chair as she pushed the throttle full forward, eking out every last bit of the sixty-four kilometers per hour for this model. She could almost be impressed by the speed with which the Regulars had cut down trees and built a 'Mech-sized wooden barricade, if it hadn't been blocking their path.

Weapons fire blazed from a half-dozen 'Mechs directly behind the makeshift wall, most hammering into her *Thunderbolt*'s armor, tearing off plates and splashing molten droplets to sizzle and flashfire in the tall grass; her armor diagrams screamed in yellows and reds. While other 'Mechs were faster, none could take this punishment. And she couldn't go around this barricade, because the river was too deep both upstream and down. No, the crossing had to happen right here and right now if they were going to hold open the gap for the rest of the Light Horse.

Another savage smile lit Ryana's face as she neared the barricade and, once more, put Chief Olfson's accomplishment to work, igniting those jump jets, lofting the brutish brick up and over.

Once more, the anthropomorphic enemy machines displayed the shock of their pilots in their weapons drifting off target, and movement slowing...until she came down in their midst in an explosive rush of superheated air, knees taking up the shock of landing, and immediately laid about her as though in a bar fight with a bunch of fools taking her for granted.

She kicked out with the *Thunderbolt*'s right leg, crushing a *Wasp*'s leg and sending it tumbling to the ground. She lashed out with her left arm, hammering straight into a *Vulcan*'s shoulder brace, which she managed to snag, and tore the entire arm assembly away from the machine. Her right arm rammed its massive laser barrel into the left torso of a *Javelin*, and she triggered the laser, regardless of the consequences of the damage she might have done to the lens or aligning crystals. The beam burned directly into the enemy 'Mech's torso, flash-heating the ammunition to explosion. The machine tore itself apart in a *boom* that hammered into her *Thunderbolt*, knocking her machine backward, destroying its large laser and crumpling half the right arm like a tin can; only stumbling up against the wooden barricade kept her upright.

She swallowed the blood-filled bile in her mouth, shaking away the dizziness, and prepared to lay about her again when she noted the remaining defenders were retreating away to the left and right, just as another BattleMech came crashing down beside her.

She nearly attacked the machine before she realized it was another Light Horse *Thunderbolt*.

"Blake's Blood, Campbell," Major Nigel said on the comm. "Should've had you with us the last two days. You might have held them off all by yourself."

She colored slightly at the praise, but ultimately the relief that the trailing Horsemen had finally reached them blotted out any discomfort. "About time you showed up. We've been practically crawling here, sir."

"I know. In direct contradiction of my orders, I believe."

"You said to keep moving. We never stopped."

The sigh actually came across the comm. "We'll discuss the letter versus the spirit of the law latter. Right now, we've got a battalion about to hit us from behind."

She slowly maneuvered her 'Mech around to look back up the rolling hills; a paltry stream of Light Horsemen raced just ahead of a much larger force, weapons stabbing out at maximum ranges to try catching them.

"How bad has it been?" she finally asked.

"Bad."

"We can't let them hit us when we're trying to cross the river. And the terrain still won't let the DropShips evac us here."

"No."

"We're going to have to make a stand."

"These machines are brutes," he responded. "I'm thinking a mobile withdrawal, using all four *Thunderbolt*s. Make them concentrate on trying to break us while the rest speed across the river and get to the DropShips."

She slowly sighed before gritting her teeth and sitting straighter, ignoring the back strain and exhaustion. "Let's get as many Horsemen out of this as we can."

The Snakes struck again and again and again at the fleeing Light Horse.

"Major Nigel, on your right!" Ryana yelled through a throat filled with painful razor blades of heat and exhaustion.

In a *V*-pattern, the four heavy BattleMechs formed a bulwark against the attackers that kept trying to shatter their line. This time, however, as the primary force hit their line dead on, a flanker force of four medium BattleMechs burst from the right-side tree line to strike the end of the *V*, anchored by Major Nigel. His *Thunderbolt* seemed stuck in molasses as it slowly turned, and laser and autocannon fire chewed into his already savaged right side. It jerked as minor explosions went off, spewing black clouds and detritus out of the pockmarked torso.

"Campbell," Major Nigel's voice sounded across the comm; he hacked for a moment, wet and pain-filled. "You will get the rest of the Light Horse off this world."

Rage replaced all fear. "Sir, I am not going to abandon—"

"Major!" he barked, cutting her off. "For good God once you will do as commanded, and follow the letter of the law! *Save* this command, Campbell!"

Despite her anger and grief, in that moment she was in awe of the major. Under the Damocles sword of coming death, he still struck out, his large laser finding a weakened knee joint on a running *Locust* and shearing the leg right off, while keeping enough of a head to transfer temporary command and keep her on task.

A long pause tortuously stretched as her penchant for disobeying reared its head. Gritting her teeth until her jaw ached, Ryana carefully folded it back down to be used another day. Hollowness replaced all emotions. She stomped onto her pedals, igniting her jump jets as she jumped away from the maelstrom engulfing the three *Thunderbolt*s—a tsunami desperately trying to crush a rocky outcrop that refused to die.

"The Seventh Striker will live, Major," she said finally. Just as she vanished back into the trees, following the other Horsemen, she saw the first of the *Thunderbolt*s fall.

Ryana somehow managed to walk her devastated *Thunderbolt* up the DropShip ramp, and maneuver it into its cradle, where personnel quickly began webbing it into place for emergency liftoff at her command.

She shut down her machine, the darkness a needed friend in the pain of the moment, as the tears began. She'd expected to cry over the death of a company of Light Horsemen; she'd not expected that over the death of Major Nigel or the other two *Thunderbolt* pilots who had given their last full measure so she could escape. How could she face his son, Jameson?

The blackness rode her misery into oblivion, even as the itch demanded vengeance.

**ARLUM VALLEY
HOFF
DRACONIS MARCH
FEDERATED SUNS
7 JUNE 3000**

"You sent us in outnumbered!" Ryana yelled into Leftenant Colonel de Santos' face. Alone in the Quonset with the liaison, she opened up on him with both barrels.

The other man smoothed his mustache—*I knew I hated it!*—cocked his head, and waited several moments through her heavy breathing before responding.

"You have lost many of your brothers- and sisters-in-arms, including your commanding officer. I know that pain myself. And so I will forgive this lack of decorum. But really, Major, you saw all of the same intelligence I did. You agreed with the choice of targets as much as I."

She ground her teeth, knowing he was likely telling the truth, but that there was also a lie. *There has to be a lie*! "Then how did you know to send the Fox's Teeth to Crossing? Now the Seventh Crucis Lancers has taken that world in the name of House Davion."

He shrugged easily. "That was simply good guesswork on my part. Just as you were to disrupt activities on Benet, McKinnon's Company was sent to disrupt operations on Crossing. When it became clear that Crossing was practically defenseless, I happened to have the transport available to immediately move the Seventh there."

You just happened to have…? Smile. Go ahead, smile, and I'll strike it off your face, consequences be damned! "Why didn't you send reinforcements if you knew the entire First Pesht Regulars were on Benet?" she ground out, trying desperately to get her voice back under control.

He again touched his mustache, then smoothed down the front of his jacket. "Major, are you saying that the vaunted Eridani Light Horse, in their first actions for the Federated Suns, could not deliver? This was never a planetary invasion. This was a reconnaissance-in-force. If you could destroy the supply depot we believe is on-world, excellent. But this was about disrupting their supply lines, damaging the enemy, and returning with as much intelligence as you can on their operations and deployments. As far as I'm concerned, you've achieved that objective in spades. You've more than satisfied the bonus hazard-pay clause. And your actions directly resulted in House Davion taking back one of our lost worlds. Are you saying that is not what the Light Horse accomplished?"

Ryana almost did strike him them, thinking that feeling her fist crunching into Santos' face like her *Thunderbolt* decapitating that enemy *Panther* would feel *so* good. But she had absolutely nothing. Nothing but the itch that he'd somehow orchestrated the whole thing. A gambit to strike at Harrow's Sun once more and right ancient wrongs, making him such the conquering hero? But she knew instinctively how Colonel Winston and Brevet General Kerston would respond. *We can't fight the hand that feeds us. Not without direct evidence.*

When the Light Horse had broken their contract with the Draconis Combine centuries ago, it had been due to the Kentares Massacre. And when they didn't renew with House Steiner, it was due to a long series of well-documented egregious command decisions. But here?

She gazed into Santos' eyes for a long moment before her anger abruptly collapsed, and she managed to keep a shiver at bay. For herself, for those who had survived the operation, for the entire Light Horse, she managed to do one of the most difficult things she'd ever done in her life: "I apologize for my discourtesy," she got out through gritted teeth, almost sounding sincere. "I'm glad the Light Horse fulfilled the objectives of this raid."

"Excellent. You'll want a few weeks of rest and refit, of course. But I'll be back in three months for a new objective. I already have some ideas on the next strike."

Ryana watched him reach the door and slip confidently outside. *I thought the Elsies' social generals were dangerous because of their stupidity. But this is a whole other kind of dangerous.*

She scratched ruthlessly at her scalp for long moments before letting out a pent-up breath of tension and exhaustion. Despite her desire to curl up into a ball and sleep for days—she'd barely caught a wink due to anger, despite weeks of interstellar transit—and then lie in a tub for another day, she squared her shoulders.

We survived the death of the Star League. We survived the destruction of the Nineteenth. No trumped-up wannabe lord is gonna lay us low.

She stepped out into the sun, ready to get funeral arrangements underway for those lost; then to bolster her command's morale; then prepare a report that would warn the general they'd need to be careful around these Davions.

She caught sight of the banner flapping in the wind, and found her own morale boosted as she set about her work.

We're the Light Horse!

PANTHER
Light—35 tons

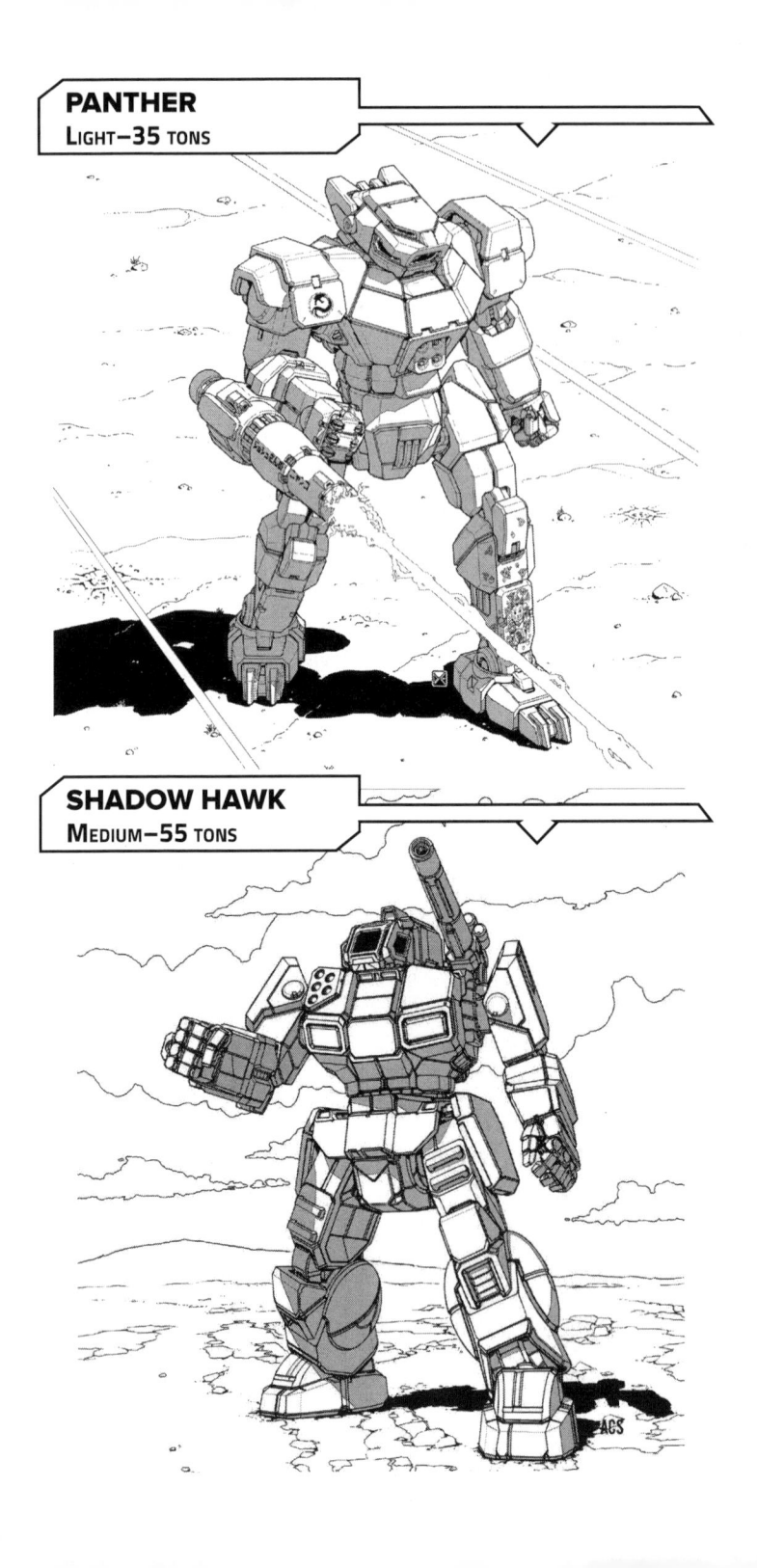

SHADOW HAWK
Medium—55 tons

THUNDERBOLT
Heavy—65 tons

THERE'S NO "WE" IN "MERCENARY"

JASON HANSA

AVALON CITY, NEW AVALON
NEW AVALON COMBAT REGION
CRUCIS MARCH
FEDERATED SUNS
3 MARCH 3029

The guards in the corridor leading to the First Prince's office eyed the approaching three mercenaries and their escorting officer with suspicious stares. Even though the previous set of guards had radioed ahead, these were the last guards before the Prince's inner sanctum, and they took their responsibility seriously.

"IDs and pass, gentlemen, ma'am," the senior infantryman said while his partner covered them with a weapon not quite pointed at anyone in particular.

Behind the infantrymen, a door opened, and out strode a bear of a man. "Brevet General Armstrong! It's good to see you," he said as the mercenaries and guards all stiffened to attention. Duke Morgan Hasek-Davion, heir to the Davion throne, was a tall and muscular man, and sported a shock of long, unbound, red-gold hair. His face was distracted, but he managed a slight smile for the mercenaries.

"Duke Hasek-Davion, it's good to see you as well," Armstrong replied, "have you met Colonel Winston, commanding my Twenty-First Striker regiment?" Armstrong was tall, pale, and wiry, with a sharply angular face, wise eyes, and thin wisps of brown hair covering his balding scalp. Winston, beside him, was a medium-brown man with the full muscular build of a former rugby star and a thick goatee on a face that had laugh and sorrow lines carved into it in equal measure.

"No, I haven't, I'm afraid," he replied, shaking their hands.

"And may I also introduce Major Cynthia Paulson, commander, First Armored Infantry Battalion." Morgan turned to her—late thirties, athletic, with long, dark hair and the tan complexion of a woman who grew up under a bright sun. She nodded respectfully to the duke.

After he shook her hand, Armstrong continued, "Your Highness, we saw the First Prince's news conference downstairs. We're very sorry for your loss."

The duke's face clouded, and his smile disappeared. "Thank you, General," Hasek-Davion replied formally, his eyes distant. Then he refocused on them. "Are you here to brief Hanse? What about?"

Armstrong paused and glanced at Winston. "The defense of Kawich, Your Highness."

"Back in January?" At their nods, Hasek-Davion paused, read both of their faces, then said, "I wasn't aware something had happened to warrant a command-circuit back to New Avalon."

A polite cough sounded from down the hall. The group turned to see Quintus Allard, Prince Davion's white-haired head of intelligence, waiting outside the Prince's office.

Hasek-Davion nodded at Quintus and turned back to them. "If Hanse allows it, please come brief me as well."

"Of course, Your Highness," replied Armstrong. "If you'll excuse us?" Saying their goodbyes, they left their escort officer with the guards and met Quintus at the end of the hall. Allard shook their hands as well, then opened the gold leaf-trimmed door to Hanse's personal chambers. The door to Hanse's larger sitting room was closed, and three high-backed sitting chairs were arranged in front of his large wooden desk.

Hanse Davion, leader of the Federated Suns, was a fit, dark-haired man in his early forties with the shape and bearing of a lifelong soldier. He sat behind his desk, watching the officers approach, and with the barest of pleasantries, asked them to sit.

Pulling out a thin folder of documents, Hanse arrayed them on his desk, then looked up and said, "Please begin."

**EAST OF SAMANAN
KAWICH, ADDICKS PDZ
FEDERATED SUNS
12 JANUARY 3029**

Captain Cynthia Paulson had wedged herself in the narrow area between her BattleMech's fusion-engine shielding and its armor. With one leg bracing her inside the 'Mech and the other hooked on the access panel for balance, she grunted as she finished tightening a wiring harness running up the center of her *Trebuchet*'s chest.

Taking a deep breath and rebalancing herself, she wriggled out the access panel and sat on the edge of the armor, next to the chain ladder that ran from the cockpit of her 10-meter-tall, 50-ton medium BattleMech to the ground.

Air inside always tastes like metal, she thought, taking a deep breath and feeling a hot, dry breeze rustle her long dark hair. *This is nice.*

She looked around the perimeter of her little outpost. Twelve 'Mechs, two-thirds of them from her Fourteenth "Roadrunner" Company, defined an oval about 300 meters long and half that wide. It was a consolidated perimeter: her *Trebuchet* and seven others of her company faced outward, with her final four 'Mechs on patrol. They shared the perimeter with "Boomer" Company, which consisted of one lance of BattleMechs for antiaircraft duties, and a demi-battery of three Long Tom Mobile artillery pieces. The three pieces were facing southeast, so they could swing in either cardinal direction toward the anticipated and secondary enemy attack vectors, firing over the ridge lines surrounding their position. Both companies had one MechWarrior in their 'Mech at all times, with the rest either sleeping, conducting maintenance or—she smiled as she saw her best friend lying on a beach towel next to her 'Mech—on personal time.

Paulson shimmied down the ladder and unzipped her maintenance coveralls to her waist, then tied them around her slim belly. BattleMechs generated tremendous amounts of waste heat in battle, so MechWarriors wore as little as possible in the cockpit. Under her coveralls, Cynthia was wearing her standard MechWarrior togs, consisting of a pair of spandex shorts and a sweat-wicking sports bra. Her best friend, she noted with a wry smile, was wearing even less.

"Catching some rays, Rowan?" she asked, plopping down to the ground beside her. Kawich was a mineral-heavy world—barely arable, but self-sufficient. In this area, though, the dirt was unsuitable for farming and was covered with fine, tan grass. Rowan's eyes remained closed as she replied with a grunt, but Cynthia could see her smile.

Rowan Avellar, niece to the President of the Outworlds Alliance and tenth in line for the throne, was a black sheep who wanted to be a MechWarrior in a nation that revered aerospace pilots. As her academy graduation day had approached, her uncle placed a call to the Outworlds-based Mountain Wolf BattleMech facility, her parents wrote a check, and fifteen months later she on arrived on Galatea, the legendary "Mercenary's Star," a naive nineteen-year-old piloting a *Merlin* BattleMech down the DropShip ramp.

Most BattleMechs in the Inner Sphere were centuries old, passed down from parent to child, and the facilities that produced new ones were running the same lines since the fall of the Star League in the 2700s. But the *Merlin* was new, the first BattleMech production line fired up in more than a century, and Rowan's arrival caused a sensation.

She'd had her pick of units—all of them wanting the rare 'Mech on their roster more than her—so she picked one she knew to be reputable. The Eridani Light Horse recruiter signed her on the spot, putting her back on the very same DropShip to send her to the unit headquarters, which had assigned Rowan to the Twenty-First Striker, where Colonel Winston immediately punted her to Cynthia.

The Paulsons had known the Winstons for decades, and Cynthia had grown up essentially as the colonel's adopted niece. As she'd matured, he leaned on her for difficult projects; when she became a company commander, he leaned on her for "project" people. Any number of "unique" people joined mercenary units: smaller units tended to gather criminals, ne'er-do-wells, and the desperate with nowhere else to go.

The Light Horse, with its reputation for excellence, attracted the opposite: rich kids, nobles trying their hand at the mercenary trade with their parents' money, arrogant and cocky hotshots who thought the rules of state-run armies didn't apply to them. When they appeared in the Twenty-First, Winston sent them to Cynthia, and she'd figure out if they were teachable; if not, he'd send them on their way.

Most project people only stayed for a year or so, but every so often, a diamond in the rough would walk their skinny butt into Paulson's company and prove to be worth their weight in gold. Barely 160 centimeters tall and almost forty-three kilograms soaking wet, the two had become fast friends, despite their age difference.

Cynthia gently fixed one of Rowan's braids and sighed. Like many MechWarriors, both women kept the sides of their heads shaved to facilitate better contact with the neurohelmet they wore to help pilot their BattleMechs. However, compared to Cynthia's long tresses, Rowan kept her red hair short and in three wide braids, the strands weaving in and out of small gold rings and each ending in a marriage promissory clasp, two featuring sapphires and the other sporting rubies.

Cynthia knew Rowan's parents—all of them—were Gregorians, a religion that encouraged multiple marriages to stabilize the Alliance's severe population decline. However, of all the topics the gregarious young woman would discuss at length, her fiancés and when—if ever—she planned on marrying one or more of them was the only area off-limits.

Rowan cracked one eye open. Lying on the beach towel facedown in a bikini, the top untied with laces splayed to her sides, Rowan had a thermos of cold water sitting on a T-shirt, a pair of MechWarrior booties, and a pistol all within easy reach.

The naive kid had grown up quickly in the eighteen months since arriving. "What?"

Cynthia ran her fingers over Rowan's braids, smoothing the rings so they all fell the same direction, and then leaned back, looking at the clear Kawich sky. "I got word about upcoming personnel reassignments," she said. "Your work at the exercise got noticed—Major Fallehy wants you in his lance."

The Light Horse was a combined-arms unit, all three regiments organized down into the battalion, and even sometimes company levels with a mix of aerofighters, armor, infantry, and BattleMechs. Though they had fewer BattleMechs than similarly sized units, they had more personnel overall, and knew how to use their organic combined arms to best effect.

Their Third Striker Battalion had recently conducted a battalion-level exercise against Seventh Striker—including Third Striker's pure aerospace company, the Eighty-Fifth. Rowan's entire family save her were aerospace pilots, and she'd been practicing calling for close-air support with her six brothers and sisters since she was eight: her years of experience gave her almost uncanny precision when calling in the Eighty-Fifth, bringing the exercise to an unscheduled early end with a Third Striker victory and making her, once again, a hot commodity. In this case, her battalion commander demanded right of first refusal, and was pulling her up into his command lance.

Rowan was quiet as Cynthia relayed all the internal regimental drama and politicking, then asked, "You ever feel crappy about a good thing?"

Cynthia chuckled. "I'm gonna miss you too, kiddo. But we won't..." She trailed off as she saw diamond formations of stars appearing in the daytime sky.

MechWarrior Ciensinski, on watch inside his *Centurion* BattleMech, turned around and broadcast on his loudspeakers, "Captain, they want you on the battalion net. Those are Capellan DropShips."

Behind her, Rowan rose to her knees, threw on her T-shirt, slipped into her MechWarrior booties, and started collecting her gear. Paulson rose and brushed herself off.

"Rowan, go wake up Strike Lance," she said. Rowan nodded, and Paulson turned to Ciensinski. "Understood," she replied, loud enough to be heard by his external microphones. "Tell battalion I need sixty seconds to mount up."

Colonel Charles Winston stroked his graying goatee as he studied the holotable inside of his headquarters in the city of Samanan. The Twenty-First had taken over this unoccupied office complex—even signed a month-to-month lease and planted their traditional three flagpoles outside—for use during their garrison of Kawich.

He studied the holotable and stifled a half-smile—he hadn't counted on taking the Twenty-First Striker Regiment through another Succession War, but it wasn't like Hanse Davion ran things by him first. He was over sixty, and had planned to retire after his youngest daughter certified as a MechWarrior later this year.

"Sir, the battalion commanders are online and waiting for our briefing," said Lieutenant Sarah Clemly, his aide. A short woman who kept the sides of her head shaved and the top braided in a brown weave halfway down her back, she managed his administrative actions so he could focus on command. They'd been told Davion Intelligence expected a Capellan counterattack at the various supply warehouses on-world, but Intelligence only expected about a battalion plus support to attack each location. This far exceeded their worst-case projections.

Outside of Samanan ran four northeast-to-southwest ridge lines, locally nicknamed the "fish ribs." Each was about thirty kilometers long, and had a one-to-two-kilometer gap in the middle where an ancient, dried riverbed split them. The first ridge was about three kilometers to the east of the city, and then each of the following three ridges were about four to five kilometers apart, heading east. Their slight western concave curve toward Samanan and their regular intervals gave them the nickname, along with the fact that just past the ribs was the Middle Sea, a vast expanse with moderate waves and excellent fishing.

In the city, Winston had his command company and elements of both Third Striker and the First Armored Infantry battalions; to the east was Paulson's Fourteenth alongside Boomer Company, their guns able to almost reach the Middle Sea's beaches; and on the farthest ridge line, his Alpha infantry company. Alpha happened to be out on a planned patrol toward the coast, which was how he already had personnel watching a Capellan Warrior House disembarking.

Fanatical and well-trained, a short battalion of BattleMechs in the greenish-silver with black trim of House Hiritsu—plus about a battalion each of infantry and hovercraft in support—were forming up outside multiple dark-green DropShips. They were an estimated two hours out. By the numbers, the Light Horse would have had a two-to-one advantage in BattleMechs over the Capellans, though that ratio dropped to one-to-one in armor, and behind-the-ratio in infantry.

But the Warrior House wasn't the only unit that had landed. A mercenary unit, identified as the Forty-Second Armored Lightning Regiment, had dropped to both the east and west of Samanan. One battalion landed alongside the Warrior House, their BattleMechs resplendent in their cobalt blue-on-black paint scheme, "XLII" emblazoned in golden lightning bolts on their 'Mech's left side.

To the west, the Light Horse's heavy aerofighter complement had chased the Lightnings from their original landing zone, so they were on the far side of a heavy forest. Leaving their combined-arms battalion to guard their DropShips, the Forty-Second had another full battalion of BattleMechs heading into the forest, giving them an ETA of reaching Samanan in three hours.

Compounding the problem, the Forty-Second, after a rough decade fighting the Draconis Combine, had spent two years rebuilding on Sudeten, acquiring an abnormally high number of heavy *Warhammer*s and *Thunderbolt*s. The medium-weight Light Horse regiment was outnumbered, outmassed, and worst of all, out of position.

AVALON CITY, NEW AVALON
3 MARCH 3029

Winston stopped his report as Quintus Allard glanced at Hanse. The duke's face remained a stone mask, so Quintus turned back to Winston and quietly asked, "Why were you out of position, Colonel?"

Winston glanced at Armstrong; seeing a nod from his commander, he replied, "Your Highness, intelligence we received from our AFFS liaison said to expect a Capellan line unit to attack from the south. I had positioned the Fourteenth and Boomer company to the east to deny the enemy an easy flanking maneuver, however, we didn't anticipate it becoming the main axis of attack. I had some scouts to the north and west, and nearly two full Striker battalions positioned south of Samanan to repulse an attack that never came."

Hanse threw a knowing glance at Quintus, who simply nodded. Davion looked back at Winston; interweaving his fingers in front of his face, the duke stared at him with icy blue eyes.

"Continue, Colonel."

KAWICH
12 JANUARY 3029

Paulson heard her callsign over the battalion command frequency, so she flicked on the radio with one hand while maintaining control of her BattleMech with the other. Her company was running east along the riverbed, her recon lance up front and pulling away, her strike lance directly behind her.

"Roadrunner actual," she said into her microphone.

"Plague actual," replied Major Fallehy, her battalion commander. "Cindy, I'm with Ninth Company, leaving Samanan now. I've linked up with Major Perrow's command lance, and we're going to cross the ridge lines to the north. Our goal is to let the Capellans pass us by and then hit the mercs, see if we can spread them apart.

"Understood."

"You run down the middle, back up Alpha Company, and try to slow the Capellans down. Seventh Striker is coming up the middle ribs from the south, and Fifth Striker is cutting up then through Samanan to set up fallback positions, but we have to buy them time."

"Yes, sir."

"I'm giving you tactical control over the entire Eighty-Fifth Company. Once they've reloaded, get Avellar somewhere high and have her rain hell. Buy the colonel time, Cynthia."

Cynthia nodded to herself. "We will, sir. We won't let him down."

"I know. Good hunting. Plague actual out."

※

Fourteen kilometers to the east, Captain Lila Oakwood lay behind a large boulder on the easternmost ridge line, next to her Third Platoon leader—Lieutenant Diego—and half of his platoon. Twenty-five, stocky, and supremely fit, Oakwood had excelled in lacrosse and rugby before joining the Light Horse's First Armored Battalion as an infantry officer, eventually earning her promotion to Alpha Company commander. All of her exposed skin was camouflaged with grease paint in browns and tans to match the scrubby dirt mountains of the fish ribs, and she was looking east with her binoculars, watching the enemy battalions shake themselves into march formation.

She hid her frustration—the only reason her company was this far east was because they'd expected to "patrol" into the coastal villages for some fishing and hopefully bring back some monster catches for the battalion's cooks to grill. Instead, she was going to be the first Light Horse ground commander to try slowing down a combined-arms regiment. *Lucky me.*

Lila swung her binoculars left, looking at the northern half of the ridge line: she didn't see any movement, and hadn't wanted to. Her XO was with half a platoon on the north ridge, and her whole force was trying to stay undetected for as long as possible. The rest of the company had moved into small patches of woods to the north and south of the valley, about halfway between the first and second ribs. She'd had her platoon leaders lay a command-detonatable minefield directly in front of both forests, to protect them from what she anticipated would be the Capellans' most probable response. *Now to start drawing blood.*

She lowered the binoculars and glanced at Lieutenant Diego, who was holding a radio handset, his radio operator wearing the large set lying next to him on the other side. "The big guns ready?" she asked. All three of Boomer Company's Long Tom artillery pieces were tasked to fire in support of her company; they'd just been waiting for the Capellans to finally get into range.

"Yes, ma'am."

She raised the binoculars to her eyes to watch the Capellans and replied, "Hit them."

Diego called in the pre-laid coordinates, and they waited for the volley to land. The Capellans were just a kilometer away from the gap between the first ribs, Hiritsu hovercraft out front and BattleMechs following. To the left and right of the BattleMechs were four infantry companies: one company each, like hers, on motorcycles and dirt bikes, followed by another in light APCs. Only one infantry company was in Hiritsu colors, the rest in a mishmash of camouflages that led her to believe they were a conglomeration of orphaned militias assigned to reinforce the Warrior House for this battle.

Boomer Company had targeted a six-round volley into a militia motorized company directly in front of her. A volley landing in the middle of a BattleMech lance could do some damage, but they were hard to hit even for an artillery ambush. Once artillery started falling, BattleMechs would spread out and start randomizing their movements, making targeting difficult. Hitting moving hovercraft was even more challenging, though successful strikes would generally put the lightly armored and vulnerable vehicles out of action.

But infantry in the open were vulnerable and slow, and as such, had remained the prime targets for artillery for well over a millennium. The artillery barrage—two rounds per gun—landed simultaneously amid the Capellan infantry company, and the unit ceased to exist. One round had drifted east and landed in the follow-on unit, blowing an APC onto its side and setting it alight, but the rest landed in and among the three platoons, leaving wounded and dead scattered across the dusty Kawich plains. Motorcycles started catching on fire, and she could see ambulances heading toward the company.

If her soldiers felt any emotion toward destroying a unit that was essentially their twin, they didn't show it: Lila felt little but the satisfaction of a trap well executed. Only the infantry and BattleMechs could scale the ribs, and she'd just eliminated one fourth of the infantry able to chase down her troops and force them off the ridge lines. If bleeding the Capellans dry was the cost to keep her troops safe, she'd gladly pay it.

She listened as her XO took over, calling in fire against the infantry on the northern side of the valley: they were scattering now, as expected, but as a whole, the formation had slowed—which was the mission. The lead hovercraft company, however, had accelerated into the valley and split into two groups, two platoons coming south toward her side, one heading north toward her XO's troops. The two lead lances of BattleMechs had run for the ridge lines, and a few were even firing lasers blindly up the slopes at her and the XO's positions.

All perfectly standard and doctrinal: the barrage was far too accurate to have been random, so the Capellans rightly assumed there were spotters on the ridge lines. The standard method to clear the heights of infantry were to find and fix them with fighters and VTOLs if available, with BattleMechs or infantry if not. The hovercraft, as per doctrine, were going to swing behind the ridge and attempt to catch her and her spotters as they retreated from the BattleMechs.

The problem for the Capellans was that it *was* a perfectly doctrinal response: competent, yes, but *predictable*. Lila and her spotters half-ran, half-slid down the mountain to their off-road motorcycles and started racing down the rib toward the safety of the forest, rooster tails of dirt rising up behind them. The southernmost of the hovercraft platoons saw her and angled to intercept them where they would hit the valley floor. Three hundred meters from her, but only a third of that from the forest, the lead hovercraft platoon hit the minefield her soldiers had laid before the attack.

Three Capellan hovercraft came to a screeching halt, white and gray smoke billowing from underneath them while another turned and headed back the way it came, leaking dark-black smoke. As soon as its rear faced the forest, however, Third Platoon lashed into it with disposable light anti-tank rockets. They didn't do much damage, but a few hit the rear skirt, dropping the tank's tail enough that it physically dragged across the dirt as the driver attempted to accelerate.

The second hovercraft platoon were J. Edgars, all four firing their twin SRM-2 racks at her team from extreme range: of the sixteen short-range missiles, most undershot, the rest overshot, and Lila's team raced through the smoke trails into the safety of the forest. She heard a pine explode behind her as the tanks' lasers shot into the forest, but a quick check confirmed no casualties.

After parking their bikes in a small clearing with the rest of Third and Fourth Platoon's, she jogged north to see what was happening. Sneaking from tree to tree the last thirty meters to lie down beside Lieutenant Diego, she whispered, "Status?"

"The J. Edgars pulled back, ma'am, but they're clearly looking for us. Crews are bailing from the struck tanks. We could snipe a couple?"

"No," she said, "we want them to think we're gone, so they won't notice when we actually leave." She took his binoculars to check on the northern woods. The four hovercraft whipping around that side had either been warned or were simply luckier than her side, with only one striking the northern minefield.

She sucked in her breath: *Saracens*! Sporting a ten-tube long-range missile system and three twin short-range systems, they could throw an unholy amount of high-explosives into infantry units. She didn't anticipate her troops engaging such dangerous foes, but something set the tanks off, and they unleashed full volleys into the woods. She could see the trees exploding, and a cloud of smoke started to rise from both the missiles and the forest as it caught fire.

"XO, report!" she whispered into her radio, wary of the tank crews that might hear her. "Hector? Report!"

"Ma'am, Lieutenant Miller here," Second Platoon's leader said. "Lieutenant Torres is dead. We took a lot of casualties.

I'm pulling everyone deeper into the woods, and we'll call for medevac."

"How many's a lot, Tuck?" she asked, concern in her voice.

"We're checking. Right now we have seven KIA, almost triple that in wounded. First Platoon was hit pretty hard, ma'am."

She took a second to collect her thoughts, then said, "Understood. You've got command of that flank. Priorities are to evac the wounded and hunker down. Call in barrages on the 'Mechs if you see opportunities. Otherwise bug out and withdraw to Samanan."

"Roger, ma'am."

Lila looked at the hovertanks drifting back toward the valley floor; in the distance, over the sound of burning tanks and trees, she could hear but not see the approaching BattleMechs.

She glanced at Diego. "We've done all we can here. Pull everyone back to the bikes, and then we make a run for the next rib."

"Roadrunner actual, Mighty actual," Cynthia heard over the main frequency.

"Go ahead, Mighty."

"Cindy, Lila's having trouble getting out," Major Samuel Perrow said. Often called "the Rock" for his imposing statue and his willingness to use his BattleMech lance as an anchor for his whole First Armored Infantry Battalion to pivot around, he'd been "raised in the saddle" like Cynthia, a Light Horse brat his entire life. He'd entered the Twenty-First just a year ahead of her; they were good friends, and he was a strong advocate pushing for her to gain battalion command as soon as one was available. "Lila's got two platoons in APCs heading toward you, but there's hovercraft on her tail. She's having Boomer drop smoke and high explosive behind her as they run, but they could use an assist."

"We're on it, Sam," she replied, then flicked back to the company frequency. "Recon Lance, go! Get up there! We'll follow as best as we can. Strike Lance, stay here, keep our back door open!"

With a chorus of acknowledgments, her company started to separate.

Colonel Winston sagged into his command chair, breathing heavily. His heart raced from the climb up his *BattleMaster*, and he felt his left arm shake as he seated his neurohelmet on his head. He breathed deep to regain his bearings as he brought his 'Mech from standby to active.

He'd remained at the command post as long as he could, coordinating the actions of his battalion commanders, but now had to join the fight himself. To the west, Seventh Striker commander Major Nigel had his command lance and Twelfth Company delaying the Forty-Second's first BattleMech battalion, the one bright spot of the day. By conducting hit-and-runs and setting part of the forest on fire, Major Nigel had delayed the Forty-Second's progress from the west. Contact with Nigel was sporadic, but the reports were optimistic.

To the east, though, the force hadn't slowed much. The Warrior House still had their hovercraft out front, their 'Mech battalion on their heels, and the Forty-Second trailing behind. Because of the mercenaries' heavier overall composition, now almost three kilometers separated the two BattleMech battalions, which Third Striker commander and regimental XO Major Fallehy planned to take advantage of. With his battalion command lance, Major Perrow's battalion command lance, and Ninth Company, Fallehy had a combined five BattleMech lances to take on the Forty-Second's nine. If they timed their attack right and hit on a flank, Winston hoped to achieve local numerical superiority, cause some damage, and force the whole enemy battalion to pause.

But someone still had to stop House Hiritsu. He had two battalions en route, but they wouldn't make it in time, and once the Capellans forced their way through Cynthia's spread-out company, the only ones between them and Samanan was his command lance, his security lance, and the reinforced company of armor they called "Tin Can" Company.

Tin Can Company rolled through Samanan's east gate, and he ordered his two lances of BattleMechs to follow. Once they were clear, Bravo infantry company, the last Light Horse unit left in Samanan to guard the warehouses and artillery, closed the massive town gates behind them.

Seventeen tanks and eight 'Mechs weren't enough to stop a Warrior House.

But it was all he had.

AVALON CITY, NEW AVALON
3 MARCH 3029

"You did not consider the idea of fighting in the city proper, Colonel?" Quintus asked.

"We prefer not to put civilians at risk if we can help it," Armstrong cut in. "Fighting in cities is something we only consider as a last resort."

Davion's icy blue eyes narrowed at the explanation, but then he nodded curtly. "Continue, Colonel."

KAWICH
12 JANUARY 3029

Cynthia ordered her recon lance to pull up 500 meters short of Alpha Company and wait for her so the two lances could hit the Capellans together. Toward them screamed the hover APC carrying two platoons of Lila's troops. She had contacted Lila and confirmed the other surviving members of Alpha had escaped north: out of danger, but also out of the fight.

She saw another wall of smoke land directly behind the hovercraft, blocking her view of any Capellans in pursuit of her friend. Flicking her secondary radio to First Armored's frequency, she said, "Lila, Cindy. Drop another wall one hundred meters in front of us and we'll hit them as they come through."

"Got it." A pause, then, "Cindy, I'm glad to see you, but there's a lot of them. Don't try to hold them all yourself," Lila warned.

"We won't," she confirmed. "Just a couple volleys to cover you and make them slow down, then we fall back and repeat as necessary. Where are you heading?"

As they talked, the hovercraft passed her, and she could see Lila halfway out of the troop hatch of the rearmost APC, waving at her. "Second-to-last rib. We're going to get high, keep calling in fire from Boomer Company."

Cynthia raised one hand of her *Trebuchet* in salute as the infantry went by, then said, "Understood. I'll send Avellar up to you in a bit to call down close-air from Eighty-Fifth."

"Understood. Stay safe, Alpha actual out."

Cynthia flipped the radio back to her company frequency as another volley of smoke landed 100 meters in front of her two lances. "Steady, everyone, wait for them to appear." Another smoke volley landed, extending the duration of the wall, and it seemed if the valley got very still.

Then, in swirling vortices that proceeded them by seconds, a pair of Savannah Master hovercraft appeared, screaming out of the smoke. They immediately turned and ran for the safety of the cloud—one of the two *Wasp*s in her recon lance scored a hit with a medium laser on one of the tiny craft, but in a tornado of disrupted smoke, they were gone.

Cynthia's external microphones told her the story: the hovercraft were withdrawing, and the pounding of BattleMech feet grew closer. "Lieutenant Lyon, give Boomer Company our coordinates," she ordered her recon lance commander. "Tell them we need a mixed HE and smoke barrage when we give the order."

"*On* our position, Captain?"

"We'll fall back before it hits, trust me."

"Roger."

There was a moment before he said, "Coordinates called in, Captain."

Before she could reply, the smoke began swirling again—a lot, and a lot bigger eddies than the hovercraft had kicked up. BattleMechs, she realized. To Lyon she said, "Just in time."

Out of the smoke walked a line of twelve BattleMechs: a light lance to the left and right, and a medium lance anchored by a heavy *Catapult* in the middle. In her mind's eye, she could see the battalion formation: a heavy company in the middle behind the medium lance, waiting on word from the lead elements to assess and see how best to get around her small line.

She took a second to glance at the map as firing began: the fish ribs ran northeast to southwest, and because of their particular positioning, the northern lance was closer to the ridge than the southernmost Capellan lance. *They'll swing south*, she thought, and immediately aimed at the heaviest 'Mech in the southern lance, a *Phoenix Hawk*.

"Focus fire to the south, begin backing up! Lyon, get me that fire from Boomer Company!" It was out of range for her medium lasers, so she triggered both of her *Trebuchet*'s long-range missile racks, her 50-ton 'Mech throwing 30 missiles at the Capellan *Phoenix Hawk*. It dodged one salvo, but its maneuvering meant it went directly into the path of her second LRM-15 flight and both ten-racks from her lancemate Ralph Goodson's *Whitworth*. A few missed, but most hit, a total of twenty-six missiles crashing into the *'Hawk*'s torso and arms. Rowan hit a jumping *Stinger* on their left knee with her PPC, which cut through the joint, sending the leg one direction and the rest of the 'Mech falling in the other.

Cynthia grunted in approval of the lucky shot—Rowan was a genius with targeting, administration, and any number of other duties, but her gunnery was average at best. Triggering the microphone, she said, "Nice shot, Rowan! Victor, get your lance out of here! That heavy lance will chew you up!"

"They already have," Lyon reported back. "Middaugh's dead, PPC to the cockpit, and Millay ejected. MacCormac is scooping him up and we're falling back now!"

Cynthia hissed. *Both* lightly armored *Wasp* BattleMechs in her recon lance were destroyed? *Lyon's* Ostscout *can probably outrun any danger*, she thought, *and MacCormac's* Griffin *is heavy enough to take a hit or two while breaking contact, but we'll never hold the Capellans at this rate.*

"Rounds twenty seconds out," Ciensinski reminded her, firing his *Centurion*'s autocannon at another member of the southern lance.

Before she could respond, the *Phoenix Hawk* had finally regained its bearings and hit her with its large laser, scoring up her left torso from hip to shoulder. Nearly all her armor melted away, her wire-frame diagram on a secondary monitor flipping from green to black.

"Fall back, everyone!" she shouted, backpedaling. She barely missed thirty long-range missiles from the *Catapult*, but its lancemate, a *Vindicator*, hit her right leg with a PPC and melted away nearly all that limb's armor as well. Her BattleMech staggered from the hit, but she managed to keep herself upright. *Falling here is a death sentence*, she reminded herself. The other two 'Mechs of the enemy's center lance, a *Whitworth* and a second *Vindicator*, lashed into Rowan, her sturdy, heavy *Merlin* absorbing a dozen missiles and the PPC strike in its broad chest.

The Capellans advanced slowly, leery of outrunning the rest of their battalion, still somewhere behind the smoke. Her half-dozen remaining 'Mechs exchanged another volley of long-range fire with the enemy, and she saw MacCormac strike a Capellan *Stinger* on the north flank, slicing deep into its center torso and detonating the ammunition there. The *Stinger* exploded in a fireball, and the Capellan line paused for a moment to take stock of their losses. In that second of hesitation, Boomer's rounds came screaming in, a mix of smoke and high explosive putting a wall between her company and the Capellans.

"Fall back to Strike Lance, go!" she shouted, turning her 'Mech all the way around and starting to sprint. The artillery interference worked, and her lance was already several hundred meters west by the time the first Capellan 'Mechs tentatively poked through the smoke to find them. The Capellans fell back behind the smoke—*probably to regroup,* she figured—while her lances met up with Strike Lance and did the same.

"Stonewall, this is Roadrunner actual. I bought you a few more minutes, but lost two 'Mechs. A couple more victories like that and I won't have a unit left."

"Roadrunner, Stonewall actual. Understood—fall back to the last ridge. I've already ordered Boomer to withdraw, and I have repair and reload teams here so you can reset and then fall in with me."

"Understood, falling back," she replied, and passed along the instructions to her unit, her two damaged lances running to the linkup point while Strike Lance fell back in a bounding overwatch.

Cynthia switched her radio to a private frequency and then quietly asked, "Are you okay, Uncle Chuck?"

Winston flexed the numbness out of his left hand and keyed his microphone. "You know me, Cindy, I'll tough it out."

"Your family is going to *kill* you for being out here. Hell, they might kill *me*," Cynthia replied.

Winston grunted, and for a split second, thought about the machine mounted behind him. His wife—part of the Light Horse field hospital staff—and his daughter Ariana before the regiment hit Kawich, had installed a brightly colored CPR machine, affectionately referred to as a "jolter," to the wall at the rear of his cockpit, "just in case." Very few people currently knew about his heart problems—Cynthia was one, as well as General Armstrong and his doctor—but if the jolter ever *was* needed, at that point he wouldn't be concerned with who found out.

He prayed that it wouldn't come to that, but the tingle in his left hand told him his heart might finish whatever the Capellans had started.

"Just get the Roadrunners back here, Cynthia, and let me worry about me."

"That's not how families work, Uncle Chuck," he heard her mutter before disconnecting.

"*Ernsthaft?*" asked Lieutenant Diego, then rolled his eyes and muttered, "MechWarriors."

Lila grunted questioningly, turned around, and then sighed.

They were lying on the second-to-last ridge, using their elevation to call in both smoke and explosive rounds from regimental artillery. So far, it hadn't done much to slow down the 'Mechs, but it was something. Cynthia had sent her a MechWarrior to call in air support, and as Lila requested, she'd parked her 'Mech on the lee side of the ridge where it couldn't be seen.

But the MechWarrior, on the other hand, stood out against the brown scrub with her pale skin, red hair, and hair jewelry glittering in the afternoon sunlight. Lila slid—half on her heels, half on her rump—down the mountain fifty meters to the young woman.

The MechWarrior had already swapped her coolant vest for a flak jacket from her 'Mech's ankle locker, and turned around on Lila's approach.

"Stop," she ordered. She pulled a black knit cap from a cargo pocket, tossed it to the MechWarrior, and then pulled a tube of grease-camo from a smaller pocket. "They can see you from orbit, Red. Put that on and close your eyes."

Rowan did as she was told, and within thirty seconds, Lila covered her exposed face, neck, and arms in a brown camouflage. "Not sure I have enough for your legs," she said, looking at her near-empty tube and then Rowan's spandex bikini briefs.

Rowan smiled. "Normally when someone wants to goop up my legs, they buy me a drink first."

Lila barked a laugh. "So noted," she said with a smile. The smile fell as she heard several Long Tom rounds scream through the air, the distinctive screech and ripping noise of outbound artillery discernible above the din of battle. "Okay, when we get near the top, we'll crawl the last part so we're not skylighted. I'll put you next to my radio operator so you can do your magic. We'll just hide your legs behind a rock or something. Follow me and stay low!"

The two women scurried up the ridge, often on all fours, before they finally crawled into position, Lila on one side of Rowan, the radio operator on the other.

"Here," Lila said, passing Rowan a pair of binoculars and a map. "Boomer's displacing. We're currently directing fire for the four Long Toms at regiment, call sign Thunder."

Rowan nodded gratefully. Using the binoculars to confirm the Capellan location against the map, she keyed the handheld microphone and said, "Bomber Lead, this is Roadrunner Four, stand by for attack patterns."

Lila nodded in approval as Rowan recited instructions, and she turned her focus to the Capellans: they'd returned to a hovercraft-out-front formation since Cynthia's company had withdrawn. A few scouts would punch through each wall of smoke, and upon confirming it was safe, they'd lead the battalion through.

"Thunder, this is Roadrunner Four, check fire. I say again, all Thunder elements, check fire, airstrike inbound," Rowan said, and Lila started.

"You don't want them to keep dropping smoke?" she asked.

The younger woman shook her head, and then stared intently through the binoculars. "No, for two reasons. One, there's an infinitesimally small chance the fighters can run into a round in-flight, and it's not worth the risk. Two, I want *less* smoke out there so the pilots can find and then hit their targets." She put the binocs down, and flashed Lila a brilliant smile. "It's counterintuitive, I know—but tell you what: if they disable less than a platoon on this first pass, the first round's on me."

Lila quirked a smile back. "First round over dinner and dancing."

Rowan laughed, put the binocs back up. "You're on."

The smoke lifted, dissipating in the slight wind running down the valley. Lila could see the surviving two dozen or so Capellan hovercraft running down the valley in a large wedge, about a thousand meters ahead of the 'Mech battalion.

"Here they come," Rowan warned, and from the left and right, screaming down between the second and third fish ribs, came the eight aerofighters of the Eighty-Fifth Company, four each from the north and south.

Lasers flashed as the fighters streaked by on strafing runs. Lila watched as the southern flights passed over the northern flights by less than fifty meters, all eight of them below her position on rib two. She felt almost dizzy as she stared down into a cockpit of an Eighty-Fifth *Shilone*, so close she felt like she could have hit it with a rock, and then, just that fast, the fighters were gone.

Down in the valley, five hovercraft were immobile and burning, five more were smoking but still moving, and the rest of the formation circled as if dazed. The 'Mech battalion slowed almost to a halt, raising their weapons to the sky and watching for another attack.

Lila whistled appreciatively. "Forget dinner and dancing—we live through this, Red, I'll wife you up," she kidded.

The young MechWarrior put the binoculars down, studiously looked her over from head-to-toe, and then nodded. "Okay," Rowan finally said, then turned back to the Capellans, using the binoculars to compare the hovercraft's new positions to the map. "But I gotta warn you, Captain," she added, "you're fourth in line."

Cynthia's troops were still getting hurriedly repaired when Colonel Winston's voice came over the battalion frequency: "Roadrunner, Stonewall actual. Send your strike and recon lances to me, and take your command lance up rib one. I'll have Alpha infantry fall back and meet you there. Tin Cans will hold the northern ridge."

Cynthia looked at a secondary monitor to confirm the status of her company: reloading only took moments, so it had been completed first, but armor repairs depended on damage taken, and could take a while. All of her 'Mechs were only about half-repaired—*that'll have to do*, she thought—and she ordered the technicians to finish up whatever they were working on so the company could move. Then she switched to the battalion frequency and replied, "Stonewall, Roadrunner—my command lance is heavier. I should be down in the valley with you."

As she waited for a response, she watched her monitors: Boomer Company's AA lance joined up with the colonel, and the three mobile artillery pieces continued past the repair site, heading to their next firing positions a half kilometer west.

"Roadrunner, that's exactly why I want you on the ridge," Colonel Winston replied. "Once we pin them in place, you need to charge down and hit their flank. With a bit of luck, it'll be enough to make them fall back for a few minutes. That's all we need, Cindy—Seventh Striker will be here in thirty minutes, we just have to hold them that long."

"Understood," she replied, and pointed her command lance toward the western lee side of the ridge. Within a minute, she was at the peak, stepping forward just enough to raise her cockpit above the ridge; the rest of her *Trebuchet*, Goodson's *Whitworth*, and Ciensinski's *Centurion* were hidden from Capellan sight.

To the east, racing from the second ridge toward her, was Alpha Company in their hover APCs, the extra-wide vehicles designed for riders to ride the dirt bikes directly up rear ramps. Pacing the APCs was Avellar's *Merlin*, with a thick wall of smoke shielding their movements from Capellan sight.

The lead elements of the Warrior House were passing the second fish rib, now just 4,000 meters away from Colonel Winston's thin line of defense. Far to the east, she could see the dust kicked up by the Forty-Second, the distance between the two enemy battalions growing with every step. Alpha's APCs started to swing around the rib to offload Lila's platoons on the ridge's lee side; Rowan, in contrast, just headed her *Merlin* straight up the ridge toward Cynthia.

Touching a secondary monitor, Cynthia tagged everything she could see and squirted it out to the regiment. "Stonewall, Roadrunner. Looks like you'll have company in about ten minutes."

"Understood," Winston replied. "Plague actual, Stonewall. Status?"

"Stonewall, this is Mighty actual. Jamal ejected and was wounded, he's with the medics. We're down by half, the Forty-Second's down a company, and they're about eight kilometers behind the Warrior House. We're falling back, we can't—"

Major Perrow was cut off in a blast of static and then, silence.

Winston's blood ran cold: there were a few reasons radio comms might get cut, but unfortunately many of them were fatal. "Mighty, Stonewall, come in," he called over the command frequency.

"Sir, this is Lieutenant Armstrong!" came a new voice, "The major's down, the captain's down, they're everywhere! I think we're cut off!" Colonel Winston heard the near-panic in the lieutenant's voice and sympathized: every lieutenant in the Light Horse was a battle-tested veteran, but getting shoved into command while pursued by an enemy BattleMech battalion would test even the best of lance commanders.

Winston flipped through a mental roster and tagged the name with a face. "Okay, David, I understand. Start falling back, help is coming, okay? Fall back in pairs, by the book. Roadrunner Four, can you see the Forty-Second from the top of rib one?"

"Uh, barely, sir?" came the tentative voice of Avellar. He could see the *Merlin* standing on rib one's highest peak, skylighted in front of the whole Warrior House, trying to get line of sight on the invading mercenaries.

"Good enough. Hit them, Roadrunner. Thunder and Bomber squadron both—if it's painted blue, hit it with a bomb and have Thunder bounce the rubble. How copy?"

"Good copy, Stonewall."

"You hear that, Lieutenant Armstrong? Wait for the bombs to fall, and get your lances out of there."

"Roger, Stonewall," Armstrong replied, relief evident in his voice.

"Tin Can actual, Stonewall actual," Winston said, watching the Capellans approach. *Three thousand meters now*, he thought, watching the hovercraft starting to break north toward Tin Can Company. Almost as one, the Warrior House started to compact, tightening up once they realized the Light Horse artillery and aerospace fighters were no longer focused on them.

"Stonewall, Tin Can actual."

"Captain Hesse, you're now both the acting commander of First Armored and my acting XO. Looks like the Capellans are sending the fast-movers at you to keep you out of our little brawl. Be careful, those SRMs can bust your tracks and turn your heavies into pillboxes in moments."

"*Verstanden*, we won't let you down."

"I know you won't, Stonewall out."

The Warrior House was now only 2,000 meters away, and of the thirty BattleMechs they had started their assault with, Cynthia's relayed feed showed two dozen remaining. The seventeen MechWarriors with him found large rocks and boulders on the valley floor to position their BattleMechs behind, finding the best cover they could on the mostly featureless plain.

"About two minutes, everyone," he said. "Engage at maximum range. They have numbers, but they're hurt. If we can do enough damage at range, we can hopefully whittle these odds down some."

He heard the four lance commanders voice their agreements—the six Roadrunners had consolidated into one lance—then he flipped back to the Roadrunner frequency for a moment. "Roadrunner Four, I need you to divert Bomber squadron for one run at the Warrior House when the heavies hit five hundred meters. We'll have their attention, and they'll still be far enough away to prevent fratricide. After that, task the Eighty-Fifth as you see fit."

"Stonewall actual, Boomer actual," a new voice interrupted, "guns are laid and awaiting orders."

All seven *guns are up*? He felt a glimmer of hope. "Roadrunner Four, they're yours, too!" Winston said, a little too loud.

He heard the young woman acknowledge, and a sharp pain went up his left arm. "*Not now*, damn it!" he whispered. He saw the range dropping. "One minute," he broadcast on the regimental frequency.

The Capellans started to speed up, their light lances leaving their slower compatriots behind and drifting north and south, trying to flank Winston's line. The first ranging shots from his composite company rang out, Lieutenant Liesen in his *Rifleman* firing his autocannon at a distant *Vindicator*. As if Liesen had broken a magic spell, the entire Warrior House battalion began to run at them.

Winston raised his handheld PPC, and the moment a Capellan *Cataphract* came into range, he fired. The cerulean beam raced from his *BattleMaster* and struck the Capellan dead center. The heavy 'Mech staggered and fired back, its PPC missing Winston by meters.

"Stonewall elements, check fire. Bomber squadron attacking now, now, now," came the call across the main frequency. As it did, the six surviving fighters of the Eighty-Fifth came in by pairs, wingtip to wingtip, crimson lasers and cobalt PPC blasts chewing up the Capellan line from north to south. A pair of 'Mechs fell, another one exploded—and they continued to close.

"Cindy, come down the ridge and close the door behind them," he ordered, firing his PPC again at the same *Cataphract*. Again, the Capellan heavy took the hit, and returned fire with its autocannon and PPC, both of which hit the *BattleMaster* this time.

Winston grunted as his 'Mech shook and swayed from losing more than a ton of armor in seconds, and he felt his chest tighten, his pulse beating thunderously in his ears. His vision started to gray, and through the cloud he saw an ancient *Highlander* raise its autocannon toward him.

Enemy commander, Winston thought. Spinning and firing more on muscle memory than vision, he registered the hit from his PPC.

"Tin Can actual, Stonewall," he gasped, trying to keep his 'Mech upright. The *Highlander* reeled from impacts, and Winston breathed deep. *Cindy, has to be*, he thought.

A sharp pain stabbed through his chest.

"Stonewall, Tin Can actual is dismounted and injured," he heard over the radio.

Winston fired again at a form he believed to be the *Highlander* as his vision grayed over. He felt his *BattleMaster* falling forward, he wasn't sure why.

"Cindy, take command." was his last order before he died.

"Sir! *Uncle Chuck*!" Cynthia cried over the command frequency as the *BattleMaster* crashed into the brown dirt and remained still. Rowan was in a long-range duel with a severely damaged *Cataphract*, and both Goodson and Ciensinski were combining their fire with Cynthia against the Capellan *Highlander*.

As planned, the attack down the ridge had thrown the Capellan assault into confusion, halting their advance and forcing them to react to the Light Horse on the fly. The remaining dozen and a half Capellans started to form into a tight oval, backing off the Light Horse line about 100 meters.

Which was just enough. "Bomber squadron attacking now, now, now!" Rowan sang out over the main frequency, and diving from the sky with the sun at their backs was the Eighty-Fifth. The *Highlander* and three other silver-green Capellans fell, the damaged *Cataphract* exploded, and Cynthia ran her *Trebuchet* next to the *BattleMaster*'s fallen form.

"Rowan, keep it up. Lila, I'm dismounting to check on Stonewall Actual!" she said, as she laid her *Trebuchet* prone next to Winston's *BattleMaster*.

She heard an "Understood" from the radio, though she wasn't sure who said it, then unbuckled and disconnected her coolant suit before shucking her neurohelmet. Carrying a first aid kit, she popped the cockpit hatch and climbed out in her spandex togs.

Battle, she'd learned long ago, sounded incredibly different on the ground than from inside her 'Mech. The screech of overheard artillery, the distinct whine of aerospace fighter engines, the closer roar of missiles and the whip-*snap* of lasers cutting through the air—war was loud and confusing and terrifying when not wrapped in the safety of her *Trebuchet*.

She shook off her fear and sprinted the twenty meters to the fallen *BattleMaster*'s cockpit, dust kicking up and caking her sweat-laden thighs. Grabbing a handhold, she could see Colonel Winston hanging forward in his command chair, held in place by his restraints. She punched in the daily emergency-access code every Light Horse soldier was taught, and the bulbous canopy pivoted upward. She quickly felt for breathing and a pulse—finding neither, she gasped and immediately went for the jolter.

She followed the pictograms on the cover, charged it; then, opening his coolant vest, placed the paddles against his chest. It took three tries, but finally the machine blinked green, and she heard faint breathing. She sagged against the transparisteel cockpit glass and saw the reflection of a giant explosion gleaming from every monitor.

She turned around, staring at a huge ball of smoke and fire falling from the sky about thirty kilometers away, and finally heard the explosion roll down the valley.

Glancing at the monitors to get a read on where all the forces were, she grabbed the auxiliary handset off the command console and said, "Lila, the colonel's alive. What just blew up?"

**AVALON CITY, NEW AVALON
3 MARCH 3029**

"So that part of the report was accurate?" Quintus asked. "You *did* die."

Winston nodded. "Yes, sir."

The room was deathly silent before Paulson said, "But, he got better?" The joke fell flat, and the three mercenaries shrank slightly beneath Hanse's glare.

"What blew up?" Quintus asked Paulson, breaking the tension.

"A Capellan DropShip. A Warrior House *Gazelle* tried to make a run for it, but the Eighty-Fifth shot it out of the sky as a warning to the rest."

"Tell me what the monitors showed you," Hanse demanded. "Who was doing what?"

Paulson nodded. "Yes, Your Highness. Seventh Striker hadn't arrived yet, but the Forty-Second was starting to contract and react to them. Lieutenant Armstrong was swinging back out of the north to join up with my lance on the Capellan's east side, the colonel's ad-hoc company was pushing from the west, and the Tin Cans were sniping from the north ridge. Boomer and Thunder were pounding House Hiritsu, and the Eighty-Fifth went where they were needed."

Hanse nodded. "Yes, I saw from the reports. Excellent positioning and tactics—tell me, Major Paulson, who gave those orders?"

The three mercenaries fidgeted. "Your Highness," General Armstrong began, "in the Light Horse, we encourage initiative from our junior leaders in situations where the chain of command has been disrupted."

"Oh, I'm well aware," Hanse replied testily. "That's one of the reasons I have you teaching classes at NAIS. I encourage initiative from my troops as well. No, let me be more *specific*:

Who, exactly, was in command at that point? We've pulled the logs and comm chatter, and if this report is right..." Hanse pulled out a specific flimsy, "when that *Gazelle* lifted off, Major Fallehy and Captain Hess were injured, and both Major Perrow and *you*, Colonel Winston, were *dead*. Major Paulson, who, *exactly*, was in command of Third Striker Battalion, First Armored Infantry Battalion, and by extension, the entire eastern defense of Samanan?"

Paulson straightened her spine. "I was, Your Highness."

Hanse leaned forward. "And who, exactly, was *running* the defense of Samanan? Because if I was a betting man..." he said, glancing at Quintus.

"You are a betting man, Your Highness," Quintus pointed out.

Hanse half-chuckled. "You're right, Quintus, I *am*. What's in my junk drawer?" he asked, almost to himself. After pulling open the bottom-right drawer of his desk, he began to rummage through it. "Pens, flimsies, pistol with spare mags—ah!"

He pulled out a wrapped stack of bills and slammed it on the desk, then withdrew a flimsy. He skimmed it quickly. "Forgot this was in there. So, I'll bet a quarter-million pounds and this title to a forest moon with—" he looked at it again for reference, reading out loud, "—'a growing logging industry and excellent sport fishing' versus everything in your pockets that the defense of *my* storehouses was, in fact, being run by a wet-behind-the-ears MechWarrior from the Outworlds Alliance."

The room was silent.

"General, let me be clear," Hanse began quietly. "I am in no way angry at MechWarrior Avellar. In fact—" he nodded to Quintus, who passed Armstrong an envelope, "—this is a copy of an invitation I have sent to her, via ComStar, for her and a plus-one to visit me here on New Avalon. I want to thank her personally, and will extend to her an AFFS leftenant commission for any posting she wants."

He leaned forward. "No, General, this is about you and your unit. This was *not* Avellar taking initiative in the absence of orders. This is the *complete* abrogation of responsibility by her chain of command.

"You, General," Hanse continued, looking at Armstrong, "should have demanded Colonel Winston's retirement before sending the unit to Kawich. If you didn't know he was medically unfit, you're an idiot; if you knew and sent him anyway, it was a blisteringly terrible decision—and I *know* you're not an idiot, Nathan."

He turned his glare to Colonel Winston. "You, Colonel, should have retired when the war broke out, and you most *certainly* should have retired before defending Kawich. You put your entire unit *and* the mission at risk out of pride, and there is no excuse for it.

"And you, Major Paulson…" he said, turning to her. "You are an officer with responsibilities to your subordinates. No matter how close you are to Colonel Winston, you should have commanded your battalions—*plural*—and *let him die.*"

The room was deathly still. Paulson looked sick at Hanse's statement, and Winston blanched.

Armstrong coughed once and said, "Your Highness, that's not really how we do business—"

"'*Not how we do business*'?" Hanse all but roared. "There is no '*we*' in 'mercenary,' General, but there is '*me*'! 'Me,' as in your employer." He slammed his finger into the desk for emphasis. "Me, a field marshal who has expectations from brigade and regimental commanders that you all apparently *chose* to *ignore*, and me, the man who has extended you an *incredibly* long line of trust these past few years to find it *exploding* in my face the moment difficult choices needed to be made!"

Hanse leaned back for a moment, took a deep breath, and continued with his emotions reined in. "Gentlemen, Major, I just had to tell my nation that one of their March leaders, a duke, was killed by the Capellans. He was betrayed by an aide, and your bad intelligence was part of that betrayal. It is because I do not want the public to know how much damage the Capellan agent did, or to make my heir, Duke Morgan Hasek-Davion, suffer any further, that I am going to classify the defense of Kawich at the highest levels. As far as the public knows, this disaster never happened. Again, let me be clear: I am exceedingly pleased with the valor and skill your troops fought with. I am incredibly disappointed in all of *you.*"

He let the words hang in the air for a moment, and then nodded to Quintus, who passed over another envelope. "Your orders. Colonel Winston, you will remain in command until Major Fallehy returns from recuperative leave and is fully trained, and you will take the Twenty-First Striker regiment to Sudeten, where you are, officially, listed as 'on loan' to the LCAF to defend the Olivetti Weapons facility.

"Right now," he continued, "the survivors of the Forty-Second Armored are sitting in prisoner-of-war camps. The Capellans have refused to pay ransom or the remainder of their contracts, so they are, for all practical purposes, destroyed. You will take their personnel and equipment with you to Sudeten and absorb the best of them into the Light Horse Brigade, primarily the Twenty-First, bringing you back up to strength."

"That's not really how we rebuild—" Armstrong quietly began before Hanse silenced him with a glare, then relented slightly.

"Nathan, if spies see the Twenty-First at anything less than full strength, questions will be asked, and the story will fall apart. The Forty-Second is experienced, it's available, and it's dead broke. Doing this will mislead or confuse enemy intelligence efforts while you also defend an ally's strategic asset."

Armstrong nodded.

"Any questions?"

"Your Highness, we ran into Duke Hasek-Davion on the way in, and he asked us to brief him after our meeting with you," Armstrong said.

Davion shook his head. "Absolutely not. I'll send Quintus over with the cover story, and I'll tell him the truth in a couple of years. Anything else?"

They shook their heads, and Colonel Winston said, "Your Highness, you have my sincerest apologies for letting you down."

Hanse leaned back. "I know it's polite and traditional to accept apologies when offered, but Colonel, you let me, your unit, and *most* importantly, your junior leaders and troopers down. You command a regiment, so you are expected to set the example...and you should have known better."

He nodded to Quintus, who stood, and the mercenaries immediately stood as well. He slid the moon's deed to Quintus and said, "Quintus will provide you a copy of that to take with you. Please tell Avellar it's hers if she accepts my commission."

After Paulson nodded, Hanse turned to Armstrong, and his eyes narrowed. "I will be keeping a close eye on your brigade for the foreseeable future, General, and if lapses like this happen again, *we* will have a very long, *very* uncomfortable one-way discussion about your unit's continued employment. Understood?"

When Armstrong nodded, Hanse said, "Good. Quintus will show you out."

BATTLEMASTER
Assault—85 tons

HIGHLANDER
Assault—90 tons

MERLIN
HEAVY—60 TONS

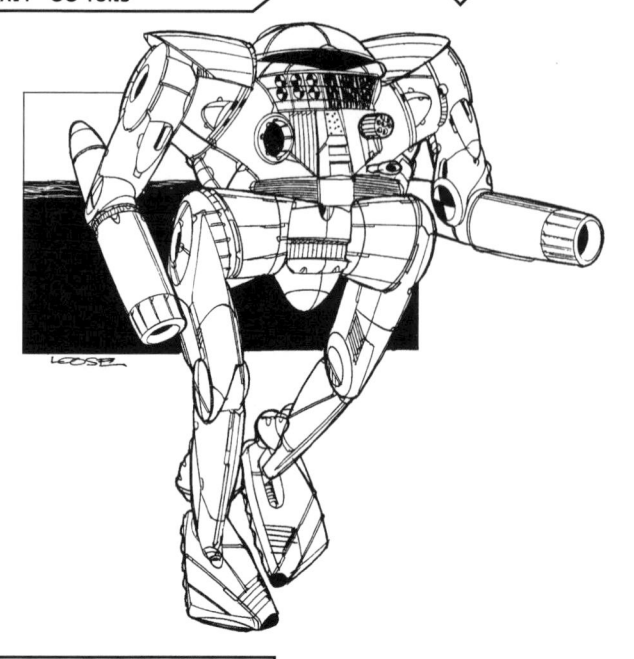

PHOENIX HAWK
MEDIUM—45 TONS

TREBUCHET
MEDIUM—50 TONS

FAILINGS IN TEACHING

DANIEL ISBERNER

**LECTURE HALL 22, COLLEGE OF MILITARY SCIENCE
NEW AVALON INSTITUTE OF SCIENCE
NEW AVALON
CRUCIS MARCH
FEDERATED COMMONWEALTH
3 OCTOBER 3051**

Captain Maxwell Parish stood in front of his tactics class and tried to stand still. Thankfully, his lectern gave him something to hold on to.

"Now as you can see in the image, your troops are surrounded. Help is on its way, but you have to hold out. What are you going to do?"

Quite a few hands went up in the air, but Parish wasn't in the mood to listen to his students. Or cadets. It didn't matter what they were called, they all got on his nerves when they talked. They were all too loud...

"Your jump-capable 'Mechs will jump behind the enemy lines and—"

"Professor Parish?" It was Claudia Endris, one of his very loud students. *Always talking, always talking...* "Five minutes ago, you said all our jump-capable units got destroyed. Aside from that, even if our jump-capable units were still available, for them to actually be able to jump *behind* enemy lines, they would have to cross open terrain first and—"

"Are you teaching this class or am I?!" Parish yelled at the young woman.

"You...you are. Of course. Professor, but I thought—"

"You aren't here to *think*. You are here to *learn*."

That doesn't change the fact that she is right and you are an asshole, his inner voice chided him.

A half-hour later, he dismissed his class. He had tried to correct his mistakes, act like it was intentional. None of the cadets had bought it, he knew that. He didn't usually go out the night before he gave a class, but last night... He had ended up in a bar.

"Captain Parish?"

Cadet Claudia Endris stood in front of him, looking at him like she was worried.

"Yes, Cadet Endris?"

"Are you all right, sir?"

"Yes. I'm sorry for yelling at you before, Cadet. You were right, of course."

"That's not what I meant."

That's what you get for being friendly with the cadets and even taking part in group activities. They start caring about you.

"It's nothing, really."

"You sure?"

"Yes, I'm sure. Go. If memory serves, you have simulator hours coming up, and Captain Farraday hates when cadets are late."

She looked at him a few moments longer, then turned around and left. When she had exited the lecture hall, he grabbed two aspirin from his bag and swallowed them dry.

You'll find out what's going on once the news hits the NAIS.

He had been surprised the Eridani Light Horse had been able to get the information before it reached New Avalon proper. When it showed up in his files last evening, he had gone out and drunk himself into a stupor.

It wasn't enough that he had to teach in the NAIS instead of seeing combat because House Davion was holding a tight leash on their income, leveraging "repair bonuses" against teaching time.

"Repair bonus," my ass. It's a Company Store scam. We all know it.

No. They had finally found out where the Clans were coming from. The invaders from the Deep Periphery were no one else but the descendants of Aleksandr Kerensky and the Star League Defense Force.

For centuries, we have waited for them to return. To bring peace to the Inner Sphere, and now…

"Professor Parish? What are you still doing here?" Professor String looked at him like he had broken her expensive glasses. "Your class let out a half-hour ago. I would like to set up mine now!"

"Sorry. I'll leave."

He gathered his things and left. He didn't like Professor String, and she didn't like him. She had been teaching weapons-spec classes for fifty years, and hadn't been happy about Eridani Light Horse officers starting to teach at the NAIS.

You and me both, sister. I'd prefer shooting at another 'Mech over teaching tactics any day of the week.

When he entered the Eridani Light Horse compound, he tried to look at the ground. The Light Horse would set up three flagpoles at all of their facilities: one for the unit flag at half-mast, one for their employer, and an empty one for the long-dead Star League—reminding everyone what had been taken from them. Usually, he would stand and salute the flagpoles, but… He just couldn't do it. He didn't even want to see them. He wanted to get inside and get another drink.

No! That's not a good idea. You need to clear your head. You need to figure out where to go.

His rank afforded him a four-room apartment. Living room, bedroom, and an office, all connected to his own kitchen. None of the rooms was very big, but the office had its own door, allowing cadets to meet with him without having to enter his actual apartment. He had been offered an office in the NAIS office building, but decided against it. He liked the fact that his students had to sit and look outside the window behind his desk when they wanted to talk to him. Looking directly at the flagpoles, showing them just who the Eridani Light Horse are. What an honor it was to be taught by them.

Now he closed the blinds and switched on the light before he powered up his computer and went to the kitchen to make himself tea.

When it was done, he reached toward the whiskey, but stopped himself. *One drunken night is enough. Those traitors to their own legacy aren't worth more.*

When he got to his messages, he almost spilled hot tea into his lap.

To all Eridani Light Horse personnel,

After deliberation with the command staff and listening to the problems concerning the recent revelation about who the Clans are, we have come to a decision.

With a heavy heart, I have requested all Eridani Light Horse personnel be granted a leave from active duty for at least one year and to stop all preparations for troop movements toward the northern border of the Lyran half of the Federated Commonwealth. This will give us time to find out where we stand and how we want to deal with the new information presented to us by Wolf's Dragoons and the Federated Commonwealth.

All personnel will remain at their current post and continue serving the Federated Commonwealth in the capacity they were assigned.

I know not all of you will be happy with this decision. I also know quite a few of you hold reservations against the way the Federated Commonwealth has been dealing with us. Whether these concerns are justified is of no matter right now, for we will serve the Commonwealth until our contract expires.

A year of sabbatical and reflection will allow us to focus and to come back stronger than ever before.

Be strong,
Brevet General Ariana Winston

He had to read the message thrice before he could believe it. *We are pulling back. We...*

Then it hit him. *I have to keep teaching for at least another year.*

It had to be a bad dream. His orders were to finish all his classes before Christmas, then he would have shipped toward the front lines.

This cannot be happening!

When his office bell rang, he decided to ignore it.

HOLY PONY BAR
MORGAN, NEW AVALON
CRUCIS MARCH
FEDERATED COMMONWEALTH
4 OCTOBER 3051

Parish had decided to spend the evening somewhere where no one would know him. The small town of Morgan was just such a place. Located halfway between Jeratha and Avalon City, it was mostly populated by middle-class workers who worked in either of those cities and preferred the quiet of the small town over the constant noise in the big cities. That was exactly what he was seeking tonight.

In civilian clothing, he sat quietly in a corner, drinking whiskey and beer.

"Can you turn up the volume?" another patron asked the barkeeper. Some interesting news item must have come up on the big screen above the bar, but it was impossible for Parish to see from his seat.

While the barkeeper looked under the counter for the remote, Parish turned his attention back to his whiskey. Maple and smoky notes dominated this one, with just a hint of peach.

"*—Kerensky's offspring.*" He finally heard the newscaster's voice. *Ah, shit!*

"*From what we hear, the news of the origins of the Clan invaders currently ransacking the Lyran half of the Federated Commonwealth—*" He could hear rumbling and quite a few hostile comments toward the Lyrans. "*—has not only impacted* civilians all around the Inner Sphere. Even the venerable Eridani Light Horse mercenary unit has been shocked to the core."

Parish tried to sink deeper into his corner.

"With the unit tracing its origins back to the Star League, that does not come as a surprise. Earlier today we have tried to contact Captain Maxwell Parish, the ranking Light Horse officer on-planet, for comment on the rumors that Eridani Light Horse personnel have requested time off from active duty, but we have not heard back. We will update this story as soon as..."

He no longer listened, instead he chugged his whole glass and signaled the barkeeper to bring him another. *Couldn't have just one evening in peace.*

"Hey, it's you!" one of the other half-drunk patrons shouted and suddenly stood in front of him. "Y'knew, didn't ya? Y'knew who the Clans are!" Alcohol made the man slur his words. "You're workin' with 'em!"

What the hell?

Parish finally looked up, calmly stood, and came out of the corner. Then he punched the man straight in his face, breaking his nose and sending him to the floor. More people got up. Some backed away, but three of them came right at him.

A shot went out and stopped them in their tracks. The barkeeper's right hand had an antique revolver pointed at the ceiling, while his left held a stunner, pointed at them.

"The first shot was a blank. But the others aren't. And the stunner's always fully charged. Now everyone sit down!"

The men retreated and the barkeeper put his gun away before he came over to Parish. "Pay up, then get out!"

Parish did as he was told. He didn't leave a tip.

Outside, he went for a walk. He had arrived via bus, deciding against a Light Horse vehicle, to be less conspicuous. Now he regretted his decision. With his face on the news, taking a bus might be worse than arriving in town in a vehicle with military plates. He had also opted not to take a communicator or anything that would let anyone on base reach him, so he couldn't just call someone to pick him up.

At least, not if I want to avoid answering unwanted questions. That leaves two options. Get on the bus and just hope no one on it watched the news, or...

He decided he would go for option two and went looking for another bar. Things couldn't get any worse anyway.

When he woke up the next morning, his back hurt from lying on a wooden bench, his head felt like someone had hit it with a PPC, his mouth tasted like three weeks in a cockpit, and he had no idea where he was.

He tried to sit up, which led to another PPC slamming into his head. Opening his eyes did the same, and finally realizing where he was...

A real PPC would have been better.

Bars separated his accommodations from the rest of the small office. A man and a woman in police uniform turned to him when they heard his groan.

"Look who's finally up," the woman declared.

"What happened?" Parish asked. "Can I get some water?"

To his surprise, the female officer actually brought him a glass. He didn't know any military police who would have brought an actual glass cup to anyone in a holding cell, but the police station seemed very small, and small-town law enforcement usually didn't follow the same rules as MPs.

"You trashed a bar and broke a few noses," the male officer finally said. "But you're in luck. The owner said he wouldn't press charges if you covered his damages, and from what he told us, the other patrons involved won't press any charges either, if you cover their bar tabs for the next week."

"Sounds expensive."

"You're probably right," the female officer replied. "And, knowing the guys, there's actually a good chance they attacked first. The fact that we require video surveillance in bars might help you a lot, but the simple question is, do you want your liaison officer to know?"

He looked up. She didn't have a threatening look on her face; quite the contrary. She almost seemed to sympathize. But she was also right. If nobody pressed charges, no one would find out and he wouldn't get into trouble. He would pay the local police for his stay and the fines, and as long as he paid cash, they wouldn't even have to put his name into a file.

**LECTURE HALL 22, COLLEGE OF MILITARY SCIENCE
NEW AVALON INSTITUTE OF SCIENCE
NEW AVALON
CRUCIS MARCH
FEDERATED COMMONWEALTH
17 DECEMBER 3051**

Parish looked at the rows of cadets, all with their heads down, all concentrating on the written exam. Thanks to a multi-day combat simulation starting tomorrow, it would have been his final class before he was supposed to ship out to the front line. Now…

He drank from his cup of spiked coffee. Only a shot of whiskey in it, but it dulled his grinding frustration.

When he looked up again, one of his students had her hand raised. Claudia Endris, of course. He acknowledged having seen her, then put a very minty piece of gum in his mouth and went over to her seat. Unsurprisingly, she had chosen a spot at the end of a row, making it easy for him to answer any questions she might have. Over the last two months, those questions had become more and more.

He picked up a chair on his way over and sat down beside her. "How can I help you?"

"This question." She pointed to the third to last. "It makes no sense."

He forcefully swallowed down an angry shout. Yelling during an exam would get him into the doghouse. "Why?" he asked calmly instead.

"Part Three of the question," she whispered. "You ask about positioning of an infantry platoon to support the 'Mechs the best way possible. The problem is, Part One classified the planetary conditions as extremely hostile, and you want us to answer how 'Mechs will operate under these conditions. Part Two specifies that all supplies, including the hazardous environment gear, are destroyed, making it impossible for anyone to leave their 'Mech."

"Yes?"

"Sir, under these conditions, positioning the infantry platoon will be moot. They are all dead."

"Then let them fight as zombies!" he said loud enough for all of the cadets to lift their heads, only to lower them quickly, hoping he wouldn't notice.

He went back to his desk, sat down, and emptied his cup of spiked coffee before he refilled it from his thermos. He didn't even notice he'd swallowed the gum.

That was a rookie mistake, Max, his inner voice chided him. *Why did you refuse to let any of your TAs look over the test?*

You can't blame this on me. *She should've come up with a solution. It's not my fault they are traitors...dead.*

Well, you *wrote the test. So technically it is your fault. Also, you cannot blame your students for Kerensky's traitors.*

For three hundred years, my family has served in the Light Horse, waiting for the Star League Defense Force to return. You just watch me blame whomever I want.

These inner dialogues had occurred more and more often over the last two months. Usually when he was drunk. But he felt far from drunk. Only a few cups of spiked coffee, really. Nothing worth mentioning.

Claudia Endris handed in her test early and looked furious. The last couple weeks had turned her from actually caring about him into being mostly angry. It was her fault, really.

None of the other cadets asked a question, and when everyone had turned their test in, he packed up his things and went to his apartment.

He dumped the tests on the desk in his office and went to the bedroom. To his surprise, Claudia Endris sat on his bed, still furious.

"You were drunk."

"What? No."

"Don't lie to me. I've seen you drink more and more over the last couple months. Ever since you found out what the Clans are."

"So?"

"I care about you. I hate seeing you throw your life away."

Now I'm getting chastised by a nineteen-year-old.

"And don't look at me like I'm a little kid," she said. "I'm pretty sure we've done enough to scrub that thought out of your head."

He took off his shirt and threw it into the hamper, or at least close to it. "Why are you here?"

"I told you. I care about you. Despite your recent behavior."

"I don't need your pity."

"Perhaps you do. Perhaps you don't. But I'm pretty sure you need someone to talk to. Not just the ever-growing pile of empty whiskey bottles you hide under the bed."

"So, you want to know what's going on?"

"I *know* what's going on. I want *you* to know. I don't think you do. At least not really. I also don't think I can help you. You need someone who knows what they're doing. Not a hobby psychologist like me."

"I'm not going to see a shrink."

"I don't care who you see. For all I care, you can lay your sorrows down at the feet of a prostitute. From all I hear, they're good listeners, possibly even better than shrinks. But I need you to talk to *someone*."

She got up and went for the door. "Please," she said with sorrow in her voice before she left.

He looked at the bottle of whiskey in his hand. He hadn't even remembered picking it up before going into his bedroom. He took a sip, then a few more, put the bottle on his dresser, changed into something more casual, took a few more sips, and went out.

When he passed the flagpoles, he looked the other way and almost stumbled over a rock in the grass next to the walkway.

Who puts rocks on grass?

THE HIGH TIDE
AVALON CITY
NEW AVALON

Parish sat in his usual corner, sipping a beer and alternating between staring at a shot of whiskey and his noteputer as he ran the numbers for his people and their equipment on planet.

House Davion charged the Eridani Light Horse a maintenance fee even though on-planet Light Horse personnel kept their 'Mechs and other equipment running. He was pushing his case through the court system, but until it was resolved, he still had to pay.

Then there was the reduced pay for not being on the front lines. Not even listed as militias because of their teaching duties. This pay had been further reduced ever since October, which House Davion had explained was necessary, because now there wasn't even a chance the unit would see military engagements. He had asked his legal advisors if he could fight that part in the courts, but the chances they gave him were slim to none. Contrary to the maintenance fee, their reasoning was somewhat sound.

It's just another sleazy Company Store ploy. We all know it.

There was nothing he could do about it, though, and the Davions knew that.

He downed his glass of whiskey and ordered a new one.

Right now, he was bleeding C-bills. Not a lot, but enough to have him worried. At some point, he would have to either cut salaries or do what House Davion wanted him to do: sell them his unit's equipment, and then lease it back.

"Screw the Davions!" he said, not caring who heard him.

That was a mistake. The bar was filled with proud Federated Commonwealth soldiers.

"What did you just say?" The guy standing in front of Parish's corner was in his early twenties and wearing a neatly pressed dress uniform with the rank of subaltern.

This boy has never even seen combat, and was either unable to finish military academy in regular time or he's incapable of even reaching the rank of leftenant.

"You heard me just right!" Parish fired back.

"Say it again."

"Screw the Davions!" he proclaimed louder than before and pushed himself to his feet, having to steady himself when the bench he was sitting on didn't slide backward like he would have expected from a chair.

More heads turned his way, and the subaltern's face reddened. Then the boy threw a punch. Parish ducked away, a bit clumsily due to the alcohol and the fact that he was somewhat boxed in between bench and table. Parish tried to get out of the corner, and the next punch hit the side of his head.

His ears rang, but now he was out of the corner and returned the favor. His fist connected with the boy's jaw, making his head hit the pillar between two benches. To Parish's surprise, the subaltern stayed on his feet. Still, the hit must have jiggled his brains because the next punch was so clumsy, Parish didn't even have to duck away. Instead, he hit the boy again. This time he went down.

Before Parish could finish his work, another fist connected with his stomach. Thanks to the alcohol, he barely felt it, but it also took him too long to locate his new attacker. When he finally found her, the woman hit him with an uppercut, and he fell to the ground next to the stunned boy.

"Get your hands off my boyfriend!" the woman yelled at him. She was also wearing a dress uniform, but her patches identified her as a leftenant.

He kicked at her knees and felt his shoe connect. The woman crashed down and hit her nose and forehead on the side of his table. Blood spattered his face and clothes and began pooling on the floor under her.

Multiple hands grabbed Parish by his jacket and pulled him up. He was now ringed by multiple men and women, all with murder on their faces.

"Enough!" someone yelled, making them all turn toward the voice. "Let go of the asshole. I don't want any fights in my bar. He might be an asshole, but he didn't throw the first punch."

When nothing happened, Parish heard a shotgun being racked.

"I said. Let. Go. Of. The. Asshole!"

This time they let go of him, and he landed on his rear, sending numbed pain all the way up through his spine.

The barkeeper knelt beside Parish. He was a big man in his sixties with gray hair, lots of muscles, and a shotgun that looked almost like a toy in his hands.

"Those two idiots are going to pay your tab." He pointed toward Parish's two attackers, who were still lying on the floor. "But you're leaving and not coming back. Have I made myself clear?"

"Yes."

"Good. You're lucky I'm not like most military bar owners. But you must be stupid five ways to Sunday to say what you said in here. Either that, or you need help. Up to you which one you want it to be." He got back to his feet and turned around. "Now get the hell out before either of those two decide to follow you outside. I can't control what happens outside my bar."

It sounded like good advice, and Parish did as he was told.

**NEW AVALON
20 JUNE 3052**

When Parish woke up, his back hurt from lying on a metal bench, his head felt like someone had hit it with three PPCs, his mouth tasted like ten weeks in a cockpit, and he had absolutely no idea where he was.

He tried to sit up, which led to two more PPCs hitting his head. Opening his eyes did the same. Before he could register where he was, he threw up. He couldn't turn on his side quick enough, so some of the vomit landed on himself.

Real PPCs would have been better.

Three sides of his accommodations were made of gray plaster walls. One of them had a small, barred window. The fourth side was made up of metal bars.

Not again…

He tried to remember what had gotten him here but couldn't. His brain hurt.

On the plus side, I've never seen this cell before.

With some luck, he could bribe his way out. That had worked so far. None of his jail cell mornings had ended up in his file.

At least not one I can access. He was sure the Davions kept another private file about him.

Parish tried to get up, but the world around him spun, so he decided it would be better to fall back on his bench.

He heard a lock turn loudly, then turn again, and an even louder door was opened. Each of those sounds sent another PPC through his ears, directly into his brain.

Major Madeleine Rose, New Avalon's liaison officer for the Light Horse, came into view, and all his hopes for getting out of this shattered immediately. He didn't dare get up again, but instead saluted her from a sitting position.

"Captain Parish..." Her voice was not angry but carried disappointment, making him feel like a six-year-old. "I hope your behavior last night is not a reflection of the proud Eridani Light Horse Regiment in general."

"No, ma'am! It is not," he said between clenched teeth.

"Good. So far I have turned a blind eye to your behavior." *So much for them not having found out.* "But if you continue down this path, bribery will not help you much longer."

She was still not angry, but kept her disappointed-mom voice going. It was working far better on him than anger ever could.

"Yes, ma'am!"

"Very good." She pulled over a chair and sat down. "Now. You have two possible solutions here. One, this incident and quite a few more go on the record..." She paused. Even with his headache, he knew what was coming, though. "Two, we forget about all of this, and you withdraw your legal challenge to the maintenance fee."

She got up. "I expect an answer in the afternoon, an hour after the police let you out. Don't make me wait."

He could've thrown quite a few snarky remarks at her, but even in his hungover state, he was not stupid enough to utter them out loud. Still, mental images of him grinding her to a pulp under the foot of his 'Mech made him smile.

When he was back in his office, he sat down and started thinking. Major Rose had backed him into a corner and she knew it. He could either withdraw the lawsuit or flush his career down the crapper.

She's trying to destroy me!

No, you *did this to yourself. She's just using the weapons you gave her.*

I didn't give her anything. She *prepared an ambush.* She *probably paid the ones who attacked me in the bar.* She *has been waiting for the right moment. She must have known for months...*

While he grew more furious with every new thought, his mind came to a dead stop at the last. *She's known for* months!

He dialed her number, but to his surprise, he only got an answering machine. That just made him even more furious.

"You want a fight?" he started after the beep. "You can have a fight. I will not back down. I will come at you. Personally. You want to take me down? I will take you with me. You think you have something to blackmail me with? Something you have been hiding from your superiors for months? What else might you be hiding from them? Do you think they will be happy with you keeping something from them? You come at me, and we will both go down. But you will *never* get the Eridani Light Horse to withdraw from a fight. *We* are the true descendants of the Star League. We will fight this battle.

"I will rather die than let my unit suffer."

After he hung up, he took an expensive half-empty bottle of whiskey out of his desk drawer and emptied it without putting it down. Then he went out for a walk.

He went around the compound and out the back, so he wouldn't have to pass the flagpoles. Someone kept putting rocks on the grass.

**LECTURE HALL 22, COLLEGE OF MILITARY SCIENCE
NEW AVALON INSTITUTE OF SCIENCE
NEW AVALON
CRUCIS MARCH
FEDERATED COMMONWEALTH
7 OCTOBER 3052**

Parish looked at the cadets in front of him. These were the ones who hadn't passed the exam last semester, and were now trying to make up for it by taking a block course during their summer vacation. The whole semester crammed into four weeks of nonstop lectures and seminars.

Because almost half his students hadn't passed the test, the NAIS was blaming it all on him. *Why is it my fault? If I forget something, they should notice and not just sit there*—so now he had to make up for it.

What the last semester had been missing was a student like Claudia Endris. She had made valedictorian, and was currently pondering which unit she would join. She had gotten quite a few offers from premier regiments, but had not decided on one yet.

He drank his Irish coffee and looked at the cadets in front of him. They were all looking at the papers in front of them, thinking about the problem he had presented them.

To avoid the NAIS putting more pressure on him, Claudia had demanded she prepare his classes and everything he handed to the students. In exchange, he'd promised to see a psychiatrist. She had made it clear she would have been out of the door and out of his life, had he dared to refuse. He had not.

One of the students raised his hand.

"Yes?"

"Professor, I..." He was clearly afraid to speak up. Parish's temper had become legend in the NAIS, but he had also promised Claudia he'd ease up on the cadets.

"Come on, I don't have all day." He tried not to be angry, but it didn't work completely. *One of you guys is reporting back to Claudia. I know she has friends in here.*

"The situation in front of us is unsolvable."

"Why do you think that?"

The problem on their noteputers presented a basic situation, and depending on what answers the students chose, they would get different situations with different questions as a response to it until the situation was resolved.

"Our patrol lance receives a distress call from civilians within enemy territory. Obviously being attacked by pirates who tried to cash in on the conflict."

"Go on."

"We then have four choices. First, ignore the distress call, because we think it is a trap. Which will get us demoted when we get back to base. Second, we call for help, but that help will be twenty minutes out. When they arrive and we finally engage, the civilians are all dead and the pirates are gone. We won't get demoted, but we will still get chewed out and have to live with dead civilians on our conscience. Three, we send in a scout to find out what's going on. And finally, four, we run in blindly to take out the pirates."

Parish had put down his mug and was now listening closely. "You have established the basic situation. Go on."

"If we choose option three, the scouts will find a beat-up pirate lance we can take out easily. But when the rest of our lance arrives, Draconis Combine units will emerge from hiding and kill us all. The same happens when we barge in without a scout."

"That is correct."

"Why?"

Now he was annoyed, and emptied his mug before answering. "What do you mean, 'why'?"

"It is not fair."

"*Fair?*" He was yelling now. "*Fair?*! Boy, this is a wartime scenario. And you are demanding *fair*? War is not fair. If you want *fair*, you should go back home and start training for the games on Solaris. There is no *fair* in war."

"But—"

"No 'but.'" With an effort, Parish calmed down a bit. "If...*if* you ever get to command a lance, you will run into situations that have *no* good response. Whatever you choose, someone will *die*. And it could be you, your comrades, or civilians. *Fair* is for games."

Another cadet was raising his hand.

"Yes?"

"Why is there no fifth solution?"

"What would that solution be?"

"Send in a scout, but also call for reinforcements because we see a potential trap."

Ah, someone got it. "It's not there because I wanted someone to come up with it by themself."

Claudia had set up the problem, so that had been her idea, but he couldn't tell the cadet that.

"How would it end, in that case?"

"Impossible to say. But I am open to ideas."

Now he was having fun. The cadets came up with quite a few ideas how the situation would develop from there. Parish refilled his mug, but only twice.

Back in his office he went over the final exam he would present to his students tomorrow. A fresh bottle of whiskey next to his keyboard.

Claudia wasn't there, but when he was finished with the last tweaks to the exam she had prepared, he looked at his messages. There were two. One was from earlier in the day when he was in class. It was from Brevet General Ariana Winston. The other one was from Claudia, marked important. He picked up the whiskey bottle and read her message first.

> *Maxwell,*
>
> *I'm off to pack my things, because I will ship off-planet in a couple days, and I need to get everything in order.*
>
> *I have narrowed my choices down to two units I would like to join. The decision is in your hands, if you will.*
>
> *One of them is the First Davion Guards. They have a slot open, and their offer is more than generous for someone fresh out of the academy.*
>
> *The other one is not an offer, but an unsolicited application I am hereby presenting to you. I would like to join the Seventy-First Light Horse regiment and serve under your command. I know you have an open spot in your company, and I also know you will be shipping to the front lines very soon.*
>
> *This also means I have to apologize. When I prepared my application to the First Davion Guards earlier today, you received a message from Brevet General Ariana Winston. I read it.*
>
> *I don't want you to go to war without me. I hope I can be honest with you, but without me I am afraid you will drink more and more and get yourself and the people under your command killed. With me there, I hope I can help you.*

But perhaps I won't be needed, because I'm pretty sure the brevet general's message will help you, too.

No matter what, I want to be at the front lines. I want to beat Kerensky's Clans—and I would prefer to do it with you.

Attached you will find a full application, even though I know you won't need it to make up your mind.

Please send me your answer the moment you have made a decision.

Yours,
Claudia

He sat there for a few minutes and just stared at the screen. The bottle of whiskey that was halfway to his mouth hung in midair.

She...we... We are moving to the front lines?

The reply he sent her was short:

Yes!

Then he opened the brevet general's message. The bottle of whiskey was set back on the table.

When he finished reading, he grabbed the bottle and went outside. Captain Maxwell Parish stopped in front of the flagpoles and stared at them.

"Time to grab them by the short hairs and twist!" he declared with a strength he had forgotten he possessed.

Then he threw the full bottle of whiskey at the empty flagpole, shattering the glass and spilling its contents on the ground.

VIEW FROM THE GROUND

ALAN BRUNDAGE

BASE STOCKADE, FORT WINSTON
DIERON
DIERON MILITARY DISTRICT
DRACONIS COMBINE
28 OCTOBER 3061

A steady and irritating *ting-ting-ting* brought with it a reluctant return to consciousness. Lisette Swann, sergeant in the Eridani Light Horse, rolled over on the narrow, uncomfortable cot. Swiping unruly brown locks out of her face, she looked toward the bars of her cell. Her hangover-blurred vision made out the short, slim form of Tanon Ino, her fellow sergeant, standing in the doorway. Even back during their training days at Fort Telemar on Kikuyu, he'd always been disgustingly prim, pressed, and sober. She suspected he'd been born that way. He seemed to take it as a point of pride. His knowing smirk wasn't helping either.

"Busy night, I see," he quipped, continuing to tap his stylus on the bars.

Lisette levered herself into a sitting position and swayed unsteadily for a second. "You could say that. It was fun, though I don't think I'll try it again. You getting me out of here?"

"I might be." He narrowed his eyes. "What kicked everything off this time?"

"There was a slight...difference of opinion."

Tanon's eyebrows slowly crept up his forehead. "Seriously? A 'difference of opinion' is what you're going with?" He looked pointedly around the cell. It wasn't the first time they'd been here during their long friendship.

Lisette leaned back and expelled an exasperated sigh. "Fine, I know the drill. I was angry, per usual. I was also…kinda drunk. Which I suppose is also per usual these days. I hit on a guy who wasn't interested, then hit on his girlfriend who was. Guy took exception to that and tried to get me to leave, I declined, he took a swing at me, and so I hit him with a barstool. Bar fight ensued, wacky shenanigans, and I guess the Snakes' 'Friendly Persuaders' took exception, so here I am."

Tanon winced when she called them Snakes, but was otherwise silent for a moment. The Light Horse were guests on a Combine world after all, practically permanent residents, according to the rumor mill. "That's not exactly how it went down. Officially, no one knows about the fight. You got thrown in here because you puked on the gate guard's boots when you got back to base. Nice boots, he was quite upset. I had to give him my next day pass to calm him down. He figured you could sleep it off in here, and I wasn't going to argue. This time."

"My luck strikes again." She rose to her feet, only swaying a little. "Can we get out of here then?"

Nodding, Tanon slid the door open. "Yeah, but we *will* talk about this later."

Pouncing up from the cot, Lisette raced over and rubbed his cheeks affectionately. "You're my best friend ever!"

"I'm your only friend," he countered dryly, pushing her away.

"It's too early to logic me. C'mon." She grabbed his arm and exited the building with a quick wave to the guard.

"Don't do that," Tanon said with a pleading edge to his voice.

She sighed. "Fine."

"In the meantime, we've got to get you presentable. In case you've forgotten, we've been assigned a lance, and the lieutenant wants a meet and greet today."

BARRACKS COMPLEX, FORT WINSTON
DIERON

To say Fort Winston needed some work was an understatement. Although technically it was a part of the Fortress Dieron complex, it had been virtually abandoned in the centuries after the Exodus, and there were many areas where that neglect showed. Luckily, the above-average technical staff of the Eridani Light Horse, with some support from local Dieronese contractors, was making excellent headway in transforming the place from a historical curiosity into a functional base of operations. There was still much left to accomplish, with some estimating it might be years before the base would approach full operation, but the progress so far had been remarkable.

Ground cars, as with so much else, were in short supply, so Lisette and Tanon were forced to cross the complex on foot, which was just as well. Supply shipments from all the Second Star League signatory states clogged the streets, creating congestion and confusion as the different labels and languages were sorted. Thankfully, Lisette wasn't suffering from a lengthy hangover, and the walk was even helping to clear her head.

Like most Light Horse members, she had her own quarters, thanks to the extreme size of Fort Winston, which had been designed to house a force much larger than the present-day Light Horse. The small rooms were private and functional, containing a simple bed, a desk, a small table, and a chair. Hers had virtually nothing for decoration, just a full technical poster of an *Owens* OmniMech—the 'Mech of her dreams—and a picture of her adoptive parents from back in '58, before they'd shipped out with Task Force Serpent. Neither had returned from that mission, their deaths just two more logs in the fire of resurrecting the Star League, leaving her to carry on the family legacy alone. Fairly or not, she resented them a bit for dying with so many others Light Horse members. The losses had left the survivors confused, broken, and in desperate need of bodies for the ranks. The Light Horse had always brought in outsiders, but for the first time, new blood nearly outweighed the old.

She pushed such morbid thoughts aside and quickly got ready. Hastily donning a relatively wrinkle-free, olive-drab duty uniform, she moved to the mirror, tied her hair back into a ponytail, and checked her face for dirt. The face in the mirror was young, freckled, dark-eyed, and starting to bruise, but should pass muster for today. She nodded with satisfaction and left her quarters.

Tanon was waiting for her outside, reading something on his noteputer. He tucked it away and gave her a cursory inspection. "A tad better at least. Let's go. Don't want to be late, do we?"

She rolled her eyes, but followed his lead.

ERIDANI LIGHT HORSE COMMAND AND CONTROL
FORT WINSTON
DIERON

To enter the command complex, they needed to pass several checkpoints, all of which required different levels of identification, both high- and low-tech, and took an obscene amount of time to pass through. Between those checkpoints were kilometer upon kilometer of reinforced stone-and-ferrocrete halls, following a slightly rounded, maze-like pattern. Lisette and Tanon passed through all of this just to end up in an unimpressively generic conference room. It was amazing how the bureaucratic thinking for some things never changed.

Grabbing a coffee and some kind of scone from the side table, she took stock of her surroundings. The room was dominated by a faux-wood table, shiny new and locally made, from the looks of the pattern on it. A wall-mounted flatscreen display, not quite top of the line but sufficient for smaller briefings like this one, dominated one wall. The opposite wall held two portraits: one of Chancellor and First Lord Sun-Tzu Liao, and one of General Edwin Amis, commander of the Eridani Light Horse. Elevated above both was the Cameron Star, the symbol of the Star League. The new Cameron Star looked somehow sharper than the one she'd seen in records, like it was ready to draw its share of blood before it could be comfortably blunted.

She spun her chair around for a few rotations, her head draped over the backrest, taking note of the two doors and the position of the two men in the room with her. Tanon was ensconced in his noteputer again, reviewing some kind of new weapon specs. Not for the first time she thought he would have been happier as a tech.

The other man was laser-focused on the Star League symbol on the wall, like he was trying to sear it into his retinas. He was muscular, but not overly so, and sat rigidly in his chair. His skin shone like polished teak. His hair was styled into a short, yellow crest on his head, leaving his temples clear for access to a neurohelmet. He flicked vivid green eyes her way briefly before dismissing her.

She was just gathering herself to pester the idiot when the door opened and the new lieutenant entered. A fit woman, older than everyone else in the room, clad in cleanly pressed duty attire. *Maybe she and Tanon can bond over that.* Her dark hair was cut short, forgoing the usual buzzed temples most MechWarriors favored. She glanced around the room, taking note of everyone, lingering specifically on Lisette.

"I'm glad to see everyone found the room with no problem," she began in a rich contralto. "I'm Lieutenant Natalya Mah, your new lance commander. I know the three of you have been waiting for assignments for quite a while, trapped in the amber of reorganizational paperwork, as it were. As of today, consider yourselves officially members of the Nineteenth Cavalry Regiment. We'll join them on their next deployment once Training Command certifies us as active."

Lisette snapped her eyes over to Tanon, who looked even more shocked than she felt.

"I see some of you know what that means, the honor it conveys. Now, I've reviewed your records. You're all exceptional in some way—if a little rough around the edges—which is why you're part of my recon lance. 'Mech assignments were jumbled in the preparations for the Milos operation, so I've taken the opportunity to reassign you replacements." She glanced at her own noteputer. "Sergeant Ino, you're getting a *Wasp*. Corporal Razan—" she peered at the yellow-haired man, "—I don't have a *Dasher* for you, but there is a *Clint* available. It should suit your skill set. And Sergeant Swann—" she pivoted to Lisette, "—you've been assigned a *Jenner*."

"I want to apologize in advance. None of these 'Mechs are quite what you're used to, but they're serviceable, and will be upgraded as new equipment becomes available. Familiarize yourself with them; we have a training exercise against Bravo's recon lance next week. And before you ask, they're in the same boat as us."

Mah snagged a chair of her own and sat. "But for now, let's get to know one another a little better. Don't worry, I'm not asking for detailed histories, just a sense of who you are. I'll even take pity on you and go first. I'm from the Federated Commonwealth, back when that was a thing that mattered. No history of military service in the family, it just seemed the right thing to do. I spent most of my service in St. Ives before being stationed on the Clan border, where I earned my spurs in raids into the Clans' occupation zones. When the call came that the Star League was re-formed and in need of troops, I jumped at the opportunity. And here I am."

An uncomfortably long silence passed before Tanon sighed, then spoke. "My, uh, my family has been a part of the Light Horse since the days of the Star League...the first one, that is. Not always as MechWarriors, though. We've had people in every branch of service, serving where our abilities mattered, always trying to honor the ideals of the League. I'm fulfilling tradition, sure, but it's also a chance to see the galaxy and maybe do some good in the process."

Razan rolled his head around on his shoulders, looking bored. "I am Razan, formerly of Clan Jade Falcon. I was taken bondsman seven years ago, when my Trinary raided Kikuyu. Since that time, I have provided intelligence and worked as a technician. I have only recently earned my right to be a warrior once more. Raised within the tradition of the Clans, I dreamed of one day resurrecting the Star League. Now that a Star League has been reformed, my blood tells me to serve, and I am most curious to see where it leads."

That left only Lisette. "I'm an orphan of the War of '39. As far as anyone can tell, my family was killed by Combine forces. No other relatives could be found, so the Swanns took pity on me and adopted me. The Light Horse has been the only life I've ever known. Being a MechWarrior and living up to the ideals of the Star League are all I've ever wanted, so I enlisted. The new Star League demanded the blood of my parents and thousands of others on Huntress, to wipe out an enemy to make a point. We accomplished that, but the first Star League stood for more than victory. It stood for hope and greatness, for peace. This new League…I don't know what it stands for, at least not yet… I don't know where the Light Horse fits in anymore either."

The lieutenant looked around the table. "Well, this is certainly going to be interesting."

**BATTLEMECH HANGARS, FORT WINSTON
DIERON
DIERON MILITARY DISTRICT
DRACONIS COMBINE
29 OCTOBER 3061**

The scent of ozone filled the air, wafting up to dissipate in the high ceilings of the hangars. Sparks shot out in all directions, accompanied by the sounds of heavy equipment moving around, and the shouting of techs.

Lisette dodged around a pair of said techs working on what looked to be a disassembled gyro. Continuing on led her past a dozen BattleMechs in various stages of repair, which made sense, given that the Milos mission had required swapping out some of the more damaged machines for those ready to go. Her own *Stinger*, for example, had been shipped off to the 151st.

At last, she reached her assigned berth and looked up, ready to be underwhelmed. She was not disappointed.

The *Jenner* was a Draconis Combine machine. Designed as the Star League was collapsing, it represented the failure of the ideals of the old League, at least to her. A light 'Mech built and deployed almost exclusively by the Draconis Combine Mustered Soldiery, it was second in ubiquitousness only to the *Panther*.

Lisette was intimately familiar with the *Jenner*, having studied it thoroughly back when the Combine was the enemy, and more recently because she might have to coordinate with DCMS forces as part of the Star League. This one was definitely old and worn by heavy use. Several of the armor plates were cracked or dented, but apparently not damaged enough to be replaced. A few old laser scars remained visible beneath the fresh coat of paint. The Nineteenth had opted to stick with olive drab, which had been hastily applied except for the right leg, which was still primer gray. The patterning of the armor plates made her think the leg might be a more recent vintage than the rest of it. The only marking on it was the Light Horse symbol of a prancing pony, painted high on the left thigh.

"Quite the looker, ain't it?"

Lisette jumped at the sudden voice beside her, whipping around to face a stocky older man in grease-smeared coveralls. He was chewing on a cigar and peering up at her through smudged goggles.

"It's...something, that's for sure," she offered cautiously.

The man chuckled. "No need to sugarcoat it. Ol' *Ramshackle* here will never win any beauty contests. That doesn't matter so long as she does the job." He stuck out his hand. "I'm Marius, by the way, and if you're Lisette Swann, then I'm your chief tech."

Taking his hand and shaking it firmly, Lisette turned back to the *Jenner*. "I am. Glad to meet you, Chief. I read my orders. They say this is a JR7-F model? Give me the rundown." She already knew most of what he would say, but it was a good bonding experience between tech and MechWarrior.

"Sure thing, ma'am. They didn't make these for very long, was something of an experiment, so it's been in storage for, oh, longer than was probably healthy. As you can see, we've had to completely replace the right leg. The internals were compromised, which is why this beast was in storage in the first place, but everything with the new leg tied in well enough, though expect a hiccup or two. Benefits of centuries of unchanged design," he added with a wink.

"I've taken the liberty of ordering some double-capacity heat sinks, but for now you're limited to singles. Shouldn't be an issue for training, but I'll get it converted as quickly as I can. That gives you more than enough heat dissipation to handle your quartet of medium lasers, which if you're very lucky, I can replace with the pulse variety.

"Now, this little beast was meant as a scout and raider, so they removed the short-range missile mount and used the excess space for armor. Nothing I can do about that right now, but I do have a fun idea or two for after we upgrade your armor and free up some space. Don't tell anyone, but we have a spare anti-missile system just sitting around…"

"As for the engine, it's in surprisingly good shape. It didn't require much beyond basic maintenance. I'm honestly surprised they didn't bother salvaging it for another 'Mech. It's got a bit of a rumble and an odd hitch now and then, but that's just this ol' beast ready to get back into action, know what I mean? Ready to head up and get calibrated?"

"You know it." Suiting action to word, Lisette climbed up the gantry and to the back of the *Jenner*'s domelike head. The hatch stood open already, and she ducked inside. The tang of dust, old sweat, blood, coolant, and heated electronics assailed her nose, not unexpected in a 'Mech as ancient as this. A few panels were still off, and a testing kit lay nearby. The walls were coated in a thin layer of soot and grime; only token efforts to clean them had been made. On a bulkhead to the right, someone had used a torch to burn ramshackle into the metal. She smiled, knowing a named 'Mech was a lucky 'Mech.

She headed forward and dropped into the pristine command couch. It had been replaced during the refit; the firmness of the padding alone told her that. Oddly, that firmness made it less comfortable. She wanted to be able to sink into the couch, to bond with all the previous pilots. Even though they were a collection of unknown Dracs, they were still MechWarriors, which made them siblings of a sort. She settled into the couch and pulled down the sleek new neurohelmet.

Leaning forward to examine the panel, she saw a new plastic overlay had been placed on the controls, all thankfully marked in Star League English. She hit the power switch to bring the fusion engine off standby. It rumbled to life with an unexpected kick. Her command screens booted up, briefly covered in the Japanese favored by the Combine before also switching to Star League English.

"*Please enter security code*," the computer asked in oddly off-key tones.

"The future is uncertain, the past forgotten." Her passcode accurately expressed her mood most days.

"*Authorized*."

A quick scan of her panels revealed nothing of concern, so she signaled a thumb-up to Marius down below.

"We've got your patterns from your records loaded in, so just let us know if anything feels strange." Marius' voice sounded tinny over the comm unit.

"Roger that," Lisette acknowledged. She leaned back in the couch and closed her eyes, letting the wave of vertigo pass over her. It was blessedly brief. She looked at her readouts. "I'm showing synchronization on my end. What about down there?"

"Looks good. Just a few more tests and we'll call it a day."

"A few more tests" turned out to be almost two hours of calibration, movement, and weapons checks, but it was worth it. In the end, she had a decent grasp of the 'Mech and its foibles. It was almost enough to make her forget her obsession with the *Owens*. Almost.

After unplugging and stowing the neurohelmet, she exited the cockpit and scrambled down the chain ladder, testing its worthiness in the process, and then stood, looking up at her new ride.

Marius came up beside her. "Nice job. I know *Ramshackle* is old, dinged up, and a little quirky, but she's all yours. Try to keep her in one piece, yeah?"

"I'll do my best, but no promises. We wouldn't want you to get bored, would we?" she replied with a sly grin.

**180 KM SOUTH OF MOUNT SHANYU,
　SCALES OF THE DRAGONET
DIERON
DIERON MILITARY DISTRICT
DRACONIS COMBINE
1 NOVEMBER 3061**

The day was clear and bright, the pale blue sky marred by only the faintest wisps of white clouds. Brilliant sunbeams shone down on the craggy peaks of the mountain range, giving life to the scrub and trees. Small clumps of snow still lay hidden, not yet melted by exposure to the sun. It was beautiful. Too bad Lisette couldn't really enjoy it.

She ran her tongue over teeth fuzzy from three days in the field, eyes firmly on her scanners as she trampled scrub and brush in her search for the last member of Bravo's recon lance.

"Hide and seek, they said. It'll be *fun*, they said," she muttered. "Three days on, it's not so much fun."

"Say again, Charlie Three," Razan's voice crackled over the radio. "Your transmission was garbled."

Eyes squeezed shut in embarrassment, Lisette replied, "Sorry, just talking to myself. I said I was enjoying the run."

"Hm. Perhaps you should focus on your duty. Charlie Four out."

That arrogant Clanner... But he had a point.

Sprinting her *Jenner* forward, Lisette came into range of a picturesque scene. There was a copse of trees, a glassy, smooth lake, and a massive outcropping of the mountain's stone. She slowed to a fraction of her speed, focusing her attention on the lake. If it were her, that's where she'd hide. It had total cover and was deep enough to provide free "coolant" to 'Mechs that waded in. She checked her lasers to make sure they were powered up at training levels, then kicked in some speed to approach, noticing a slight hitch in her gait.

It wasn't until she approached closer that she saw the cave in the mountainside—and more importantly the outline of a BattleMech crouched within. She picked up a sudden reactor spike, then a target lock. She reacted instantly, kicking in her jump jets, and soared clear across the lake, feathering her jets in midair to spin around and stay face to face with her opponent.

"Contact, grid Epsilon Twenty-Three!" she yelled into her mic.

The Bravo lance 'Mech, a *Battle Hawk*, came leaping out of the cave, firing its own powered-down medium lasers, then using its jump jets to close the distance. Lisette triggered her quartet of mediums, watching her heat spike. Only half her shots connected, but the simulated damage was reasonable.

The two light 'Mechs bounced around each other, strange insects engaged in an even stranger dance, jump jets flaring, lasers strobing. Lisette managed to score a shot that disabled the *Battle Hawk*'s anti-missile system, a victory that didn't really help her much in this fight, given her *Jenner*'s lack of missiles.

Whoever was in the *Battle Hawk* was good. Running down the side of the mountain, they still managed to land several shots, despite her *Jenner*'s own speed advantage. Lisette leaped, landed, then spun and leaped again, *Ramshackle*'s gyro, frame, and myomers groaning and straining to keep up with her commands. While she was in the air, the *Battle Hawk* landed a solid hit with its Streak SRM. Dirty white smoke erupted from the training charge, registering as head and torso damage on her schematic.

The hazy cloud of smoke briefly obscured her vision before her jets carried her clear. The *'Hawk* pilot realized her intention at the last minute and jetted sideways, leaving her *Jenner* to land unopposed in the space it had just occupied. She stumbled a bit upon landing, the ancient left leg sagging compared to the new one, but caught her balance just in time to ride out the impact of two more missiles. The computer registered them as having destroyed her two right-side lasers.

Grinding her teeth, Lisette spun and charged, her remaining lasers blazing, and readied herself to jump again. The *Battle Hawk* pilot saw her charge, snapped off a shot with their trio of lasers, then tried to bolt, jumping left. Lisette pounced, soaring through to air, low-powered lasers peppering the opposing 'Mech, before her superior speed carried her forward to slam into the *Battle Hawk*.

The impact pitched her forward in her harness as both machines smashed to the ground, registering real damage this time. She felt blood trickle down her face; looking forward, she saw the fracture in the ferroglass had worsened, sending splinters ricocheting around the cockpit.

She managed to lever *Ramshackle* back to its feet and turned to examine her foe. The *Battle Hawk* was also standing back up, so she triggered her remaining lasers again and again, concentrating on its left leg, ignoring her heat warnings until finally the battle computer registered the *Battle Hawk*'s leg as destroyed and the exercise complete.

"That stunt was completely uncalled for, Swann!" Lieutenant Mah shouted at Lisette. "You almost cost us the exercise, not to mention the potential injury to yourself and the MechWarrior from Bravo. What were you thinking?"

Lisette stood at attention, enduring Mah's tirade while Tanon and Razan observed from the sidelines.

"Ma'am, I was thinking about victory. I knew I needed to keep the *Battle Hawk* in place. I'd already signaled Razan of my location, so even if the *'Hawk* managed to take me out, Razan would be able to finish the job."

"It was needlessly reckless for a training exercise," Mah ground out.

"Perhaps," Razan said unexpectedly, "but it did secure our victory. Results matter."

"To an extent. In the field, her actions probably would have gotten her killed. On top of that, what if intel had been wrong? The rest of the lance could then have been facing unknown odds with depleted numbers. The Eridani Light Horse doesn't need more dead heroes, Swann. I thought you would have figured that out by now."

Lisette paled, thinking about her parents. "What's that supposed to mean?"

Mah shook her head slowly. "That's not what this is about." Somehow, she knew what Lisette had referred to. "It's about your inability to be a team player. If you'd waited for Razan, the two of you would have taken down that *Battle Hawk* together *and* remained viable combatants."

Mah was about to continue when her comm piped up with an emergency signal. She pointed at Lisette to stay put, then grabbed her headset and stepped aside. She spoke quietly, then stiffened at whatever reply she received. A mumbled back and forth ensued before Mah returned, looking grim.

"A civilian passenger DropShip has encountered an emergency on approach, suffering near-total drive failure. They've gone down somewhere southwest of Newbury, in sector J16. The ship itself has been found, but several escape pods were launched and have disappeared, no transponders. We're close enough to be re-tasked as part of the search and rescue effort. Saddle up! There's people to rescue. Everything else can wait."

**712 KM SOUTH OF MOUNT SHANYU,
    SCALES OF THE DRAGONET
DIERON
DIERON MILITARY DISTRICT
DRACONIS COMBINE
2 NOVEMBER 3061**

The rolling gait of the *Jenner* chewed up the terrain as Lisette kept it moving at top speed. Her comm systems were wide open, searching for any sign of the escape pod's emergency beacon. Her eyes scanned the horizon for smoke, but there was only clear sky.

She signaled the rest of the lance. "Grid Theta-Four clear, moving on to Theta-Five."

Mah sounded distracted as she replied, "Acknowledged, Charlie Three. Be aware, Newbury Search and Rescue is now on scene to assist. If you find any pods, signal them for an immediate assist."

"Roger that, Lieutenant."

Lisette clicked off and resumed her search pattern. She was entering a region of uneven terrain, crevasses, canyons, and random stone spires. The magnetic properties of the rocks caused shadows and glitches on her scanners and interfered with her comms. She slowed her speed, both to get a more thorough scan and to avoid accidentally shattering the legs of her 'Mech.

An hour of hard searching left her ready to proceed onward when she detected a faint signal. She tried narrowing it down, running through the different channels. It seemed to be the right pattern, but the interference made it difficult to tell.

"Charlie actual, this is Charlie Three. I might have something here."

She was answered by nothing but static.

"Charlie actual, this is Charlie Three, over."

Still nothing.

It was more important to find the pod first, so she continued.

Trial and error eventually led her to a crevasse she'd passed a half-dozen times already. The signal seemed to be coming from down inside it.

Maneuvering ever so carefully, she halted the *Jenner* right at the edge and scanned down. Sure enough, there was the pod, wedged precariously into a fissure whose depth she could only guess at. She had no idea how to get them out.

She was still brainstorming when Razan's *Clint* jetted in, unexpectedly landing beside her. "Lisette! The lieutenant has been trying to reach you for a status report."

She would never let him know how much she'd jumped when his voice barked out of her speakers. Calmly, she replied, "Status report is that I've found a pod. I'm just in the process of figuring out how to extract it."

"We should wait for search and rescue. They have the necessary equipment."

"Or we could try something now. How deep do you think that is?"

There was a pause before he answered. "Several dozen meters at least. Why?"

She felt the spark of imagination. "I'm just spitballing here, but do you think you could shimmy your *Clint* down under them and use your jump jets to give them a boost?"

Razan's reply came after a hesitation. "I could, but only if there is no other choice. My 'Mech has only one hand, and the weight will likely exceed my lift capability. Waiting would be safer for the occupants. Is the pod in imminent danger?"

Lisette frowned. "No, but it would be faster. We could beat the search and rescue teams, save them some time. We're already here."

"Is not the purpose of having experts to utilize them when their expertise is required? I am a skilled warrior, but I believe this operation is better left to those experts."

Lisette couldn't believe a Clanner, of all people, was recommending the safe play. "I thought you Clan types were all about the glory?"

"*Aff*, that is often true. But we also act for the greater good and strive to limit civilian casualties. I believe Lieutenant Mah would call that being a 'team player,' *quiaff?*"

She sighed and couldn't help feeling a little deflated, even knowing it was the right call. "All right, you get clear of the interference and signal for the search and rescue teams. I'll stay here just in case anything changes."

"*Aff.* You have made a wise decision today. Unexpected, but wise."

"Don't get used to it." The words were out of her mouth before she could even think to stop them, so she was surprised when he chuckled.

"I would not think of it. I shall return shortly."

The search and rescue team arrived in the form of a heavy lift VTOL and a smaller ambulance VTOL. The expert crews were able to latch on to the pod easily and safely, managing to retrieve the occupants less than two hours after Lisette had located them. Overall, it was a better idea than her "squeeze a 'Mech under the pod and fire the jump jets" plan.

The survivors, tourists from the Combine periphery, thanked her profusely. Lisette wasn't quite sure how to react, so she settled on smiling and nodding. It seemed to work.

At some point Lieutenant Mah arrived. "Give me more good work like today, rather than yesterday's display, and you may find yourself getting some actual commendations in your record for a change."

Damn, but that simple praise felt good.

Mah clapped Lisette on the shoulder. "We're done here. Between us, Bravo, volunteers, and search and rescue, all pods have been accounted for. We'll return to base, and you can all have a few days off. To decompress."

"Yes, ma'am. Thank you, ma'am."

**PARADE GROUNDS, FORT WINSTON
DIERON
DIERON MILITARY DISTRICT
DRACONIS COMBINE
5 NOVEMBER 3061**

The men and women of the Eridani Light Horse, at least those not occupied with unavoidable duty, had gathered on the parade grounds. It was controlled chaos, no real formation, nor was there supposed to be.

Lisette stood with Razan, who had surprised her by expressing a desire to attend. "Why come this year?" she asked. "Why not before?"

He paused, collecting his thoughts before answering. "It is the first year after my return to warrior status. It did not feel proper to celebrate alone. Today—Exodus Day—is one of the few holidays our people share. We may honor Aleksandr Kerensky's legacy in different ways, and for different reasons, but we both honor him all the same. If we are to truly be the Star League reborn, we must find that which binds us together, such as this day, not that which divides us."

Lisette blinked in shock. "I think that's the most I've ever heard you say at one time."

"Please do not mock me on this hallowed occasion," he answered with what sounded like genuine exasperation.

"Fine, I'll save it for tomorrow."

"Bargained well and done." Razan may even have smiled a bit.

A collected hush fell over the crowd as Major Gregory Ostroff of the Training Command took up position by the flagstaffs, ordering the Light Horse flag to half-mast, and the Star League flag removed with honors. He then read out Colonel Bradley's final message to General Kerensky. As the ceremony ended and the last words of hope were recited, the gathered crowd watched as the Light Horse banner was run back up to full-staff and the Star League banner returned to pride of place as well, fluttering high above in the wind of Dieron.

"That was a moving ceremony," Razan said. "Before this, I had only ever read Colonel Bradley's words, never heard them spoken. Powerful." He looked thoughtful.

Lisette hesitated before turning to him. "This ceremony is one of my earliest memories. My parents would bring me with them, to instill a sense of history in me. But now... Now I wonder. Should we still be mourning the Star League? It's back, forged anew. Can you still feel the loss of something you currently serve? Something that's right in front of you?"

Razan pursed his lips and looked up at the Star League pennant. "I do not know. You feel the loss of the Star League as something personal, twined with the loss of your...parents." He stumbled over the unfamiliar concept. "*The Remembrance* taught us the history of the Star League, not the emotion. Each Clan emphasizes the importance of resurrecting the Star League. It was only during my time here in the Inner Sphere that I realized we did not know what to do should we ever succeed." He took a deep breath. "Should we mourn it? *Aff*, lest we forget the past. But we should also celebrate its rebirth."

"Wise words," she whispered.

"Do not get used to it."

SWIFT IZAKAYA, ALDINGA
DIERON
DIERON MILITARY DISTRICT
DRACONIS COMBINE
6 NOVEMBER 3061

Lisette sat at a small table with Tanon and Razan. She looked at both of them, and the sea of faces around her, content. A thick but pleasant fog filled the *izakaya*—a particularly Combine flavor of pub—a mixed aroma from cooking food, spices, smoke, and drinks. Soft lights enhanced the mood, illuminating the bar but leaving the tables dim. The noise level was high but celebratory.

The local newscast was on a loop, showing nothing but the scene of Theodore Kurita being elected First Lord of the Star League. "*And welcome your new First Lord, Coordinator Theodore Kurita!*" the announcer declared again, to loud cheers in the crowded restaurant. On screen, Theodore bowed as he acknowledged the honor bestowed on him with his typical poise and grace. The Dieronese were ecstatic, and showed no signs of slowing down.

"He'll do a great job," Tanon opined, just barely audible over the din of the crowd. He was sipping something Razan called a fusionnaire.

Lisette took a slug of her own drink, a local brand of sake the *izakaya* owner swore by. "It'd be hard for him to do worse than Sun-Tzu using the Star League Defense Force to reclaim his lost worlds. Here's to a peaceful three years!" She raised her drink in salute.

"Hear, hear!" agreed Tanon.

Razan merely lifted his glass in acknowledgment.

Lieutenant Mah returned to the table with another round of drinks and a platter of finger foods for the table. "These are all compliments of the house, apparently."

That got a rowdy approval from the table. Even Razan seemed to be loosening up and enjoying himself, something Lisette had once thought impossible.

Spinning her two cups, she smiled at the table and nodded to Razan. "But you know, today—yesterday now, I guess—is special for other reasons. It's Exodus Day. I know times have changed. We know what happened to Kerensky after he left for the dark. And we have a Star League again. I think, maybe, it's time for us to stop focusing on the losses of the past. To take time to reflect on what has been, on what's been lost, but also to look toward the future. A future where a war orphan raised by mercenaries works together with a Clanner, not to kill, but to save the lives of their traditional enemies. That's a future I want to work toward. That's what *this* Star League can be."

She looked around at her lance, who were all nodding in agreement. She raised her glass.

"To a better tomorrow!"

BATTLE HAWK
LIGHT—30 TONS

CLINT
MEDIUM—40 TONS

JENNER
Light—35 tons

NO DUST, NO WEAR

JASON HANSA

**STAR LEAGUE DEFENSE FORCE ENCLAVE
LOOTERA
HUNTRESS
CLAN HOMEWORLDS
14 DECEMBER 3067**

Colonel Sandra Barclay rubbed her eyes, ran a hand through her bobbed brown hair, and then asked, "Say again, Lieutenant Young?"

Barclay, commander of the Seventy-First Light Horse Regiment, Eridani Light Horse Brigade, Star League Defense Force, had paused her review of increasingly gloomy logistical reports at her aide's call. The Light Horse was receiving at least one Trial of Possession challenge a day from four of the five Clans on-planet, usually for personnel or equipment. The personnel they could sometimes replace, but the equipment was already getting difficult to repair, and replacing it was next to impossible.

She hated these combat trials, and it was getting harder and harder to pretend otherwise. Colonel Antonescu—commander of her sister regiment, the 151st—had warned her during their changeover that if her unit proved themselves in the first month or so, the trials would slow down. If they didn't, or if she blew the challengers off, it would be almost impossible to be taken seriously at the Star League embassy, or to even purchase foodstuffs from the local markets. Combat trials were required to survive in Clan space—but she wasn't required to like them.

Barclay was in her mid-forties and almost two meters tall, lanky, and kept fit through a regime of regular exercise and BattleMech piloting, and surviving on mostly coffee while at the office. Her office was relatively spartan, a room just big enough for her desk, some chairs for visitors, and some shelves she kept knickknacks and memorabilia on. Lieutenant Young had recently set up a few strands of Christmas lights on the shelves, and put up a small, one-meter-tall Christmas tree in the corner that was gaining a small spread of gifts to and from her senior leaders.

Instead of the intercom activating, a figure barely 160 centimeters tall walked into the office. Ebony-skinned and bald, Lieutenant Young was a communications expert that served as her aide in her command lance.

"There's a pair of Goliath Scorpions out here, and the leader says it's not about a trial," he said quietly. "One's in their version of a daily uniform, and seems to be a logistician? But the other? He's...something," he finished with a nervous titter.

Barclay's eyebrow rose. *What's this, then?* "Send them in, Lieutenant, and put some coffee on."

"Roger, ma'am, and a fresh pot just brewed," Young replied.

A few seconds later, the two men entered her office. The rearward man was as Young described: middle-aged, moderately athletic, and wearing a flowing gray shirt over black pants and calf-high black boots. But the lead warrior was in what she recognized as the Scorpion field uniform: black pants tucked into stiff, black knee-high boots, an armored black tunic over a dark gray top, a pair of wickedly curved knives tucked into sheaths on the belt, and a hooded black mask that left only the warrior's eyes visible.

With deliberate movements, the warrior removed the hood, and she could see he was about thirty, handsome, and possessed the calm look of an experienced veteran.

"Colonel Barclay, I am Star Commander Nerran of the Crimson Seeker Star, Clan Goliath Scorpion. This is Merchant Factor Palos, and on behalf of my Khan, I thank you for seeing me on such short notice."

She nodded. "Welcome, and please sit, gentlemen. This is my aide, Lieutenant Pascal Young. Would you like some coffee?"

Both Palos and Nerran accepted, and Sandra passed over her half-full cup for a refill.

As Young left, Nerran steepled his fingers and said, "Colonel, may I first begin by apologizing if I have given offense. My Khan would never offer such disrespect as sending one of my rank to parley with you. My mission was to meet an officer of equivalent rank and set up a future meeting—I was not expecting your aide to show me directly in."

Barclay smiled. "No disrespect assumed or taken, Star Commander."

As Nerran nodded his thanks, Young walked back in carrying a tray and three coffee cups. After distributing the drinks, he took a seat in the corner and pulled out his noteputer.

Sandra continued, "Since you said 'parley,' Star Commander, I take it you're not here to declare a trial like the other Clans?"

Nerran shook his head. "My Khan sent me here to open a dialogue between your unit and our Clan. She believes we have a lot to offer each other, and suggests discussion and cooperation would gain us both more than a constant series of trials." While she considered his words, he sipped his coffee, and raised an eyebrow. "This is quite good, Colonel."

Sandra smiled. "If your Khan is after my coffee, Star Commander, I immediately bid everything I have to defend it. Good coffee's harder to replace than BattleMechs."

Both Scorpions laughed, Nerran's a deep, genuine one.

Sandra leaned back, sipped her own coffee, then asked, "Star Commander, can you explain a bit more about your Khan's intent?"

Nerran smiled and said with some pride, "We are a Clan that studies and appreciates the past. We want to learn about the Inner Sphere and your people. We want to know more about the worlds and their history since the Great Father and his followers departed on their Exodus. We want to exchange personnel as liaisons and observers, and to what we will provide in exchange, well…" He trailed off and turned to Palos.

"What do you need?" the merchant asked bluntly.

Sandra barked a laugh. "Mr. Palos, the list of what we need runs as long as my arm. Was your Khan a bit more specific?"

Nerran smiled. "*Neg*, Colonel. Though our purse is not unlimited, our Khan was quite clear on the leeway she is giving Palos, and to quote her instructions—" he nodded at the small tree in the corner, "—she said, 'Get me their holiday wish list.' So, in accordance with the *direct* orders of my Khan, what do you need, and how can we help?"

Sandra took a long drink of coffee, studying the men, and her office was silent save for Young's fidgeting. She glanced at her aide, who looked about ready to jump out of his chair. He knew the reports as well as Sandra did, and the strain their logistics were under. Young had the desperate look of a drowning swimmer thrown a lifeline.

A quote she learned at the academy came back to her: "*Jaw, jaw is better than war, war.*" Barclay put her cup down. "Lieutenant, grab my noteputer and yesterday's maintenance and ammunition status reports, then call Master Sergeant Brady and ask him to report here immediately."

"Yes, *ma'am*," he replied, jumping to his feet.

"Also, may I trouble you for another cup?" Nerran asked, raising his mug with a smile. "This coffee is *quite* good."

**STAR LEAGUE ENCLAVE
HUNTRESS
CLAN HOMEWORLDS
20 DECEMBER 3067**

Colonel Barclay stood in the Eleventh Reconnaissance Company's 'Mech bay and watched the last Clan Star Adder truck, carrying a Light Horse BattleMech, roll through the open bay doors. The various Clans challenged her unit differently: the Jade Falcons and Ice Hellions trialed for equipment only, eschewing taking any Light Horse members prisoner. The Fire Mandrills and Star Adders would trial for personnel and equipment, but only the Mandrills had any intention of returning her warriors to duty. The Adders took them out of principle, immediately dropping them into the technician caste—or lower, she'd heard from the Scorpions—once they arrived at the Adder enclave. She watched the last of her former MechWarriors get into the van that would take them to the Adder Dropship, denied even the dignity of piloting their own equipment one last time.

She watched the van leave, then slowly turned around. To her right was Master Sergeant Brady, Lieutenant Young, and Star Captain Archibald Ben-Shimon, the Goliath Scorpion liaison. To her left were the technicians assigned to the Eleventh. After the first couple disastrous years of garrisoning Huntress, the Star League realized the best way to rebuild Lootera was to dump money into it. From that point forward, the SLDF hired hundreds of former Smoke Jaguars for any task that didn't require them to fight: construction crews, janitors, security guards, facility maintenance, and technicians: three quarters of the personnel in the room wore civilian jumpsuits, a handful in threadbare Smoke Jaguar gray.

And they were, to a person, silent. No, more than that: the whole *bay* was silent. There was no background hum of generators or air compressors or the other equipment she'd associated with 'Mech bays from decades as a MechWarrior. There were no technicians climbing or repairing things or swearing because of dropped tools. It was *silent*: their last charges had rolled out the door, and the technicians had nothing to do. The cold winter breeze flowed in through the open bay door, gently rustling her short hair, and she took a deep breath.

"Fall them in, Master Sergeant." Her words shocked everyone, but the master sergeant moved quickly to respond. There were only a few former-Jaguar civilians in the group, but the veterans quickly showed them where to stand. While that was occurring, Sandra turned to Young and said, "Retrieve the colors."

Every unit in the Eridani Light Horse—and nearly every unit across the Inner Sphere since time immemorial—had their own set of colors. Every command from company on up had a small flag to designate where their headquarters was and to march alongside other flags in parades.

The Light Horse's colors were old. The Eleventh Recon Company had been activated during the original Star League, and their colors, like most of the Light Horse's, were faded and patched over. Sometimes a unit's colors were destroyed through enemy action, though never had an enemy captured one. But—from time to time—there was a solemn ceremony to perform.

The formation was silent as Young brought the Eleventh Recon's colors in from outside the main entrance: a prancing white unicorn on a field of yellow and blue, which stood out as one of the more unique in the regiment. At the top of the dark, oaken staff were attached battle streamers in a rainbow of colors representing the Great Houses the Light Horse had been employed under during the past centuries. Young also held a long, slim canvas carrying case for the colors, and as Sandra took the case, she told him to give the master sergeant the colors and then fall in.

The master sergeant stood with the colors at attention in front of the formation as she approached. He saluted her with them, and then, dropping them horizontal to the ferrocrete bay floor, held them still as Sandra slid the carrying case over the flag and streamers, about three-quarters of the way down the staff. The deed done, the master sergeant brought the cased flag vertical with a *snap* that seemed loud in the bay. Sandra saw tears on a few of the technicians' faces, the rest quiet and somber.

She paused for a second and found her voice. "Strip this place bare. Move everything serviceable to the main Eleventh Battalion bay, and we'll redistribute it from there. For those of you on contracts, I will release any who wish to find other employment. But, if you're willing to stay on, I promise to keep you gainfully employed." She saw tentative smiles and nods: they were former Jaguars, but most had built families here in the past eight years, and she felt it important to alleviate their concerns upfront.

"And once everything is moved, Colonel?" the senior technician asked.

She sighed and turned slightly away, looking at the setting Huntress sun. "Kill the power and lock the doors. We'll keep it on standby in case we need to reopen it."

He nodded, but she didn't think anyone believed that event would ever come about.

She glanced over at Ben-Shimon, wearing his field uniform. He was an aerospace pilot, barely taller than Young, and deep in thought; he started slightly when he noticed her looking at him. He nodded respectfully, and when his eyes moved past her, she heard the master sergeant approaching. She turned around and saw he was still carrying the cased colors.

"If you don't mind, Colonel, I'll take these over to regiment and get them cleaned before we case them for good."

She nodded. "Put them somewhere safe, Master Sergeant. We'll uncase them again one day. Maybe here, maybe back on Dieron. But eventually."

"Yes, ma'am."

Star Captain Ben-Shimon watched the exchange, and after the master sergeant left, he said, "How old is that guidon? It looked quite worn."

Barclay nodded. "It's a couple decades old, at least. But you can tell a lot about a unit with a new guidon, Star Captain."

Ben-Shimon turned to her with interest. "Colonel?"

She nodded. "It's true. Now, accepting the fact that almost every guidon wears out eventually and has to be replaced, a unit with a new guidon is new. They have no heritage, no history. Their legacy is what they make it—which can be a good thing for a hungry unit trying to make a name for themselves. But if the unit's been around a while?"

She looked around the bay for a second, watching her people work, then turned back. "Colors with no dust and no wear have no glory, Star Captain. It's either a unit with no legacy or a pack of cowards that refuse to take the field. You see a guidon like the Eleventh's, you know you're in for a fight." She glanced over at him with a slight smile. "Remember that the next time you bid against someone: demand to see their colors."

Ben-Shimon opened his mouth to reply, closed it, looked away thoughtfully, and then back at her. "That is excellent advice, Colonel. Thank you."

She turned back toward her troops, and the smile slid from her face. "Glad I could help someone," was her only reply.

**STAR LEAGUE ENCLAVE
HUNTRESS
CLAN HOMEWORLDS
22 DECEMBER 3067**

Goliath Scorpion Khan Ariel Suvorov could see the stares and whispering among the Light Horse personnel as she followed Ben-Shimon through their main headquarters. She did not bother to hide a smile, since no one could see it behind her full-faced helmet.

He was in his dress uniform—dark gray shirt, long black vest-coat made of ballistic cloth, and gold pants with a pair of *zulkari*, the curved daggers, on his belt—but Suvorov was wearing her full ceremonial uniform. Over a silky catsuit to keep the uniform from chafing, she wore a glossy black-leather uniform highlighted with gray piping that gave it the segmented look of a scorpion carapace, a glossy black helmet with a plume of black horsehair and golden daggerstars for eyeholes, the ubiquitous *zulkari* on her belt, and a gold-trimmed black cape that swayed and tapped the back of her ankles as she walked.

Wearing the full ceremonial uniform was Ben-Shimon's idea, to remind the Light Horse of her position as Khan. *Aff, I've come*, she thought to a pair of soldiers eyeing her from down a hallway. *Not as an enemy, but not yet a friend.*

They approached a closed conference room door, with a dress-uniformed Light Horse lieutenant barely taller than her standing next to it.

"My Khan, this is Lieutenant Pascal Young, Colonel Barclay's aide-de-camp." After they greeted each other, Ben-Shimon asked, "Is your colonel ready?"

"Yes, sir," Young replied, and with a confirmation glance toward Suvorov, he opened the door, walked in, and stepped to the side.

"Colonel Barclay, may I introduce Khan Ariel Suvorov of Clan Goliath Scorpion," Young announced in a loud voice.

Suvorov strode into the conference room. The oval-shaped table in the center was a dark wood; at its head was a small flag with her rank on it, placed next to where Colonel Barclay stood. Down the opposite side were the Light Horse battalion commanders and other senior leaders, while on her side was

Star Captain Madsen, who commanded the elite Crimson Seeker Star, Nerran, and her aide, Johnathan.

Barclay waited until Suvorov took off her helmet before saying, "It is nice to finally meet you in person, Khan Suvorov."

Just shy of fifty, Suvorov was petite and extraordinarily fit, both genetic traits of her aerospace-pilot heritage. She kept her raven hair in a pointed bob, the tips of her hair appearing in her peripheral vision as she nodded to the colonel.

"It is nice to finally meet you as well, Colonel Barclay. Thank you for welcoming me to the Star League facility."

Barclay nodded and took something from her master sergeant, then turned back toward her. Suvorov hid a flash of anger. Her own aide had not thought to ask if there was going to be an exchange of welcoming gifts. Instead, Lieutenant Young had pulled Ben-Shimon aside a few days ago for a worried conversation about making sure the gifts matched in respectability, warning that this was an expected custom. Luckily, they had come up with something appropriate, but it had been a close call.

"Khan Suvorov, distinguished guests, this is a bottle of 3028 Timbiqui whiskey. It is one of their limited-edition Melissa Steiner marriage-celebration labels. These are increasingly hard to find, and I am proud to present it as a token of welcoming and goodwill."

Suvorov accepted the bottle and looked at the label. Prominently visible was a young blond bride with a brilliant smile, with *"3028"* etched in gold script on the bottle. She thanked Barclay, and passed the bottle to Madsen, who handed her a small briefcase.

Once Young had informed Ben-Shimon of the gift and its age, Suvorov knew they had to match it in rarity. Her Clan boasted no vintners or distilleries with quality equal to the Inner Sphere, but they did have something they believed could match the whiskey.

"Colonel Barclay, assembled warriors, you may note that we carry daggers on our hips. In our Clan, precision strikes are valued as a testament of skill, and if we are dishonored, we will challenge our enemy to 'dance the scars.' There is an artisan in our labor caste named Maximilian, and he forges *zulkari* with unmatched craftsmanship." She paused, letting her words fill the room.

"You, Colonel Sandra Barclay, led this regiment as it destroyed Clan Smoke Jaguar, and as a token of goodwill and in recognition of glory earned, I present to you a pair of Maximilian *zulkari*."

Suvorov opened the case and displayed the contents for the room to see. Inside, packed in form-fitted red velvet, were a pair of curved daggers in gleaming worked-silver sheaths: one with a black hilt and gold tassels, the other with the colors reversed.

The room took a collective breath at the sight; even the Light Horse warriors appreciated the artistry on display.

Barclay solemnly took the case and gently stroked her fingers over one of the knives. "Khan Suvorov," she said, "I am honored beyond words."

The master sergeant started clapping, at which the rest of the room joined in. Colonel Barclay passed the case to Young, who also stroked the daggers before closing it, and the colonel addressed the room. "Please, everyone, sit. Khan Suvorov, we have a short presentation of our history and heritage for you, and then it would be my pleasure to escort you on a tour of the facility."

As Suvorov sat, she noticed the carafes on the table. She smiled at her glass—her aide *had* remembered to bring Scorpion mugs, so they would not have to borrow cups—and as the lights dimmed and a screen on the far wall lit up with the Light Horse logo, she poured herself a cup of coffee.

Sipping it as the old Star League anthem played, Light Horse BattleMechs marching across the screen, she raised an eyebrow in delight. *My warriors were right—this* is *good coffee.*

STAR LEAGUE ENCLAVE
HUNTRESS
CLAN HOMEWORLDS
27 DECEMBER 3067

Colonel Barclay stood in the hardened hangar that had housed the company headquarters of the 101st Air Cavalry company.

Two aerospace fighters had taxied out this morning just before dawn, along with the rest of their company from matching hangars to the left and right, answering a challenge from Clan Fire Mandrill. The half-dozen had left in pairs, departing in dramatic fashion—full-power combat takeoffs on pillars of white fire against the dark-gray predawn sky.

The six fighters would never return: two pilots had been killed in space above Huntress, and the other four had surrendered to the Mandrills and followed them to the Clan enclave to receive their bondcords.

Another two dead. That ate at her as she stood in the cold and watched the sun rise, waiting for the master sergeant to form up the unit. The challenges were eating away at her regiment's strength, but more than that, her people were dying. *Dying for what? For Clan honor? For the honor of the Star League?*

Her thoughts remained dark until she heard a voice say, "The storage case, Colonel."

She turned to Young, walking up to her with casing for the 101st's colors. He nodded respectfully and quietly said, "The unit is formed, ma'am. Master Sergeant Brady has the colors."

Setting her jaw, Sandra solemnly walked to her spot and deactivated another company.

**LOOTERA
HUNTRESS
CLAN HOMEWORLDS
31 DECEMBER 3067**

Sandra lay on a chaise longue, occupying a corner of the brewery's roof by herself as she looked at the stars. The Light Horse were throwing a New Year's celebration in what had become an undeclared part of the SLDF compound. First discovered by the 151st regiment years ago, the large, two-story complex had a brewery and restaurant on the first floor and an event hall on the second. The Light Horse had immediately started renting it for every occasion, with many of the troops gravitating there on weekends as well.

The party was a formal one, with yearly invitations sent to all on-word Clan leaders as, theoretically, a way for the SLDF to better understand their neighbors. Until this year, when Ariel had accepted on behalf of herself, her saKhan, and her Crimson Seeker Star, only the Cloud Cobra ambassador had ever attended.

The roof's patio was an open layout of tables and chairs extending across half of the building, with a covered bar near the elevator. Only a score of patrons were on the roof—mostly in pairs, canoodling in the darkness—and clustered around the propane heaters scattered around to heat the chilly night air. The view was fantastic: the sky was clear, and since the brewery was located on the outskirts of town, there were no city lights or other buildings to mask the stars or hide the dark Jaguar Fang mountains in the distance.

"Good evening, Khan Suvorov," the bartender said. "May I get you something?"

Sandra was nursing a glass of champagne, with a bottle in an ice bucket next to her, and though she didn't hear Ariel's reply, she wasn't surprised when the Khan appeared out of the darkness.

"May I join you?"

Sandra glanced over. Lieutenant Young had reported that the Scorpions had originally had a rough time finding appropriate outfits. Khan Suvorov had ordered them to follow the Cloud Cobras' lead and wear "civilian" outfits to better blend in, but the Scorpions didn't have a wide selection in their enclave. But then Lieutenant Young introduced Suvorov's Merchant Factor Palos to guild members he knew in Lootera's upscale district, and the results were outstanding.

A black velvet off-the-shoulder sheath dress fit Ariel's petite pilot frame like a second skin. A three-centimeter vee went below her navel, and side slits rose up over her hips. Combined with black peekaboo pumps and centuries-old jewelry discovered by one of her Seekers years ago in a forgotten, burned-out ruin, Ariel's look had drawn admiring glances from Clan and Light Horse alike. She held a small clutch in one hand and a pair of tumblers in the other.

Sandra waved toward the matching chaise on the other side of the bucket. "Kick off your shoes and stay awhile, Ariel. Champagne?"

At her invitation, Suvorov placed the tumblers next to the bucket, slipped out of her shoes, and moaned in relief. "Truly, these are torture devices. I do not know how Star Captain Madsen is managing in her heels."

Barclay laughed as the Goliath Scorpion Khan sat and stretched out her legs, wiggling her toes at the distant mountains. "Me neither. I can barely manage high heels, much less what she has on. Too many years in boots, I guess."

"Agreed. You look splendid, by the way. Pascal helped you shop as well, *quiaff*?"

Sandra looked down—she was in a deep violet half-mermaid gown, with an impressive train and accented with diamond jewelry her late husband had given her. "*Neg*, my friend, but thank you. My eldest daughter Grace did before they left—she's in the 151st under Colonel Antonescu. I'm hopeful she'll pin captain this year."

Ariel turned. "I hope you were able to see her before they departed?"

Sandra nodded, smiling at the memories. "We did get some time together. All of us went out for dinner a couple of times, had some time to visit. My middle daughter Chloë and her husband are both MechWarriors in my Sixth Assault, and my youngest, also named Ariel—"

"A very good name."

"I thought you would approve," Sandra said, laughing. "She's a technician assigned to my command lance. She's downstairs with her girlfriend, dancing up a storm."

Suvorov sat up. "I am glad you had time together. And if she is anything like you, Grace's promotion is inevitable." After snapping open her clutch, she pulled out a large flask and held up the tumblers. "A toast?"

Barclay sat up and slid her legs off the chaise. "Ah, the good stuff. What's in there?"

"Thirty-nine-year-old Timbiqui."

Sandra gasped. "You *opened* it?" she whispered loud enough to cut across the roof. A few nearby couples turned for a moment; seeing nothing amiss, they went back to their own affairs.

"Only the bottle is collectable, Sandra, and it is already on its way to our museum. It would be a waste of good whiskey to let it sit inside untasted," Ariel said as she poured two doubles, passing one to Sandra.

"Is it good?"

Ariel smiled. "It is magnificent. To Grace," she said, then sipped her drink.

Sandra sipped hers and moaned at the smooth, smoky taste. "Oh my God, Ariel, you were right. Best whiskey I've ever had, by far."

The two women leaned back in their chairs, relaxing and enjoying their drinks.

"I'm glad you came tonight, Ariel," Sandra said, finally. "Command is a lonely position, and it's good to have someone to talk to. God knows it's hard to make new friends at my age..."

"At *our* age," Ariel interrupted, saluting her with the tumbler.

Sandra laughed and saluted back. "I stand corrected, at *our* age, and I've enjoyed our talks this week."

"You are welcome," Ariel said, then was quiet for a second. "We are of the same age, in similar positions, and with similar issues. Anyone I could talk to in my *touman* might later use my words against me. It had been nice to just...talk."

Sandra smiled and nodded. "I'm not going to lie, I needed it. Last week was a rough one, with both the 101st's deactivation and visiting my husband's grave with the girls on Christmas, so I just wanted to say thank you."

"I am sorry for the loss of your husband, Sandra. I am sure he fought the Jaguars with honor."

"Second husband." Sandra finished her drink and passed it back to Ariel for a refill. "My first husband—the girls' genetic father—died on Kikuyu fighting the Falcons."

Ariel refilled and passed back the glass, then refilled her own. "Then I am sorry for that loss as well. Our Clans do not get along very well; I cannot stand the Falcons and their constant preening."

"Thank you." Sandra took a deep sip before continuing, "No, William survived the Jaguars, but the day Prince Victor was fighting on Strana Mechty, that very day, he started coughing up blood..." She paused—the whiskey was flowing through her system, and the pain she'd locked away, pain she'd dealt with by burying it under layers of duty, all threatened to come out now.

She pushed some back down as she glanced over. She could see Suvorov, patient and listening, waiting for her to continue.

Sandra took a breath. *It's been too long since I've talked this out.* "Cancer. It was cancer. Thousands of years of medical technology on this world, and there's still ways for our own bodies to kill us, you know?" She coughed once to hide a sob, then steadied herself. "I sat here on Huntress for *months*, watching him slip away. My XO took the regiment back to Dieron to start rebuilding, and I stayed. Oh, William was okay for a while, we could walk through town, we could drive out of the city and see the beauty of the world. It's not until someone's dying you realize how beautiful life can be, you know?"

She took a deep drink of whiskey, tears starting to flow. "But every week, he got a little bit worse. He was strong, Ariel, he was a beast! He could bench press me, and in bed? Good Lord. We broke a headboard once. He ripped it off the wall, and the damn thing fell on my face and broke my nose! We laughed as he bandaged me up—and now this man, this man I loved, this...wonderful, amazing man was dying, right before my eyes."

"He lost weight, he wasted away, and then he couldn't walk or shower or do anything without my help. He was so embarrassed, and I kept telling him I swore 'in sickness and in health,' and then he couldn't even leave the bed. When the end came, it was almost a mercy."

She finished her drink, wiped her face, and Ariel silently passed over the flask. Sandra poured another large measure and passed it back to the Khan, who poured the remainder into her tumbler.

"I got back to Dieron, moved in with my mom and the kids, and got to work, rebuilding my regiment *again*, after building us back up after Kikuyu *and* Coventry! This unit has become my home, my family—my everything since then."

Suvorov turned her head. "Your everything? You..." She paused—the Clans didn't really understand the concept of love, Sandra knew, so she could see the Khan struggling to phrase her question. "You did not find anyone new?" she finished with a shrug.

Sandra chuckled, wiping tears off her face. *Oh, God, this feels good. To just talk it through and laugh and remember and just release part of the pain.* "I'm widowed, not dead, Ariel," she said with a slight smile. "There's been shenanigans here and there these past seven years, but no one I wanted back in my heart. I have the regiment and I have my family, and that's enough for now."

They both fell silent, and then both women lay back down, sipping their whiskey and thinking. It was Ariel who broke the comfortable silence first, as the ten-second countdown began. "Thank you for sharing that with me, Sandra."

"Thank you for listening."

The crowd hit zero, the band downstairs began to play, and couples started kissing on the rooftop. Ariel watched them for a moment, bemused, and then turned back. "Happy New Year, Sandra."

"You too, Ariel. Happy New Year to you too."

**STAR LEAGUE ENCLAVE
HUNTRESS
CLAN HOMEWORLDS
19 JANUARY 3068**

Sandra Barclay scowled as she tapped a finger on her office desk, waiting for the techs to establish communications. Within moments, the screen flickered from the Star League emblem to the Goliath Scorpion insignia, and then she was looking at Khan Suvorov in the middle of her operations center.

"Good afternoon, Colonel Barclay. I hope all is well in Lootera?" Ariel Suvorov said with a smile, and Sandra froze. They'd met and talked numerous times since New Year's Eve, and she could read Ariel's body language. *She doesn't know.*

"Khan Suvorov," Sandra said calmly, "may we speak in private?"

Ariel nodded and walked off-screen. Half a minute later, the camera angle changed, and Ariel was seated in a room that looked nearly identical to Sandra's office. "Is everything okay?"

Sandra took a deep breath. "Ariel, your Galaxy Commander Rik Myers just challenged me for possession of a battalion of troops and the entire embassy."

"He did *what*? For the embassy on Strana Mechty and a battalion?" Sandra could see Ariel growing livid. She wasn't sure of the history between Suvorov and Myers, but she knew it was long and tense.

"Not just Strana Mechty—for all of it. The description of the 'embassy' makes it clear he considers our Huntress enclave as embassy land."

"I should kill him *myself*," Ariel growled. "I just returned him to Galaxy command, and this is what he does?" She let loose an impressive howl of rage, then shouted, "*All* of it? I *will* kill him!"

Sandra laughed at her friend's reaction, then took a deep breath to calm herself. "I'll admit, I was pretty pissed this morning. I couldn't believe that after all our talks, the tours, and the private moments that you'd suddenly betray me by trying to absorb my troops. I know you've been trialing the other Clans to regain my warriors, but I didn't think—what?"

As Sandra was speaking, Suvorov had grown quiet and her body language had changed.

Sandra slumped. "This *is* your plan," she whispered. "You *do* want to absorb us."

Ariel waved frantically. "*Neg*, Sandra, he does *not* have my authorization." Then she paused, looked away, and then brushed her hair back before continuing, "But, *aff*, I was going to talk to you about it later this month: I do want you and your unit to join my Clan."

Sandra felt a knife stab at her heart. "Ariel—"

Suvorov leaned forward. "Sandra, listen to me. You have nowhere to go, and you are getting chewed up, piece by piece. Your regiment is *dying* around you, and I want to help. We can offer you a new home, a home among friends."

Barclay leaned back in her chair, staring at the ceiling, then closed her eyes and remembered the sound of her boots echoing in the empty hangar as she cased the Eleventh Recon

Company's colors. *We're dying, slowly.* She shuddered. *I can't do this again.*

She sobbed once as she remembered everything she'd done to reach this point. *I rebuilt this command three times*! Three! *This is* more *than my regiment; this is my* family. She stifled a sob again, then breathed deep to pull her emotions under control. *I will not see my regiment ripped apart, not again. No more.*

Sandra opened her eyes, and then looked at Ariel, who'd been silently watching her. "Can you nullify this trial? I am open to discussing—" a deep breath, "—open to discussing absorption with you."

Suvorov looked pained. "Sandra...Colonel Barclay, I cannot. As Khan, I must allow my Galaxy Commanders a level of independent command authority. I *will* chastise him in private, but to order a halt to this would undermine my entire Clan. I am sorry."

Sandra took another deep breath, focusing. "Then I'll just have to beat this sonofabitch, won't I? Any suggestions or advice?"

Ariel looked away for a moment, then said, "Remember, as the Hunted, you have your choice of terrain. Choose wisely, bid your forces well, and we shall celebrate your victory afterward." She smiled, nodded once politely, then cut the feed.

Sandra was quiet for a moment, then bellowed, "Young!"

"Ma'am!" her aide called from the outside office.

"Notify the battalion commanders, conference room, one hour!" She heard his acknowledgment, and pulled up the challenge again. *We're the Hunted, so we can choose the terrain.* She felt a *click* in her head, something she remembered about Clan customs.

Ariel didn't say our *terrain, she said choice* of *terrain.* She flicked to a map of Huntress. *So, where do we* want *to fight, and who hates the Scorpions enough to let us to use their land*?

She studied the map, thinking of the weaknesses in Clan BattleMechs and their organizations. After a moment, she made a decision.

"Young!"

"Ma'am!"

"Get me the Falcon Eyrie!"

**EASTERN SHIKARI JUNGLE
JADE FALCON TERRITORY
HUNTRESS
CLAN HOMEWORLDS
30 JANUARY 3068**

"Phantom, this is Backstab. Target secured, and they didn't get a warning off. We warned them to stay quiet or we blow the trucks in place. How copy?"

Sandra Barclay smiled as she slid her 95-ton *Cerberus* BattleMech behind a thick tree for cover. She keyed her radio. "Backstab, Phantom actual. Well done, stay there. Take down anyone that tries a link-up."

She could almost see the smile on the young lieutenant's face as he replied, "Roger Phantom. Backstab out."

Glancing at the map, she saw Lieutenant Phillip Heptig had updated his position: his *Tarantula* and his lancemate's *Hitman* were kilometers to her east, well behind Scorpion lines and sitting on their ammunition and repair point. Galaxy Commander Myers hadn't moved his logistics teams forward to follow the battle when she'd retreated, leaving it even more vulnerable than they'd estimated when they planned the two-'Mech deep strike.

She briefly wondered if Myers would notice or even care that his support troops were now out of the fight—when she'd finally answered Myers' challenge, she replied with her bid, which consisted of her command company and her stepfather's old unit, the Forty-First Support Company, both companies containing two lances of 'Mechs and one platoon of VTOLs; the Twelfth Mechanized Infantry Company, a mix of battle armor and light troops; and her heavy hitters, the double-fisted punch of the Fourth and Sixth Heavy Assault Companies. Along with the Forty-First, they'd sat out the 3060 invasion of Huntress to finish rebuilding on Dieron. She'd told Myers the units she was going to use, and passed along their heritage and battle honors as per Clan custom; but since half the battalion had *never* fought on Huntress, she hoped Myers would underestimate them.

She'd started the trial on the edge of the Kerensky Plains at dusk, the four BattleMech lances of her command company and the Forty-First staring through the waves of heat rising from the plains at the Nova and five BattleMech Stars he'd bid against her. The sixteen Light Horse BattleMechs had exchanged two salvos with the thirty BattleMechs facing them, and before the Scorpions could close, she'd retreated her force into the Shikari Jungle.

With a roar and a stream of insults, Myers had followed her in. Now it was time to make him pay for that mistake.

"Elephant actual, Rainbow actual, this is Phantom actual. Begin your press. Mule actual, get ready. The brunt of their counterattack will likely come at us."

With a chorus of acknowledgments, her trap snapped shut.

**LOOTERA
HUNTRESS
CLAN HOMEWORLDS
1 FEBRUARY 3068**

"So, both the Fourth *and* Sixth Assault companies are pure Clan-tech?" Ariel Suvorov asked Sandra after sipping her fusionnaire.

They were back on the brewery roof in what had become "their" corner, and downstairs was a raucous Saturday-night party. After months of mixed results at various combat trials, to trounce an opponent so thoroughly had put the Light Horse into a jubilant mood.

"Yup," Sandra said cheerfully. She saw a waitress approaching with another Medium Laser, so she finished off the one in her hand and exchanged it. "How long on the appetizers?"

Ariel laughed brightly. "You just ate!"

Sandra laughed as well. "I need carbs to absorb the alcohol. Where was I?"

"The trap snapped shut."

"Right," Sandra said, and sipped her fresh Medium Laser, enjoying the chilled gin-and-bourbon drink as it went down. "He *knew* it was a trap, but he kept boasting about how he'd defeat us anyway. So, we had him surrounded, and cut off from his supplies—"

"And you had plenty of supplies."

Sandra laughed. "That's one of the blind spots in Clan bidding, you can bring as much or as little logistics tail as you can protect. I brought nearly my entire team, plus every former Jaguar willing to go. We kept reloading and repairing and then heading back into the fight while we chased Myers around the jungle. I'm sorry, Ariel. They're your troops, but they were led by an overconfident man, and I used that against them."

Suvorov was silent for a moment, then she finished her drink in one go, coughing once at the schnapps and vodka settling in her stomach. She signaled the waitress for another, and then asked, "Where are your daughters? Downstairs?"

"Yes, both of them and my son-in-law, dancing their heads off. Ariel was on my command lance's repair team. They all earned a night to blow off some steam."

Suvorov nodded. "A couple more drinks, and I may join them. I have not danced since…" She paused to think, then shrugged. "It has been awhile."

"Then you're overdue," Sandra replied with a wicked smile.

The waitress brought Ariel a fresh drink, and she studied it for a moment before saying, "I am surprised you bid both of your daughters and yourself into the same battle."

Sandra was silent for a long moment, staring at the stars before quietly answering, "If I lost, at least we'd get absorbed together."

Ariel nodded, leaned back, studied the stars herself, and slowly sipped her drink. Finally she said, "Tell me how you killed him."

**SHIKARI JUNGLE
HUNTRESS
CLAN HOMEWORLDS
31 JANUARY 3068**

Sandra pushed through the jungle, her command lance pacing her as they headed toward the Scorpion lines. The battle had raged for seven hours, pushing the Scorpions back to a small circle in the deepest part of the Shikari: Battered and tired, ten BattleMechs and a handful of Elementals were all that remained.

Now, after nightfall, her forces were pushing the Scorpions into an ever-decreasing perimeter. However, that meant for every meter of space gained, the defending fire increased in volume and accuracy.

Sandra was rotating her units out for repairs and rearming; she had finally taken a turn at one of her hidden sites, the team hiding under camouflage tarps strung between trees. Her daughter had personally welded on replacement armor while the *Cerberus* was reloaded.

She flicked her secondary radio to an unencrypted frequency and broadcast, "Galaxy Commander Myers, this is Colonel Barclay. I'm asking you again to accept *hegira* and stand down. You've fought well and honorably today. No more of your troops have to die for your stubbornness."

"Do not patronize me, *freebirth*. I would sooner die than accept *hegira* from you. I offered you an honorable challenge, and you used ambushes and treachery."

Sandra barked a laugh. "I answered your challenge honorably and fairly, Galaxy Commander. You failed to research my units, you failed to understand how my choice of terrain would negate your range advantages, and you will fail at this trial. The moon has set, the night has gone long. End this now. Power down, and return to your Clan with your honor intact."

He growled. "Big talk for the so-called leader I last saw retreating into this jungle. You have had too much influence on my Khan, and your unit's decadent, consumerist ways are corrupting my Clan. Once I defeat you, I will challenge the Khan, take command, and preserve the Goliath Scorpion's ideals."

A red dot appeared on her map. "Face me, Sandra. Granting you an honorable death above your station is the first step in rebuilding my Clan's honor."

"I am on my way, Galaxy Commander," she replied coldly, and snapped the channel off. Her primary radio lit up with voices, but she silenced them with a loud, "This is Phantom actual. Clear this channel." There was a moment of silence, after which she broadcast, "Does anyone have a visual on that clearing?"

Instead of using the Twelfth Infantry Company to fight the Scorpions, she'd had them broken into squads and hidden throughout the jungle as spotters. A few had been discovered, but for the most part, she'd had near-continuous visibility on the Scorpions' movements.

"Phantom actual, Kingpin actual," the Twelfth Infantry Company's commander called in. "A Third Platoon squad has eyes-on, and the clearing's empty. They report the target passed through it about five minutes ago."

"Thanks, Kingpin. Command lance, on me," she ordered, pushing her *Cerberus* forward. Lieutenant Young immediately moved to her side in his *Nightstar*, and ahead of her was Master Sergeant Brady's *Bandersnatch* and Sandra's bodyguard, Sergeant Petty, in a *Cronus* so new Petty liked to joke it was still under warranty.

Reports trickled in that the Scorpions were starting to fall back and were holding their fire. *They heard our exchange and are waiting*, she realized.

Clicking to a secondary frequency, she broadcast, "Commanders, this is Phantom actual. If the Scorpions facing you are quiet, then cease fire. Continue rotations for rearming and repair, but do not press without instruction." She paused as acknowledgments rolled in. "Major Endris: remember, Claudia, if I fall, you're in command. We must not lose. Your orders are to prosecute the attack."

There was a pause before Endris, the commander of the Eighty-Second Battalion, came over the comm with a quiet "Yes, ma'am."

Then the comm fell silent. Sandra knew the company frequencies would be nonstop chatter as commanders rotated 'Mechs in and out of the line. But no one jumped onto the command frequency as she led her lance toward the clearing.

Then: "Phantom actual, Kingpin Three-Three-One. You have a pair of Clan assaults heading to intercept you."

Sandra's hands tightened on her joysticks. *Finally.*

The *Cronus* was the first to enter the 300-meter-wide circular clearing from the western edge, covered in two-meter ferns and elephant grass. Petty continued her scouting run across it as the other three 'Mechs all entered.

"Spread out," Sandra commanded. "They'll be here soon enough." She continued east to link up with Petty while the master sergeant and her aide moved toward the center and faced north and south.

"Contact!" Young sang out. "Oh, bloody hell," was his next statement as a 95-ton *Gladiator* followed a 100-ton *Scylla* physically pushing apart a pair of trees on the clearing's south side.

"The ugly one's mine!" Petty shouted gleefully, triggering her jump jets and hitting the *Scylla* with her PPC.

The Scorpion wasted no time returning fire with a score of missiles from a long-range-missile rack, then a large laser and a pair of medium lasers. The *Cronus* staggered in midair from the hits before landing hard and falling onto its left side.

"They're *both* ugly," Young muttered as he braced his 95-ton *Nightstar* in front of the *Gladiator* and fired.

Both his Gauss rifles and his PPC struck the Scorpion assault 'Mech. Sandra saw infantry spotters fire a pair of man-portable short-range missiles out of the tree line into the *Gladiator* as well, adding to the damage. The Scorpion 'Mech shook under the barrage, losing almost three tons of armor in as many seconds, then it fired back. Three large pulse lasers lashed across the *Nightstar*'s torso, melting armor but failing to penetrate to the internal structure. The *Gladiator* followed up by lining up the quad-pack of medium lasers in its right arm; all four struck the *Nightstar*'s left arm, melting nearly all its armor off in seconds.

As Young tried, and failed, to keep his 'Mech upright, Sandra fired into the *Scylla*, her twin Gauss rifles both hitting the assault 'Mech's right torso. The impact knocked the Scorpion backward slightly, enough to throw off their follow-up shots at Petty—*lasers only*, Sandra noted.

As the master sergeant moved forward to engage the *Gladiator*, Sandra heard "There you are!" over an unencrypted frequency. From the northwest, several small trees were knocked over as a *Fire Scorpion* entered the clearing 100 meters behind her.

The low-slung quadrupedal 'Mech had an armored but cosmetic tail over its back and a pair of armored "mandibles" to protect its cockpit. In her 360-degree monitor, Sandra could see the Galaxy Commander launching a double-pack of ten LRMs before firing his massive Ultra-class autocannon.

The stream of rounds hit her first, the heavy autocannon fire chewing through the armor of her 'Mech's left arm and the left rear torso, the secondary monitor showing her armor status immediately flipping from green to red. One of the medium pulse lasers mounted there went offline as she heard her head-mounted anti-missile system whirl into action. Ten of Myers' missiles went wide, and her defensive system caught many of the rest, leaving only three to smash into the back of her left leg.

"We end this now, *freebirth*. First, I kill you and claim this battalion, then the rest of your mercenary regiment. No longer shall Huntress entertain *surats* from a sham Star League."

Sandra twisted her *Cerberus*' torso left, swinging her targeting pip toward the Scorpion as he crab-walked to his left, directly into her line of fire. Aiming at center of mass, she fired her left-arm Gauss rifle the instant her pip turned gold, not waiting for her torso-mounted pulse lasers to bear.

The watermelon-sized ferro-nickel slug ran the gap between the mandibles and slammed into the *Fire Scorpion*'s cockpit, and the 'Mech fell directly onto its belly, all four legs splayed out into the grass.

Sandra swung her attention back toward the west, where the *Scylla* was rising to its feet and the *Gladiator* faced her.

There was a pause, and then over an unencrypted frequency she heard, "Colonel Barclay, this is Star Colonel Malachi Posavatz before you." The *Gladiator* blinked its running lights in the darkness. "We accept your offer of *hegira*."

**STAR LEAGUE ENCLAVE
HUNTRESS
CLAN HOMEWORLDS
2 FEBRUARY 3068**

Ariel Suvorov slowly woke up and groaned, her head pounding in the distinctive drumbeat of a hangover. She realized two things at the same time—she was naked, and in a bed that was not hers. She froze for a second, then heard the reassuring sounds of Archibald Ben-Shimon softly grunting in his sleep next to her.

She opened her eyes and looked around the room before sighing. *Oh, I remember.* She vaguely recalled passing through Sandra's living room hours earlier before spending some quality time with Ben-Shimon. *This is young Ariel Barclay's room.*

Ariel slid out from under the comforter and, seeing a pile of folded clothes on top of a dresser, swiped an *Immortal Warrior* nightshirt to throw on. Walking quietly as to not wake Archibald, she slipped over to the door and slid it open. To the left were two closed doors, with another to her right, and down the hall she saw Sandra cooking in a kitchenette that looked almost identical to hers. *The Smoke Jaguars must have used the same floor plan for all their facilities.*

Sandra turned from the stove and waved Suvorov to come closer. Sandra was in standard utility jumpsuit, barefoot, with her short brown hair still damp from a shower.

"Good morning," she said cheerfully as Suvorov entered the living room. "Your aide came by with your day-bag about half an hour ago."

Suvorov thanked her and grabbed the small rucksack containing spare uniforms she'd left with her aide. There were several flights heading between the enclaves daily now; as Khan, she could always call up a personal one, but she didn't like to flaunt her authority unless she needed to. Last night, after their talk, Sandra and Suvorov had headed down into the brewery to drink, dance, and celebrate with the Light Horse and her Seeker Star, missing the last shuttle by hours.

"Refresher?"

"Down the hall, first door on the right," Sandra replied. "Second door is my office if you need to check in with anyone, the last on the left is my bedroom. The coffee is hot, the Dutch baby will be ready in about ten minutes, and I'll put some eggs on when I hear you turn the shower off."

Eight minutes later, Ariel padded barefoot down the hallway toward the living room, hair slightly damp and dripping onto her black jumpsuit. Putting her boots and socks down by the couch, she walked to the kitchen table and gratefully accepted a cup of coffee. She sipped it as Sandra moved around the kitchen, and she bounced her leg gently in time with some music playing quietly in the background. She heard a door open down the hall, and Ben-Shimon came out, yawning as he pulled last night's shirt back on.

"My Khan, Sandra. Good morning," Archibald said.

Ariel said good morning back while Sandra checked on something in the oven. Satisfied, she reached in with a pot holder and pulled it out, and Suvorov breathed deep at the tantalizing aroma.

"Sandra, that smells amazing," she said, watching her friend slide a large, crispy brown pastry from a pie dish to a cooling platter.

"I am afraid I cannot stay," said Ben-Shimon. "I should head back on the morning shuttle."

Barclay's bedroom door opened down the hall, and Suvorov hid a smile as she saw Nerran walk out, dressed in last night's clothes and tightening his belt. *I was hoping things went well*, she thought.

"Sandra, my Khan." Nerran nodded in greeting. "I will accompany you, Archibald."

Sandra said, "Wait, guys." She pulled out a pair of lidded travel cups, quickly filled them, and passed one to each. "Hot coffee. Those are not disposable, so I want them back."

After thanking her and saying their goodbyes, they departed, and Suvorov got up to pour herself another cup of coffee while staying out of Sandra's way. A moment later, Sandra brought over a pair of plates, each loaded with scrambled eggs and a large wedge of pastry dusted with powdered sugar, and placed a carafe of coffee on the table between them.

Ariel looked at Sandra over her coffee cup. "So, shenanigans with Nerran?"

Sandra blushed. "He's handsome, and I figured, why the hell not?"

Ariel laughed. "Life is too short to stay chaste," she replied, then took a bite of the pastry. She closed her eyes and sighed. "This is very good, Sandra."

"Thanks. I've always loved to cook."

"Is your Ariel coming home for breakfast?"

"No, she's been staying with her girlfriend lately. I probably won't see her until the funeral."

Suvorov nodded, taking another bite. "That is tomorrow?"

Sandra growled. "Tomorrow morning, yes. We bury ten MechWarriors, a pair of VTOL pilots, and fifteen infantrymen because of that damn Galaxy Commander."

"I know, and I am sorry—"

Sandra cut her off with a hand. "No, you *don't* know." She took a deep breath, looked at the ceiling. "I am not going to buy us a new home with more graves. I *cannot* kill my soldiers trying to save them."

Suvorov nodded, took a bite of pastry and eggs, thinking as she chewed. She finished off her coffee and sat back. "What do you propose?"

Sandra finished hers as well, and as she refilled their cups, she said, "The infantry and armor do a series of contests. We conduct special-forces testing for the infantry and crew-certification competitions for the tanks. Whoever scores the highest overall wins those matches. Then, the aerospace pilots and MechWarriors head into the simulators—"

"*Neg*," Suvorov said forcefully. She leaned forward. "I can sell my Clan Council on nonlethal trials for the support branches, as killing potential new warriors in a trial is wasteful. But the trials for MechWarriors and pilots *must* be live fire."

Sandra frowned slightly, took a long drink, and said, "Then... we do it your way, a 'dance of the scars' type challenge? Direct-fire weapons only, no physical attacks, no aimed headshots? Massed fire allowed, because that's how we fight, but otherwise, we keep this as clean as possible?"

Suvorov smiled. "This is acceptable."

"When?"

Suvorov sipped her coffee, then said, "This year on Huntress, the eleventh of July is the longest day of the year. It is an important day on some worlds?"

Sandra thought for a moment, then shook her head. "No. How about the tenth, so the sun rises over a brand-new Huntress on the eleventh?"

"Well bargained and done," Ariel said, and with a clink of coffee cups, the agreement was sealed.

**OUTSIDE LOOTERA
HUNTRESS
CLAN HOMEWORLDS
10 JULY 3068**

Just before noon, with Huntress' sun high in the sky, Sandra looked down the rows of BattleMechs stretching to her left and right, the BattleMechs of the Seventy-First Light Horse Regiment, Eridani Light Horse, assembled for what everyone knew, one way or the other, was the regiment's last battle on this planet.

The day after she'd clinked cups with the Khan, she'd assembled the entire regiment in their largest 'Mech bay and announced her intention to declare a winner-take-all trial against the Scorpions. She invited anyone who would rather take their chances returning to the Inner Sphere earlier to ride home with the ambassador and his staff in late February, with no one shaming or judging their decision.

Only a handful had left, most of them with dependents on Dieron assuming they could eventually link up with them. As spring turned into summer, though, word started trickling back from the Inner Sphere about the attacks on Dieron, and grief ran through the unit. The regiment, as one, understood there was no going back.

She watched the Light Horse and Scorpions growing closer, learning about each other before the final trial. The intermingling trickled down through everything: more and more Scorpions began to explore the streets and shops of Lootera, and many of the Light Horse stopped using contractions.

Through it all, the technicians worked, stripping missile launchers from the force. Sandra formally adopted any former Smoke Jaguar who wanted to stay with the unit through the trial. Her daughter Ariel had volunteered for a technician exchange-program, helping the Scorpions modify their 'Mechs. Her daughter gleefully told her over dinner one night that the Scorpions were excited about the upcoming trial, pulling vintage and legacy BattleMechs out of storage for use as a sign of respect.

"Mom, I spent today putting chemical lasers into an OmniMech!" she'd said, a wide smile on her face. "And tomorrow? A *blazer*. I cannot even *imagine* where they got that! This trial is going to be *amazing*."

Sandra had laughed at Ariel's excitement, but looking down the rows, waiting for the chrono to hit noon, she felt it herself. Her troops had lost the infantry competition—though it was closer than the Scorpions had expected—but her armor crews had handily won their challenge. Master Sergeant Brady informed her that most of her troops and their counterparts were already at the brewery and other pubs across Lootera, watching the upcoming battle on vidscreens together.

The aerospace contest had finished just after eleven, Khan Suvorov personally leading her Scorpions to victory in another tight match. Despite the precautions, both sides still lost a pilot each, but Sandra knew that had she not come to an arrangement with Khan Suvorov, she would have eventually lost all of her pilots through trials or burial.

"There sure are a lot of them, ma'am," Petty commented on an internal lance frequency. "You get so used to Clan underbidding, it just looks weird when they bring a bunch."

Sandra smiled. Brady had swapped his *Bandersnatch* for the *Gladiator* they'd taken as *isorla* in the jungle, but Petty refused to modify her *Cronus*, simply keeping the SRM rack unloaded. Young's *Nightstar* needed no modifications, and Sandra had also decided to not swap BattleMechs: her *Cerberus* had carried her through battles on Coventry and Huntress, and she knew it would carry her through today.

"Since I trialed for everything in system, including the JumpShips to take us home, they get to bring everything they have," Sandra replied. Still, she shook her head at the eclectic collection the Scorpions were fielding. A *Fenris*; a 'Mech she didn't recognize, but her computer identified as a *Predator*; a pair of *Black Lanner*s; an ancient *Corvis*; a brace of presumably vintage *Starslayer*s; and what her daughter reverently referred to as "the last *Sun Bear*."

In total, she had a consolidated nineteen lances facing down Alpha Galaxy's fifteen BattleMech Stars plus the Crimson Seeker Star's MechWarriors. Because of the Light Horse's Clan salvage, both the numbers and technology were nearly equal: 150-some BattleMechs would face each other in a fight of skill and tenacity. Medical teams were on standby off to the side and in the air, but no technicians: the first side to 50 percent mobility killed or destroyed would immediately lose the trial.

"*Trothkin*, hear me!" Scorpion Loremaster Kyrie Ben-Shimon called out over an open frequency.

Sandra swung her targeting pip onto the BattleMech directly across from her, 600 meters away. She'd instructed her unit to not fire until she did: the responsibility of this trial fell on her, and she would initiate it.

Her pip flashed gold on Nerran's customized 90-ton mixed-tech *Emperor*. She pinged it with a comms laser, requesting a private frequency. He connected immediately.

"Well, hello, lover. Fancy meeting you here," she said lightly.

"—This trial was honorably offered and honorably accepted—"

"It is Friday, you know," she continued. "If you have no plans, the Khan and I are meeting for drinks tonight at the brewery."

"—Let this trial be fought with honor and skill—"

"I will see you there."

"—and let none interfere!"

A chorus of "*Seyla*!" from the Clan side—and a few from her own, she noted—flooded the frequency.

Sandra's targeting pip flashing gold, and she fired, both Gauss slugs striking the *Emperor* in the center torso. Nerran immediately returned fire, his Gauss round slamming into her right torso and his large laser drawing a scar down the *Cerberus*, from left shoulder to hip.

The air lit in a rainbow of colors as every BattleMech began firing on their own targets, beginning her regiment's final battle.

CRONUS
MEDIUM—55 TONS

CERBERUS
ASSAULT—95 TONS

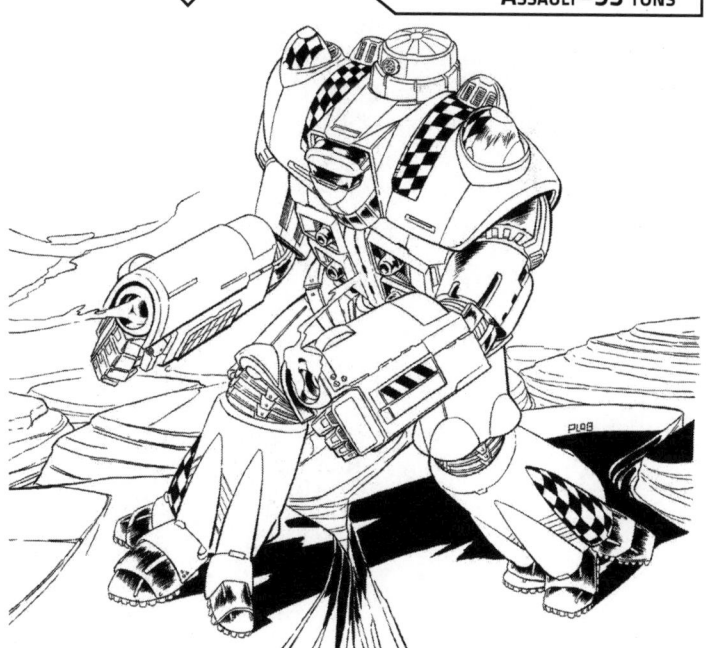

FIRE SCORPION
Heavy—65 tons

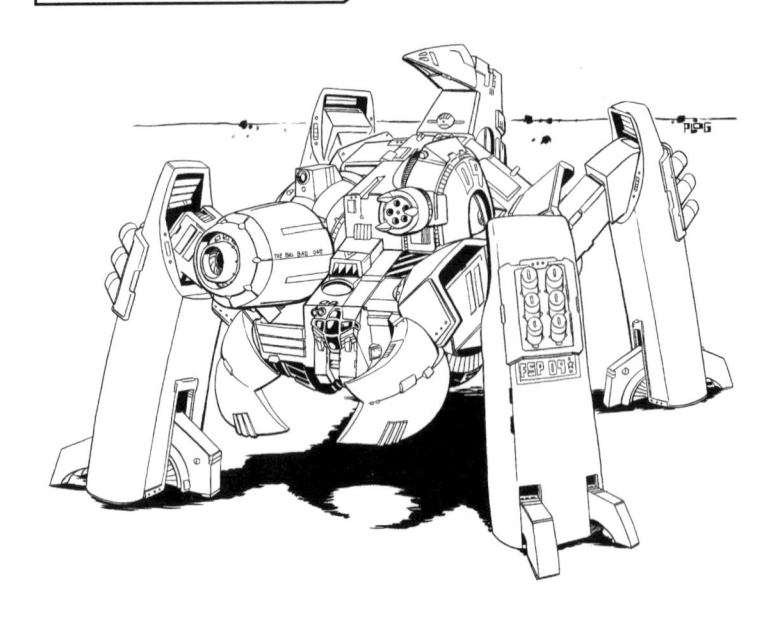

GLADIATOR (EXECUTIONER)
Assault—95 tons

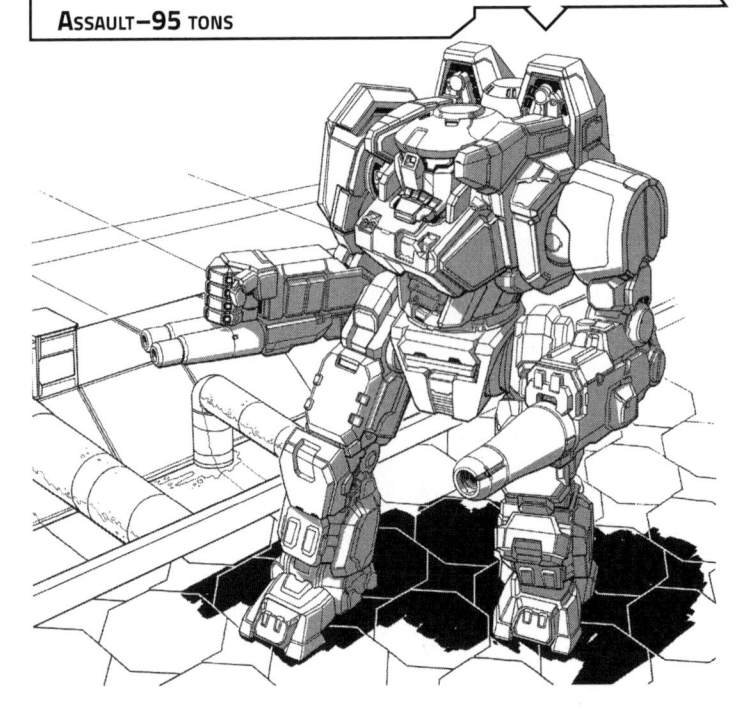

NIGHTSTAR
Assault—95 tons

SCYLLA
Assault—100 tons

THE DAY
WHEN HEAVEN WAS FALLING

JASON SCHMETZER

**MYOO MOUNTAINS
HESPERUS II
LYRAN COMMONWEALTH
30 DECEMBER 3144**

Leutnant Gilda Pennon died smiling.

She saw the yellow-and-gray *Victor* BattleMech raise its arm, saw the maw of the 100mm autocannon swing into line with her 'Mech, and grinned.

"You sack of shit," she said, just as the *Victor* fired.

The seemingly unending stream of shells *ka-blam-blam-blammed* across the front of her *Zeus* and tracked upward, finally crossing her cockpit. Her 'Mech halted immediately; her screens went dark, and a bright red "*KIA*" flashed in her HUD.

The *Victor*'s MechWarrior laughed at her death. "Got to keep moving, girl," Lieutenant Thomas Cole said. "End sim."

At Cole's words the *Zeus*' HUD fired back up, showing the 80-ton *Victor* standing there, tall and imposing in the early-morning Hesperan sunlight. The prancing horse of the Eridani Light Horse stood out in the bright light.

"I don't have to keep moving, thank you," Gilda said. "I'm Self-Protection Force, remember? We don't run around the badlands chasing every little thing. We stand between the factory and whoever comes against it, and mostly watch while the turrets blast them into tiny little pieces that regret ever getting on the other end of an improved heavy Gauss rifle."

Cole chuckled. "If you say so. If that were true, I reckon you wouldn't have come out here with me this morning." The *Victor* started moving, angling its path to pass on her *Zeus*' left side. She pivoted and fell into step with the other machine; the navs were already set to return them to the factory complex.

Her *Zeus* was of the weight and quality of Thom Cole's 'Mech, but his *Victor* had been places. The Eridani Light Horse was a storied mercenary unit. It had been around for centuries, since the Star League. She heard stories off Galatea every other week about some two-bit crew of mercenaries running out on their employers or double-crossing the people they were supposed to be protecting, but the Light Horse wasn't like that. They were true to their salt, as the saying went.

When Gilda had learned the Light Horse was coming to Hesperus II to help garrison the factories, she'd done a lot of reading and watching about them. She knew their history, backward and forward. She knew their traditions. And when they arrived, and the kommandant had asked for volunteers to liaise with them, she'd made sure her name was on the list.

Her *Zeus* had been built right up there, beneath those mountains, in the Defiance Industries factories that made Hesperus II such an important world to the Lyran Commonwealth. She'd grown up here; her mother worked the *Ghost* line, and her dad ran an armor forge. Gilda's first job had been driving exoskeletons in the warehouses before she worked up to moving 'Mechs off the lines and then, finally, trying for a slot with the Self-Protection Force. She wasn't really interested in going off-world to fight for someone else's home.

"You're good," Cole said, "but you need to keep stretching your wings. Could be sometime you get someone comes in here and hits the factories in a way you don't expect. You need to be ready for that. Even," and here she heard his chuckle, "if that means you need to move around some."

"I get what you're saying," Gilda told him. She opened her mouth to say more, but a clutch of new blue icons appeared on her HUD. She frowned as she read the unit ID. A lance of four friendly BattleMechs, all light 'Mechs looking like something that'd get someone fired if it came off the line looking like that, was coming toward them. The *Zeus*' computer helpfully threw up a sidebar of the lance's unit.

A lot of mercenaries, not just the Light Horse, had landed on Hesperus recently. Rundle's Renegades was a double-lance outfit with beaten-down 'Mechs just barely better than IndustrialMechs with bolted-on weapons and armor. They had pranced around the factories and Defiance Self-Protection Force barracks like they owned the place, because *they* had been hired to come and do the job the DSPF couldn't.

A lot of Gilda's fellow DSPF MechWarriors had been put out of sorts. She'd looked to them, feeling the same, but then seen the Light Horse just ignore it all and go out every morning to train. After a couple minutes of self-reflection, she realized the Light Horse had the right attitude about it. A week later, she'd approached Lieutenant Cole about joining them. Which was how she had gotten here.

Apparently, some of that was starting to rub off on the lesser mercenary groups like the Renegades.

"I wonder if we should stick around, watch for a while," Cole said. When Gilda snort-laughed, Cole chuckled as well. "Well, it was just an idea. Everyone needs negative role models, my old man used to say."

"I think I have enough of those." Gilda waved the *Zeus*' right arm at the now-passing lance of Renegade 'Mechs. All four ignored her, as she knew they would. Those jocks were all braggarts, but they needed the audience to make it work.

She and Cole kept moving; thirty minutes later, they were back in one of the cavernous bays cut into the heart of the Myoo Mountains complex. As soon as she racked her *Zeus* in its bay, alerts called all MechWarriors to their ready rooms.

"There's no easy way to say this," Kommandant Heutzel said, "so I'm just going to say it. The Jade Falcons are coming, and the Third Royals just pulled out."

To their credit, the MechWarriors of the Self-Protection Force didn't erupt in shouting, but Gilda saw and felt the ripple of shock that ran through the room. Beside her, her best friend Ilhan Mesrubbi looked at her sidelong, mouth open. Gilda gave her a Gallic shrug, then turned back to listen.

"It gets worse," Heutzel said. "LIC says the Hell's Horses are coming, too."

"And the Third Royals are gone?" asked a MechWarrior in the front row.

"And the Hesperus militia," Heutzel said. Gilda didn't know the Self-Protection Force commander well; they'd been introduced, of course, but he let the company hauptmanns run their companies pretty much on their own. Heutzel showed up at big functions. He was well into late middle age, but somehow still looked like he was in his thirties. Good Asian genes, her mother would have said.

He let the company leaders lead, but he always—*always*—gave the bad news.

"The militia," Hauptmann Cardenas said. "The *Hesperus* militia. The people who *live* here. They're gone."

"It didn't make sense to me either," Heutzel allowed. "DefHes wasn't in on the decision, I'm told."

"Why would you be?" Cardenas snorted. "You're only the defense force commander for the single most important BattleMech factory in the entire Commonwealth."

"What about the Light Horse?" Gilda asked, raising her voice above the noise of hushed side conversations and snide remarks. "And the other mercenaries?"

"Still here," Heutzel confirmed. "I spoke with General Eichler. He assured me their orders haven't changed. I expect the other, lesser groups will fall into line with them." He leaned down to answer a quiet question from the front row Gilda couldn't hear.

In the moment of distraction. Mesrubbi leaned closer. "This is jacked," her friend said. When Gilda only nodded, Mesrubbi went on. "The Clans are coming. Okay, sure. They're Clans. That's what they do. But the Third Royal Guards turned tail and ran? And somehow convinced a bunch of part-timers to board ship and leave their homes and families behind to Malvina Hazen's tender mercies?" Mesrubbi leaned back, shook her head, and spread her hands over her lap. "This smells wrong."

"It sure does," Gilda agreed.

"How much time do we have?" a loud voice shouted from the back.

Heutzel straightened up. The room quieted, anxious to hear the answer.

"I've only known about this for a couple hours," he said. Gilda glanced at Mesrubbi. He was stalling. That meant the news was bad for sure. Heutzel made a face like he'd tasted something sour. "They'll be down in four days."

The room erupted in shouting.

MYOO MOUNTAINS
HESPERUS II
LYRAN COMMONWEALTH
3 JANUARY 3145

Ilhan Mesrubbi leaned through the doorway. "They're down," she said. "The Jade Falcons."

Gilda pulled the towel down from where she'd been drying her short hair. It felt decidedly weird to be doing something as domestic as showering when invaders were landing on Hesperus II, but it had felt weirder to not begin her morning with a shower.

"Turns out not all the Third Royals and the militia pulled out," Mesrubbi went on. "Scuttlebutt is like a company of them stuck around long enough to scratch the Falcons' paint jobs. Then they burned for orbit, too."

"You're kidding," Gilda said. That made even less sense than the rest of the regimental combat team pulling out weeks earlier. "You think maybe they never really left? It's three weeks to a standard jump point. What if they're out there, waiting to combat-drop in behind the Falcons or something?"

"Could be," Mesrubbi agreed. She stepped fully into the doorway so she could lean against the doorjamb. "You ever know the LCAF to be that sneaky, though? On purpose, I mean."

Gilda chuckled. "I guess not." She gave her hair one more swipe, then dropped the towel on the sink. "What's the word from the kommandant?"

"Mount up, but interior defensive positions only."

Gilda frowned. "Interior."

"Those're the orders."

"That doesn't make sense." She waited until Mesrubbi made way, then moved out of her bathroom into her tiny one-room suite. "There's not enough room in here for us, the Light Horse, and the other mercs."

"Word is the Light Horse is forming up outside the gates," Mesrubbi said.

"That doesn't make sense," Gilda repeated.

"What about all this does?"

By the time Gilda got her *Zeus* to its assigned position inside the defensive walls, Mesrubbi's *Fafnir* was already there. The pair of assault 'Mechs stood on a BattleMech-scale ferrocrete firing step that was high enough that their arm and torso-mounted weapons could fire over, while the wall protected their legs. The wall in front of them was two meters thick, reinforced armor composite thicker than any BattleMech could carry. Cut into the mountain cliffs above and behind them were turrets, bunkers, and weapons installations that could claw a DropShip out of the sky. The most advanced war machines in the Lyran Commonwealth were constructed inside that mountain.

Looking at it in her vision strip, Gilda felt like it wasn't enough.

"There they are," Mesrubbi said.

Gilda's computer painted a rash of red carets across the cleared kill zone in front of the factory: Clan 'Mechs and tanks coming up over the horizon. They were still several kilometers away, but she frowned, then looked at the mountain again, behind her. It was quiet, no puffs of smoke or eye-searing pulses of laser light.

"Why isn't the artillery firing?" she asked.

"Who knows..." Mesrubbi's voice trailed off. "Better question, where are *they* going?"

Gilda looked at her forward screens. The yellow-and-brown 'Mechs of the Eridani Light Horse were drawn up in serried ranks just outside the wall, in the kill zone. But on their flanks, small units of 'Mechs and tanks moved forward.

She centered her sensors on one and read the name: it was one of the smaller mercenary groups that had come to defend the factory, like the Renegades. *Speaking of which...* Gilda keyed a search into her HUD. A group of green-highlighted icons moving on the right caught her attention. Rundle's Renegades.

"Flank attack?" Gilda asked, but she knew that couldn't be it.

"In plain sight of the gods and radar?" Mesrubbi scoffed. "Not even those fools are that stupid."

Gilda didn't know what else it could have been. She clicked over to the company channel and listened for a moment; no one else knew, either. Licking her lips, she dialed a specific frequency and held her breath. "Thom?"

"Not a good time, Gilda," Thom Cole said. Somewhere out there, his *Victor* stood at the head of its lance.

"Where are the mercs going?"

"The cowards, you mean?"

"Do I?"

"They're surrendering."

Gilda almost choked. "They're *what*?"

"General Eichler sent word. The smaller groups decided to surrender en masse. They don't think we can hold the Falcons and the Hell's Horses both." Gilda could hear the scorn in Thom's voice, and that let her imagine the expression on his face.

"Is that going to work?"

"We're about to find out. I have to work now, Gilda."

"Me too."

Gilda quickly filled Mesrubbi in, and then sent a message to her company CO. He didn't reply. Gilda didn't try again. The mercenaries were getting close to the Jade Falcon lines. Too far away for the Light Horse to support even if the elite mercenaries were so inclined. Which Gilda didn't think they were. She wished she could hear what the mercenaries were saying. "Hi. We took the Lyrans' money, but we're scared. Can we please hide with you and pay a fee or something?"

Whatever it was, it wasn't a long conversation.

The Jade Falcons and Hell's Horses fired en masse. It was over in less than a minute. The few mercenary 'Mechs and tanks that broke back toward the Defiance defenses were run down and obliterated.

"Guess we won't be surrendering," Ilhan Mesrubbi deadpanned.

"The orders stand, Pennon," Hauptmann Sradebovic said flatly.

"Sir," Gilda persisted, "if we don't go out there and support them, the Light Horse is as dead as the rest of that rabble." She glared at the image of the hauptmann's *Atlas* in her HUD, thankful the conversion was voice-only. "Together, we might have enough strength to draw the Clans in, where the mountain's defenses can engage them."

"And that is still not the plan," Sradebovic said, again. "Hold your place."

"Sir—"

"Do you want to be relieved, Leutnant?"

"No, sir," Pennon said. The company commander cut the channel before she could say anything else.

"He said no?" Mesrubbi asked.

"He said no."

"Maybe he's right," her friend offered. "Maybe there is a plan. It's like you said. The Third Royals could still be out there."

Gilda wanted to believe her, but in her mind all she saw were the mercenary 'Mechs and tanks getting cut down by the Clans. The smoke from the wrecked machines still climbed into the sky. The Jade Falcon and Hell's Horses vanguards had paused just long enough to pry any survivors out of their cockpits and execute them before resuming their resolute pace toward the factories.

Toward the assembled companies of the Eridani Light Horse.

Gilda frowned and punched her comm board. "Thom."

"Still not a good time, Gilda," Thomas Cole replied.

"You need to come back inside," she said.

"Can't do that," Cole said. "You stand and deliver, remember? We keep moving."

"Where are you going to move with all of that in front of you?"

"Maria's Elegy," Cole said.

Gilda blinked. The planetary capital also hosted the planet's primary spaceport; she knew the Light Horse's DropShips were there. The tiny port at the factory was too small to host a regiment's transports. It was barely large enough for the DefHes executives' DropShuttles. You couldn't even get a 'Mech up there.

"You're running?"

"Can't fight," Cole said after a minute. "Can't surrender. Don't see what other options we have."

"You can come back inside the walls," Gilda said firmly.

"Your bosses won't let us. The general asked."

"What?"

"Can't go back. Can't stay here. Our only way out is through."

Gilda stared at the backs of the Light Horse 'Mechs in front of her. Across the field the Jade Falcon 'Mechs were well over the horizon and getting larger. Even at a glance she could tell the Light Horse was badly outnumbered. The mercenaries had taken the Commonwealth's kroner and tried to stay true to their salt, but this was suicide.

"Who said you can't come in?" Gilda demanded.

"Your CEO."

"I'll go to the kommandant," Gilda began, but Cole stopped her.

"No time." The front edge of the Light Horse line rippled as the 'Mechs shifted their weight. They were getting ready to move. "You were a good friend, Gilda. If we don't both come through this, thanks for that."

If we don't both come through this. The very abstract concept of death in battle suddenly got very real for Gilda. More real even than watching the other mercenaries die. There was a very good chance Thom Cole, who she'd come to admire and consider a friend, was about to die. And she'd have to watch, safe behind the impenetrable walls and turrets and bunkers.

No.

"Hang on," Gilda said. "I'll get a door open."

"Good-bye, Gilda," Cole sent, and closed the channel.

Gilda stared out across the field for a minute longer, then jerked her controls to the side and stepped the *Zeus* down off the firing step. "Come on," she said to Mesrubbi. "We're going to do something."

"What?"

"The LCAF hung the Light Horse out to dry. They're going to die like those other mercenaries if we don't help them."

Mesrubbi turned her *Fafnir* off the step and followed; if Hauptmann Sradebovic noticed two of his 'Mechs leaving, he didn't say anything.

Gilda took the *Zeus* back toward the 'Mech hangars. Cole was right. There wasn't time for her to try speaking with the hauptmann or even Kommandant Heutzel.

"Gilda," Mesrubbi hissed, "think about this. They'll *fire* us. They might *shoot* us."

"I'm not letting them die out there," Gilda said.

"Gilda—"

"Go back if you need to. But I'm doing this."

"You're an idiot," Mesrubbi said. But her *Fafnir* trudged doggedly behind her the whole way.

By the time Gilda found the access port she was looking for and got it open, the leading edges of the Light Horse and the Clans had already engaged. Gilda had her *Zeus* moving as fast as it could—which wasn't very fast, as 'Mechs measured such things—and was leaving Mesrubbi behind, but she couldn't shake this conviction that she needed to do this, to save as many of the Light Horse as she could. She *had* to. Or she wouldn't be able to live with herself.

"Thom, I've got a gate open!" she sent. A touch transmitted the nav coordinates. "Pull back this way and we can screen you back inside the mountain." She waited, but there was no response. Gilda ground her teeth and urged the *Zeus* to go faster.

A few minutes later, alarms screamed at her. A cluster of red carets lit her HUD: Clan 'Mechs and tanks. None of the machines were as heavy as her *Zeus*, but there were four of them. They were painted in browns and grays; Hell's Horses then, and not the emerald green of the Jade Falcons.

All four of the contacts had been cutting across in front of her, but their sensors must have caught her, because all four turned toward her *Zeus*. Gilda stopped her 'Mech and reversed throttle. Four against one was a serious disadvantage, and she couldn't help the Light Horse if she was dead.

The first Hell's Horses 'Mech to come into range was a fast-moving *Kuma*. Gilda knew about *Kuma*s from her training. They were powerfully armed with a heavy large laser that hit harder than her own Gauss rifle, could jump as far as a *Spider* less than half their mass, and were almost as fast on the ground. Gilda's best chance against it was to hold the range open and hurt it at long range, where her *Zeus* was built to fight.

The *Zeus*' extended-range large laser blasted out at the *Kuma* almost before Gilda knew she was going to fire. The ruby beam missed, but it was close enough that the *Kuma* staggered a few steps as the Hell's Horses MechWarrior jerked their machine to the side. They corrected almost immediately.

"Well, okay then," Gilda murmured.

Behind the *Kuma*, the other Hell's Horses machines didn't slow.

The *Kuma* was fast enough that it was almost inside the range bracket of its own primary weapon by the time Gilda adjusted her aim and fired again. This time she added her Gauss rifle and LRM 15 to the ER large laser. The laser missed again, but almost all of her long-range missiles scattered explosions across the charging 'Mech, and the Gauss slug hit the 65-ton machine dead-center in the chest. To their credit, though, the Hell's Horses MechWarrior just leaned into the damage and continued their sprint forward, raining broken armor plates as they came.

The *Kuma* was more than twice as fast going forward as Gilda's *Zeus* was going backward. It was going to catch her if she didn't put it down quick, and the 'Mech was too fast and too strong to go down that quick unless she got unbelievably lucky. Gilda clutched her gunnery controls, watching the reload and recharge indicators, and tried to imagine if she'd earned that much luck recently.

"On your right," Mesrubbi said.

Gilda sidestepped the *Zeus* a few steps to the left, clearing the line of fire. In her HUD Mesrubbi's *Fafnir* stomped forward, not slowing, and triggered both the huge cannons built into its chest. The *Zeus'* sensors flared with incredible power readings, and the air crashed with paired sonic booms as the improved heavy Gauss rifles slammed two incredibly huge rounds downrange. Both took the *Kuma* in the chest.

The 'Mech simply came apart.

"Nice shooting," Gilda gasped.

"Thanks," Mesrubbi said. "But there's more."

The next 'Mech was a 65-ton *Hellbringer*, but two Epona hovertanks whipped around its legs before it could fire, and arrowed toward the Self-Protection Force 'Mechs. Gilda adjusted her aim toward the right-side tank. Eponas were built to Omni standards; the blower she targeted was configured with a pair of LRM 20 launchers. Both pods belched fire and missiles at her as the driver drove straight in. Gilda saw the launch and knew she had maybe a second; she squeezed all her ready triggers.

Her laser scored a bright weal across the Epona's turret but didn't penetrate. Her Gauss rifle put a slug into the ground next to the speeding tank, and her missiles scattered to the wind. Not that she saw anything except the laser; by the time the rest of her rounds arrived, the Epona's LRMs were falling around her.

Far more hit her than missed. The *Zeus* shook, lurching, and it was only luck that Gilda kept her machine on its feet.

Which was when the other Epona cut to the left, across her nose, turret cranked to the side, and hit her with its dual plasma cannons. Light and heat enveloped her 'Mech. Alarms screamed in her cockpit, and her cooling suit stiffened as the 'Mech's life support system pushed fresh coolant through its spaghetti tubes. More and more alarms lit. Gilda looked down, slapping overrides. The missile magazine showed dangerous heat levels. If those missile bodies cooked off...

Most of the lights in her cockpit went off.

The *Zeus* lurched to a halt, off-balance. Its reactor had succumbed to the heat override protocols and shut down. Gilda was helpless.

And falling. She barely had time to brace herself before 80 tons of BattleMech hit the ground in a limp mass. Gilda rocked in her restraints, feeling muscles twinge in her neck as the impact threatened to rip the heavy neurohelmet off her head.

Emergency power and basic sensors kept her HUD up as she beat at her controls in a futile attempt to speed up the emergency restart process. It would only be seconds, but in combat every second was precious.

The *Hellbringer* leveled its PPC arms at Mesrubbi's *Fafnir* and cut loose; the two 'Mechs were infinitesimally linked by blue-white actinics, and then the *Fafnir* was stumbling back on its stubby legs. Her return fire, another pair of Gauss slugs, cracked harmlessly into the sky. Behind them, past where Gilda had fallen, the pair of Eponas skirled into sliding turns to come around again.

More and more green lights lit up on her boards as the *Zeus*' laboring heat sinks slowly got the waste heat from her weapons and the Epona's plasma cannons under control. Only another second or two…

The 80-ton 'Mech shuddered into motion. Gilda started it getting upright, already searching her HUD for the tanks.

Missiles crashed down on the *Zeus* as it found its feet, more impacts throwing her still-logy 'Mech off balance and destroying more of her precious armor. A *Zeus* was an assault 'Mech, liberally protected; Gilda wasn't used to thinking about her armor as something that could run out, but now she was. The Hell's Horses assaults were brutal.

"Gilda, look out!" Mesrubbi cried.

Gilda looked, but it was too late. The damned two-barrel Epona was charging straight at her again. The *Zeus*' weapons were too far out of line…for that tank. The other one, the missile carrier, was crossing in front of her, relying on speed to escape her fire basket. She fired her Gauss rifle and missiles, missiles first. The warheads went wide again, missing the fast blower, but she corrected her aim before triggering the Gauss rifle.

That ferrous slug ripped straight through the Epona's plenum chamber, dumping air out. That destroyed its lift cushion, which meant the tank dug into the sandy ground at well over

100 kph; the sleek tank became a rolling cloud of smoke and debris spread across a couple hundred meters of desert.

Incredibly, Mesrubbi's sluggish *Fafnir* somehow interposed itself between the Epona and Gilda's *Zeus* before the Hell's Horses gunner could hit their foot trip. The eye-searing pulses of plasma hit the *Fafnir* squarely. Gilda's IR detectors pegged their readings as the ions recombined. The *Fafnir* staggered, then fell still. Amazingly, Mesrubbi had managed to hold her 'Mech upright as it shut down.

The *Zeus* was fully back up; Gilda slammed her throttle to the stops and cut along to follow the Epona. The swift blower was already past her and sprinting to clear the distance so it could come around; her missiles and rifle were still reloading, but when those indicators turned green there was a chance it would still be in range…

The *Hellbringer* fired, both PPCs again. One missed.

The other reached between the *Fafnir*'s blocky shoulders and obliterated the squat cockpit assembly.

And Ilhan Mesrubbi.

Gilda screamed, the Epona forgotten. Her arms and legs spasmed. The *Zeus* couldn't turn fast enough. Eyes burning, Gilda dragged her sights around to bear on the *Hellbringer*. She triggered her missiles too fast; they scattered across the desert. The Gauss rifle reloaded a moment later; she triggered it, but the slug missed, digging a furrow through a sand dune beyond the Hell's Horses 'Mech. Only her laser hit, digging a glowing weal across the blocky 'Mech's chest.

Heat, far below what the Epona had done to her, suffused her cockpit, but Gilda didn't feel it. She screamed and screamed, seeing the *Fafnir* fall during every blink of her burning eyes. The reload indicators were all red. It took time, precious seconds to feed in new missiles, to load a heavy metal slug, for laser capacitors to gather up enough charge to fire a damaging beam. It was all too slow.

She'd been too slow.

"Gilda, go back inside," a scratchy voice said.

Gilda looked through her tears, slapping controls. "Thom!"

"We couldn't get back now even if we tried. The Jade Falcons—" The broadcast cut out.

"Thom!"

"—are cutting us down. They wouldn't even take the bid the general offered them. Save yourself, Gil—" The signal cut off again.

Gilda gasped, suddenly unable to breathe beneath the weight pressing on her chest. Thom was gone. Ilhan was gone. Her weapons' indicators blinked green; her hands, well-trained even while her conscious mind was screaming, had kept the *Hellbringer* in her sights. She triggered all of them again. This time all three hit.

Her large laser painted its hellish touch across the *Hellbringer*'s side chest; a moment later the Gauss rifle put its slug through the still-hot, already softened armor, crushing through the remainder and all but obliterating the internal framework holding that side of the OmniMech together. Its return paired PPCs crashed into the *Zeus* like thunderbolts, but Gilda saw a handful of her LRMs hit the same spot, finally collapsing the *Hellbringer*'s side and destroying the extra-light engine components there.

The *Hellbringer* turned away. Gilda crowed hoarsely in triumph.

She was still crowing when the Epona she'd forgotten hit her again with its plasma cannons. The *Zeus* locked up around her, and she barely had time to see the warning lights flash about her remaining LRM ammunition when her auto-eject system ripped the *Zeus*' head apart and flung her clear of the 'Mech.

It took an hour for a skimmer to find Gilda, trapped in the wreckage of her cockpit couch. The Epona had scurried off to screen the *Hellbringer* back to support.

She spent most of that hour sobbing.

Gilda barely remembered the skimmer ride back into the factory. Before she knew it, she found herself standing in her cooling suit in front of Kommandant Heutzel, who was also in his cooling suit. The Hell's Horses had settled into a holding pattern; the Jade Falcons were busy chasing the scraps of the Eridani Light Horse into the hills.

"I don't know if you heard," Heutzel finally said, "but Clan Wolf is here. They hit a pirate point a day out and their DropShips are already burning in."

The kommandant always gives the bad news, Gilda remembered. "I hadn't heard, sir."

"So that's coming," Heutzel said. The kommandant looked around the small office; it was the bay manager's office, small and crumpled, with broken components and discarded noteputers and hardcopy. The air was thick with the cloying scent of overheated lubricant. Gilda realized her eyes burned, but she didn't know if it was from the air or from— *No.* She squeezed her eyes shut. It wasn't time to think about that.

"You're out of the battalion," Heutzel said.

Gilda opened her eyes, but the CO was still staring at the side wall. "Yes, sir."

"Obviously. You nearly jeopardized our entire plan here." Heutzel sniffed, clearing his sinuses, then snort-sneezed. Hesperus' fine dust did that to sinuses. "And you got MechWarrior Mesrubbi killed."

Gilda ground her teeth. "Sir—"

"You don't think we *all* wanted to be out there?" Heutzel blurted. His face twisted back around to face her. To her surprise, his expression wasn't angry. Or at least, the anger in it wasn't directed at her. "You don't think every single member of this battalion doesn't know what you did and why, and doesn't wish they had a crystal ball to go back in time and go with you?"

"Sir—"

"I did *not* give you permission to speak," Heutzel barked. He swiped a hand across his upper lip, blinked hard. "I shouldn't even be talking to you." His face, never florid, was almost purple. "If we could find a single damn Lyran provost, you'd be under arrest."

Gilda didn't speak.

"You're out of the battalion," he said again. "If we're all alive in a few days, there will probably be charges. Destruction of company property, at the very least." Heutzel sneezed again. "Anything to say for yourself?"

Gilda opened and closed her mouth but couldn't speak. She cleared her throat. "I wish it had come out differently."

"We all do," Heutzel said.

"Sir..."

"What?"

"Is there any word, sir? About the Light Horse?"

Heutzel stood. At his sides, his fists clenched and unclenched. "Only bad ones," he replied. "Now get out of my sight."

There hadn't been room inside the walls for the Light Horse 'Mechs, but the advance party support staff had carved a small compound out of a disused corner of the parade field. The hard-shell tents and pseudo-Quonsets were already coming down when Gilda stepped around the corner and saw them. She'd been wandering aimlessly and realized that even if the 'Mechs had made it through the Jade Falcons and Hell's Horses, the support staff—the technicians, astechs, administrators and logistics pogues—wouldn't have anywhere to go.

The only spot of calm in the chaos was the small assembly area on the front edge of the encampment. A pair of temporary flagpoles had been driven into the ground; one mast was bare, and the other flew the prancing Eridani Light Horse guidon. Gilda stopped a few meters away, watching the fabric flutter in the tepid breeze.

A technician in khaki ELH battledress stepped up next to her. He snapped to attention as if he were on parade, rendered the flag an academy-precise salute, and then stood there. The muscle in his jaw worked as he ground his teeth.

"Is there any word?" Gilda whispered.

"No good ones," the technician ground out. Then he did a careful about-face and marched away. Gilda watched him, then glanced past him at the chaos. The camp was coming apart. In the absence of the combat units they were here to support, Gilda expected almost all of them would be on company payroll before tomorrow morning. In a couple days, there'd be no trace this camp was ever here.

She turned back to look up at the flag. Thom Cole had explained the empty flagpole, a bare post for the long-dead Star League flag. The prancing pony flew half-mast like that and had for centuries, because the Eridani Light Horse still mourned the death of the ancient league their ancestors had fought for.

Gilda sniffed. She'd grinned wryly at Cole's conviction when he'd told her that story. The Self-Protection Force was a job, one she loved—had loved—to be sure, but it was just a job. She couldn't see herself flying the corporate flag at half-mast any longer than the memo said to.

But today she felt different. Today she'd watched an entire regiment charge toward death because they'd signed a piece of paper saying they would.

Today she'd seen her best friend killed because of a choice Gilda had made.

Maybe two best friends.

Gilda looked around. No one was near her. She stepped close to the flagpole, undid the rope, and dragged the Light Horse flag down. She bundled it quickly beneath one arm, put her head down, and turned back toward the building. No one stopped her. Gilda didn't know if it was because no one cared, or because she knew they'd all be at least putative Defiance Industries employees in a few hours.

If the Clans made it inside the perimeter, no one would want to be caught with mercenary paraphernalia. A Light Horse flag would be a death sentence.

Gilda wasn't going to let that happen.

Somewhere out there, someone would want to keep the traditions of the Eridani Light Horse alive. The dream of that organization had endured more than three centuries already. It was a light kept burning by the will of men and women that it should continue. Thom Cole had carried that light, in his way.

Gilda would carry it forward.

She shouldered her away around a stream of astechs coming out of the nearby building, ducking inside. She knew where she had to go. And it wasn't inside the Defiance Industries building, but the way out was through.

A bit of verse stuck in her mind.

"Followed their mercenary calling," she whispered, "and took their wages and are dead."

FAFNIR
Assault–100 tons

LOKI (HELLBRINGER)
Heavy–65 tons

KUMA
Heavy—**60** tons

VICTOR
Assault—**80** tons

ZEUS
Assault—**80** tons

STRONG AS STEEL

MICHAEL J. CIARAVELLA

FORT PASUACK
MIRACH
FEDERATED SUNS
20 MARCH 3151

This is going to be even simpler than I imagined!

From where he lay, deep in the underbrush dotting the tree line, Jonathan Sparrow could easily observe the war games going on just below the ridge. While others might have been concerned to be so close to the hulking behemoths known as BattleMechs that had dominated warfare for centuries, Sparrow was confident in both his camouflage and that he was safely outside of the boundaries of the exercise. Not only that, but he'd been researching them since he had gotten this assignment, had been watching his quarry for weeks since arriving on the planet, and had heard stories of them since he had been a child on New Avalon.

The Eridani Light Horse.

Once one of the largest and most revered mercenary units under contract, the ELH could trace its grand history back to the original Star League, serving with honor and distinction on battlefields throughout the Inner Sphere. While elements of the ELH had been beaten down and shattered again and again, they rose back up each time, like the legendary phoenix, to be reborn and once again hold high the best ideals of a bygone era.

From where he watched, Sparrow wondered if he was watching the beginning of such a rebirth once again.

After nearly thirteen months on Mirach under an uneventful garrison contract for the planetary government, the ELH had been maintaining a nearly constant series of training exercises as they prepared for their contract to end. Despite technically being a part of the Federated Suns, Mirach had always prided itself on protecting itself, creating such units as the Mirach Home Guard to ensure its safety. Unfortunately, that also made it a target, and raiders regularly preyed on the planet, knowing the government would be slow to seek outside help. Raiders, suspected to be Republic deserters fleeing from the besieged, fragmenting nation, had swept down and struck the Home Guard hard, overwhelming them with numbers and advanced technology. The Home Guard eventually drove them off, but at a terrible cost. The Eridani Light Horse 11th Recon Battalion, the Alley Cats, had been hired to prevent other raiders from taking advantage of the planet's momentary weakness, and from all indications, the plan had been successful.

However, from the news recently received around the capitol, the planetary militia had finally built itself back up to the point where they could once again take over the protection of Mirach and save the government the cost of hiring such elite mercenaries. Seeing the writing on the wall as clearly as Sparrow did, the ELH commander, Colonel Amelia Donovan, had stepped up their training regimen to prepare for their next contract, conducting a series of exercises to ensure that the unit was still in top form.

When Sparrow had heard about the most recent set of night exercises, he knew this would be the ideal time to execute the next phase of his mission. The mercenaries' attention would be focused elsewhere for the duration of his intrusion, and when they did return, the victorious forces would be celebrating while the losers would be eager to drown their sorrows at the nearby pub...assuming they weren't assigned to a punishment detail immediately afterward. Either way, his insertion would go unnoticed, and he should be in and out quickly enough to deliver his message and get clear before he was noticed. His superiors trusted him enough to leave the operational specifics to him, so now it just required him to wait for the opportune moment.

Until then, he could afford to take a little time to watch and see how the once-legendary mercenaries fared.

From what he had gathered from his sources, the exercise was between Captain Denise Bezos' Striker Lance and Lieutenant Andrew Sacrow's Support Lance. Both sides had been supplemented with forces to augment where the other was weakest: Bezos had a lance of JES Missile Carriers to provide long-range fire support, while the Support Lance had a mixed bag of Pegasus scout tanks and Fulcrum hovertanks to rival the Strikers' speed.

From his position, Sparrow was able to see the Striker lance as it swept the area, each BattleMech carefully positioned to provide support to its lancemates. Captain Bezos led in her *War Dog*, while the remaining three units, a *Marauder*, a *Thunderbolt*, and a *Warhammer*, maintained a rough diamond formation as they advanced across the field.

Interestingly, the ELH seemed to be foregoing its recent focus on full mixed units, as infantry units had apparently not been included in the exercise—a fortunate circumstance for Sparrow. While he had no doubt the infantry would have gained valuable knowledge by engaging in the night exercises, having the two forces on the alert for possible camouflaged humans on the field would have complicated the situation far too much for his liking.

Unsettled by that particular thought, Sparrow glanced around, verifying he neither heard nor saw any telltale signs of BattleMechs in his vicinity. While he was confident his sneak suit's visual camouflage could conceal him from the base's sensor suite, advanced BattleMech sensors were a far greater threat.

Any further thoughts on the subject were superseded as the battle began in earnest. From the south side of the exercise area, two Pegasus hovertanks shot out over a nearby hill, quickly closing the distance to their opponents. The Striker forces began spacing out, ignoring the light tanks for the moment as they prepared to respond to the new threat they knew would be coming.

However, the Strikers also seemed determined not to allow their opponents to get away with it scot-free, however. In unison, the JES missile carriers spat hundreds of missiles into the area, saturating the area with simulated death. The closer of the two tanks managed to evade the barrage, but the other was pelted with paint-rounds, turning the camouflage pattern into a hellish red kaleidoscope. The umpire must have determined the tank had been damaged, as it abruptly slowed down, and then cut away at a sharp angle, clearly fleeing the scene at the maximum speed it was now able to attain. For a moment, Sparrow thought the missile carriers would finish off the light tank, but it appeared the Strikers were waiting for bigger fish.

They were not long in coming. Two BattleMechs, a *Crusader* and a *Penetrator*, stomped forward. While the *Penetrator* was painted in the standard ELH camouflage pattern, the *Crusader* was a true work of art, with flames about the canopy, chains entwined along the length of its arms, and a green-hued tiger lying next to a white lamb adoring the chest. From his research, this unique BattleMech, *Fearful Symmetry*, could only belong to Master Sergeant Hisui "The Jade Tyger" Kamiya.

The *Crusader*, with its missile-heavy armament, seemed like a natural member of the support lance, but the *Penetrator* normally wouldn't have taken on such a role, especially with its primarily laser-based armament. The *Penetrator* quickly showed its worth, however, lancing out with its two large lasers, firing each in succession, and cutting armor from the left arm and leg of the Striker *Warhammer*. As the two forces closed, the *Crusader*'s LRMs would be of limited use, but the *Penetrator*'s bevy of medium pulse lasers would make even the largest Striker 'Mech hesitate to close the range too quickly.

Captain Bezos clearly thought the same thing, and ordered her closest BattleMechs to rush them, hoping the numerical advantage would dissuade the Supports from moving forward too eagerly. Dropping her *War Dog* back, she allowed her lancemates to close with the laser-heavy BattleMech, focusing their fire upon it in the hope of dropping one of the enemy BattleMechs while the enemy forces were split, hopefully drawing the other Support Mechs out from cover.

Laser fire and PPC lighting reached out, scouring simulated armor from the *Penetrator*. One arm dropped limply as it was deemed lost from heavy damage to the left torso, and the 'Mech dropped to one knee as the umpire apparently decided it had taken too much damage to keep its balance.

The Striker gambit appeared to have worked, however. Seeing the *Penetrator* drop, the remaining two Support Lance BattleMechs, a venerable *Archer* and a *Crossbow*, stepped out from cover. The two missile-heavy 'Mechs launched salvoes at the *Warhammer*, buffeting it with missiles. The heavy 'Mech suddenly slumped over, having reached the limit of its endurance, and shut down.

With the Support BattleMechs having abandoned their cover, they were now the perfect targets for the JES armor, which replied with a vengeance, sending a veritable storm of missiles towards the new 'Mechs. Both were soon covered in paint, and the *Crossbow* seemed to sway for a moment, but stayed up. The Striker lance, sensing blood, closed the distance, moving in for the kill.

Until one of the JES carriers went up in a furrow of orange paint.

Quickly shifting his rangefinder, Sparrow found the source of the attack: The two Pegasus tanks had linked back up and attacked the rearmost JESsie with lasers and short-range missiles, taking it out in a single salvo. The other tanks were trying to maneuver to fire as well, but their lack of close-range weapons left them at a severe disadvantage, locked into place by the two circling Pegasuses.

The Striker commander, quick to respond to the new threat, turned the lightest unit of his lance, an *Enforcer* III, back on the hovertanks, but it was struck by a pair of PPC blasts before it could fully turn, the fractional-powered blasts burning away paint and destroying its right arm, which now hung uselessly at its side. Instead of sneaking the Fulcrum tanks into the background, Lieutenant Sacrow had held them in reserve to pin the BattleMechs right where he wanted them. It probably wouldn't turn the tide, as the other three BattleMechs quickly savaged the closer of the two Fulcrums, but it did change the nature of the battlefield. While all of the Support 'Mechs were damaged, the *Penetrator* had regained its feet, and they were now going toe-to-toe with five units to three, while the attacking hovercraft kept the JESsies from providing support.

Sparrow nodded in professional appreciation, and lowered his binoculars, knowing the exercise would soon be over. Even if the Strikers managed to rally, they would lose at least two more of their tanks, and probably one of their Battlemechs—the *Marauder* now being savaged by paint missiles, if he were to venture a guess. It was likely that the Support lance would pull back to the forest cover, allowing them to once again provide mutual support as the Strikers were forced to either close to continue the engagement or redeploy to support their tank forces.

Either way, he was fairly sure the umpires would call this a success for the Support Lance: The Pegasus Scout Tanks could clearly disengage at will, and it would be a far smaller Striker force going after the Support 'Mechs now. He had no doubt the captain would have some choice words for his clever subordinate, but Sparrow was happy he had gotten the chance to see it.

Moving stealthily through the tall grass, he pressed on under the ground radar the ELH had placed in the area. It was mounted about a meter and a half up, to ensure animals and ground-clutter didn't set it off all night long, but roving patrols and an extensive camera system more than made up for that. Sparrow hoped his sneak suit would help with the cameras, and his examination of the patrol routes should guarantee no other issues. He'd paid the local contractors that had worked on the compound handsomely, and while they didn't have all the answers, it was enough to ensure he had a good running start on the situation.

He moved slowly, taking nearly fifteen minutes to cover the short distance, glad the dim moon cast no more than a pale shadow in the sky as he crept closer to the compound.

It was all working perfectly—until he felt the rifle muzzle press against the side of his head.

Sparrow froze, instinctively moving to grab for the muzzle, but was forced to shut his eyes as a blinding light pinned him to the ground, clearly one of the wall-mounted spotlights from the compound. Pressing his head to the dirt, he very slowly pressed his hands against the ground to either side of him, only lacing his fingers over his head when ordered to by the ELH infantryman who had captured him.

Glancing up, his eyes finally adjusted against the light, Sparrow found himself ringed by not just one, but nearly a full squad of the ELH's elite Pathfinder infantry. As he listened, he heard the rush of air from several turboprop support vehicles approaching, potentially the twins of the Pegasus scout tanks he had seen earlier. From how quickly they'd appeared, he suspected they had been engaged in a night exercise of their own, but he wasn't willing to see if the rifles they were holding only held paintball rounds.

The more he thought about it, it was clearly not just the exercise that had done him in. The warriors around him had snuck up professionally, and from how quickly and carefully they had focused on him without searching for other intruders, he knew he must have been spotted a lot sooner than he'd realized.

When they finally hauled him up, securing his hands behind his back, Sparrow waited quietly as a Maxim hover transport pulled up, and a hulking bear of a man stepped out, his two sharp brown eyes narrowing under an enormous pair of eyebrows. Sparrow recognized him instantly—Captain Daniel "Bear" Blonsky was one of Colonel Donovan's longest-serving officers—and nodded respectfully at him.

Taking in Sparrow's stealth-suit, the Bear looked carefully at him before speaking in a deep bass rumble, "And what do you have to say for yourself?"

For a brief moment, Sparrow thought of trying to bluff his way in, but supposed it would be more efficient to just come clean, and take the inevitable embarrassment in stride.

He smiled, and gave the best shrug he could with his arms secured.

"Take me to your leader?"

From where she stood at the front of the classroom, Colonel Amelia Donovan, commander of the 11th Recon Battalion of the famed 71st Eridani Light Horse, looked over the various MechWarrior trainees gathered in the classroom for a live viewing of the war games on the large monitor behind her. While she would normally have observed the mission from the field or in the command center several buildings over, their instructor, Captain Twofalls, had suggested the trainees might benefit more from hearing from their commander instead of him.

Glancing over at the instructor, who stood stoically at the back of the classroom, she wondered for the dozenth time whether it had been his idea or whether the suggestion had been made to him. It was true that the duties of running the company, so long the responsibility of her father, had taken her away from her true love, the education of the next generation of the Eridani Light Horse. The more she thought about it, the more likely she figured one of her loyal subordinates may have suggested just such a course of action to the instructor, and while she resented being handled like that on one level, she also could not help but recognize how much more peaceful she felt in this setting.

When the small alarm buzzed on her communicator, Donovan was tempted to depart early, her first instinct to personally deal with the situation. If Alexa or Ron had been there, she might have done so, but the married officers who handled her operations and personal security respectively had not yet landed since entering the system on their return from Galatea, leaving her a bit shorthanded. Her S2, Gordon Temple, had assured her that he could handle the situation from the command center in his role as head of intelligence for the unit, and Bear had brought some of the Pathfinders with him to look into the situation personally. Amelia had no doubt that not even one of the famed Word of Blake Manei Domini could take on such a force when they were forewarned, and the fact that no other alerts had been raised seemed to indicate she was right.

Glancing at the assembled students again, Donovan clasped her hands behind her back, making sure that they could all see her crisp fatigues and the ELH patch on her arm. "All right, ladies and gentlemen: Can someone tell me what the Striker lance could have done better?"

A flurry of hands shot up, and she smiled as she chose one of the cadets she had seen taking furious notes during the exercise. The young man shot to his feet, coming to attention. "Ma'am, the Striker lance should not have lost track of enemy armor units, even if they were damaged."

"Very true." Donovan replied. "Still, we need to remember that combat is a fluid thing. While their commander could have used some of her resources to ensure they were no longer an active threat, and clearly should have, there are times when you only have so much bandwidth. To the Support team's credit, they did pull those units nearly entirely from the battlefield, and bringing both damaged units back cost them the use of the tanks. In a real battle, we would want to be more careful with such losses, as each comes with a body count. What else?"

Another cadet stood when pointed at. "The Support commander should have pulled back when the rest of the lance appeared, to better assess the situation."

Donovan tilted her head slightly, giving him a tolerant smile. "Don't let the captain hear you say that…no, that choice was probably the best one. Sometimes there isn't time to go with the perfect answer, and not closing the range would have given the support units an ideal range advantage and the chance to take the initiative. While I might agree there were other ways to move in to keep their options open, I don't think it was the wrong call. Give me five pages on two unit commanders who would agree, no more recent than 3100, and the pros and cons of both by the end of the week."

To his credit, the cadet didn't groan, but his eyes almost looked betrayed by the extra work. Donovan had been notorious for such assignments during her tenure as the head of the training cadre. Such assignments gave the cadets important face time with her, which usually allowed some of the best the chance to shine and get recognized when it came time to graduate.

Donovan was about to choose another student when Bear returned, stepping into the room surprisingly quietly for his size. His expression was carefully neutral, but Donovan had known him long enough to know she was needed. Giving a small smile to the trainees, she watched several hands go down slowly.

"It appears I have been called away, but I am going to take one more question." She gestured to the trainee, the wiry young woman who had put down her hand last. "You."

The trainee took to her feet instantly, and ensured her posture was perfect before responding, "Colonel, when you stated you did not think it was the wrong call... What would you have done?"

Donovan glanced at the instructor, sharing a small smile of approval, and then turned to the young woman with a serious but not stern expression. It did not come easy to question the wisdom of a superior, and she appreciated the deft way the cadet had managed it.

"I probably would have swung my left flank to keep my movement up and take an extra moment to see if there were any other surprises coming for me, but otherwise...I would have done the same damn thing," she replied, getting a surprised burst of chuckles from the room. "The Eridani Light Horse has not gotten to be where we are by being predictable." Turning to depart, she looked back at the young woman. "However, when I do it, I would have called it an abrupt tactical relocation."

Donovan allowed the laughter to follow her to the door, and Bonderevsky stepped into lockstep with her as they walked out the door.

With Bear having brought her up to speed on their unexpected visitor, Donovan was careful to seem unhurried as she headed down to the area of the compound designated as the brig. It had been set up to hold rowdy drunks, but it had also been constructed to ensure it could do more in a pinch, although there had been little call for it on this most recent contract.

As she arrived at the control room, she stepped up beside Temple, who was watching the intruder as he sat chained to a table, watched over by two armed guards. "Has he said anything?"

Temple shook his head, not taking his eyes off the prisoner. "Nothing except to ask for you. We haven't asked him anything more, as he seems content to just wait patiently."

"What does he think happened?"

"I am assuming he thought we caught him on a camera he did not see." Temple replied. "I doubt he's even considered that the other tradesman sold him out."

Donovan smiled. The ELH had good contacts in the city, and Temple's people had become suspicious when someone had been sniffing around for the specifications on the compound. The ELH paid their workers well, and two of the former workers had reached out to inform them of the stranger looking for information on the ELH outpost. With the impending exercise, Donovan had expected something like this might happen, and had prepared for it.

Temple shrugged after a moment. "Normally, I would brush him off as a crank, interrogate him, and then hand him over to the local constabulary. This doesn't smell right, though...no identification, top-of-the-line sneaksuit, and from what we heard, plenty of cash to burn. If we had not been forewarned, there's a good chance he would have gotten in, and who knows where we would be then."

"Did he have any weapons on him?"

"Just a low-voltage stunner, nothing that would have given our boys anything more than an ugly nap. It is one of the other reasons we went so light on him...if this was an assassination attempt, it was a damn strange one, but that doesn't feel right to me. No, I think this is something else, but damned if I know what it is."

"It almost seems like a test," Bear replied from the other side of her. "To see exactly what we would do."

"The question is..." Amelia replied. "Did we pass?"

Temple shrugged slightly. "Only one way to find out."

Donovan gave him a wan smile and nodded before schooling her expression into something more suitable for what would come next. Standing slowly, she allowed the two men to precede her into the room.

Sparrow had finished berating himself for the hundredth time, and had moved on to a mental review of the locations the additional scanners could have been hidden when the heavy metal door creaked open. Without shifting their eyes from him, his guards spread themselves out further toward the walls, allowing space for the additional visitors to enter the room.

They would need it. The first to enter was Bear, and for a moment Sparrow could have believed he was facing a warrior of pure Clan Elemental stock, with arms that could have doubled as cargo grapples. His sharp, no-nonsense expression seemed to say he would have been happier to be conducting a far more active interrogation than Sparrow had endured so far. He stepped up to the left side of the table and leaned against the far wall, watching their captive for any sign of a threat.

The second man was almost more frightening in his own way, entering with a quiet, careful dignity, and cutting immediately to the right. His blond hair was carefully coiffed, and his small, pencil-thin mustache might have seemed silly on another warrior. There was an air of gravitas to him, however, that made Sparrow think he was the one behind his capture, and he quickly resolved not to underestimate this man. From the cursory glance he gave his prisoner, it was clear he had already studied Sparrow to the extent remote cameras could do so, and it was not difficult to recognize another in his own field.

The arrival of the third guest, however, was almost enough to bring him to his feet, if the shackles that bound him to the table would have allowed it. Even if the rank insignia on her green battle fatigues did not show her to be the highest-ranking member of the famed Eridani Light Horse on planet, the way she carried herself would have identified his visitor as Colonel Amelia Donovan, commanding officer of the Alley Cats, and by extension, the Eridani Light Horse. Unlike her two companions, she made no effort to hide that she was watching him curiously, waiting only for the door to close before taking the single metal chair opposite him.

Donovan continued to give him a long, appraising glance, and he was tempted to say something, despite his previous reticence in the face of his captors. She allowed the game to play out for nearly a full minute, confirming she knew exactly what she was doing, before gesturing to him. "I was told you wanted to see me?"

"Yes, Colonel," Sparrow replied. "I hope you will forgive the unorthodox method of my arrival."

"In the future, you might consider making an appointment with my staff," Donovan replied. "At the very least, it will reduce the chance of you being shot by our perimeter security."

"Slightly," Bear growled from the far side of the room, and Donovan struggled not to smile.

Sparrow smiled, which he hoped would come across as ingratiating. "I do apologize, ma'am. Due to the nature of the message I bear, I thought it would be more prudent to attempt a more—surreptitious approach." His eyes flicked over to the blond man. "I seem to have overestimated my abilities in that area, however."

The glance Donovan gave the blond man confirmed him as her S2. Sparrow waited for the colonel to focus back on him. "You stated you have a message?"

"Yes, ma'am," he replied. "I come bearing a special offer of employment."

Once again, there was the shadow of a smile from the mercenary commander. "Then you certainly should have made an appointment," Donovan replied. "I have an entire dedicated staff that handles our contract negotiations. While I appreciate the...unorthodox methods you used to come to see me, I recommend that you go through regular channels."

Sparrow shrugged slightly. "I would have liked nothing better, for convenience's sake at the very least, but I fear my mission is a bit more urgent than I would like." He glanced among the three people in the room before focusing back on the colonel. "And my superiors sought to begin this discussion with the utmost discretion."

Now the larger man guffawed, appropriate for his barrel chest. "They may wish to have a bit of a chat with you, then."

Sparrow turned slightly toward the other man, gracing him with a thin smile. "No doubt you will be right, but there are many different types of discretion. I believe I still might have managed to keep any observers from knowing too much."

Donovan leaned back, considering Sparrow for a moment. While she seemed to be enjoying the verbal fencing for its own sake, it was clear she was not going to allow herself—or him—to indulge in it all evening. "You still have not introduced yourself, sir, or told us who you are representing."

Turning back to her, Sparrow bowed his head slightly in apology. "An oversight, I assure you. My name is Jonathan Sparrow, and I come bearing a message from Prince Julian Davion of the Federated Suns."

In an instant, all traces of humor left the three visitors, and he also sensed the intense interest of the two guards in the room. Seeming to also sense their attention, the S2 gave a nearly imperceptible nod, and the two guards departed, leaving the four of them alone. While Sparrow was sure they were still being watched over the monitors, and that the guards had gone no further than outside the door, Bear straightened, moving away from the wall to take the place of departing soldiers.

Everyone waited until the door sealed up again, and then Donovan fixed him with an intent expression. "That is a very interesting statement, Mr...Sparrow," she finally replied. "Do you have any confirmation of who you are, or who you purport to represent? When we invited you into the compound, we did not find any identification upon you."

"A conscious choice, I assure you," he replied. "As I mentioned, I was concerned that I might be intercepted before we had the chance to speak, and I did not want to affect our discussion if I should be delayed in arriving. However, you should have a message in your master buffer from one of your vendors, Tydon Unlimited. If you use the proper name of the third item ordered on the list, it will provide you with the code key for the attached document, which is meant to look like a corrupted invoice. The document will both support my bonafides and confirm my authority to speak to you on behalf of the Federated Suns."

No one moved for a moment, but Sparrow was sure the S2's team was working on the decryption as quickly as he had spoken.

Without waiting for confirmation, Donovan said, "Assuming that is true, it once again seems like you have gone to a great deal of trouble to keep your arrival quiet. Is there a reason for that?"

"My employer believes it is of the utmost importance to bring the Eridani Light Horse regiments back under contract with the Federated Suns, the realm they had served so faithfully for decades."

Donovan went very still, and he thought he saw a flicker in her eyes before she continued speaking. "That would be a very worthy goal. However, I am not sure how attainable it might be. As I am sure you know, there has been a bit of difficulty in that regard."

Sparrow's lips thinned in displeasure, silently confirming that he knew all about those particular difficulties. "The First Prince is aware of the…challenges you have found in the past, ma'am."

Donovan's eyes narrowed slightly, and for a moment thought he might have overplayed his hand. "You mean the challenges my father encountered, Mr. Sparrow."

Sparrow nearly kicked himself, remembering that her father had passed several months ago, leaving her in command of the unit. It had been the elder Donovan's dream to reform the Eridani Light Horse as a full mercenary regiment, but they had been stymied at every turn by bureaucratic holdups.

When offered to join Task Force Serpent in 3058, General Adriana Winston, commander of the Eridani Light Horse, had bargained hard for the ELH's place in the historic mission. Jumping into the unknown, following unreliable intelligence from a Clan traitor, there was no guarantee they would ever find the Smoke Jaguar homeworld of Huntress, nor that any of them would ever return.

As a term of their contract, General Winston had ensured that their pay would be maintained in the Inner Sphere, a staggering sum that would have guaranteed any remaining ELH forces could rebuild and maintain their legacy, even if the unit was destroyed to the last warrior. Naturally skeptical of what might happen while they were away, the general had ensured that the funds would be split into three pieces, invested in the Federated Suns, the Lyran Commonwealth, and with ComStar on Terra. While such redundancy did cost them in interest, it also ensured that a sizable portion of the funds would be immediately available if anything happened.

As fate would have it, however, the unit would survive Task Force Serpent, and would not come to their demise in the Clan Homeworlds.

At the time.

While the strike at the Clan Homeworlds would not destroy the unit, the Word of Blake Jihad would decimate the Eridani Light Horse regiments: The 21st Striker and 19th Cavalry regiments would be shattered on Dieron, losing over 90% of their forces, and the 151st would be destroyed by orbital bombardment on the planet Columbus. Contact with the 71st on Huntress had been lost when communication with the Clan Homeworlds was severed, but later intelligence would reveal that the unit had been battered in constant Trials of Possession from the various Clans, eventually causing them to be defeated and absorbed into Clan Goliath Scorpion. For all intents and purposes, many thought the Eridani Light Horse had perished in the fires of the Jihad.

The spirit of the ELH continued, however, with some of the units that had been left behind. One such unit, the 11th Recon Battalion of the 71st Light Horse Regiment, had remained behind in the Federated Suns on training cadre duty, under the command of Colonel Richard Donovan, who had been on rear detachment at the time the rest of the unit had left the Inner Sphere. During the post-Jihad era, Colonel Donovan had lobbied ceaselessly to access the funds held by the various nations, arguing that they were rightfully his to use to rebuild the regiments.

Unfortunately, while ComStar had received confirmation of the destruction of the 71st Light Horse on Huntress, the Great Houses refused to believe it without evidence. Neither the Federated Suns nor the Lyran Commonwealth would agree to release the funds held in their care until there was confirmation that the 71st was no longer viable, despite what ComStar had decreed. In hindsight, it only made sense: Neither nation wanted the other to have the advantage of the ELH working for them, and if something had happened to Donovan's unit in the meantime, the money would have no clear beneficiary.

With the outbreak of the unrest after Gray Monday, the elder Donovan had even gone to First Prince Harrison Davion to request his support in reforming the regiments, and received tentative encouragement for the project. Unfortunately, Davion wanted the ELH to work solely for the Federated Suns, and that was a line Donovan was not willing to cross. While amiable, the negotiations had outlasted both men, and Caleb Davion, Harrison's son and successor, had not even been willing to consider the possibility, seemingly dashing the hopes of the Alley Cats at seeing their dream become a reality.

"If the First Prince is looking for a full ELH regiment, he might do best to reach out to the Lyran Commonwealth. Lieutenant General Eichler may be willing to negotiate with them." The Lyran Commonwealth, seeking to rebuild their own depleted forces in the wake of the Clan attacks on their worlds, had allowed some of the ELH survivors from Dieron that had taken refuge in the Commonwealth to form a unit they had called the Eridani Light Horse. While their pedigree was not as strong as that of the 11th Recon, neither Donovan had ever contested it.

"Eichler is dead," Sparrow quietly replied, and the others looked at him in surprise. "I am sure you know they were savaged by the Jade Falcons on Hesperus II, but the truth is the unit was destroyed to the last man. The Commonwealth has been keeping it quiet for political reasons, but Eichler's unit is, for all intents and purposes, defunct." He straightened. "But the First Prince has been in negotiations with the Archon...if you accept his offer, Archon Trillian Steiner will not only promise not to contest the legitimacy of your claim, but she will support it fully."

For a moment, the room went completely still, and Sparrow was conscious of increased scrutiny from all three of the ELH officers. He knew the relatively recent ascension of Julian Davion to the throne had ushered in a new opportunity for hope for many for return to a more traditional form of Davion leadership, but the relentless strikes by two of the Suns' historic enemies, the Draconis Combine and the Capellan Confederation, had precluded anything but a brutal fight for the nation's very survival.

"That is an extremely generous offer." Donovan finally replied. "You will understand if I am a bit surprised at how it came to be in the first place. Our previous attempts to move forward on claiming our birthright in the Federated Suns have been...complicated at best. What made Prince Davion change his mind?"

"I cannot speak for the First Prince," Sparrow replied, "But I do know he has always had nothing but the greatest respect for the historic skills of the Eridani Light Horse. It would be a great coup for all involved if the ELH would once again be able to rise from the ashes and serve the goals of the Inner Sphere."

Donovan clearly heard the phrasing he'd chosen to use, and nodded briefly. "As a Federated Suns unit?"

"As an independent mercenary command, as it has been since the fall of the First Star League," Sparrow corrected, and saw her chin rise slightly at the acknowledgment. "The First Prince is well aware of the course of negotiations with his predecessors, and while he would like nothing more than to have the Eridani Light Horse back under contract with the Federated Suns, he knows that will not be possible until the Eridani Light Horse is reformed."

"The First Prince might find that a little more challenging than he expects." The S2 finally spoke, giving the other man a careful stare. "At last count, there are at least three colonel claimants to the Light Horse mantle, and a half-dozen minor units who seem happy to use the name as well."

"A situation that need not remain true," Sparrow replied. "If you should agree to the First Prince's terms, he will instruct the courts that after full consideration and with the support of the Lyran government, it is confirmed that you are the true Eridani Light Horse."

Sparrow could see the wheels turning in the colonel's head, and managed to keep from smiling. If the Federated Suns and the Lyran Commonwealth both supported the Eridani Light Horse's claim to the throne, it would be enough for most of the rest of the Inner Sphere. The fractured states of the former Free Worlds League would never agree upon anything, and neither the Draconis Combine nor the Capellan Confederation, traditional recipients of the damage caused by the ELH, would support the choice anyway. When it came down to it, if the Federated Suns said they were the Eridani Light Horse, they would be.

"I had not imagined the First Prince to be so generous," Donovan finally replied.

"I cannot claim this to be pure altruism, Colonel," Sparrow replied. "The Federated Suns is in dire need of assistance, and the First Prince is willing to make a deal with some caveats. While he does not want to lock the ELH into a company store, he is asking for you to take on a two-year defense contract with the Federated Suns as the cost of his support."

"And how do we know he will not try to change the terms of the deal later?" Temple asked, watching the other man carefully.

Sparrow looked carefully at the S2 for a moment, and then slowly turned back to Donovan. "I think we both know, ma'am, that the Federated Suns is fighting for its very survival at this moment. If you place everything else aside, First Prince Davion is looking to his friends. The Eridani Light Horse has never refused to support the Suns when it is in need. I am hoping the same remains true now."

"Well, what do we think?"

Donovan had not spoken since departing the interrogation room, heading up two floors to the space she had chosen as her office during their time on Mirach. She waited until Bear closed the heavy soundproof door behind them before turning to her fellow officers. Donovan noted that out of the sight of the prisoner, both of their expressions were very different than the careful reserve they'd maintained in front of Sparrow. Temple's expression had taken a decided turn toward the thoughtful, and it was clear he was as surprised by the options before them as she was. Bear, on the other hand, seemed almost giddy with excitement.

To her surprise, Bear spoke first. "What do we think? Colonel, this is our chance! If the FedSuns have chosen to support us, we will have finally gotten exactly what we wanted, what your father fought for! It's the chance of a lifetime!"

"Yes, it is." She replied. "Unfortunately, is it the right time? We know the First Prince is only doing this because his nation is on the brink of collapse and he has no other options. Not to mention, our own independent operations have been doing well. We're ready to form another company, and we have no shortage of offers. If we take our time, we could make a whole new legacy for ourselves, without the Federated Suns."

Bear looked scandalized by her suggested course of action, but Temple clearly saw her attempt to play devil's advocate as he replied, "Which also raises the question of whether we want to tie our star to the Davions again anyway? What if we do, and the nation should fall? We would certainly not find work in the Combine or the Confederation, and both the Commonwealth and the Free Worlds factions are in little better condition. We might actually find ourselves worse off afterward than before."

"Amy…" The tone Bear used was one she'd heard far too infrequently as of late. "You can't really be thinking of passing up this opportunity. The regiments reformed…the ELH banner flying high again…this is everything your family has worked toward for decades!"

Donovan closed her eyes for a moment, tilted her head down, and took a moment before she responded, "Alexa and Ron are almost back."

Major Alexa Newman was her executive officer, currently tasked with finding new contracts on Galatea, and her husband Ron was a member of Donovan's command lance, acting as her personal security while in the field. They had recently secured several excellent offers on the Mercenary's Star before leaving the newly formed office in the hands of Captain Mortimer Jones. "We are not going to make any decisions until we've all had the chance to discuss this. For now, verify his bonafides. At the very least, we'll want to keep him as our guest for a little while, and see what else he has for us."

It was at that moment when one of the young officers knocked, and she let him into the room. "My apologies, Colonel, but the prisoner informed us he has something else for you."

The three ELH officers turned to the security monitors to see Sparrow smiling up at them. "He said it was a more tangible confirmation of his story."

The "tangible confirmation" was the location of a privately owned warehouse at the spaceport. The next day, Bear had accompanied her, along with several of his best people, and they found it with little trouble. The code-key Sparrow had given her had opened the small entry door, and once the Pathfinders had verified the space was secure, she entered, her eyes widening in surprise at what was inside.

Looking up at the immense war machine in front of her, she could barely keep from whistling in appreciation. While BattleMechs were considered the premier war machines ever developed, Clan OmniMechs remained the top of the line, with technology that was some of the best humanity had ever managed to field. Staring up at the *Cauldron-Born*—or *Ebon Jaguar*, as it was known in the Clans—that loomed over her, she was awed by the sheer size of the behemoth, despite the fact that her own BattleMech was both taller and heavier than this mighty beast.

No, it was the sight of the golden ELH emblems on its torso and lower legs that drew her attention, and she instantly knew she had a big decision to make.

Despite her hopes to have Alexa and Ron back in person before making a final decision, Amelia knew she had no time to waste if they wanted to capitalize on the opportunity before them. Messages had gone out to the other ELH units the day after Sparrow's revelations, asking the commanders to meet for a conclave on Mirach. While Donovan didn't reveal details of the First Prince's offer, she had alluded to the possibility of their financial difficulties being resolved, knowing that would be enough for the other commanders to respond.

Supported by the full remaining HPG network available by the Federated Suns and whatever JumpShips they could use, the messages sped off at top priority to the various postings of the other units that claimed heritage with the Eridani Light Horse. Even as wounded as they were by the attacks by the Draconis Combine that had nearly decimated their nation, the Federated Suns still had impressive resources, including funding only a major Great House could manage.

14 APRIL 3151

Colonel Amelia Donovan sat at the head of the table in her ready room and smiled at having her command staff fully assembled once again.

To her right, Major Alexa Newsom watched her steadily, her long brown hair perfectly coiffed and her expression poised and controlled. Despite having only given birth to a daughter only months ago, she had already returned to her pre-pregnancy uniform, an effort Donovan still attributed to some sort of witchcraft. Seated across from her and one seat down, beside Temple, her husband Ron still managed to find himself maintaining the unit's uniform regulations, but his light-brown beard was far fuller than she remembered from before his departure.

Giving them both a friendly welcome nod, Donovan turned to Temple. "What have we got?"

"Four of the units have responded so far, and are on their way," he replied. "Two headed out immediately, two will be sending emissaries to speak with us."

Amelia nodded, having expected as much. "And the 'Eridani Warhorses'?"

"They have declined to send anyone, as we expected."

"Did they even send a reply?"

"They did, but I will save it for you to read later. The gist was that they do not see any reason to join with us. They know who they are, they know their history and they intend to make their own way."

Amelia nodded. "It's only to be expected. Hell, I'm still surprised the others did not feel that way as well."

"Colonel Tappan is with us. Covir is a bit more reticent, which is why I believe he is coming in person, but I think he will come around. McMasters is sending his XO, which we expected: They're in the middle of a garrison contract, and can not abandon it in good conscience."

"Does that mean we're going to have to do this with him all over again?"

The intelligence officer shook his head. "I highly doubt it. Major Sills has been with the Colonel for years, and her opinion carries a lot of weight with him. In fact, I take it as a very good sign that he's sending her. McMasters can be both a bit prickly and more conservative in his thinking, but he is also smart enough to know that such an attitude is only going to get him so far. By sending his XO, who is widely respected and believed to be a bit more open-minded, he's showing he's willing to listen. If she recommends that they work with us, I have little doubt he'll disagree. I think we're in as good of a place as we can be with them, at least for now. It's Colonel Goss I am most surprised by. Of all of the commanders, I consider him the most likely to balk at reforming under your command. He is also known to take the role of a mercenary a little more joyfully than many of the other commanders."

Ron nodded. "I know Goss, and have worked with some of his people before, and he's right. The only reason he holds onto the Eridani Light Horse banner is because of the additional money and prestige it gets him, not out of any sense of history or honor. I'd watch him carefully, because I doubt he can see anyone else in charge other than himself."

"Then why do you think he's coming in?" Alexa asked, turning towards her husband. "Surely he doesn't think he's going to gain the support of the others. You know none of us would follow him, even if there was a vote."

"To survey the battlefield," Amelia replied. "And whatever we may think of him as a person, he survived the last few years as well as we have, and he has a keen sense of tactics. I have no doubt if a vote were called, and he felt he had the right to it, he would do what he must...and we would be forced by our honor to go along with it."

"Which would be the death of the Eridani Light Horse," Bear replied quietly, making everyone turn to him. "I know what you mean, Colonel, and the theory is a noble one, but we are still mercenaries, and the Alley Cats, at the very least, are not going to take orders that go against our sense of honor. I can see our people leaving in droves, and if the people that make up the spirit of the Light Horse are gone..." He shrugged, shaking his head sadly. "We've all seen it...dozens of units bringing themselves back from the abyss with new faces, new tech, but it is the spirit of those units that keep things alive. Wolf's Dragoons, the Gray Death Legion...they're more than just an emblem or a flag, they are a history of service, of sacrifice, of loss...these units have fought and clawed their way back to their rightful place, and I truly believe we deserve to be among them." He smiled at her. "I also think there is no person I would trust at the helm other than you, Colonel."

Amelia smiled slightly at the older man, nodding in thanks.

"We also need to remember you are the last, best hope for the Federated Suns," Sparrow said from his seat against one of the far walls. Donovan had freed him following her return from the warehouse, but he was still escorted by a Pathfinder at all times. "The Draconis Combine is the major threat, but they are already overextended. The Capellan Confederation is too busy gobbling up what is left of the Republic of the Sphere to do anything against the FedSuns, but they both have the coin to hire mercenaries to do their dirty work. This is the ideal moment for everyone: Small and lesser-known mercenary units can take on light garrison forces or under-equipped mainline units at a fraction of the cost of a major house military. Hell, we heard about members of Hanson's Roughriders being ravaged by a unit called Dylan's Doomsayers, which I never even heard of until the briefing this morning."

"I read that," Alexa said with a nod. "I heard some good things about them, even if they are new. Ex-Lyran warriors, for the most part, several right off the Jade Falcon front. Not only that, but the Roughriders had been shattered by the Wolves several months ago, they got hit while still undergoing repairs. Hardly the best showing of what they can achieve."

"Granted, Captain," the intelligence agent replied, his tone showing he wasn't giving up on his train of thought. "However, that doesn't matter. The Doomsayers have been barraged with new contract opportunities, and wounded prey or not, they took on a storied unit and beat them. That's a big feather in their cap."

"So, we need to make sure no one gets to use us for the same purpose," Amelia replied, sliding her gaze around the table.

"Horse feathers?" Ron replied, and his wife gave him a withering glare.

Seeing they had reached the end of their information, Donovan dismissed them, sending them off with orders to prepare for their visitors. Turning toward the window, she glanced out at the triple flagpoles outside of the window, with the ELH flag hanging high, the Alley Cats flag beside it, and the third flagpole conspicuously bare.

1 MAY 3151

Two more weeks went by, and when the various commanders had all arrived, they convened in the main conference room around a large, round table. It had taken some time to find one of sufficient size, but the facilities staff had been up to the task. Temple had joked that if it was good enough for King Arthur, it was good enough for the ELH.

The various colonels of the Eridani Light Horse units were a mixed lot. Colonel Eric Tappan and Colonel Arthur Covir, with wildly different complexions, Tappan being tall and lanky, and Covir shaped like a spark plug. Major Rachel Sills, her long, plaited blond hair hanging over her shoulders, sat across from them beside Colonel Lyle Goss. The other ELH warriors all wore their stock fatigues, but Goss wore a battle jacket with the sleeves ripped off, showing the tattoos that wrapped up both his arms. While he may not have fit Donovan's mental conception of a mercenary commander, he did look every inch a mercenary.

The initial greetings went well, and the formal explanation of the First Prince's offer was well-received by everyone around the table. All of those assembled seemed to see the benefits in the offer itself, but the specifics of how it would work were the focus of discussion. The recent news that Clan Sea Fox was apparently willing to begin bonding mercenary companies, securing their contracts as the MRBC had once done, only added to the potential benefits.

Unfortunately, things began to come off the rails exactly where expected, namely when it came to who would command the ELH if all of the units were to come under a single command. While several of the commanders seemed willing to have Donovan take the lead, others seemed to be just as comfortable with Goss as the more proven military commander.

"There is always the chance of some survivors in the Clan Homeworlds…" Colonel Tappan interjected, hoping to take a new tack on the leadership debate. It was going into the second hour on that topic, and tempers were starting to wear thin enough where a break seemed to be in order. "We might be able to get more guidance there."

"No." For the first time, the voice was from Sparrow, who had become the de facto Federated Suns liaison. He glanced up with hooded eyes and took in those around the table. "I can tell you quite definitively that there is nothing left of the Eridani Light Horse in the Clan Homeworlds."

Amelia took a moment, moderating her voice before she said something out of turn, and focused on the intelligence agent. "Do you have something to share, Mr. Sparrow?"

"Thank you, Colonel." Sparrow leaned forward, his gaze taking in everyone in the room. "My superiors believe there was a good chance this point would be raised, so we wanted to ensure there was no question: We have been in contact with some of our limited remaining intelligence assets in the Clan Homeworlds, and the report is definitive. On Huntress, Colonel Sandra Barclay's 71st Light Horse Regiment was challenged to a series of Trials of Possession as they prepared to return to the Inner Sphere in 3068. While they were initially successful against several Clans, they were quickly worn down by the constant fighting, and eventually were forced to join Clan Goliath Scorpion. The Scorpions, who did not follow *zellbrigen*, immediately took the surviving warriors as *abtakha*, eventually using them as the core of two new units, the 1st and 2nd Eridani Lancers."

"That sounds like we actually have members of the 71st still alive and active!" Goss replied. "Once a Horseman, always a Horseman."

Sparrow shook his head sadly. "There is little more I would prefer to say on the matter. We were hoping to find some of the members of the unit there to make this particular discussion even easier, but with the communications difficulties, it was hard enough to get as much as we did. Apparently there was a rebellion of sorts during the Jihad in the Clan Homeworlds. It is a little unclear who was involved, or many of the specifics, but it appears some of the Clan scientists were involved, and the death toll was significant. Unfortunately, both Eridani Lancer units were decimated in the conflict, and any survivors were scattered throughout the Goliath Scorpions or taken as bondsmen by other Clans."

He looked directly at Amelia. "With their clear martial skill and their vaunted history tracing back to the First Star League, they were eagerly sought after, and the Clans are understandably reluctant to risk losing them. Even if we could find any of the survivors, it is doubtful we could get them back to the Inner Sphere, and it certainly would not be in time." He shook his head again. "No, I am afraid there is nothing left of the 71st Light Horse Regiment: If we are ever to see the White Horses ride again, it will have to be after you rebuild them here."

The hall was silent for a long moment.

"You said, 'in time.'" Colonel Corvir's voice broke the stillness. "That makes it sound like there's a running clock on this."

"There is," Sparrow replied. "As the colonel has explained, the Federated Suns is facing a grave threat to its very existence. If we are to succeed in repelling the forces threatening us, we need to keep them from engaging mercenary forces to deplete us further. The best way to do that is to hire the best mercenary unit out there, and to make sure everyone knows we have done so."

"And you think by showing we are the reformed Eridani Light Horse, we'll able to fight off the hordes or mercenaries the other Great Houses could send our way?" Goss replied. "We're good, but I don't want you to count on too much here, Mr. Sparrow."

Sparrow smiled thinly, nodding at his point. "I don't doubt you are correct, Colonel. However, I think we may be getting ahead of ourselves. At the moment, the Clans are too busy with the Republic to have anything to do with The Federated Suns, which is an immense relief to us all. The Lyran Commonwealth is too busy with their other fronts to risk a conflict with us, and while the Free Worlds League states are still having some issues with us on a minor level, it is a regional problem that is no true threat to us or our survival. No, it is the Draconis Combine and the Capellan Confederation we need to worry about, and Daoshen Liao is focused on gobbling up the remains of the Republic of the Sphere as quickly as he can. That leaves only the Draconis Combine to worry about, and I can assure you they have problems of their own. Not everyone in their command structure is thrilled with how the Warlord is prosecuting his war, and a number of other threats on their borders have been making them slightly more circumspect than usual. If you couple that with the notorious Combine disdain for mercenaries, you may find things far more comfortable than you were expecting.

"I also don't think you realize how far your reputation still goes," he concluded. "Yes, there are a lot of smaller units that want to take a swing at you and make their bones, but at that same time the Eridani Light Horse is a name to conjure with. Two major houses have put aside their differences to give this unit new life again, all because of the great service you have given us in the past, and the noble lineage that has have espoused since the time of the Camerons. I cannot think of another unit I would be prouder to ride into battle with, and I can not think of one better suited for this particular task. This is not showing the flag, ladies and gentlemen...this is making sure there is a Federated Suns to return to when you are done."

The various members of the unit looked around, and then gave a series of nods. What part of Sparrow's speech had caught their attention was unknown, but it seemed he had made his point.

Major Sills leaned forward. Being the lowest ranked representative for a unit at the table, she had kept her own counsel for the most part. Now everyone turned to her as she spoke, "It seems like we all agree that this would be a good course of action, but it seems the real question is whether Colonel Donovan is the right person to lead us." Several of the officers, mostly her own, seemed to bristle at this, but Amelia nodded, knowing that the other woman was correct. "I also propose there might be some way to find out…"

"Are you really sure this is a good idea?"

Amelia allowed her gaze to flick over to Sparrow, who had followed her out of the conference room, forcing down her instinctive flash of resentment at his question. She allowed her gaze to hold on Ron for a moment, letting him know she had this, then turned to the younger man, her gaze steady. "Am I sure about what, Mr. Sparrow?"

To his credit, the FedSuns officer did not shy away from his gaze. "With all due respect, Colonel, you're betting a great deal on your unit's ability to take on other units. The Federated Suns needs the Eridani Light Horse—the *entire* Eridani Light Horse—and we need them as soon as possible." He shook his head slightly. "I just don't see how this is getting us any closer to that goal."

Amelia nodded, understanding the undercurrent in the other man's voice and using it to calm her own annoyance. "I can see how you would feel that way, Mr. Sparrow, but I assure you that this is both vital and necessary. Some of the other commanders raise valid points: While the Alley Cats have done very well for themselves, so have the other ELH factions, and several of them have as valid a claim to the mantle of the unit as ours. While we're the direct descendants, there are enough descendants of the rest of the unit to justify a certain amount of question as to who should step up."

She took a deep breath. "Perhaps if my father were still alive, the situation would be a bit more cut-and-dried, but to be fair, some of them do raise important points."

"I understand that, ma'am," Sparrow replied, but clearly was not going to give up the point. "However, I don't understand why you feel the need to court all of them. Even if one or two of the other units join on, you'll be able to make up their numbers with your own hiring efforts and the support the First Prince will be giving you. We don't need to convert all their hearts and minds."

"Actually, we do." Captain Alexa Neuman came around the corner, earning a wide grin from her husband. Turning to Amelia first, she nodded respectfully, her features a careful professional mask. "What I was saying, Mr. Sparrow, is the problem we face is the same one we've dealt with for more than a century: With the original ELH shattered into fragments, and with so many of those fragments having a valid claim to the mantle, it is imperative we do what we can to settle any concerns about our pedigree. Having two ELH units did not work for anyone in the past, and despite the support either the Federated Suns or the Commonwealth might put forward, we need to convince the other colonels that we're a force to be reckoned with. Every other unit claiming the mantle diminishes us, and from the brief I read on the way here, it seems your First Prince is relying upon our reputation as much as our fighting skills. As good as we are, we need to provide incentive for other mercenaries not to seek conflict in the FedSuns, and to hopefully seek out safer pastures. If we can keep the other mercenaries out of it, we all win."

She turned back to the others, taking all four under her gaze. "I don't like it any more than you do, Mr. Sparrow…but if we need to play their game…we need to play to win."

Colonel Amelia Donovan moved her *Cauldron-Born* through a copse of trees, careful to use the lanes that had been prepared for them. A pair of ForestryMechs maintained the routes on a weekly basis, maintaining emergency routes her command team had planned to use in case of a strike upon the planet by enemy forces. While she knew she should feel slightly bad about using her familiarity with the terrain to gain an advantage in this exercise, she was fairly sure it was better for her to use everything she could in this particular mission, allowing her to gain the support of her entire unit.

Behind her, the rest of her command lance and her pursuit lance followed, also careful to follow the trail. Like the other exercises they'd been conducting, the laser weapons were dialed down to non-hazardous levels, and autocannons and missiles were replaced with paint and tracer rounds to ensure damage could be tracked by a master unit, a Morningstar City Command Unit overseeing the exercise from the nearby hill. The other commanders were watching from the Morningstar, except for Goss and herself, both out in the field. Bear remained with them, while Alexa continued preparations for departure back at the Fort.

"I am coming up on the enemy force," Ron said, his *Beowulf IIC* leading the pack as they located the edge of the trees. The Clan 'Mech had been recently acquired as salvage, and despite only recently getting acquainted with it, the warrior had quickly taken to the unfamiliar chassis. "Striker Two has the enemy command lance on sensors. No sign of the armor lance."

Amelia nodded, although she was troubled by the absence of the Fulcrums that made up Goss' armor lance. The fleet hovertanks were next to useless in the tight confines of the trees, but they were devilishly fast, carried a fair mix of weaponry, and could shift the course of the battle whenever they chose to show themselves.

Since Goss only had a lance of armor and his command lance disembarked as an honor guard, Amelia had tried to match the battle valuations of the two units as closely as possible to ensure the test was a fair one. While the Clan technology most of her command lance boasted made for a slight differential in tonnage in the enemy's favor, she felt confident the training of her units would more than even the field for them. "Alright, let's make sure we have this handled. Command lance, engage at will. Pursuit lance, stay in the trees and provide harassing fire."

A chorus of affirmative responses came instantly, and she moved her unit to the edge of the tree line, led by Lawrence Maxwell in his *Thor*. The MechWarrior fired a PPC at a nearby *Nightstar*, singeing it with light, but nothing more. Instantly, the readout showed heavy damage on the arm.

"First blood goes to us—!" Maxwell began, but his voice cut off sharply. Whirling on the Clan OmniMech more quickly than an assault 'Mech had any right to, the *Nightstar* fired its full complement of heavy weapons: two Gauss rifles and an ER PPC. To Donovan's shock, the first Gauss round and the PPC caused visible damage to both torsos, while the second Gauss round decapitated the 'Mech. With no pilot to provide balance or control of the OmniMech, the *Thor* crashed into a cluster of nearby trees.

"I am sorry, Colonel." Goss' voice sounded tinny through the neurohelmet speakers, but his gloating tone came across clearly. "Unfortunately, I am the one who will be teaching the lesson today."

"Pull back!" Amelia shouted, sending her units into a controlled retrograde maneuver as they tried to gain concealment. "Command actual to base, emergency priority."

She only heard the buzz of static in her helmet, and Amelia was not surprised to find Goss had blocked their communications back to the Fort. Swearing, she opened the channel back up, relying on the short-wave directional broadcasts her forces had been using to keep in contact. "All units, cycle your weapons back to full power, emergency code Sierra Five Alpha."

Fighting down her instinctive horror and revulsion for the actions of a man who could murder one of her warriors while claiming to be a member of the Eridani Light Horse, she concentrated on the situation at hand. While Amelia had never truly expected a situation like this, she did not believe in keeping her warriors out of the fight, so she had coding prepped into all BattleMechs to allow her warriors to be brought back to full power on command authority. While it would do nothing for her warriors' lack of actual autocannon ammunition or missiles, it would help her to get their energy weapons into the fight.

Energy weapons she had in abundance. Configured in the B-configuration, the *Cauldron-Born* boasted Clan extended-range particle projection cannons and lasers to avoid relying upon ammunition that might become scarce during an extended campaign. Typing in the command to release her own safety interlocks, she snarled in malicious glee as her weapons came back to full power.

Taking a brief moment to analyze the tactical situation, Donovan assessed her remaining forces. With Maxwell's *Thor* out of the fight, that left only Ron in his *Beowulf IIC* and Avery Underwood in his *BattleMaster* from her Command lance. Goss, commanding his lance from his *Atlas* AS7-K, sported a *Berserker*, a *Sagittaire*, and the *Nightstar* that had killed her lancemate.

While she did have her Pursuit lance, the *Vindicator, Jenner, Commando,* and *Panther* barely exceeded the tonnage of one of the hulking assault BattleMechs arrayed against them, and the lack of missiles and autocannon ammunition would be telling.

"Ron, can you spare someone to get word back to the base? We need to make sure Alexa is prepared if the other units are heading there."

"I can get back there faster than most—" he replied, but didn't seem surprised when she cut him off.

"I need you here. See if you can get that *Nightstar*'s attention."

If Ron was shocked to be ordered to go after a 'Mech nearly 50 tons heavier than his own, he didn't say anything about it. "Confirmed, Colonel." was his only reply as he lunged forward, firing off a quick blast from his ER large pulse laser that cut armor away from the *Nightstar*'s rear center torso.

Using Ron's distraction, Dan Hackley's *Commando* shot into the trees, headed back to the Fort as quickly as he could. Donovan silently approved the choice: without short-range missiles, the light 'Mech couldn't hurt any of the opponents they were up against.

With a new target in their sights, Goss' command lance quickly turned on Ron's *Beowulf IIC*. The *Nightstar* fired another Gauss slug that narrowly missed the lighter 'Mech, but it was enough to keep Ron from attempting another shot. Seeing Goss' *Atlas* moving to support his lancemate, Donovan fired one of her *Cauldron-Born*'s PPCs and large pulse lasers, striking the *Atlas* in its left torso, carving away armor from the side of the assault 'Mech. The *Atlas* shifted its focus to her as she sent a blast from her other PPC into its leg, making it shudder. Donovan felt heat rise in her cockpit faster than even the OmniMech's double heat sinks could abate, then was thrown against her restraints as an answering shot from the *Atlas*' Imperator Dragon's Fire Gauss rifle ripped armor plates from her right torso.

With Goss engaged with Donovan, and the *Nightstar* still focused on Ron, the two remaining enemy BattleMechs, the *Berserker* and the *Sagittaire,* focused on the three light 'Mechs firing from the tree line, preparing to flush them from cover. Both moved forward to engage the pursuit lance—

—When the *Nightstar* crashed to the ground.

Avery Underwood, the final member of her command lance, had finally entered into range. Having been in the position of Tail-End Charlie, the *BattleMaster* pilot had forgone using his PPC, his sole long-range weapon, to approach nearly unnoticed. The *Nightstar* pilot, focused completely on Ron, had unwittingly shown his back to the other 'Mech, allowing Avery to line up a careful shot into the 'Mech's back with his PPC and quartet of medium lasers, capitalizing on the damage Ron had done earlier.

The energy weapons seared into the internal structure of the *Nightstar*'s chest, coring deep into it and destroying the gyro that allowed the massive BattleMech to maintain its balance.

Despite the horrific damage it had taken, the *Nightstar* wasn't completely out of the fight—not until Ron and the three remaining pursuit 'Mechs concentrated their fire on it, cutting away the left leg and arm. Seeing it was no longer combat capable, the enemy pilot shut down his engine in a gesture of submission.

The victory came at a cost, however. Closing quickly, the *Berserker* staggered the ELH *Panther* with its ER PPC, then followed up with their large pulse lasers. While the first laser cut an ugly scar across the *Panther*'s left leg, the ER PPC and second laser cut deep into the right arm, severing the lower half of the limb. Without any weapons, Donovan quickly ordered the pilot to pull back.

The *Sagittaire* pilot, taking a page from Underwood's playbook, fired its full complement of energy weapons at the *Vindicator*, pinning it against a tree from the sheer weight of fire. While the enemy pilot must have been roasting in his cockpit, the *Vindicator* dropped to the ground in a smoldering heap of armor and damaged actuators.

With two more ELH BattleMechs out of the battle, the advantage seemed to be with the attackers, especially with the continuing disparity in weaponry. As one, the remaining three BattleMechs focused on Donovan's *Cauldron-Born*, and she felt her 'Mech stagger as concentrated fire rippled over her torso. The bright flash of laser fire caused her left torso to flare yellow on the wireframe diagnostic, while the distinctive impact of a Gauss rifle round caused it to shift to red. Clearly Goss wanted to end this by ending her, and she squared off with his 'Mech.

Ron's voice rang out over the command channel, rallying the other 'Mechs to her aid, and she saw him take charge of her force, engaging the *Atlas* and hoping to overwhelm it with a sheer weight of fire. While the damage they caused was negligible, it had the desired effect of pulling the focus of Goss' lancemates to her three remaining 'Mechs, leaving him with only the largest enemy to deal with.

As she watched Goss continue to stride toward her in his immense *Atlas*, she wondered how the others were faring.

Sparrow was in the command center, observing the battle, when all of the screens suddenly went to static. Alexa was on top of the situation instantly, switching to the satellite network and bringing up the scene of the battle, where she saw the treachery by Goss' forces.

"All hands to Condition One! Warriors to your BattleMechs. Stand by for orders!" She whirled on one of the lance commanders. "Get your unit loaded for bear and send them after the Colonel."

Sparrow stepped over to her, his expression polite but focused. "Colonel, with all due respect, we may want to be cautious. I have seen no sign of either of the other lances Colonel Goss should have with them, and if they are not engaging the Colonel…"

Alexa glared at him for only an instant, but quickly turned back to the command center technician. "Bring up local oversight of the region, tag all unusual movements."

"Colonel," a technician said. "We have several BattleMechs moving from the spaceport toward our position. A scheduled repair request that came through after the Colonel departed."

"Who approved it?" she asked, her eyes narrowing, but Chief Technician Baneville stepped forward.

"I did, Colonel. The Skipper told us we should provide every courtesy…"

"Understood." Alexa nodded. "Get our defenses up and running. I have a funny feeling they're looking to cause more damage than to repair it, and I want to be ready. Also, get my *Excalibur* prepped."

The Chief's eyes widened. "Are you sure, ma'am? You haven't—"

"Trained in her since I had the baby," Alexa responded. "True, but I'm sure I remember which end of the PPC to point at the enemy." She softened her voice slightly. "I also happen to be the senior warrior here on property, which means my place is with our defenders. The colonel left me in charge of the complex in her absence, we are not going to lose it for her."

"Yes, ma'am," the technician replied, then turned to Sparrow. "Is there any way you can get to the *Morningstar*, or communicate with the support lance?" Since the support lance had not been needed for the exercise, the colonel had made them act as escort for the other commanders, which meant they were the closest support either unit could call upon.

"I can try," he replied, only to be interrupted by the arrival of an urgent message from the *Commando*, warning of Goss' betrayal. Despite being torn to send him back to support her husband and her best friend, Alexa forced herself to put him into the Fort's defensive formation before heading down to the 'Mech Bay herself.

The choices of command suddenly did not seem so pleasant.

Trying to move as quickly as her damaged right leg would allow, Donovan felt a sheet of armor on her left torso rip clean off under a blast from one of Goss' large lasers. Her *Cauldron-Born* had taken a hellacious beating in the intervening minutes, its left arm now missing, heavy armor damage all over, and a damaged foot actuator causing a pronounced limp.

The enemy *Atlas*, however, just shrugged off all her incoming attacks. While it showed several damaged spots, some cutting all the way into the internal structure, the assault 'Mech's immense size served it well, and it remained combat ready.

Not only that, but her own forces were dwindling. Working in tandem with MechWarrior Ahlya Martinez's *Jenner*, Ron had the two 'Mechs trade hyper-accurate laser fire with the *Sagittaire*, the speed of the two lighter 'Mechs somewhat offsetting the heavy armor of the assault 'Mech. Unfortunately, their battle was balanced on a knife's edge; the *Sagittaire* only needed to get moderately lucky, while the two ELH warriors had to make a lot of specific shots to even the score.

Meanwhile, the *BattleMaster* and the *Berserker* continued beating at each other with their remaining weapons, but it was slow going. The *Berserker* pilot clearly wanted to close the range and use its greater mass against Underwood, but the *BattleMaster*'s close-range weapons made that a dicey proposition, especially since the *Berserker* had lost both its hatchet and one of its large pulse lasers during its last attempt to close with the ELH warrior.

Triggering her large pulse lasers in sequence to try to keep her heat down, Donovan tried to radio for support again, but the silence continued due to the jamming.

Suddenly, she felt her entire 'Mech shift to one side as the *Atlas*' latest Gauss rifle shot smashed through the remaining armor on her right hip, making her internal schematic flash red. Another shot like that would finish her, and the *Atlas* still moved inexorably forward, its lasers glowing in preparation.

Heedless of her heat, Amelia fired both PPCs at point-blank range. The two blasts seemed to merge into one and cored the *Atlas*' left knee. The assault 'Mech listed to one side, coming down and shattering the bole of a nearby pine tree as it fell. Amelia immediately switched to her lasers, unable to keep a satisfied grin off her face as her targeting computer spotted the weakened knee joint, and she cut into it with precision pulse laser fire, severing the lower half of the leg.

To her horror, she saw Goss trying to push his *Atlas* back up, but this time the range was to her advantage. Rearing back a thick leg, her *Cauldron-Born* kicked out, smashing into the *Atlas*' damaged arm and crushing the shoulder. The larger 'Mech smashed back into the ground face-first, and she lined up her weapons on it.

For all his faults, Goss knew when he was beaten. Her sensors quickly registered the fusion engine going dark.

She gasped through the heat, quickly taking stock of the battlefield in the brief lull gained by the end of the *Atlas*. The *Sagittaire* was nearly in as bad of shape as her *Cauldron-Born*, missing an arm and with a heavily damaged leg, allowing Ron and Ahlya to get behind it, like sharks awaiting the kill. Both the *Berserker* and *BattleMaster* were battered, but still combat capable.

For a moment, she thought that the battle was going to continue, but the steady beeping of the approaching sensor response of other 'Mechs made everyone pause. When

Lieutenant Sacrow's *Archer* entered the clearing, she couldn't help but sigh in relief.

At this close of range, the tightbeam message came through clearly. "Apologies, Commander. We had to deal with an armor lance on the way in, or we would have been here sooner."

Amelia smiled, almost despite herself, and nodded. "Just in time, Lieutenant." She switched over to a general channel. "MechWarriors, your commander is down, and you are charged to shut down immediately or be destroyed. This will be your only warning."

There was no hesitation as both of Goss' remaining lancemates shut down their reactors, ending the battle… for now.

Leaving the enemy 'Mechs under the watch of Underwood and Martinez, Amelia led the rest of her forces back to the Fort at full speed.

She needn't have bothered. The battle had already ended by the time she arrived, with Alexa leading a valiant defense of the Fort. With the advantage of surprise taken away, she had let them get just outside the fort before ordering them to surrender. Goss' pilots had made a fight of it…but not a long one.

The relief they'd felt was short-lived, however, as they tallied the dead. Aside from four killed from her forces, one of the Support lance members was critically injured, and Alexa had lost three more at the battle for the Fort…the death of eight Horsemen was more than Amelia was comfortable with, and as soon as she had ensured everything had been taken care of, she headed to her office alone, leaving orders to only let her know when the other commanders, traveling back on the Morningstar, had returned.

Taking a brief moment to check on his wife—and chide her for going into battle without him—Ron immediately moved to follow the orders, while the others all waited to see exactly what the next few hours would bring.

The other commanders, absent Colonel Goss, were already in the conference room when Donovan entered, being briefed by Alexa and Sparrow.

"—From what intel we've gathered," Sparrow continued, nodding to Donovan, "Colonel Goss had been hired by Warlord Toranaga to ensure that the Eridani Light Horse did not get into the fray. The Combine military has enough difficulties with the regular Federated Suns military, the last thing they need is for us to open up a new front and stretch their forces even thinner. Goss brought a newly formed mercenary unit, Forge's Firestarters, with him when they came for the Conclave. The Firestarters were the actual force that struck at the Fort. They had been tucked away in the DropShip instead of the forces Goss had promised to bring. As far as we know, his own unit is still safely back at his temporary headquarters.

"Apparently, the plan was that with you dead—" Sparrow nodded at Donovan again, "—they could claim the Davions had been false to them, and lead all of you into an ambush under the guise of reunion talks. Once victorious, he would gather the support of the rest of the unit and try to turn the ELH against the Davions." He looked around the room. "I've already sent a message to his second in command. I am hoping he will choose to join us once his commander's treachery is confirmed...especially since we will not be considering them in the future if they do not."

"Surely they didn't think we'd work for the Dracs against the Suns!" Covir replied, his expression still stunned.

"Not for an instant," Sparrow replied. "However, it seems like the hope was to at least keep you off the battlefield, which would have been enough of a victory for Toranaga. He must be pretty concerned if you caused him to go to this much trouble to keep you out of the fight."

"The ELH is a name to conjure with," Talbin replied. "Sounds like we need to prove it again!"

Covir still shook his head. "Still, there is a lot to consider here—"

"No." The voice, coming from the head of the table, surprised them all. It seemed almost too deep for Donovan's voice, coming up from the depths of her soul. "We have debated and pondered long enough. It is time to choose."

For the first time, it became clear she was wearing her sidearm, the only one in the room to be doing so.

Sills blanched slightly. "You really think we're going to allow ourselves to be threatened at gunpoint—"

"I don't care what you think," Amelia replied, shocking the other woman to silence. Although Bear was sure the others could not hear it, he was sure he caught the same flicker of concern in Alexa's eyes, at the very least. Their commander sounded exhausted, as if she had finally moved past any semblance of diplomacy. "As for threatening, I am not threatening any of you with anything. If I was, you would know it—" Her gaze seemed to harden even more, "—and you would deal with it, as I would expect from those who believe themselves to have the right to the legacy of the Eridani Light Horse."

Stepping around the table, Amelia continued speaking, but she did not deign to look at any of the officers seated around the table. Occasionally, her gaze would flicker to one of her own officers, along the walls, but her expression never changed. "I have made the questions I've asked of us far too complicated, and I blame myself for that. I don't know about anyone else in this room, but I know what I have to do.

"First Prince Julian Davion has sent us an emissary, and a contract, to protect his worlds from others like us. He promises to pay us, in coin and care, and in exchange he wishes us to use our skills to protect that which he holds dear." She looked around the room. "He asks us to risk our lives and our legacy for his nation, to be used against others so his forces can reinforce and rebuild."

She saw the nods and grim expressions around the room, and knew she had their attention now.

"As is his *right!*" Her voice cracked out like a gunshot, and several around the table instinctively straightened as Donovan's tone of command was fully on display. There was no question now, despite their respective ranks or commands, as to who was running this meeting.

"The First Prince needs to protect his own, and that is his right as given to him by powers we do not need to understand.

He offers us coin for our blood, which we will take, as we are mercenaries.

"However, we are also more than that. We are the grand legacy of a unit that served the greatest nations humankind has ever known. The Eridani Light Horse served the first Star League, protecting humanity against all that would threaten it, and it shall again. The Light Horse fought back invaders from beyond the known worlds, following them back to their homeworlds and informing them that we would not allow anyone to shatter what we treasured.

"Yet still darker times lay ahead. The Jihad. Gray Monday. The fall of the Republic. Despite everything we could do, civilization found itself shattered, again and again, without cease. Countless history books tell of the times when the ELH was destroyed, although few can agree when... Many choose to believe the ELH keeps rising like a phoenix from the ashes, gilding itself for a new flight over and over.

"Yet we know better," Amelia said, looking slowly around the room, taking in the gaze of each of the assembled warriors and holding it. "We know that as long as it is represented by a single warrior who swears to follow the tradition, the Eridani Light Horse will always stand ready.

"Some of you have asked why I think I should lead us forward, when there are so many with a claim to the mantle. I will tell you: I am going to lead us forward because I am ready to do so. I will wear the crest proudly, and tomorrow morning you will find me on the field of battle, ready to march forward to my destiny. I may die. All of those who fight with me might die. Yet no matter what happens, people will know that when the Federated Suns called, the Eridani Light Horse stood up and answered.

"Those who wish to join me will be at the staging areas at 0600 tomorrow." She looked around carefully. "If you are with us, don't be late...we ride with the dawn."

Without another word, Amelia Donovan strode out of the room, her officers at her heels.

All except for one.

Covir looked like he was going to say something snide when he noticed Bear still leaning against the transplex window at the far side of the room. Straightening his shoulders, he squared off to the other man. "Does she really think her speech is going to sway us from what we rightly deserve?"

Bear's answering smile was laconic, as if his namesake had just woken from hibernation. "Oh, I don't think she doubts for a moment that you will all get what you deserve, Colonel." From the other man, the comment sounded like an insult, but Bronson was clearly wise enough to not make an issue of it. "What she's doing is acting like the commander of the Eridani Light Horse, focusing on the mission, and ensuring the best chance of success."

He looked around, holding the gaze of some of the undecided commanders, starting with Sasson. "You know as well as I do that she could not have negotiated a better contract: The Federated Suns needs the very best in its defense right now, and will only survive with us at their side. Do you really believe abandoning the nation that helped support us is what we should be doing right now?"

Covir stubbornly shook his head. "That was a long time ago..."

Bear glared at him, his eyes smoldering with a mixture of frustration and disappointment. "That is because we have a history with this nation, with these people. We protected their ancestors so that they could be free today, and I find that as noble of a cause as any I could think of." He looked around the table and shrugged. "I don't know about the rest of you, but I know where I'll be tomorrow."

"Do you think it did any good?"

As far as Alexa could tell, these were the first words Amelia had said since she'd entered the command center. The space was quiet on the upper level, allowing the commander to take full advantage of the floor-to-ceiling windows on the far side of the room, bulletproofed and exterior-tinted to keep any ambitious assassins from taking the decision away from them.

Alexa took a spot in her favorite armchair, sitting and watching her friend and commander carefully. "Do I think what did any good? Your statements in there?" She allowed a moment for the thought to pass. "I think you accomplished more in a single diatribe than we have in months on this damned rock."

Whatever Amelia was expecting, that was clearly not it, and she turned back to her friend, stepping away from the windows. "What do you mean?"

Alexa stood up, moving to join her friend. "I mean you reminded them that while they are mercenaries, they are also the Eridani Light Horse. Not one of many, not one of the special few, they are the ones who carried the legacy of their ancestors, and the greatest hope for the nation that took us in and cared for us when the first Star League fell. They have earned our faith and our support, and you reminded them of exactly who they really are."

Amelia smiled thinly and straightened a bit. "Well, I'm glad someone thinks so. I think it means we need to see what they decide to do." Moving back toward the other armchair, she settled herself in, waiting a brief moment for her friend to settle in as well. "Where's Ron?"

"Overseeing security preparations and working with the Chief to make sure we're ready to move tomorrow. Everyone is working through the night to get us prepared, and we should be ready to go right on time."

"It helps that we've been preparing for this for a while."

"That it does," Alexa agreed. "And since we'll use the DropShips to get us where we need to go, they can rest on the way."

"Rest," Amelia repeated, as if tasting the word for the first time. "What exactly is that like?"

"You'll have to tell me when you finally know," Alexa replied. "For now, we'll just have to guess." She looked at her commander carefully. "Do you have any orders for me?"

"Yes. Speak to Sparrow, and make sure the First Prince is aware of our plans. One way or the other, the Eridani Light Horse is going to be on the field of battle, and he needs to know that. After you're done with that, we need to further our preparations: Let the recruiters know we are going full speed ahead. We are bringing the bulk of our forces to the field, but we need to prepare for the next battle."

Hearing her friend say that made Alexa smile, and she nodded. "Yes, ma'am. Who will we be leaving in command here?" She shook her head before Amelia could reply. "And do not even think of saying it will be me. I love you, I support you, but there is no way in hell I'm going to let you and my husband go into harm's way again. He knows better than to ask, you should as well."

"Alexa, the—"

"Don't." The word had steel in it, and Amelia relented. She did not want to bring her XO's daughter into this, and was glad to hear she didn't have to. Sighing heavily, she allowed herself to think for a moment. "Who do you recommend?"

Alexa did not have to think about it. "Captain Twofalls of the Training Brigade. We'll want to leave him behind to prepare the next class of MechWarriors anyway, and he's well respected by the unit. It also shows we're maintaining our roots not only as the ELH, but as the Training Cadre. No matter what happens next, we will still have a history to hold onto." She smiled. "Not to mention, he is old school Davion to the core, and trained on New Avalon. The First Prince is going to think long and hard before pulling anything on him, and it would only blow up in his face."

Amelia nodded. "I agree with your recommendation. Let him know, won't you?"

"And what will you be doing? Getting some rest?" Alexa teased.

Amelia mock-frowned at her friend. "If my people are not resting, neither am I. They need to see me out and about. Let's do a walkaround of the compound, and then I can go oversee the techs working on my OmniMech...I am sure there's some last-minute tweaking that can be done."

Alexa sighed, but allowed her friend to lead her out, the only sign of her pleasure a small smile on her lips.

UNION-CLASS DROPSHIP *FOULK'S FOLLY*
MIRACH
5 MAY 3151

From the bridge of her DropShip, Amelia Donovan looked out among the various stations, Alexa at her side. The chronometer clicked over to the appointed time, and she glanced over at her friend. They had been waiting until the last moment to prepare to lift, but so far, no messages or messengers had been forthcoming.

"Any word from the other DropShips?" Amelia asked, immediately regretting asking a question she already knew the answer to.

"Nothing yet, Colonel," Alexa replied, taking a quick flip through her channels to verify before continuing. We don't have anything on the scopes, so—"

Suddenly, a light flashed on her board. She nodded to the comm tech, who put it up on the speakers.

"—I'm sorry we are running a little late, ma'am." Covir's strong voice came over the comms, a lilt of humor and genuine abashedness leaking through the line. "I'm afraid my technicians were not as ready to move up and out as we had hoped they were. They are on the way to the DropShips, and will meet us there. The group with me is the rest of our own training battalion, which I am hoping you will accept here at the Fort. My technicians, the ones that will not be coming with us, should be here shortly. I have spoken with Colonel Telson, and his people are ready to go as well. They have a bit of a head start on us, but he is afraid he does not quite have as many ready forces as we have managed to field. His aerospace wing is pretty powerful, however, and should give us a bit more of an unexpected punch. McMasters hasn't commed in yet, but Sills is on board. You can count on us."

On the line, Amelia heard Alexa whistle with pleasure, and she glanced at the secondary monitor, where her XO had put up their new TO&E. While the other two units were not as large as theirs, Colonel Keene's unit was made up of newer, more advanced machines, and Telson had an impressive support unit of aerospace fighters and conventional aircraft and VTOLs. Coupled with her own forces, they would have a very powerful unit to field, and she looked forward to seeing what they could do.

"Thank you, Colonel…and thank the others for me. It is good to have you both here."

"It is good to be here, Lieutenant General," Covir replied, using the rank for the first time, and she was touched by the sound of true sincerity in his voice. "I know we have not always seen eye to eye on all of your command decisions, ma'am, but I also know you have done more than anyone else ever has to rebuild the unit and bring us back to the Inner Sphere. My people stand with you, and I am glad you will have us."

"We are family, Colonel," she replied, and now it was the other warrior's turn to be silent. "We will not always agree, but we know what we need to do to accomplish our goals. Welcome home."

Turning to the captain, she nodded. "Lift off at your discretion, Captain."

The thrum of the DropShips' engines were not loud enough to overwhelm the cheers coming from her people or the speakers.

"Eridani Light Horse…*we ride!*"

ATLAS
Assault—100 tons

BEOWULF IIC
Medium—45 tons

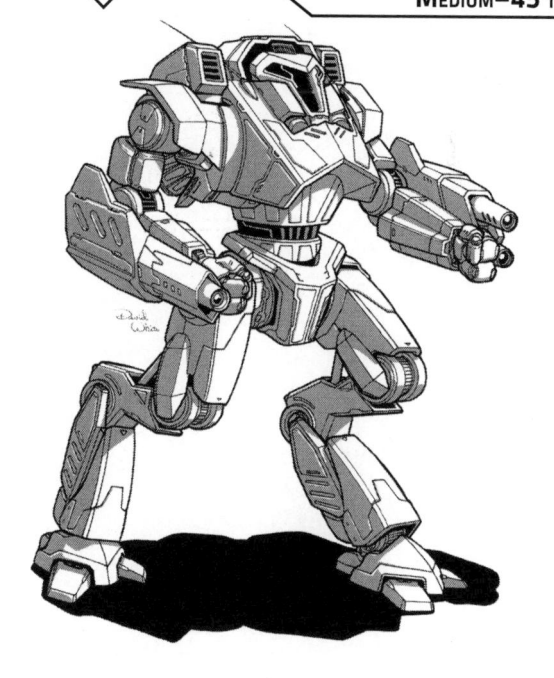

BERSERKER
Assault—100 tons

CAULDRON-BORN (EBON JAGUAR)
Heavy—65 tons

CROSSBOW
HEAVY—65 TONS

CRUSADER
HEAVY—65 TONS

PANTHER
Light—35 tons

PENETRATOR
Heavy—75 tons

SAGITTAIRE
Assault–95 tons

THOR (SUMMONER)
Heavy–70 tons

VINDICATOR
MEDIUM—45 TONS

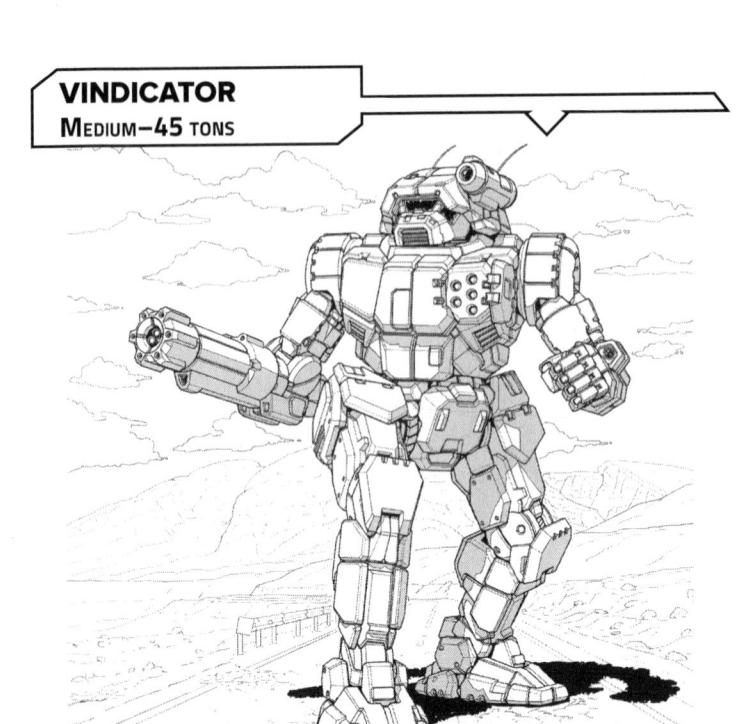

WARHAMMER
HEAVY—70 TONS

BATTLETECH GLOSSARY

AUTOCANNON
A rapid-fire, auto-loading weapon. Light autocannons range from 30 to 90 millimeter (mm), and heavy autocannons may be from 80 to 120mm or more. They fire high-speed streams of high-explosive, armor-piercing shells.

BATTLEMECH
BattleMechs are the most powerful war machines ever built. First developed by Terran scientists and engineers, these huge vehicles are faster, more mobile, better-armored and more heavily armed than any twentieth-century tank. Ten to twelve meters tall and equipped with particle projection cannons, lasers, rapid-fire autocannon and missiles, they pack enough firepower to flatten anything but another BattleMech. A small fusion reactor provides virtually unlimited power, and BattleMechs can be adapted to fight in environments ranging from sun-baked deserts to subzero arctic icefields.

DROPSHIPS
Because interstellar JumpShips must avoid entering the heart of a solar system, they must "dock" in space at a considerable distance from a system's inhabited worlds. DropShips were developed for interplanetary travel. As the name implies, a DropShip is attached to hardpoints on the JumpShip's drive core, later to be dropped from the parent vessel after in-system entry. Though incapable of FTL travel, DropShips are highly maneuverable, well-armed and sufficiently aerodynamic to take off from and land on a planetary surface. The journey from the jump point to the inhabited worlds of a system usually requires a normal-space journey of several days or weeks, depending on the type of star.

FLAMER

Flamethrowers are a small but time-honored anti-infantry weapon in vehicular arsenals. Whether fusion-based or fuel-based, flamers spew fire in a tight beam that "splashes" against a target, igniting almost anything it touches.

GAUSS RIFLE

This weapon uses magnetic coils to accelerate a solid nickel-ferrous slug about the size of a football at an enemy target, inflicting massive damage through sheer kinetic impact at long range and with little heat. However, the accelerator coils and the slug's supersonic speed mean that while the Gauss rifle is smokeless and lacks the flash of an autocannon, it has a much more potent report that can shatter glass.

INDUSTRIALMECH

Also known as WorkMechs or UtilityMechs, they are large, bipedal or quadrupedal machines used for industrial purposes (hence the name). They are similar in shape to BattleMechs, which they predate, and feature many of the same technologies, but are built for non-combat tasks such as construction, farming, and policing.

JUMPSHIPS

Interstellar travel is accomplished via JumpShips, first developed in the twenty-second century. These somewhat ungainly vessels consist of a long, thin drive core and a sail resembling an enormous parasol, which can extend up to a kilometer in width. The ship is named for its ability to "jump" instantaneously across vast distances of space. After making its jump, the ship cannot travel until it has recharged by gathering up more solar energy.

The JumpShip's enormous sail is constructed from a special metal that absorbs vast quantities of electromagnetic energy from the nearest star. When it has soaked up enough energy, the sail transfers it to the drive core, which converts it into a space-twisting field. An instant later, the ship arrives at the next jump point, a distance of up to thirty light-years. This field is known as hyperspace, and its discovery opened to mankind the gateway to the stars.

JumpShips never land on planets. Interplanetary travel is carried out by DropShips, vessels that are attached to the JumpShip until arrival at the jump point.

LASER

An acronym for "Light Amplification through Stimulated Emission of Radiation." When used as a weapon, the laser damages the target by concentrating extreme heat onto a small area. BattleMech lasers are designated as small, medium or large. Lasers are also available as shoulder-fired weapons operating from a portable backpack power unit. Certain range-finders and targeting equipment also employ low-level lasers.

LONG-RANGE MISSILE (LRM)

An indirect-fire missile with a high-explosive warhead.

MACHINE GUN

A small autocannon intended for anti-personnel assaults. Typically non-armor-penetrating, machine guns are often best used against infantry, as they can spray a large area with relatively inexpensive fire.

PARTICLE PROJECTION CANNON (PPC)

One of the most powerful and long-range energy weapons on the battlefield, a PPC fires a stream of charged particles that outwardly functions as a bright blue laser, but also throws off enough static discharge to resemble a bolt of manmade lightning. The kinetic and heat impact of a PPC is enough to cause the vaporization of armor and structure alike, and most PPCs have the power to kill a pilot in his machine through an armor-penetrating headshot.

SHORT-RANGE MISSILE (SRM)

A direct-trajectory missile with high-explosive or armor-piercing explosive warheads. They have a range of less than one kilometer and are only reliably accurate at ranges of less than 300 meters. They are more powerful, however, than LRMs.

SUCCESSOR LORDS

After the fall of the first Star League, the remaining members of the High Council each asserted his or her right to become First Lord. Their star empires became known as the Successor States and the rulers as Successor Lords. The Clan Invasion temporarily interrupted centuries of warfare known as the Succession Wars, which first began in 2786.

BATTLETECH ERAS

The *BattleTech* universe is a living, vibrant entity that grows each year as more sourcebooks and fiction are published. A dynamic universe, its setting and characters evolve over time within a highly detailed continuity framework, bringing everything to life in a way a static game universe cannot match.

To help quickly and easily convey the timeline of the universe—and to allow a player to easily "plug in" a given novel or sourcebook—we've divided *BattleTech* into eight major eras.

STAR LEAGUE
(Present–2780)

Ian Cameron, ruler of the Terran Hegemony, concludes decades of tireless effort with the creation of the Star League, a political and military alliance between all Great Houses and the Hegemony. Star League armed forces immediately launch the Reunification War, forcing the Periphery realms to join. For the next two centuries, humanity experiences a golden age across the thousand light-years of human-occupied space known as the Inner Sphere. It also sees the creation of the most powerful military in human history.

(This era also covers the centuries before the founding of the Star League in 2571, most notably the Age of War.)

SUCCESSION WARS
(2781–3049)

Every last member of First Lord Richard Cameron's family is killed during a coup launched by Stefan Amaris. Following the thirteen-year war to unseat him, the rulers of each of the five Great Houses disband the Star League. General Aleksandr Kerensky departs with eighty percent of the Star League Defense Force beyond known space and the Inner Sphere collapses into centuries of warfare known as the Succession Wars that will eventually result in a massive loss of technology across most worlds.

CLAN INVASION
(3050–3061)

A mysterious invading force strikes the coreward region of the Inner Sphere. The invaders, called the Clans, are descendants of Kerensky's SLDF troops, forged into a society dedicated to becoming the greatest fighting force in history. With vastly superior technology and warriors, the Clans conquer world after world. Eventually this outside threat will forge a new Star League, something hundreds of years of warfare failed to accomplish. In addition, the Clans will act as a catalyst for a technological renaissance.

CIVIL WAR
(3062–3067)

The Clan threat is eventually lessened with the complete destruction of a Clan. With that massive external threat apparently neutralized, internal conflicts explode around the Inner Sphere. House Liao conquers its former Commonality, the St. Ives Compact; a rebellion of military units belonging to House Kurita sparks a war with their powerful border enemy, Clan Ghost Bear; the fabulously powerful Federated Commonwealth of House Steiner and House Davion collapses into five long years of bitter civil war.

JIHAD
(3067–3080)

Following the Federated Commonwealth Civil War, the leaders of the Great Houses meet and disband the new Star League, declaring it a sham. The pseudo-religious Word of Blake—a splinter group of ComStar, the protectors and controllers of interstellar communication—launch the Jihad: an interstellar war that pits every faction against each other and even against themselves, as weapons of mass destruction are used for the first time in centuries while new and frightening technologies are also unleashed.

DARK AGE
(3081-3150)

Under the guidance of Devlin Stone, the Republic of the Sphere is born at the heart of the Inner Sphere following the Jihad. One of the more extensive periods of peace begins to break out as the 32nd century dawns. The factions, to one degree or another, embrace disarmament, and the massive armies of the Succession Wars begin to fade. However, in 3132 eighty percent of interstellar communications collapses, throwing the universe into chaos. Wars erupt almost immediately, and the factions begin rebuilding their armies.

ILCLAN
(3151-present)

The once-invulnerable Republic of the Sphere lies in ruins, torn apart by the Great Houses and the Clans as they wage war against each other on a scale not seen in nearly a century. Mercenaries flourish once more, selling their might to the highest bidder. As Fortress Republic collapses, the Clans race toward Terra to claim their long-denied birthright and create a supreme authority that will fulfill the dream of Aleksandr Kerensky and rule the Inner Sphere by any means necessary: The ilClan.

CLAN HOMEWORLDS
(2786-present)

In 2784, General Aleksandr Kerensky launched Operation Exodus, and led most of the Star League Defense Force out of the Inner Sphere in a search for a new world, far away from the strife of the Great Houses. After more than two years and thousands of light years, they arrived at the Pentagon Worlds. Over the next two-and-a-half centuries, internal dissent and civil war led to the creation of a brutal new society—the Clans. And in 3049, they returned to the Inner Sphere with one goal—the complete conquest of the Great Houses.

LOOKING FOR MORE HARD HITTING BATTLETECH FICTION?

WE'LL GET YOU RIGHT BACK INTO THE BATTLE!

Catalyst Game Labs brings you the very best in *BattleTech* fiction, available at most ebook retailers, including Amazon, Apple Books, Kobo, Barnes & Noble, and more!

NOVELS

1. *Decision at Thunder Rift* by William H. Keith Jr.
2. *Mercenary's Star* by William H. Keith Jr.
3. *The Price of Glory* by William H. Keith, Jr.
4. *Warrior: En Garde* by Michael A. Stackpole
5. *Warrior: Riposte* by Michael A. Stackpole
6. *Warrior: Coupé* by Michael A. Stackpole
7. *Wolves on the Border* by Robert N. Charrette
8. *Heir to the Dragon* by Robert N. Charrette
9. *Lethal Heritage* (*The Blood of Kerensky, Volume 1*) by Michael A. Stackpole
10. *Blood Legacy* (*The Blood of Kerensky, Volume 2*) by Michael A. Stackpole
11. *Lost Destiny* (*The Blood of Kerensky, Volume 3*) by Michael A. Stackpole
12. *Way of the Clans* (*Legend of the Jade Phoenix, Volume 1*) by Robert Thurston
13. *Bloodname* (*Legend of the Jade Phoenix, Volume 2*) by Robert Thurston
14. *Falcon Guard* (*Legend of the Jade Phoenix, Volume 3*) by Robert Thurston
15. *Wolf Pack* by Robert N. Charrette
16. *Main Event* by James D. Long
17. *Natural Selection* by Michael A. Stackpole
18. *Assumption of Risk* by Michael A. Stackpole
19. *Blood of Heroes* by Andrew Keith
20. *Close Quarters* by Victor Milán
21. *Far Country* by Peter L. Rice
22. *D.R.T.* by James D. Long
23. *Tactics of Duty* by William H. Keith
24. *Bred for War* by Michael A. Stackpole
25. *I Am Jade Falcon* by Robert Thurston
26. *Highlander Gambit* by Blaine Lee Pardoe
27. *Hearts of Chaos* by Victor Milán
28. *Operation Excalibur* by William H. Keith
29. *Malicious Intent* by Michael A. Stackpole
30. *Black Dragon* by Victor Milán
31. *Impetus of War* by Blaine Lee Pardoe
32. *Double-Blind* by Loren L. Coleman
33. *Binding Force* by Loren L. Coleman
34. *Exodus Road* (*Twilight of the Clans, Volume 1*) by Blaine Lee Pardoe
35. *Grave Covenant* (*Twilight of the Clans, Volume 2*) by Michael A. Stackpole
36. *The Hunters* (*Twilight of the Clans, Volume 3*) by Thomas S. Gressman
37. *Freebirth* (*Twilight of the Clans, Volume 4*) by Robert Thurston
38. *Sword and Fire* (*Twilight of the Clans, Volume 5*) by Thomas S. Gressman

39. *Shadows of War* (*Twilight of the Clans, Volume 6*) by Thomas S. Gressman
40. *Prince of Havoc* (*Twilight of the Clans, Volume 7*) by Michael A. Stackpole
41. *Falcon Rising* (*Twilight of the Clans, Volume 8*) by Robert Thurston
42. *Threads of Ambition* (*The Capellan Solution, Book 1*) by Loren L. Coleman
43. *The Killing Fields* (*The Capellan Solution, Book 2*) by Loren L. Coleman
44. *Dagger Point* by Thomas S. Gressman
45. *Ghost of Winter* by Stephen Kenson
46. *Roar of Honor* by Blaine Lee Pardoe
47. *By Blood Betrayed* by Blaine Lee Pardoe and Mel Odom
48. *Illusions of Victory* by Loren L. Coleman
49. *Flashpoint* by Loren L. Coleman
50. *Measure of a Hero* by Blaine Lee Pardoe
51. *Path of Glory* by Randall N. Bills
52. *Test of Vengeance* by Bryan Nystul
53. *Patriots and Tyrants* by Loren L. Coleman
54. *Call of Duty* by Blaine Lee Pardoe
55. *Initiation to War* by Robert N. Charrette
56. *The Dying Time* by Thomas S. Gressman
57. *Storms of Fate* by Loren L. Coleman
58. *Imminent Crisis* by Randall N. Bills
59. *Operation Audacity* by Blaine Lee Pardoe
60. *Endgame* by Loren L. Coleman
61. *A Bonfire of Worlds* by Steven Mohan, Jr.
62. *Ghost War* by Michael A. Stackpole
63. *A Call to Arms* by Loren L. Coleman
64. *The Ruins of Power* by Robert E. Vardeman
65. *A Silence in the Heavens* (*The Proving Grounds Trilogy,* Book 1) by Martin Delrio
66. *Truth and Shadows* (*The Proving Grounds Trilogy,* Book 2) by Martin Delrio
67. *Service for the Dead* (*The Proving Grounds Trilogy,* Book 3) by Martin Delrio
68. *By Temptations and by War* by Loren L. Coleman
69. *Fortress of Lies* by J. Steven York
70. *Patriot's Stand* by Mike Moscoe
71. *Flight of the Falcon* by Victor Milán
72. *Blood of the Isle* by Loren L. Coleman
73. *Hunters of the Deep* by Randall N. Bills
74. *Target of Opportunity* by Blaine Lee Pardoe
75. *Sword of Sedition* by Loren L. Coleman
76. *Daughter of the Dragon* by Ilsa J. Bick
77. *Heretic's Faith* by Randall N. Bills
78. *Fortress Republic* by Loren L. Coleman
79. *Blood Avatar* by Ilsa J. Bick
80. *Trial by Chaos* by J. Steven York
81. *Principles of Desolation* by Jason M. Hardy and Randall N. Bills
82. *Wolf Hunters* by Kevin Killiany
83. *A Bonfire of Worlds* by Steven Mohan, Jr.

84. *Isle of the Blessed* by Steven Mohan, Jr.
85. *Embers of War* by Jason Schmetzer
86. *Betrayal of Ideals* by Blaine Lee Pardoe
87. *Forever Faithful* by Blaine Lee Pardoe
88. *Kell Hounds Ascendant* by Michael A. Stackpole
89. *Redemption Rift* by Jason Schmetzer
90. *Grey Watch Protocol (The Highlander Covenant, Book 1)* by Michael J. Ciaravella
91. *Honor's Gauntlet* by Bryan Young
92. *Icons of War* by Craig A. Reed, Jr.
93. *Children of Kerensky* by Blaine Lee Pardoe
94. *Hour of the Wolf* by Blaine Lee Pardoe
95. *Fall From Glory (Founding of the Clans, Book 1)* by Randall N. Bills
96. *Paid in Blood (The Highlander Covenant, Book 2)* by Michael J. Ciaravella
97. *Blood Will Tell* by Jason Schmetzer
99. *Hunting Season* by Philip A. Lee
99. *A Rock and a Hard Place* by William H. Keith, Jr.
100. *Visions of Rebirth (Founding of the Clans, Book 2)* by Randall N. Bills
101. *No Substitute for Victory* by Blaine Lee Pardoe

YOUNG ADULT NOVELS

1. *The Nellus Academy Incident* by Jennifer Brozek
2. *Iron Dawn (Rogue Academy, Book 1)* by Jennifer Brozek
3. *Ghost Hour (Rogue Academy, Book 2)* by Jennifer Brozek
4. *Crimson Night (Rogue Academy, Book 3)* by Jennifer Brozek

OMNIBUSES

1. *The Gray Death Legion Trilogy* by William H. Keith, Jr.
2. *The Blood of Kerensky Trilogy* by Michael A. Stackpole

NOVELLAS/SHORT STORIES

1. *Lion's Roar* by Steven Mohan, Jr.
2. *Sniper* by Jason Schmetzer
3. *Eclipse* by Jason Schmetzer
4. *Hector* by Jason Schmetzer
5. *The Frost Advances (Operation Ice Storm, Part 1)* by Jason Schmetzer
6. *The Winds of Spring (Operation Ice Storm, Part 2)* by Jason Schmetzer
7. *Instrument of Destruction (Ghost Bear's Lament, Part 1)* by Steven Mohan, Jr.
8. *The Fading Call of Glory (Ghost Bear's Lament, Part 2)* by Steven Mohan, Jr.
9. *Vengeance* by Jason Schmetzer
10. *A Splinter of Hope* by Philip A. Lee
11. *The Anvil* by Blaine Lee Pardoe
12. *A Splinter of Hope/The Anvil* (omnibus)
13. *Not the Way the Smart Money Bets (Kell Hounds Ascendant #1)* by Michael A. Stackpole

14. *A Tiny Spot of Rebellion (Kell Hounds Ascendant #2)* by Michael A. Stackpole
15. *A Clever Bit of Fiction (Kell Hounds Ascendant #3)* by Michael A. Stackpole
16. *Break-Away (Proliferation Cycle #1)* by Ilsa J. Bick
17. *Prometheus Unbound (Proliferation Cycle #2)* by Herbert A. Beas II
18. *Nothing Ventured (Proliferation Cycle #3)* by Christoffer Trossen
19. *Fall Down Seven Times, Get Up Eight (Proliferation Cycle #4)* by Randall N. Bills
20. *A Dish Served Cold (Proliferation Cycle #5)* by Chris Hartford and Jason M. Hardy
21. *The Spider Dances (Proliferation Cycle #6)* by Jason Schmetzer
22. *Shell Games* by Jason Schmetzer
23. *Divided We Fall* by Blaine Lee Pardoe
24. *The Hunt for Jardine (Forgotten Worlds, Part One)* by Herbert A. Beas II
25. *Rock of the Republic* by Blaine Lee Pardoe
26. *Finding Jardine (Forgotten Worlds, Part Two)* by Herbert A. Beas II
27. *The Trickster (Proliferation Cycle #7)* by Blaine Lee Pardoe
28. *The Price of Duty* by Jason Schmetzer

ANTHOLOGIES

1. *The Corps (BattleCorps Anthology, Volume 1)* edited by Loren. L. Coleman
2. *First Strike (BattleCorps Anthology, Volume 2)* edited by Loren L. Coleman
3. *Weapons Free (BattleCorps Anthology, Volume 3)* edited by Jason Schmetzer
4. *Onslaught: Tales from the Clan Invasion* edited by Jason Schmetzer
5. *Edge of the Storm* by Jason Schmetzer
6. *Fire for Effect (BattleCorps Anthology, Volume 4)* edited by Jason Schmetzer
7. *Chaos Born (Chaos Irregulars, Book 1)* by Kevin Killiany
8. *Chaos Formed (Chaos Irregulars, Book 2)* by Kevin Killiany
9. *Counterattack (BattleCorps Anthology, Volume 5)* edited by Jason Schmetzer
10. *Front Lines (BattleCorps Anthology Volume 6)* edited by Jason Schmetzer and Philip A. Lee
11. *Legacy* edited by John Helfers and Philip A. Lee
12. *Kill Zone (BattleCorps Anthology Volume 7)* edited by Philip A. Lee
13. *Gray Markets (A BattleCorps Anthology),* edited by Jason Schmetzer and Philip A. Lee
14. *Slack Tide (A BattleCorps Anthology),* edited by Jason Schmetzer and Philip A. Lee
15. *The Battle of Tukayyid* edited by John Helfers
16. *The Mercenary Life* by Randall N. Bills
17. *The Proliferation Cycle* edited by John Helfers and Philip A. Lee
18. *No Greater Honor* edited by John Helfers and Philip A. Lee

MAGAZINES

1. *Shrapnel Issues #01–#07*

The march of technology across BattleTech's eras is relentless...

Some BattleMech designs never die. Each installment of *Recognition Guide: IlClan*, currently a PDF-only series, not only includes a brand new BattleMech or OmniMech, but also details Classic 'Mech designs from both the Inner Sphere and the Clans, now fully rebuilt with Dark Age technology (3085 and beyond).

RECOGNITION GUIDE: ILCLAN vol. 01
RECOGNITION GUIDE: ILCLAN vol. 02
RECOGNITION GUIDE: ILCLAN vol. 03
RECOGNITION GUIDE: ILCLAN vol. 04
RECOGNITION GUIDE: ILCLAN vol. 05
RECOGNITION GUIDE: ILCLAN vol. 06

©2020 The Topps Company, Inc. All Rights Reserved. Recognition Guide: IlClan, BattleTech, 'Mech, and BattleMech are registered trademarks and/or trademarks of The Topps Company, Inc. in the United States and/or other countries. Catalyst Game Labs and the Catalyst Game Labs logo are trademarks of InMediaRes Productions, LLC.

STORE.CATALYSTGAMELABS.COM

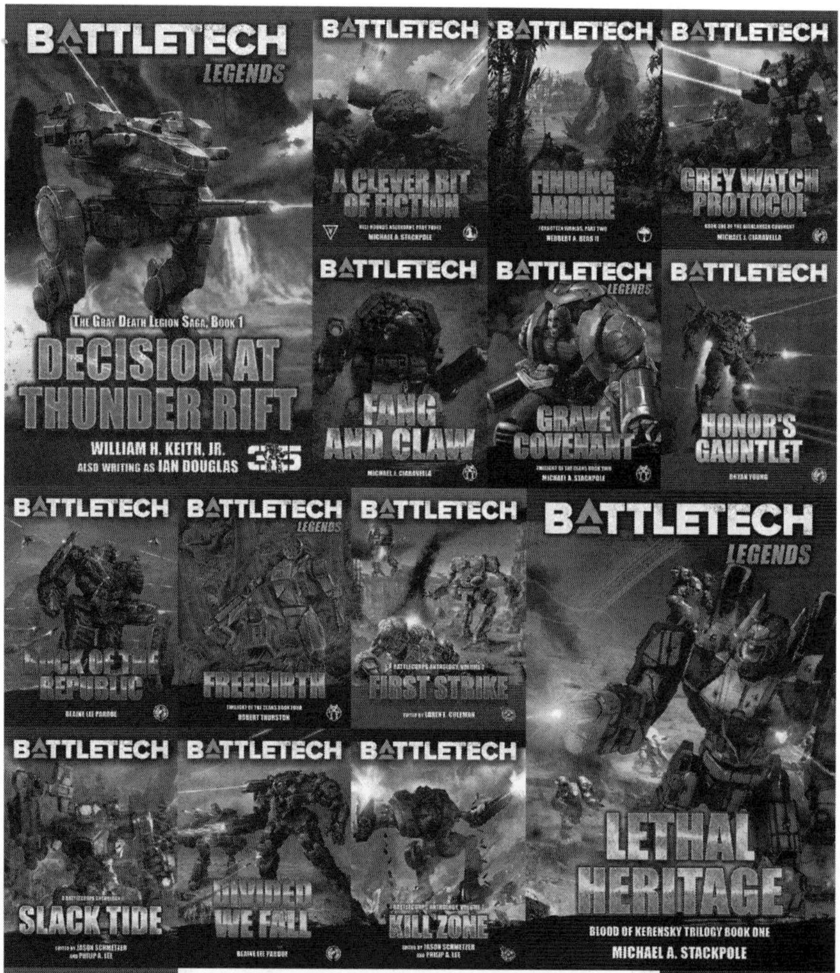

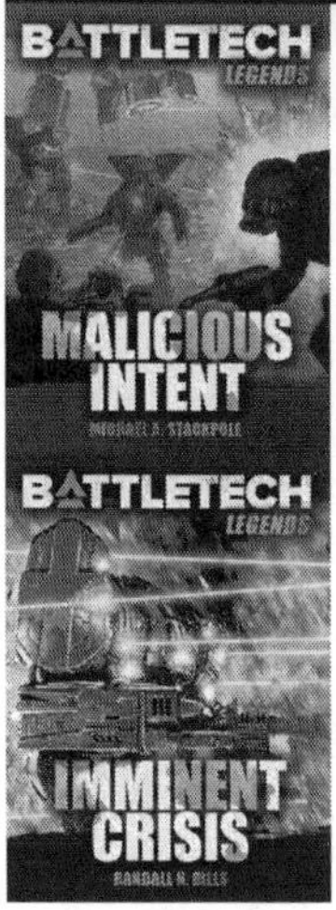

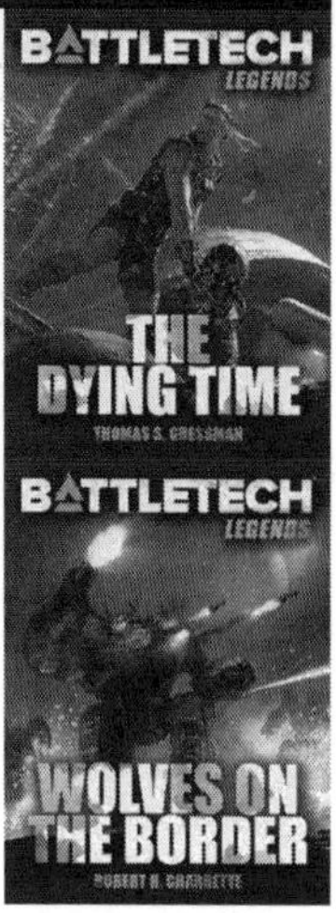

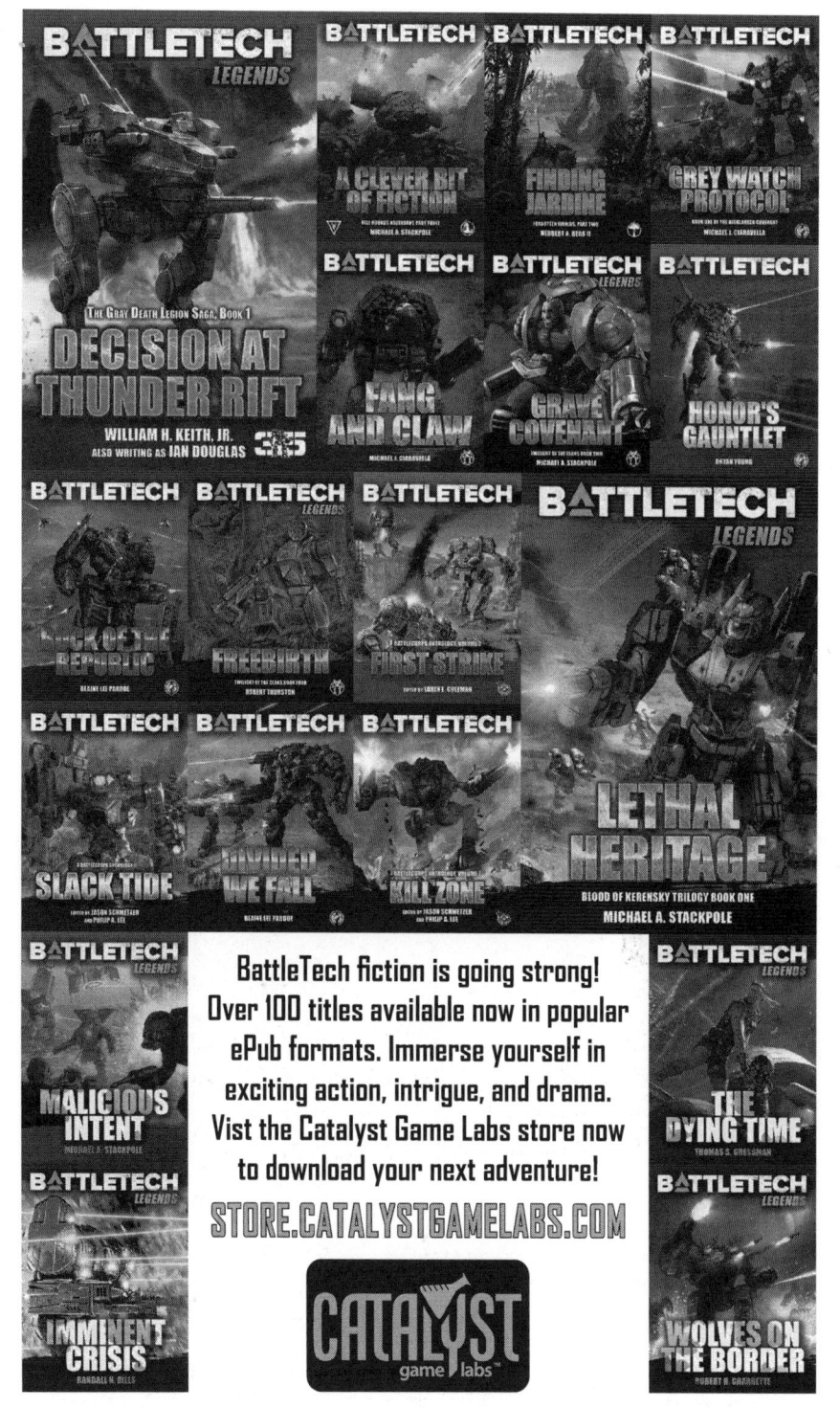

Printed in Great Britain
by Amazon